WALTER BOTTGER

RTTEN APPLE

Dedicated to

The late Hon. Maurice H. Nadjari, who lived it,

and

The late Rev. James Seth Stewart, who helped me understand it.

CHAPTER 1

Mulroy's was an East Side Irish bar. On Third Avenue, just north of 76th Street in New York City, Mulroy's beckoned customers with a green sign lettered in gold that hung over the door, perpendicular to the sidewalk. In the windows, bright neon lights announced that Guinness was on tap and that Rheingold beer could be had. Occupying half the room was a long bar of dark wood that stood in front of a mirrored, bottle-lined wall and curved to meet the wall near the door. On the other side of a low barrier parallel to the bar was a row of tables covered with green and white checkered tablecloths where patrons dined on burgers and fries or chili con carne.

Mulroy's had resisted the changes that the 1960s had brought to the East Side of Manhattan and that had transformed Third Avenue into a row of white brick and steel apartment buildings. Now in the 1970s, Mulroy's served as a reminder of the old days, not that long ago, when Third Avenue was covered by an elevated railway.

It was to Mulroy's that Henry Perkins came directly from the midtown law firm where he was an associate. He was not happy. He had just lost a summary judgment motion, which he should have won. A year or so ago, his client, Southwick Company, had hired a contractor to build an extension to its facilities. Without completing the job, the contractor had sued for the full amount of the agreement. Henry knew that an inspection report had been done for the contractor, which would have shown that the work was

1

not completed. Henry had subpoenaed the report, but the contractor had not complied. Henry had moved to compel the production of the report, but his motion had been denied by the court. Then the contractor had moved for summary judgment for the whole amount of the contract. The court had ruled for the plaintiff and awarded the contractor all the money. Henry was shocked by the decision. It did not make legal sense.

He was criticized by Allan Tubman, the partner for whom he had been working, for not having moved quickly enough to take the contractor's deposition.

Henry responded, "I was waiting for the inspection report, which I could have used at the deposition to firm up our case. Anyway, I suspect that there might be another explanation for such a baseless decision."

"What do you mean?"

"I mean, this judge. He comes out of one of those political clubhouses. And so does the contractor's lawyer. So, it might not have mattered whether I took that deposition."

Allan's face darkened. He sat up and leaned forward over his desk. "Henry," he said through tightened lips, "that is unprofessional nonsense. And you know it. Or you should. And anyway, there's nothing we can do about it now, so we'll just ignore that possibility."

Henry sat up sharply. "Allan, I'm sorry. It isn't nonsense. Unfortunately, I'm sure crap like that happens. I've seen it firsthand back in Cleveland and when I was living in Chicago. So that could be what happened here."

"Henry, you're chasing ghosts. That's not productive. I suggest that you just do your job. And stop holding back."

"What do you mean, 'Holding back?'"

Henry was considering saying more when Allan continued, "Look, I've got to get back to work."

Allan picked up his pen and moved some papers to the center of his desk. Then Allan shook his head sadly and sat back in his chair. "Henry," he began, "you're a smart, personable guy. You don't graduate from Dartmouth and Virginia Law School without a brain. But there's something's missing. I don't know what it is. But you're not operating at full throttle. I'd give this whole thing some thought, if I were you, Henry. I'm talking about the future. Your future. Just commit yourself more and make things happen."

Henry took another swallow of his beer. *Allan may not want to see it,* Henry said to himself, setting down his beer, *but I know that, unfortunately, it's for real.*

There was Judge Edwards, who lived down the street when Henry was growing up back in Cleveland. Henry's favorite teacher had been run down by the son of a rich, politically connected foreign car dealer, right in front of several witnesses. The young man had been caught immediately, drunk with an open bottle in the front seat. But Judge Edwards had found the son not guilty and the next week the judge was seen driving a brand-new Jaguar. And then there was his Uncle Daniel, with whom Henry had been parked in Chicago the year his parents were working in a hospital in Guatemala. Uncle Daniel bragged about paying off politicians and cops so he could get public contracts for his construction company and operate and park his trucks illegally. *Allan might ignore it. But it really does happen,* Henry muttered to himself.

He had just ordered another beer when he spotted a young woman sitting down with three friends at a table on the other side of the barrier. She was slender and lithe with long dark hair, big brown eyes, and a pretty mouth.

Ooh, yes, Henry thought. He shifted on his stool. *That one I'd like to meet.*

Suddenly she looked at Henry and smiled at him flirtatiously. Henry smiled back.

How do I pull this off? he thought. *First thing, I have to get her away from those three friends she's with.*

3

He thought about it for a moment. *Well,* he said to himself, *they just got here so I've got some time.*

He turned to his beer and took a swallow. Then he looked back at the young women again, sizing up the situation. They were looking at a menu. One of them, a sturdy woman with short black hair, seemed to be in charge, and was doing the talking.

She could be a problem, Henry said to himself as he turned back to his beer. *Too bad the nice one isn't alone.*

For a few minutes he kept his eyes on the television set mounted above the bar where the last minutes of another unsuccessful effort by the Mets were playing out. Then he looked back at the women. The one who seemed to lead was on her feet and the others were rising to join her.

Henry started to lift himself from the barstool. But he realized that it was too late. They were leaving.

As the women left, the one he had liked glanced back at Henry and smiled warmly. And then she was gone.

Damn. Henry shook his head. He turned and signaled the bartender. "Another beer." Then he looked back at the television set.

"Good evening," said the television. "This is Fred Mellen with the eleven o'clock news."

Henry turned on his stool, so he was facing the set.

"The Senate today promised a thorough investigation into the break-in at the Democratic headquarters in the Watergate Apartments. Senator Sam Ervin told reporters that he and his fellow lawmakers were determined to find out how much President Nixon knew about the break-in. More news after this."

Henry took a sip of his beer while the advertisements played themselves out. The newscaster returned.

"Locally, the Blinn Commission has made its report..."

Henry leaned closer to the television screen to hear over the barroom chatter.

"Winding up over a year's investigation and weeks of sensational testimony, the Blinn Commission today issued its final report on its investigation into corruption in New York City..."

The Blinn Commission, Henry recalled, had spent several months looking into reported organized corruption in the New York City Police Department, concluding with some spectacular testimony by a corrupt officer who was cooperating after being caught in the Blinn net. A burst of laughter nearby drowned out the voice for a moment, and Henry edged closer so he could hear.

"...offered three conclusions," the television went on. "First, there was, and still is, systemic, organized corruption within the police department that is beyond its capacity to erase internally. Second, corruption extends into the prosecutors' offices and even into the courthouses. And third, presently existing law enforcement cannot adequately deal with the situation."

Henry took a drink of his beer.

"...Commission recommends the appointment by the Governor of a special prosecutor, empowered to supersede local law enforcement and to investigate and prosecute corruption in all five boroughs and in all law enforcement agencies and in the courts. Len Wisener, at City Hall, spoke to the mayor..."

At that moment, the bartender climbed up on a stool and switched the television set to another channel, where a slick-looking man, aided by graphic insets, was giving the ball scores.

"Hey!" Henry blurted out, but the bartender was already gone.

"What shit," said a voice next to Henry. It was Art Clooney, one of his colleagues from the office.

"What's the problem, Arthur?" asked Henry in a challenging tone.

"There're a few rotten apples in the barrel. Find them and pull them out and then the problem will be over."

Henry shook his head. "I don't know, maybe something good may come of this thing. I guess we'll have to see, won't we?"

Two hours later, Henry turned the corner off Third Avenue and headed east. It was already Saturday morning, but Henry knew he could sleep in as long as he wanted. No work tomorrow.

At the thought of work, he felt an unpleasant sensation. He stopped and took a deep breath, filling his lungs. Then he exhaled forcefully. He sniffed. Almost clean, the late summer air. Good air. Honest. Straightforward. Especially at one in the morning when the daytime unpleasantries could be forgotten. Maybe there was a hint of the end of something. Like summer. But good. Change. Renewal. Hope.

Now he could go home and sleep.

He started walking again. Halfway down the block, he paused in front of a group of brownstones, his eye caught by a row of small, anemic-looking trees sticking up through holes in the sidewalk. A familiar city sight. Yet something about the trees moved him tonight. Perhaps it was the way the leaves still clung tenaciously to their slender branches. Hanging in there.

Suddenly it made him glad. Glad that even on a side street in a dirty city like New York, nature could still fight back. That, despite the assault from the auto fumes, the layers of incinerator effluent, the dogs, the defacers, and the unconcerned who piled garbage beneath them, trees full of tender little leaves still had the courage to emerge each spring, to stand fast through the steamy summer, and hold on until they chose to flash their special rays of color in a farewell salute, and only then depart. On their own terms.

He walked on, feeling better now. On either side of the street, dark windows hid sleeping people where dreams leavened the sludge of a day's disappointments. Ahead of him, the streetlamps cast their light onto the sidewalk, illuminating his way.

As he neared the end of the block, he looked across the street, where three cars were double-parked in a row. They seemed to be centered around the door of a small, dimly lit bar. He watched as a man, then two more, stepped briskly out the door and jumped into a double-parked black Cadillac. In an instant, it pulled away, tires squealing.

Something about that bar jogged his memory. He started walking again. Then he remembered. A friend, a federal prosecutor, had told him that the bar was owned by organized crime—that it was a hangout for "wise-guys," as he called them, along with pimps and prostitutes and even drug dealers. Heavyweight criminals frequented the place. Sometimes, Henry had been told, drugs were sold openly. He remembered asking his prosecutor friend how the police could let that kind of thing go on, but his friend had only smiled.

Henry's jaw clenched.

Cops on the take. Cops and politicians all getting rich selling themselves. He'd seen it in Cleveland. He'd seen it in Chicago. And here it was in New York. The same old "sold" sign dangling from the badges and robes of people on the public's payroll. "Public servants," they were called. The only public they served was themselves.

And now the Blinn Commission had said it clearly. Guess what—there *is* corruption. Right here in New York City in 1972. And they filed a report on it. And recommended a special prosecutor, whatever that is. Would something be done? Or would corruption go on, just as it always had?

Henry was twenty or thirty yards short of the bar now. Two cars remained, double parked in front of the bar. He fixed on one of them. It was a green and white sedan with a light and a siren on the roof. And on the door, the seal of the New York City Police Department.

Damn! There it was. Right in front of him! His jaw tightened. A bar full of crooks. And there were the cops, probably drinking free. Or buying the hoods drinks with the cash they'd just pocketed. Holy smokes! Didn't anything ever get better?

He started across the street. Then suddenly remembering where he was, he paused and glanced to his left. It was all right. No traffic. His hands clenched tightly in his pockets as he went on. Damned crooked cops. He kept up his pace, angling across the street toward the bar. Another glance back. No traffic. A look to the sides. No one on either sidewalk.

He was next to the police car now, passing along the side away from the bar. He tried to peer across the car into the bar, to spot the cops, but the lights inside were too dim. Then he stopped, right next to the hood. Drawing his foot back, he took aim and kicked as hard as he could, right into the right front tire.

"Ouch!"

CHAPTER 2

Henry sat back in his desk chair and pushed aside the brief on which he had been working. While keeping an eye on his watch, he was trying to justify rearguing the motion for summary judgment which he had lost. But he was grimly aware that, since the rules required that such a motion must be brought before the same judge that had issued the decision in question, there was no real chance to succeed, so his efforts would be in vain. Glancing at the large pile of papers in his inbox he let out a sigh. There was nothing inviting there, either.

He looked at his watch again. And this time, it gave him good news. Placing the draft of the brief on another pile, he got up. He walked to the door, put on his suitcoat which was hanging on a hook, opened the door, and stepped into the hall.

"Where're you goin', Perk?"

Henry started. He had thought that no one was looking as he slipped along the hallway of the office, toward the elevators.

"Oh, hi, Jerry." Jerry was looking out the doorway of his office. "For a beer," Henry responded.

"At three o'clock in the afternoon?"

Henry shrugged. "Sun's going to be over the yardarm. In a while. And there's something I want to catch on the tube."

Jerry laughed. "Okay. How about some company?" Jerry grabbed his coat from the back of his door. "A cold beer sounds a lot better than sixty-one pages of interrogatories."

The pub was dark and quiet as the two men entered. There were only four other people in the place. At a nearby table a couple sat with half-empty drinks, engrossed in each other. A slightly disheveled man in a rumpled glen plaid suit sat alone at the near end of the polished oak bar, nursing a glass of clear liquid on the rocks, while, at the other end, the bartender slowly shined some glasses and hummed an undistinguishable tune.

"Hi, Roy."

The bartender nodded and continued his polishing as Henry and Jerry walked the length of the bar and took seats.

"I'll have a Rheingold," said Henry. "How about you, Jerry?"

"Sure. Same thing."

The bartender turned toward the familiar red tap. In a moment he set two frosty mugs of beer in front of the lawyers.

"Jesus," said Jerry, as he looked at the size of the mug. "I'll never finish those interrogatories."

Henry lifted his mug. "Cheers."

The television mounted over the bar interrupted. "We now go live to the office of Governor James Whelan for a special press conference."

Henry looked up. "Say, Roy."

"Yeah?"

"Could you turn up the sound a bit?

"Ladies and gentlemen," said some person standing at a podium. "Governor Whelan will speak now." On the screen above the bar, the speaker, clearly the Governor's press secretary, looked out at the still-buzzing gathering of reporters and raised a hand. The room became quiet.

"The Governor will make a brief statement and then make his introduction." He turned toward the Governor. "Governor."

The press secretary stepped aside as the towering figure of Governor James A. Whelan took his place in front of the microphones. The Governor's capacious face was solemn. His jaw seemed to be at attention as his familiar voice rang out.

"Good afternoon. As governor of this great state of New York, it has shocked and saddened me to learn that elements of our law enforcement system in New York City are saddled with the taint of corruption. Evidence compiled and revealed to the public over the last year has made this conclusion inescapable. This condition is one that our state and city cannot tolerate and which I, as your governor, must address."

Oh dear, thought Henry. *Political bullshit.* From the stool next to Henry came a groan, signaling accord with Henry's thinking.

Having glanced down at his text, the Governor continued. "As the Blinn Commission recommended, I have exercised my authority under the powers granted me by the Executive Law, and have designated a Special Prosecutor, with full authority to investigate and prosecute corruption in the law enforcement and justice system in New York City, including the police departments, the prisons, the prosecutorial agencies, and the courts. The new Special Prosecutor will have full and exclusive authority in those areas, to the exclusion of the local district attorneys."

"Boy, the DAs are gonna love that," said Jerry.

"Yeah," replied Henry.

The Governor went on. "...dollars from my existing law enforcement authorization for..."

"It's crazy, man," Jerry continued. "They can't take away the DAs' authority. Not without a big fight..."

"Hey, Jerry. I want to listen. Please."

"…in the budget for next year, to be presented to the legislature in December."

The Governor was looking at his text again. He cleared his throat.

"Perk, this thing's a jerk-off, and you know it. This guy's nothin' but a politician. Just listen to him."

Henry turned. "Yeah. But let me do so."

Jerry sighed and lifted his glass of beer as the Governor continued.

"…will also appoint a single judge to hear and determine all matters…"

"…and then," added Jerry, "the appellate courts'll have their day."

"Quiet," said Henry.

The Governor had paused, bathing the staring cameras with earnestness.

Henry took another swallow of his beer.

At last, the Governor went on. "To fill the position of special prosecutor, I wanted not only a person who has demonstrated his or her ability as a lawyer and prosecutor, but someone of unimpeachable integrity whose career has shown the kind of commitment, courage, and independence needed to tackle the very difficult job ahead. In Howard Matlin I have found such a man."

"Who?" asked Jerry.

Henry shrugged. "Never heard of him."

"…as District Attorney of Fuller County for the last six years, Howard Matlin has uprooted the endemic corruption in that county and sent numerous despoilers of the public trust to jail. He has done this without regard to party or to prior public stature, even in the face of threats to his person and his own career."

Henry sat forward.

"…such a man is needed to bring those same qualities, that same zeal and dedication to New York City…"

Matlin went after corruption? *Okay,* Henry said to himself. *Maybe something will happen.*

"...and put justice back into our justice system." The Governor was looking directly into the cameras, his face now that of the commander. "And now I wish to present the man who has consented to take on the responsibilities I have outlined. Our new Special Prosecutor, Howard R. Matlin."

There was a scattering of polite applause, mostly from the Governor's aides. Then the Governor moved away, and Howard Matlin stepped toward the cluster of microphones.

"Thank you, Governor."

Matlin's voice was deep, but surprisingly gentle, unlike that of a politician. He was of smaller stature than the Governor, darker, and with features that were almost monkey-like. But even on television, the power in his neck and shoulders was apparent. As Matlin's image filled the screen, Henry could see the firm jaw, the erect head, the dark eyes meeting the cameras unblinking.

"I will root out corruption," Matlin began softly. "Literally. I don't believe in a 'rotten apple' theory of corruption. Wherever there's corruption, there are more than a few rotten apples. There are rotten trees and rotten roots."

Matlin's dark eyes kindled like black agates heated almost to incandescence. They seemed to flash from the screen, zapping Henry on his barstool. His glass stopped mid-journey.

"Healthy trees don't breed rotten apples. Rotten trees and rotten roots breed rotten apples."

Henry's eyes were now fixed to the screen.

Matlin's voice hardened. "Be warned. I will dig as far as I have to go to get at the corruption. In the police department. In the courts. In the halls of government. Wherever it is. However well-entrenched. However long-established. I make just one promise: I will dig and dig and dig. Until the rotten roots have been ripped out of the ground, so that, in their place, healthy trees can grow again."

Henry didn't move. Matlin had finished speaking, but Henry was still hearing him. The words seemed to seep into his blood stream, palliative, then analeptic. This was no ordinary man. It didn't matter that he'd never heard of him until now. Because now, having heard him, he was almost tempted to rise like a faith-healed beggar who casts away his crutches and says *Alleluia.*

"What a character," Jerry said beside him.

The bartender, who had stopped his polishing, resumed. Then, responding to some mumbled words from the other end of the bar, he began mixing another martini.

On the screen, Howard Matlin had stood up again to answer questions from the reporters. At the moment, all were shouting at once. The Governor's press secretary had risen to take charge, and he was now pointing at one of the reporters, who was also on his feet and waving his arm. As soon as he was acknowledged, the reporter began, straining to be heard over his still babbling colleagues.

"Mike Welling of the *Daily News,* Mr. Matlin," the reporter said. "I want to know whether you feel that you have the Governor's full support to pursue things, as you put it, all the way to the 'root' of the problem, whatever that is?"

Governor Whelan rose again. "I'll answer that, Mike," he said, stepping in before Matlin had a chance to speak.

"Sit down, Whelan," Henry hissed at the television.

Jerry laughed.

"Mr. Matlin has my full confidence, and he also absolutely has the full authority to pursue the wrongdoers, whoever they are and wherever they're hiding." The Governor's jaw firmed itself. "Let me make this perfectly clear," he added, raising a finger, and waving it at the cameras. "I want Howard

Matlin to go as high as he can, and as far as he need go, in order to eradicate this scourge on the public weal."

A snort from the stool next to Henry echoed his own sentiments. "Sounds like Nixon," said Jerry. "'Let me make this perfectly clear.' Ha!"

"Sabrina," said the press secretary after the Governor sat down again.

A red-haired woman stood up and addressed Matlin. "I'm Sabrina Wilcox from the *New York Times*. I'd like to ask what your salary will be?"

"Good question," said Henry's companion.

Once again, the Governor rose to answer.

"Jesus, will you sit down!" Henry picked up his nearly empty glass and emptied it.

"Isn't that a lot of money?" the reporter persisted after the Governor's answer.

Henry caught the bartender's eye and pointed to his glass.

"Shit, you having another?" Jerry asked.

"Yeah." Henry nodded. Someone was asking Matlin another question. Henry watched, hoping to hear Matlin again.

"Do you expect a lot of opposition to your efforts?"

This time the Governor remained seated. Matlin eyed the questioner. "That's up to others. We expect to be supported by everyone in a position of public trust. If any of them causes trouble, we'll be ready."

Henry nodded.

"Mr. Matlin," said a voice off camera. The new questioner was recognized, and the camera swung around as he rose slowly to his feet. The top of his head was bald, but from just below the crown, black curly hair hung loosely, almost touching the collar of an ancient tweed sport coat. The camera was able to catch most of the reporter's features. You could tell that they had become fleshy over time and good living, but still seemed sharp, like that of an aging hawk. The face was in repose, exuding the confidence of a veteran political reporter.

"Mr. Matlin, you convicted the Chairman of the Fuller County Board of Supervisors in a four-week trial a little over a year ago."

Henry smiled at the reporter paused, almost as though Matlin were expected to comment. Then he went on. He continued to speak slowly and deliberately, measuring his own words as though they were gold dust. There was a slight sneer in his voice.

"Isn't it a fact that the appellate court severely criticized your performance at that trial as, and I quote, 'overzealous' and 'overreaching?'"

The last few words were accompanied by a slight curl of the upper lip that lingered as the sounds died out. The reporter slowly raised his eyes to Matlin, keeping them partially hooded by the upper lids. The room silenced as the reporter waited for Matlin's response.

"Mister...?" Matlin looked at the reporter. His inquiring tone was left dangling in the silence that followed.

Briefly, confusion crossed the reporter's face.

"Mister...?" said Matlin, again with a rise in pitch on the second syllable.

The import of Matlin's tone suddenly appeared to strike the reporter. The man didn't know who he was!

"Copin. Toby Copin," he stated as though instructing a recalcitrant child on toilet manners. "Of the *New York Times*." A single barking laugh came from someone off camera.

"Mr. Copin," Matlin responded firmly. "The supervisor you speak of was convicted. His conviction was affirmed, and he is presently in Green Haven Prison for a term of four years."

"But Mr. Matlin..."

"George," said the press secretary, pointing in another direction.

The camera lingered for a moment on the angry face of Toby Copin. Then, as Copin sat down, it swung away.

"What an asshole," said Henry.

"Yeah. More like a masochist for taking on that job."

Henry swiveled sharply. "I mean the reporter, not Matlin."

Jerry took a drink. "Him, too."

Henry set his glass on the bar. "What's the matter, you don't like Matlin?"

Jerry shrugged his shoulders and sat his glass on the bar. "What's there to like? Some hayseed DA nobody's ever heard of comes down to the Big Apple to get his name in the papers for a year or so, until someone makes him a judge. Then he retires to his chambers with his feet up on his desk, while his law clerk does all the work."

"And what if he does what he says?"

"Whatdaya mean?"

"What if he really goes after corruption?"

"Where? In the police department?"

"And in the DAs' offices and the courts and the politicians. Wherever it is."

His friend sat up and turned on his barstool to face Henry. "You been out in the sun, my boy?"

"Of course not. You laugh." Henry's voice crept up a pitch. "You're saying nothing's going to be done. But I'll tell you something. I don't care whether this Matlin guy comes from the north pole. I like what he says. And I'll tell you something else. He just might make some real waves in this god-damned legal system of ours."

You think so, do you?" Jerry's eyes narrowed, as though peering inside Henry's head. Then he glanced at Henry's empty glass. "No wonder. Two of those things will melt the brain." He lifted his own glass and emptied it. "I'll tell you this much, Perkins." He dropped his glass to the bar and began to rise from his stool. "If that guy does make waves, it'll be him who drowns in 'em, not the big boys."

For a moment Henry was silent. He wanted to argue, to take further issue with Jerry. But he'd already said enough to surprise himself. How did he know that Jerry wasn't right? How did he know that Howard Matlin was for real? All he'd ever heard about Howard Matlin, he'd heard in the last half hour. And most of that from the Governor, a politician.

"Come on, Perk. I've got to get back to work."

But he hadn't merely heard about Matlin. He'd seen him. Seen and believed.

He left some money on the bar, climbed off his barstool, and started toward the door.

"Look," said Jerry, placing a hand on Henry's shoulder. "If you think the guy's for real, why don't you go work for him?"

Henry stopped. He shook his head. But he said nothing.

CHAPTER 3

On the day after the Governor's press conference, Henry was seated in his desk chair reading the lead editorial in the *New York Times*. It called for "a no-holds-barred cleaning of the justice system" by the new special prosecutor. "What is needed above all," the editorial asserted, "is zealousness."

"It is not enough that Mr. Matlin be well-intentioned. It is not enough that he be honest. It is not enough that he be free from compromising supervision. To have the needed effect on the diseased organ of our justice system, Howard Matlin must be more than that. He must be zealous. He must exploit every lead, squeeze every witness. He must violate the sanctuaries of the privileged as often as necessary, so that he can clean up the puss of corruption."

Henry smiled and picked up the thick jelly doughnut he had bought with his coffee and took a large bite. Sticky red filling oozed down his fingers.

On another page, Sabrina Wilcox had a feature story on the new special prosecutor. She traced Matlin's background from his youth as the oldest child of a Queens butcher through his time as an assistant district attorney in Manhattan, his six subsequent years in private practice, and his seven years in upstate Fuller County, one as chief assistant, and the next six as district attorney. She mentioned a rumor that Matlin had left the Manhattan DA's office after a dispute with the then-district attorney (now deceased), but she had been unable to uncover any details.

In his first year as district attorney of Fuller County, Matlin had indicted and convicted the mayor of the county's largest city for extortion in the letting of snow plowing contracts. Shortly thereafter, he had sent a justice of the peace and a sheriff to jail for creating traffic fines with a speed trap and then pocketing the proceeds. Three members of one of the county's local police forces were convicted of taking bribes to protect a gambling den. Then, a year before Matlin's re-election bid, he prosecuted four officials of his own political party for a scheme involving kickbacks from public employees who had gotten their jobs through the party. He even had prosecuted one of his own assistants for drug dealing. And, of course, there was the Chairman of the Fuller County Board of Supervisors, whom Matlin had convicted of bribe receiving from a public utility. There were, Wilcox concluded, several audible sighs of relief in Fuller County when Howard Matlin received his call to New York City.

Henry put down the *Times* and picked up the *Daily News*, where Mike Welling had a story about Howard Matlin's successful prosecution of the Chairman of the Board of Supervisors.

There was only one negative note in the morning's news. In the *Times*, Toby Copin — the reporter who had challenged Matlin at his press conference — continued to question Matlin's conduct in prosecuting the Chairman. He objected, among other things, to the use of wiretap evidence at trial.

"Howard Matlin is a threat to the civil liberties of all New Yorkers," Copin wailed. "The Governor would be well-advised to keep a tight rein on his new special prosecutor."

Howard Matlin had wasted no time in plunging into the morass of New York City stink. Over the next three weeks, his investigations began generating news. Three police detectives were prosecuted for shaking down a pawnbroker. An assistant district attorney in the Bronx was caught taking money to fix an arrest for driving while intoxicated. There was the indictment of a police lieutenant caught by the Blinn Commission protecting a known gambler. Henry enjoyed each juicy story of Matlin's probes. Matlin really seemed to be going somewhere.

But each morning, after he had finished reading about the investigations, Henry had to return to his work and to what he was feeling more and more, was its futility. He wished he were where the action was. But without any criminal experience, he felt he would be of no interest to the Special Prosecutor.

One morning, Henry decided to call an old friend from his first law firm. George Leary was a successful litigator whom he had always liked and with whom he had kept in regular contact. George was now a partner in a major Wall Street law firm. But before that, he had been a federal prosecutor in the United States Attorney's office in Manhattan. Henry's phone call led to an invitation to visit George in his office the next day.

"Henry, it's always good to see you. What brings you down here?"

Henry settled himself in the chair and cleared his throat. "I wanted to get your thoughts on something, George." He paused. George said nothing, so he continued. "I'm thinking about trying something new."

"What's happened?"

"Nothing, really." He didn't mind stretching the truth a bit. "But there is something else I think I might like to do a bit more."

"What might that be?"

"Well, I'm sure you've heard about that new office that's been set up to investigate corruption...the Special Prosecutor."

George nodded slightly and narrowed his eyes.

"...and I hear they might be looking for lawyers..."

George leaned forward and picked up a small glass paperweight from his desk. He began turning it in his hand. "Why at this stage of your career would you think about doing something like that?"

Henry didn't answer and George continued.

"You don't have any experience in criminal law. I'm not sure they'd hire you. Besides, the pay is lousy. Prosecutors don't make anything. And may I be a little blunt, Henry?"

Henry nodded.

"Things haven't exactly worked out for you yet, have they?"

Henry shrugged.

"What I think you need — if I may be so bold — is a little success in your life. Not a failure."

"But why do you assume I'd fail?"

"Not you. The whole operation."

"What do you mean?"

"I mean that office — the Special Prosecutor's Office — has no real chance of accomplishing anything lasting."

"I'm not sure what you mean." Henry sat up. "Have you watched Matlin? Have you read about what he did up in Fuller County? And what he's starting to do now?"

George shook his head. He looked at the paperweight in his hand as though it carried a message on its surface. Then he set it back down on his desk.

"I've read the papers. But an upstate justice of the peace or a small-time politician is hardly the kind of thing he's going to face here in the Big Apple. Even the cops. If he makes some good cases against cops, that won't matter. You know as well as I do. The corruption here in New York City is institutionalized. Organized. Ancient and, to the participants, honorable. It's been here since the Dutchmen screwed the Indians out of the island. It was old hat when Boss Tweed did his thing over a century ago. And it ain't about to go away. Not for some upstate dreamer, if that's what he really is. Not for anyone, really. And, with all due respect, my friend, not for you."

"But there hasn't been a Blinn Commission before," Henry protested.

"Of course, there has. I thought you were a history major at Dartmouth. About every twenty years or so, someone sets up a committee to clean up New York. And look where it's gotten us. There was the Lexow Committee back before the turn of the century. The Curran Committee in the late teens. The Seabury investigations in the early thirties and another big flap in the fifties over the gambler Harry Gross. But it's just like Sisyphus. Every few years, someone rolls the stone off the top of the cesspool and pushes it up a hill. And then it rolls right back, usually flattening the guys doing the pushing on its way down."

"Well, maybe that's the way it's been, George. But I think things're different now. I just feel that New York's ready for a real cleanup. I mean, we can't afford not to do it. Look at how bad it is. Cops, judges—everybody's for sale."

George rotated his chair on its axis and eyed Henry sidewise. He smiled. "So, what's new?"

"But it stinks, dammit. It just stinks."

"I agree. And so does the East River. You think someone's going to turn that into a cherry soda?"

In spite of himself, Henry smiled.

George swiveled back to face Henry and sat forward. His eyes were warm, but he was not smiling. "Henry. Let me put it straight."

Henry nodded. He was listening.

"You don't need any more failure in your life. You don't need to put two or three or four years into some venture to see it go down the tubes, flushed away by a stream a lot stronger than you are. And that's what's going to happen to this operation of Matlin's, or whatever his name is. They're going to fall on their faces. And fall hard." George took a deep breath and let it out again. "Henry, there's nothing *anyone* can do about corruption. Corruption sits in the center of the human soul. And no commission and no special prosecutor, and especially no young lawyer who's still trying to find himself is going to yank it out of there." He paused a moment. "Look, you're a Christian, right?"

Henry shrugged. He was brought up a Catholic, but he didn't spend much time in church.

"Jesus showed up two thousand years ago and said he was going to give us peace. That everybody could stop fighting and love each other. He even got himself hung on a cross to make his point. But they're still doing a big business making guns. And people are still stabbing each other in the back."

Henry said nothing.

"It's the same thing with corruption. It's here to stay. And this Howard Matlin, if he really does what he says he's going to do, is going to get himself hung on his own cross. And I don't think you want to be up there hanging next to him."

Henry shook his head. "But I just can't...I just *hate* it."

"And so do I. I don't like it any more than you do. Believe me. But I'm not about to throw away my life over it. Nor should you. Because that's got to be your first priority. Your life. Number one."

Take care of number one first, thought Henry. That's what his Uncle Daniel from Chicago used to say, defending his payoffs to politicians and cops. A picture of Uncle Daniel flashed to mind, but Henry forced it away. George wasn't his Uncle Daniel.

"Especially," George was saying, "when you're not exactly setting the world on fire. You're...how old?"

"Thirty."

"Well then, I can't see how you could consider wasting the next three or four years in a dead-end pursuit. And finding yourself heading for forty with nothing to show for it."

The next day, Henry was sitting again at his desk with the newspaper in his hand. There was a story about the latest Matlin investigation on the front page. But Henry wasn't reading it. He was staring at the wall, reviewing again in his head the conversation he had just had with Allan Tubman, one of the partners.

"Henry," Allan had said as soon as Henry had closed the door behind him, "I don't like to be the bearer of bad news, but I've been asked to do it." Allan lifted his hand as though to gesture but then lowered it.

Henry stood where he had entered the room.

"My partners have made it clear. We need a deadline for you to find something. And not a long one, I'm afraid. There is a new associate coming at the beginning of next month and we need your office for him. So, I want you to start a search—in high gear."

That was it. No further discussion. And, for Henry himself, no options. He had to get moving. He looked down at the newspaper. His eyes roamed through the article until they stopped at the last paragraph.

"Howard Matlin announced once again that he was looking for qualified lawyers to handle his expanding investigations." There was even a name and number to contact.

After what George had said, it didn't seem promising. Even Jerry had made light of the new Special Prosecutor's Office. But...

Henry reached for the phone.

It was four o'clock in the afternoon a few days later and Henry was sitting in a hard-backed chair in the reception room of the Special Prosecutor's Office in the New State Office Building waiting to meet Howard Matlin. He tried to relax, but he could still taste the pastrami sandwich he had had for lunch two hours earlier.

A few days after Henry had made his call, he met with Matlin's chief assistant, Nat Perlman, who handled the hiring. The meeting had gone well, and he apparently had passed the first test, since Perlman had called and asked him to come to the office and meet Matlin.

Would Howard Matlin really hire him? Henry had never practiced one minute of criminal law. He had even managed to avoid doing any of the *pro bono* appeals his firm provided for Legal Aid. What if Matlin asked him how to handle a lineup? Or how many votes in a grand jury were needed for an indictment?

He put those thoughts aside and looked around the waiting room. It was an almost bare, windowless room, with a few chairs and a door into the interior of the office. No pictures. No artifacts. Nothing yet to indicate any sense of presence. Each time the door opened Henry could see packing crates and other loose materials sitting in the hall.

He looked at the desk where a young man was in attendance. A young man with a leather harness slung over his chest. A gun belt, Henry could see. When Henry had announced himself, it was the young man who had nodded and pointed to the chair in which he now sat. But Henry hadn't seen the chair immediately; he was looking at the gun belt. This must be some place to work, he thought, if the front door is guarded by a man with a gun belt on his chest.

"Mr. Matlin will see you now."

It was the gun belt who spoke. As he did, the inner door opened, and a middle-aged woman leaned in and signaled to him. "Mr. Perkins?"

Henry nodded as he rose from his chair.

"I'm Harriet Winsor, Mr. Matlin's secretary. Follow me, please."

Henry entered a bare corridor that extended both to his left and right. It was painted an institutional tan. The woman turned left, but not before Henry noticed that, at both ends, the corridor ended with another corridor. Then he turned and followed the woman to the next corridor, where they turned left. Now his way opened. This corridor was wider than the first. On his right were a series of doors to offices, most of them open and unoccupied. To his left was an open bay area with desks for secretaries. None was occupied at the moment. In the bay, he noticed a pile of empty cardboard cartons and several pieces of furniture still encased in plastic sheeting. Along the hall, across from the bay, a roll of carpeting was pushed up against the corridor wall. It was wrapped in plastic. The Office of the Special Prosecutor was just getting underway.

When they reached what looked like the corner of the building, Harriet pointed Henry to a half-open door.

"Mr. Matlin is waiting for you."

Henry took a breath and entered.

It was an ample-sized room and, as Henry had guessed, a corner office. Near the corner, diagonally to it, was a large, heavy-looking desk and behind it, rising to greet him, was Howard Matlin.

"Mr. Perkins? I'm Howie Matlin."

Henry felt a jolt as the dark eyes of the Special Prosecutor met his. There he was, facing Henry. The man Henry had watched on television and seen in the newspapers. Who was going to save New York.

For a few painful seconds, Henry stood still, looking at Matlin, searching for words. Then he realized that the Special Prosecutor was leaning across his desk with his hand out. He pulled himself together and took the outstretched hand, wincing as the vise-like grip closed over his own ample hand. He wasn't prepared for the man's strength. He felt his face grow warm.

"Sit down, won't you?" Matlin gestured with a relaxed hand toward a chair in front of his desk and dropped into his own seat.

Henry sat down. He noticed that Matlin's corner office had a breathtaking view of lower Manhattan and the Hudson River. But it was the figure across the broad and heavy desk that drew his attention.

Seeing Howard Matlin in person, Henry could understand why, on television, Matlin always looked so powerful and so vital. He was. Although small of stature, Matlin's shoulders and chest were those of a weightlifter, and his face, with its dark arching eyebrows and small but forceful features, bore the vigor and determination of a much younger man.

Unlike many attorneys, Matlin did not appear to be a formal figure. His hair was close-cropped, as a small-town barber might cut it. He wore no suit coat or suspenders. His plain white dress shirt was unbuttoned at the neck, and his inexpensive-looking brown-and-tan-striped tie was loosened and dangled casually. The sleeves of his shirt were rolled up almost to his elbows, revealing his swarthy and muscular forearms, but no Rolex watch dressed his wrist. Only a simple watch of an age and style that said it might once have been his father's.

In another way, Matlin was unlike the traditional barons of the New York legal realm. There was a fire in his eyes—the same fire that Henry had seen that first day on television—that seemed to give off heat and light from some furnace burning deep within. And the simple grace of his every move-ment bespoke a profound self-certainty.

For an instant, Henry recalled his conversation with George on the fruitlessness of the Special Prosecutor's Office. But now that conversation seemed to Henry to have occurred in another dimension.

"Why do you want to work for us?" Matlin was asking.

That question Henry at least had thought about, and he relaxed as he responded.

"I think our legal system's in terrible trouble. Because of corruption. I believe the Blinn Commission when they say that the whole system's bad, and I've seen the effects of corruption myself. I want to do something about it."

As he heard himself say his words, he wondered if he sounded foolish. Certainly, if he ever said something like this to his colleagues at work, or even his buddies from college or law school, he knew that the response would be some chortling and a suggestion that he have another beer.

But Matlin was relaxed and composed. Until suddenly the Special Prosecutor's dark eyes switched on, emitting beams from some powerful source. In an instant they probed deep inside Henry's defenseless head, reading thoughts and emotions. Instinctively Henry started to raise a hand to cover his eyes as he felt the detritus of his past coming under scrutiny. But no hand rose, for, just as quickly, the searchlight switched off and a soft glow returned.

"I see from your resume that you like tennis and the opera. I'm not much for either, but my late wife used to love the opera. Do you go often?"

It was not the question Henry had expected next. But he answered.

"I have a couple of subscriptions, so I'm fairly regular."

"You worked in France for a year after college. Did you learn to speak French well?"

Now Henry was really confused. What did France or French have to do with corruption?

"Fairly well. It's never good enough for the French, though."

He tried to figure out what Matlin was searching for with this line of questioning. Did he think him a dilettante for taking a job in France? Or maybe the Office was looking for someone to speak with any French defendants.

"Nat Perlman says you're the right kind of person for us. I agree. We'd like you to join us."

What? That was it? That's all he was being asked? Was that an offer?

Then Matlin named his salary.

It took a second to sink in. It *was* an offer. With salary. Salary? Henry noted that the money offered was only a little more than half of what he was making now. He asked himself how he could accept such a low offer. How could he live?

"I accept," he heard himself say.

"When can you start?" Matlin was rising to see him out.

"Is two weeks OK?"

"That's fine. We'll see you on…" Matlin looked at his desk calendar, "Monday, December seventh." No smile or mention of Pearl Harbor.

Henry was out the door and headed for the elevator before it sank in. What had he done? He had just cut his income in half. According to people like his friend George or colleague Jerry, he may have just committed professional suicide. But he was going to work with Howard Matlin. He was going to fight corruption himself. Not by grumbling at the morning newspaper. Not by shaking his head at his Uncle Daniel or at Judge Edwards. But as part of a team embarked on a venture unlike anything Henry had seen before.

As he walked down the corridor, toward the elevators, he felt light-headed, as though he had just had several glasses of champagne. He didn't even notice the cardboard boxes and the roll of carpet along the way.

CHAPTER 4

Henry hung up his suit coat on the hook on the back of the door to his new office. He dipped into the side pocket and pulled out a folded wallet-sized case. Opening it, he looked again at the brass badge inside with embossed letters around the raised seal of the State of New York. "Assistant Special Prosecutor," it said. Henry was now a member of the Office of the Special Prosecutor, sworn to fight corruption.

Of course, he hadn't fought much corruption yet, he thought, as he dropped the case back into his pocket. This was his first day. He'd been photographed and fingerprinted, had filled out a half inch pile of forms, was introduced to a few other assistants, and had been given a tour of the office.

He sat down in his chair. It creaked; it was new. Just about everything in the Office of the Special Prosecutor was new. In fact, that morning Henry had ripped off the plastic sheeting in which his chair had been shipped. Even the New State Office Building itself was, as its name suggested, new. Rising forty-eight floors above the squat, dirty mélange of buildings along the western end of Chambers Street in lower Manhattan, the building had already become the butt of newsmen's jokes. It had been started nearly a decade before with the usual political pomp and circumstance but had, like so many public projects, taken years more than scheduled to build and had cost millions of dollars more than budgeted. The building's sorry history inspired some pundit to refer to it as a vertical Second Avenue subway, replete with forgotten promises and plenty of fraud. The irony had not gone unnoticed by the news media that among the first tenants of a building that had probably made several politicians rich was the State's new anti-corruption prosecutor.

Henry stepped to his window. It faced north. He could see upper Manhattan, the George Washington Bridge, and the Palisades of New Jersey. It was a breathtaking view, but not as breathtaking as the change in his life. Like the building, it was new—a new birth. Only a few weeks before, he had been in limbo. Given notice by his law firm. No idea where to go next. And then, as though in a dream, he was suddenly in the Office of the Special Prosecutor, hired to do something he had always wanted to do—to go after corruption.

His telephone rang, startling him. It was the first time his phone had rung, so it took a few seconds to find it on his credenza, behind his desk. "Henry Perkins here," he said, dropping into his chair.

"Henry. Welcome."

"Thanks."

"It's Howie Matlin."

Henry sat up sharply.

Matlin paused. "Are you free now?"

Free? Of course, he was free. But was he supposed to be? Should he already be at work on some project? He decided on the truth. "Yes, I am."

"Good. Could you come down to my office? We may need your help."

"I'll be right there."

In the hall he hesitated. Left or right? The Office of the Special Prosecutor occupied the entire forty-fourth floor of the building, with a hallway that encircled the floor making every office accessible from both directions. Howard Matlin's office was on the other end of the building, in the southwest corner. Henry turned right.

As he rounded a corner and headed toward Matlin's office, he recalled his earlier tour of the office. There was the technical room, with its state-of-the-art recording and copying equipment, and other paraphernalia used for penetrating the underworld. He passed the door to the file room, where dossiers on criminals, as well as records of cases were to be kept. He noted the hallway to what would become the library when they had enough books. He had been shown the grand jury room, where Manhattan grand juries would consider the evidence the investigators had gathered. He had seen the conference rooms, the inner offices, the bathrooms, and even the jail cell where they would keep prisoners who were being interviewed as witnesses.

"Hi, Harriet."

Henry smiled and nodded at Matlin's secretary, the woman who had brought him to his interview with Matlin. He was pleased that he remembered her name.

She gestured toward Matlin's door. "Go on in. He's expecting you."

Henry paused as his hand touched the door. This was it. Starting his battle against corruption. He opened the door.

"Hello, Henry. Come in."

He was surprised by the number of people already in Matlin's office. Facing Howard Matlin, in front of his desk, were Chief Assistant Nat Perlman; Matt Corey, the chief investigator; and a slender man with close-clipped, prematurely graying hair, whom he didn't recognize.

"You've met Nat and Matt, I know."

Henry nodded.

"This is Dan Nelligan. Our Assistant Chief Investigator."

"That's number three investigator, not number two," Nelligan said with a laugh as he rose from his chair.

From the relaxed way Nelligan got up to shake his hand, Henry could tell that he was someone of consequence. His appearance reinforced the impression, with a chiseled forehead, high cheekbones, and a straight nose under full eyebrows. Yet there was a warmth in his eyes and a firmness in his grip that made Henry like Nelligan at once.

"Sit down," said Matlin from behind his desk. He was in shirt sleeves, with a plain brown tie hanging down across his deep-barreled chest. His eyes were unsmiling.

"I doubt that you've heard about this yet," he began, holding up what looked like a set of legal papers. "It just came in this morning."

"What is it?"

"A summons and complaint."

"What?"

A summons and complaint were civil. This was a prosecutor's office.

"Actually, it's a…" Matlin looked at the front of the document, "…a notice of petition." He looked up. "We're being sued."

"I don't understand," said Henry.

"The Office is being sued by the five district attorneys—all together." The hardness of Matlin's voice matched his eyes.

"For what?"

"For existing. They've brought an action in the Appellate Division to have our Office declared unconstitutional."

"Unconstitutional?"

Matlin nodded.

"How so?"

Matlin looked at Perlman.

Perlman's pudgy face, behind steel-rimmed glasses, was severe. He reminded Henry of a civil procedure professor he'd had at Virginia. "The State constitution mentions only county district attorneys as public prosecutors. It doesn't mention special prosecutors superseding those district attorneys. The

DAs here are claiming that that omission means the Constitution doesn't permit special prosecutors.

"This office," Perlman continued, "was established by the Governor, pursuant to the state's Executive Law, which specifically authorizes the Governor to appoint a special prosecutor to supersede any district attorney. But, as you know, if a law like the Executive Law authorizes something unconstitutional, it is of no effect."

Henry took a breath. "So, if they're successful, we go out of business?"

"They're not going to be successful," Matlin stated.

"But you're right," Perlman added. "That's what the DAs are seeking in their suit—to put us out of business."

"Gosh..."

"Incidentally," Perlman went on, "if you're wondering how the case started off in the appellate court, the DAs have included Judge Foster, our judge, as a defendant. Suing a judge gets them directly into the Appellate Division."

"Where they may have friends," interjected Matlin. Then he looked at Henry. "With no chief of appeals on board yet, you're our resident expert in civil litigation. We'd like you to handle this."

Henry sat up sharply. Handle it? He was expecting Matlin to ask for some legal research or to help in drafting a response.

"You want me to handle the whole thing?"

"Yes."

"By myself?"

Matlin nodded. "Dan can help you with the facts. He knows the situation. And I'm always here if you have any questions." Matlin picked up the complaint, stood up, and leaned over his desk. "Here. Have a copy made and give the original to my secretary for filing. Then you can get started."

While Matlin's secretary made a copy of the papers, Henry stood and looked across the Hudson River into New Jersey. He wasn't sure what he felt. He was flattered that the Special Prosecutor had thought enough to entrust him with the whole future of the Office. But he wasn't sure he hadn't been thrown a sack of wet sand. Five district attorneys—the chief law enforcement officers of each of the five counties of the City of New York—were trying to eliminate the Special Prosecutor's Office. And he, Henry Perkins, by himself, was their opposition. If the district attorneys won this lawsuit, there would be no Special Prosecutor's Office. Some first day.

Henry started his research right away. But there wasn't much on point. There hadn't been a similar challenge in the recent past, if at all. So, there weren't many cases to give him support for his position. Or for the other side.

Two days later Henry was still at it. He was sitting at his desk, looking at his notes. He had found what he could. But from what he could find in his research, the issue could go either way; the law simply didn't indicate a clear path.

The arguments went both ways. On one hand, the Governor certainly had the legal right under the Executive Law to appoint a special prosecutor to supersede local district attorneys on whatever matters were set out in the executive order making the appointment. Since this particular executive order said the Special Prosecutor had exclusive jurisdiction over corruption in the justice system and law enforcement in each of the five counties of New York City, it followed that his office had the authority to investigate and prosecute any such corruption.

But then there was the state constitution. If you read the state constitution the way the district attorneys proposed, it mentioned only district attorneys, the district attorneys argued, meaning that the district attorneys were the only officials authorized to prosecute crime in the state courts. There was nothing in the state constitution about any special prosecutors.

But the constitution gave the Governor broad powers, not enumerated; so the Executive Law powers over district attorneys, he could argue, were supported by the constitution.

He needed a break, so he stepped into the next office, where Barry Conlon, another assistant special prosecutor to whom Henry had been introduced on his first day, had his office. Henry took a chair in front of Conlon's desk.

"Same mess?"

Henry nodded.

Conlon smiled broadly, showing his perfect white teeth. "Come on, you really think some judge's gonna declare us null and void?"

"I don't know. It's a tough one."

Conlon shrugged.

He had jet black hair, cut short, and deep blue Irish eyes that sparkled under dark eyebrows and long, curving eyelashes. Although his beard was somewhat heavy, his skin was clear, except for a hint of freckles dotting the ridges of his cheeks, just under his eyes. Henry liked Conlon, but he couldn't help being a bit jealous of his looks. *It must give him a big advantage with women,* he thought.

One thing Henry shared with Conlon was a dislike of corrupt policemen. Conlon had been an assistant district attorney before coming to the Special Prosecutor's Office. He was here because, as he had told Henry, he "got sick and tired of having my cases sold out by crooked cops," and had decided to do something about it.

"J'ya see this?" Conlon asked. He held up that morning's *Daily News.* The headlines declared "*JUDGES CORRUPT, SAYS MATLIN.*" He laughed. "Howie gets right to the point, doesn't he?"

"That isn't what Howie said," Henry protested. "All he said was he didn't plan to stop with the police—that he wasn't going to exempt the courts from a look-see, or whatever he called it."

"Ha! Welcome to the world of public service and the press. Everything you do is news." Conlon smiled again. "But half the time, what gets reported, you don't even recognize, even though it's yours." He waved a hand. "Whatever sells newspapers."

Henry shook his head. "Maybe so. But after this, Matlin'll look bad unless we catch some crooked judges soon."

"Yup."

"But that'll take time."

Conlon nodded.

"Then it's the reporter's fault, if anyone criticizes us, not Matlin's."

"You don't think the press is gonna lose any sleep over *that*, do you?" Conlon shrugged. "They say what they want. It's your problem if it isn't true. Don't worry," he said with a grin, "it'll happen to you, too."

Henry didn't smile. If the press printed things that weren't true, how was the truth going to get out? And how could Conlon smile at this kind of thing?

"Ah, well," continued Conlon, "look at it this way. The truth is that Howie *does* think the courts do have some problems. So, the reporter wasn't all wrong. And who knows, maybe someday we'll get a chance to prove Howie's right. Maybe you'll be the one. If you save the Office first, of course."

"Yeah. Right. Thanks."

"By the way," Conlon added, "who's the DAs' attorney?"

"Max Olman."

"Ooh whoo. Big guns."

"I know."

Henry was bent over his desk; he scribbled in the margin of a type-written sheet of paper. It was part of a draft of the SPO's answering papers to the lawsuit, which Henry was reworking again. He looked at what he had written, then scratched it out.

He looked at his draft: *Damn, I'm not happy with it; I didn't make it strong enough.*

He rose and stepped to his window, then he sat down again and looked at the draft. He couldn't seem to nail it down, to draft an answer that he was sure wouldn't leave the position of the Special Prosecutor's Office vulnerable. And then…what if he lost and the Special Prosecutor's Office had to close? What would Matlin say? What would his friends say? What would he say, himself? In his prior practice, when someone felt that his client's position might be vulnerable, the lawyer would sometimes try to settle the case. But how do you settle with five district attorneys who are trying to put you out of business?

He got up from his desk. He needed to think about this some more. *Maybe I'll talk with Dixon,* he said to himself. Pat Dixon was the Office's press secretary. Nicknamed "Scoop," he had been a well-known investigative reporter, with two or three books to his credit, as well. Henry found Dixon interesting, not only because of Dixon's knowledge of the workings of government, but also because Dixon made everyone feel that the Office's posture was in good hands. Despite his diminutive stature, Dixon had an authority about him that gave off a sense of seeing things as they really are.

In fact, Scoop Dixon was an integral part of this new battle against corruption. About a year and a half before, two honest policemen had gone to an assistant to the mayor with evidence they had gathered about systematic graft encountered in the police department. The mayoral assistant had

ignored the evidence and actually tried to deter the two officers from disclos-
ing it. In frustration, they had gone to Dixon, who wrote a series of articles
for the *Times* detailing the allegations, and forcing the Mayor to appoint
the Blinn Commission, which had led to the formation of the Special
Prosecutor's Office.

Henry knocked.

"Come on in."

He opened the door. Smoke billowed into his face. "Whew," he
wheezed, and immediately waved a hand. The source of the cloud was the
press secretary himself, reclining in a chair in his small, cluttered office, puffing on an unfiltered cigarette pinched between nicotine-stained fingers.

Emptying his lungs, Dixon greeted Henry. "Want a cigarette?"
he added.

"No thanks." Henry dropped into a chair.

"What's doing?"

"I just wanted to ask you a question."

"Shoot."

"Put simply, why the hell are those district attorneys trying to get rid
of us?"

Dixon took another puff of his cigarette. He let the smoke drift slowly
between his teeth while Henry waited for an answer. Then he exhaled and
sat up. "That's two questions, not one. The first question is why are they so
pissed off, and the answer's obvious. They just got slapped in the kisser by the
Governor. I mean, if you were the chief law enforcer, how would you like to
be told that you had to step aside and let someone else do your job for you?
That you couldn't cope with the corruption, so you were being superseded
and, to boot, a bulldog like Howie Matlin was going to be rooting around in
your backyard."

"But..."

Dixon raised a hand and continued. "Wait. That's why they're pissed. But the second question is whether they're serious about doing us in, or whether they just want to make some noise until their noses are back in joint."

"Aha," said Henry. It was the first time he had had such a thought— that the DAs might not be going in for the kill. He relaxed a bit. "What do you think?"

"Me? I think the same thing Howie thinks."

"Which is?"

"That they're deadly serious. That they want to put us out of business. And not just because they were humiliated by being superseded. What they're really concerned about is what Howie might turn up in those backyards of theirs. So, they want to keep him from looking."

Ten minutes later, Henry was back at his desk, reviewing the notes for his answering papers. After Scoop Dixon's remarks, his effort looked even shakier than before.

He sat back and ran a hand through his hair. What should he do? He sighed. Was there any way to avoid serving the lawsuit's answering papers on the district attorneys' lawyers and having them chopped to pieces? Was there any chance to settle? Maybe Scoop Dixon was being too cynical about the district attorneys' desire to kill the Office. He might be guessing. No one had explored the possibility of settlement. So how could anyone reject the thought out of hand? At least, it was worth a try.

He picked up his copy of the district attorneys' papers and found their attorney's phone number. Then he reached for the phone.

CHAPTER 5

The subway train lurched into Grand Central, jerked to a stop and opened its doors. Henry was on board, on his way to a meeting he had requested with the lawyer representing the district attorneys. He was going to explore the possibilities of settling the district attorneys' lawsuit.

Although it was midday, there was still a large crowd on the platform waiting for the uptown express on which Henry was arriving. No sooner had the doors opened than most of the crowd began pushing into the car. To get off, Henry had to elbow his way against the tide. With a grunt, he finally made it out and headed for the stairway. Up the stairs, just past the turnstiles, stood several beggars, each with a cup and a cardboard sign. Henry lowered his head, trying to ignore them, but guilt got the best of him. Fishing out a coin, he tossed it into one of the extended cups.

"What's wrong with me?" growled the holder of an unfavored cup. "You don't like cripples?"

Henry hadn't noticed the growler's condition. He was leaning awkwardly on a gnarled stick, his body twisted unnaturally. *Probably faking,* Henry argued with himself. But that didn't assuage his guilt, so he pulled out another coin and dropped it into the growler's cup, hurrying off before one of the others could voice a complaint.

Climbing the remaining stairs brought him onto the street where he stopped and looked at his watch. Right on time. He was about to confront District Attorney Martin Ross and Maxwell Olman, the attorney representing Ross and the four other district attorneys of New York City. He certainly didn't want to be late and give them an advantage.

Martin Ross was an immensely popular public figure. Not only with the voters of Queens who had elected him as their district attorney repeatedly, but also with the media for whom he was always ready with a piquant sound bite. He was the natural spokesman for the four other district attorneys and had assumed the lead in the suit against the Special Prosecutor's Office.

Henry had, of course, read and heard the torrent of abuse Ross had publicly directed at Matlin and the Special Prosecutor's Office. But he was trusting that Ross's words were posturing—an attempt to catch the media's attention and offset the press Matlin was getting. In that way, the public's attention might be diverted from what looked like a putdown of the district attorneys. He knew that Scoop Dixon thought that the DAs really wanted to do away with the Special Prosecutor's Office. But Scoop could be wrong. Maybe, being part of law enforcement—the district attorneys, like the Special Prosecutor's Office—would see the need for all of them to work together. At least he hoped they would.

As he entered Max Olman's building, he wondered what the well-known lawyer would be like in person. Maxwell Olman was something of an institution in the bar of New York City. His original partner, Franklin Pace, with whom he had founded his well-known law firm, Pace and Olman, had been a city commissioner under two or three mayors, and had been responsible for dozens of public works projects, some of which now bore his name. Olman himself was a frequent contributor to the *New York Law Journal* and other legal publications, and to the *New York Times*, which periodically featured a column by Olman, which he called "Tending the Bar." Olman was known for his legal puns, among other things.

Now Henry was going to meet Max Olman. He hoped that Olman would see the sense in Henry's argument. After all, he had been an officer of the Association of the Bar and chairman of its Committee on Criminal Law and the Courts for years. He was a perennial leader in the State bar association's litigation section and, as a former President of the American College of Trial Lawyers, he had national stature as well.

Of course, Olman was a defense lawyer. But leaders like Max Olman, he was sure, were above the petty fray. And Henry was aware that he himself was not without backup support. The press was behind Matlin. Virtually all the coverage of the lawsuit had supported the Special Prosecutor's Office. "Give Him A Chance," read the lead editorial in the *Daily News*, a sentiment which the *Times* and the *Post* had also expressed. Of course, Toby Copin had taken a shot at Matlin in yesterday's *Times*. "A bloodthirsty prosecutor," he had called Matlin. But the *Post* had lambasted the district attorneys for their "pettiness" in bringing the action.

Mr. Olman was tied up, the receptionist told Henry. He would be with him shortly.

Henry had almost twenty minutes to observe the impressive reception area, with its dark-paneled walls and its rich mahogany and plush furniture. He was not happy about being kept waiting. He thought it might part of a game by Olman of one-upmanship. Nevertheless, he continued to study the exquisitely framed portraits of several of the former chief judges of the Court of Appeals, along with portraits of Olman and his original partner.

At last, the receptionist indicated that Olman was free. She pressed a buzzer, which instantly produced an elderly man in a light blue clerk's coat, who guided Henry into the inner sanctum of Pace & Olman.

As Henry entered Olman's commodious office, the lawyer rose slowly from his chair and faced Henry from behind his desk. He was an icon of success. His full head of sleek gray hair was cut to precision, and it graced the angular face beneath like a silver halo. His suit cried out with expensive tailoring, and the extended hand showed the effects of a recent manicure.

Henry walked to where Olman stood to shake his hand. As he reached across Olman's desk, he could tell that the desk was some kind of antique, probably priceless. He was impressed. But he was taken back by the chilly manner in which Olman returned his greeting.

Turning to the other man present, Henry introduced himself. Ross nodded his head from his seat but made no effort to rise or to offer a hand. Henry started to put out his own hand, but, following Ross's example, he held it back.

"Sit down, young man," Olman directed.

Henry's head snapped toward Olman. The lawyer's abrupt command unnerved him. But then, he remembered, Olman *was* his opponent. And he had a client present whom he had to impress.

He sat down.

"I don't know what you have to say to us," Olman began smoothly as soon as Henry had taken his seat. "But my client, District Attorney Ross, has agreed to travel here, at great inconvenience to himself, and to the citizens of his county, who need his services. So, it had better be what we want to hear."

Henry couldn't help noticing Olman's voice. Quiet, dignified, polished. His voice box seemed like an intricate machine of impeccable mechanics. As he spoke, Olman's trimmed eyebrows rose and fell rhythmically, like the hands of an orchestra conductor, confidently directing the flow of his words. The movement of Olman's face muscles caused not a hair on his head to stray from its pre-arranged position.

"I…"

Olman cleared his throat, forestalling Henry's words. Even that eruption was artful.

Henry started again. "I know that you gentlemen are both reasonable men…"

45

Olman folded his arms in front of him. His head was tilted back slightly, so that Henry had a view of the narrow nostrils of his dominant nose.

"I asked you to meet with me," Henry continued, "because I want to give you, or rather, present you with our perspective on this matter. Not our public posture, but the things that lawyers can say off the record. To each other."

Lawyer-to-lawyer. That's the way cases were usually settled. He looked at Olman. There *was* a slight movement—a droop in the corners of Olman's mouth. Henry paused, in case Olman might have a comment. When it was clear that Olman was not moving his mouth to speak, Henry continued.

"I know that you have an obligation to defend your position, or rather the position of your five clients. We understand perfectly. We're all professionals."

Once again, nothing from Olman. He didn't move a muscle. His eyes still fixed on Henry.

Henry went on. "You've presented cogent and fair arguments to the court on your clients' position. And we're prepared to present our own arguments, which we believe are strong."

Still no movement.

"But there are other considerations. Things that might not seem as important in a set of legal papers as they are between the principals."

Olman was stone still. His failure to react was not promising.

"Do you follow me?" he asked.

"Go on," said Olman, without moving.

Henry adjusted himself in his chair. He turned his head and glanced at the man in the chair next to him. Perhaps he should address the real principal in this matter, District Attorney Ross.

Whenever Martin Ross was featured in the newspapers or on television, someone always called him "handsome." But he always reminded Henry of a hood ornament. He couldn't remember what make of car it was, but when Henry was little, he had a neighbor who owned a sedan with a silver head as its hood ornament. The head had high cheekbones, a straight nose, a severe jaw, and deep-set eyes. Like Martin Ross.

On television, in front of the press, Ross was smooth and articulate. He inspired confidence. Now that Henry was seeing Ross in person, he was struck by something else. The eyes. They were different from the hood ornament's eyes. They were colder. Colder than the chromium eyes of the figurine.

He addressed the district attorney.

"Martin." Henry felt funny calling a well-known public figure whom he had just met by his first name. But he didn't want Ross to think he was intimidated.

"Martin, in your position, you have responsibility for all the law enforcement in your county, after the police do their work."

Ross turned his icy eyes on Henry but said nothing.

"And," Henry continued, "to do that job, you need good arrests. You need honest arrests—by honest cops. And you need fair and honest officiating. From honest courts."

Ross looked away for a moment. Then he turned his eyes slowly back to Henry. There was no warmth there. Ross held Henry's gaze until Henry was the one who looked away.

"What I mean to say," Henry went on, "is that you are in a difficult position to investigate the same people you rely on for your convictions. But Howie Matlin is not. And thus, he can make sure that the field you operate in is a clear and honest one. I mean, honest cops should make your cases and honest courts should try them."

Ross made no effort to speak. Nor did Olman.

"Look..." he looked at Ross, then back to Olman. "We're basically on the same team. Our whole system depends on the honest administration of justice." It was finally coming out as he wanted. "I mean, if the courts and the cops aren't honest, there's no justice. For any of us." He lifted a hand from his lap. "I don't have to tell you that."

"Get to the point," said Olman.

Henry stopped. He thought for a moment. "That *is* the point."

"*What* point?" Olman's words were sharp.

Henry added an edge to his own remarks. "The point is that there's no reason why our office can't do its work and the district attorneys do their job, too. We see to it that the system in which all of us operate is honest and efficient. And you put the crooks in jail. As is your responsibility."

He looked back at Ross, then Olman again. There was no reaction.

Henry softened his tone. "Of course, the press will make its noise as always. But meanwhile, we in our office can do our work quietly on your behalf..."

"Quietly?" snapped Olman. "You call your Mr. Matlin's recent slanderous remarks about our judiciary 'quiet?'"

"He was quoted out of context."

"And I suppose he hasn't made similar remarks on other occasions?"

Henry hesitated. Barry Conlon had been correct. Matlin did believe that the judiciary had a problem with corruption. But Henry wasn't about to get into that with Olman. "The headline was wrong," he responded firmly.

Olman folded his hands in front on him. "Have you finished your presentation?" he asked.

Henry thought a moment as to whether there was anything he had neglected to say. "Yes," he responded. "Now I'd like to hear your thoughts."

"Young man..."

Henry straightened in his chair at Olman's provocative tone.

"You are very foolish."

Henry sat up further and looked straight at Olman as the law-yer continued.

"About your Mr. Matlin. And about the merits of this action." Olman unfolded his hands and placed them, palm down, on his desk. "Mr. Matlin is a loose cannon rolling about the deck of a ship loaded with dynamite. A dangerous man. He is also an intruder, and a crude one, who has no right, and no business, demeaning our justice system as he does. If there are imper-fections—and there are imperfections in every human endeavor—they will not be erased by fatuous and unfounded slurs played out for the delight of the tabloid press."

Henry started to protest, but Olman continued.

"As to the merits of the case, you seem ignorant. The authors of the constitution of this state were wise men." Olman's eyes still held Henry tightly. "Wiser than me." He lifted one hand a few inches off his desk and half-pointed at himself. "And certainly..." the hand dropped, "... wiser than your Mr. Matlin."

This was not good. Henry tried to think of a way to get the discussion back on track.

"In their wisdom," Olman continued in his smooth, cultured voice, "the authors of the constitution made the district attorneys of the separate counties the chief, no, the *only* officials responsible for the prosecution of crime within the boundaries of those counties. These constitutionally ordained officials are elected." Olman's eyes bore in. "*Elected*, young man, not appointed, like your Mr. Matlin. Elected by the people of a democratic gov-ernment. A government established by a constitution. A constitution which also establishes the office of district attorney but nowhere, I repeat *nowhere*, provides for a special prosecutor." Olman made the last two words sound scatological. "Nor is there a single scrap of legislative history to suggest that anyone envisioned such an animal when the constitution was adopted."

Olman was simply repeating the arguments in his papers. It wasn't helping.

"*Ergo*," Olman went on, "there is no legitimacy to an office that attempts to act in the stead of those constitutionally ordained officials." The lawyer's hands folded themselves on his desk. "That, young man, is the point. And the only point. And I wonder that any lawyer of consequence could miss it."

"Look, Mr. Olman, I've read your papers. I'm not here to discuss points of law. I'm here to try to find a resolution."

"That, I suspect, is the source of your problem," Olman cut in. "And perhaps your disability." He looked hard at Henry. "We are lawyers, and the law is our profession and our obligation. Not emotions. It seems, in an excess of sentiment, that you have neglected to examine and comprehend the law. Not unexpected in an inexperienced young lawyer, but unimpressive, nonetheless."

Henry ignored the insult and tried to take the offensive. "I had hoped, Mr. Olman," he said somewhat sharply, "that we could discuss a common-sense resolution of the situation and not just some legal technicalities."

Olman's voice was icy. "In the first place, how a lawyer can ignore legalities is beyond me. Secondly, your idea—or I presume, it is Mr. Matlin's idea—of common sense, if I perceive it from your remarks, may be common, but it lacks sense." Olman smiled at his own wit.

"Let me put it simply," Henry said, moving to his bottom line. "I suggest that the district attorneys drop the suit and let us continue with our job, with the assurance that we will be helping the district attorneys do theirs."

Olman's eyebrows lifted in a gesture of astonishment. "Drop the suit? Did I hear you correctly?" Olman sat forward in his chair. "Is that the reason you caused me to inconvenience District Attorney Ross and bring him all the way in here? Is that the reason you took up my valuable time? To ask us simply to discontinue our action?" He looked sharply at Henry. "Are you serious, young man?"

Henry swallowed. He began to see the problem in his suggestion. How could he ask the district attorneys to drop their suit while the Special Prosecutor gave up nothing? He tried to think of a way to restate his position so that it that didn't seem so one-sided.

Olman stood up. "Unless you have something else to offer, our meeting is concluded."

Henry looked at Olman. He wanted somehow to continue the discussion. He just couldn't walk away with nothing. He rose. A glance at Martin Ross showed no help there. The district attorney was in his chair, arms folded, looking out Olman's window.

Henry picked up his briefcase. "Look," he said, turning back to Olman. "there must be a way..."

Olman cut him off. "My client and I have wasted enough time on your fatuous appeal. I have better things to do. A court will decide the issues." Olman nodded at his door. "Good day."

Henry paused at the door, his briefcase dangling from his hand. "You know, you might lose..."

"A risk one takes in any litigation," Olman cut in. "Good day."

Henry hesitated as he opened the door.

"Good day," repeated Olman.

CHAPTER 6

Into the air over New York City billowed several long ugly columns of black smoke. They climbed with malevolent persistence until they reached a point high above, where they disbursed slowly and began sinking invisibly toward the lungs and bloodstreams of defenseless New Yorkers. For years, New Yorkers had simply endured the smoke. But now, in 1972, there were fines for such pollution. And no one could fail to discern the sources of the smoke. So why wasn't the City doing something about it?

Henry used to wonder about that. Now, a week after his futile trip uptown, as he stared out his office window, watching the smoke rise, he knew why. Today's press revealed that the Special Prosecutor's Office was investigating a scheme whereby certain businesses bought protection from paying fines for polluting New York's endangered air. Businessmen who had donated enough money to the right political organizations were able to have violations of the anti-pollution laws routinely dismissed by an official of the Department of Environmental Protection. The official himself and his boss apparently answered to a party district leader who collected the money from the businesses. Henry didn't know the details yet since the Office had imposed an internal security blanket on the investigation once the news media had learned of it. But he did know that Lou Morotti, one of the Office's group chiefs, was directing the investigation, and one of Lou's assistants had revealed to him that the senior hearing officer in the Department of Environmental

Protection who had actually processed the fixed summonses had been caught and had turned and was now cooperating with the investigation. So, it couldn't be long before there were some results.

It was an exhilarating sensation, being part of the solution for a change. No more helpless gnashing of teeth or grumbling over the morning paper. He knew the City was in trouble, that it was being sold out by its leaders. But now he could do something. He was on the rescue squad, able to ferret out the betrayers and drag them before the bar of justice.

But then there was his lawsuit. His confrontation with Max Olman and District Attorney Ross had convinced Henry that the district attorneys were serious about putting the Special Prosecutor's Office out of business and, in the week since the meeting, he had redoubled his effort to come up with a satisfactory response to the district attorneys' papers. He was still, however, somewhat uncertain about the effectiveness of what he had managed to put together.

"Whatcha lookin' at?" Henry started as Dan Nelligan stepped into his office.

"You scared me. I wasn't looking at anything. Just thinking."

Dan sat down, dropping nimbly into a chair across the desk. "I got a piece of news."

Henry perked up. Barry Conlon had told him that Dan Nelligan had the best sources of anyone in the office, Scoop Dixon included. Henry hoped that Nelligan was about to tell him about some juicy new development in Lou Morotti's pollution investigation. Perhaps they had already indicted someone. Or turned another witness.

"The DAs are gonna try an end-run on you."

"The DAs?" It took a second to register. "Are you talking about my lawsuit?"

"Yup."

"What do you mean by an end-run?"

"I don't know. All I know is that they're gonna try somethin' funny—something you probably aren't expecting. I just thought you oughtta know."

Henry leaned forward. "You don't have any idea what it is?"

"Nope. Just keep your eyes open, an' be ready for something comin' outta left field."

"Can't you tell me anything more than that?"

Nelligan shook his head. "Wish I could."

Henry frowned. "Thanks a lot. I'm already worried about the strength of our legal argument. And now you tell me the opposition's plotting some trick…"

"Hey, relax. You don't have to *worry*. Just be alert, that's all."

"But…"

Nelligan rose. "By the way, Matlin's gonna be on TV tonight. Channel Four, I think it is

"But…" Henry wanted more information, but he already knew Nelligan well enough to know that if he said he didn't know, he didn't. "Well, thanks for the information—whatever it means."

"Oh, you'll find out," Nelligan said with a grin. "About the same time I do."

The next morning, Henry sat down at his desk and breathed a sigh of relief. The answering papers in the district attorneys' lawsuit had finally been served at five o'clock the day before. He winced as he remembered the last hour of preparation.

"Where the hell is the answer?" Nat Perlman, Matlin's Chief Assistant, burst through Henry's door. "It's after four o'clock and it's got to be served today."

"I know," Henry responded. "I'm just making some last-minute changes."

Perlman's face reddened. "Forget the changes. Serve whatever you've got. Now. Before we're in default."

And so, the answering papers had been completed and served. Thank goodness.

A knock.

"It's open."

"Hey, man." A big grin.

"Oh, hi, Barry. Come on in."

Barry Conlon entered holding a paper container of coffee, light blue with tan drawings of Greek temples on the cup.

"Outside coffee, huh?" remarked Henry.

"You'c'n count on that. I'm not gonna be caught drinkin' that stuff the investigators brew that you drink." Conlon took a seat in front of Henry's desk. "So, d'j'ya get those papers done?"

"Yeah. Served 'em last night. We're now officially in the suit." Henry wiped his eyes and leaned back in his chair. "You know, I have to say, I still don't really understand it."

"Don't understand what?"

"The whole thing," Henry sighed.

"What d'ya mean? The legal stuff?"

"No. I mean the way they're pushing this thing. I know the DAs are ticked off that we're treading on their turf, but I don't see where they're hurt if we clean up the system."

"Ha! Obviously, you've never worked for a DA"

"I know. And you did. So maybe the question is why'd you become a prosecutor?" Henry held up a hand to forestall a wisecrack. "No, I'm serious. You wanted to do something about the bad guys. Right?"

Conlon lowered his eyes. "So?"

"So why would you object to someone wanting to clean up the playing field you were playing on?"

Conlon looked directly at Henry. "I wouldn't. And I didn't. But I only worked there. I wasn't the guy who ultimately had to get along with the cops and the judges and the politicians. The DA was. Don't forget, DAs have to rely on the precinct cops—the ones who are out there takin' money—to also go out and arrest a few people so they can try some cases and the DA can say he's doin' something about crime. And the guys from the DA's office, they gotta face the same judges every day—the ones who're gonna decide their cases. How're they gonna kick 'em in the nuts one day and then ask 'em to decide somethin' in their favor the next? And, I didn't have to run for the job *I* had; I was hired. I didn't need campaign funds every four years. I didn't need a clubhouse to hand me the nomination and get my petitions signed and collect the bucks from the real estate developers and the contractors and so forth, who're gonna keep my campaign workers in cash. All I had to do was prosecute crooks. It was my boss who had to worry about the other shit. Just like Ross and the rest of 'em do."

Henry was silent for a moment. "Well, maybe so. But Ross *is* a public officer. And I would think he might at least be a little responsive to the *public's* interest."

Conlon opened his eyes in mock astonishment. "An elected public official who gives a shit about the public? In what fairyland have you been living?"

Henry shook his head. "You're impossible."

"Only observant." Conlon sat up. "Anyway, this bullshit isn't why I came in." He smiled mischievously. "I may have somethin' for you."

"Huh?"

"A broad. A bombshell blonde. With a body that just won't quit." He lifted his hands to his chest. "Bazooms you'll die over." He lowered his hands. "And legs like a chorus girl. You free tonight? It's Friday."

"Wait a minute." Henry held up a hand. "If she's that good, how come you aren't taking care of her?"

Conlon's mouth drooped sadly. "Unfortunately, she's the roommate of a great chick I've been makin' it with. And I don't want to lose a sure thing."

Henry grinned. "Well, I'm out. At least tonight. I'm going to the opera."

"The opera?" Conlon shook his head. "Forget it, then. The only music this broad's probably heard of comes out of a boom box. Maybe some other time."

"Ouch," said Henry as he sank into his seat in the Dress Circle at the Metropolitan Opera. He was wearing a new device the tech staff had given him. Called a beeper, it would notify him if he was being paged. He found that the electronic devices the tech people had were fascinating. There were recorders you could hide...

His thoughts were interrupted by the opening chords of "Così Fan Tutte."

"*Beep, beep, beep, beep...*" Henry jumped, along with eight or ten other people who were equally enraptured by the beautiful aria. In near panic he fumbled with the offending device at his hip, jabbing and punching, desperately trying to silence it.

"Shut that thing off," came a stage whisper in front of him.

At last, he found the button and the box fell silent. Looking up, he saw several pairs of angry eyes turned toward him in the semi-darkness of the opera house. He would have to wait until the intermission to call in; he certainly couldn't create another disturbance by leaving. Just to be safe, he held the device in his hand with a finger resting lightly on the button that had silenced it.

As soon as the act ended and the house lights came on, Henry trotted to a phone booth and called the office. The call was answered on the first ring. "Special Prosecutor's Office."

"It's Henry Perkins. I was just beeped." He leaned against the panel on which the phone was mounted.

"Oh, yes. I have a message for you."

Henry could hear some paper rustling on the other end.

"Here it is. It's from Dan Nelligan. 'Looks like trouble. You have to be in the Appellate Division in Brooklyn first thing Monday morning. Come in tomorrow at nine to discuss it.' Do you understand that?"

"Yes," said Henry and hung up the phone. "Looks like trouble," Nelligan had said. But what kind of trouble? The message said that he was to be in the Appellate Division—the court that was hearing the district attorneys' lawsuit—on Monday morning. But why? Courts didn't normally call the parties Friday afternoon and summon them to a conference on Monday morning. Things didn't add up. Dan Nelligan had heard that something funny was going on. This must be it. But what? Had the district attorneys or their lawyer, Max Olman, somehow gone around end? Had they gotten to somebody? Whatever they had done, it was enough that Henry had to be in his office at nine o'clock tomorrow morning. And in court early Monday.

Snow had begun falling while Henry was still in the office on Saturday and had continued through Sunday afternoon, at which point the temperature had risen just enough to melt the would-be flakes and turn most of the accumulated snow to slush. By now, Monday morning, as Henry sloshed along to court, what remained on the sidewalks was a gray lumpy layer of matter that resembled translucent mashed potatoes sprinkled with dirt.

As he approached the white marble steps to the courthouse, Henry noticed workmen affixing conical wire contraptions to the streetlamps. It reminded Henry that Christmas was approaching. He would soon be going home to Cleveland again. For a moment, he wondered if his parents would take time off from the hospital Christmas Day so he could have dinner with them.

Then he pulled his mind back to Eagle Street in Brooklyn, where he had other things to worry about. He still had no idea why the judge had called the conference, nor did anyone else in the office on Saturday. Opinions had ranged. Dan Nelligan wondered if the judge was going to pull some trick on the Special Prosecutor's Office. Nat Perlman thought the meeting was nothing more than a hastily called scheduling conference. Henry hoped that Perlman was right.

At least Henry was ready for Max Olman this time. There would be no appeal to emotions. Legal points only. And no Mr. Nice Guy. Because this time they were in front of the judge who would hear the lawsuit. Justice Arthur Sammons.

To the legal establishment of New York, Arthur Sammons was the leading light of the Appellate Division, the intermediate appellate court in the New York State court system. This was Henry's first meeting with Sammons, but he had heard from colleagues about the judge's forbidding presence. Now he was about to find out for himself.

Max Olman was already in the anteroom when Henry arrived at Justice Sammons's chambers. Henry's "good morning" received no response. But before Henry could react, the judge himself opened his office door and invited the two men to enter.

"Ah, Mr. Justice," hailed Olman, greeting Sammons warmly. "Or Judge, I should say," with a theatrical chuckle.

Sammons smiled broadly at Olman's greeting. He obviously appreciated whatever Olman had said.

"Am I among the first?" queried Olman heartily as he pulled up a heavy wooden armchair in front of the judge's desk.

"Indeed, you are, Maxwell," replied Sammons.

Henry introduced himself and sat down in the other chair. He wondered what the two men were talking about. Not important, he decided. He sat back, ready for the discussion.

"Shall we begin?" said the judge, joining his hands. His palms pressed together with fingers upward, interlocking in a gesture that reminded Henry of a priest praying over communion wafers. Sammons, in fact, reminded Henry of a priest he had seen once on television. He had a long, gaunt face, with high cheekbones and hollows both at the temples and in the cheeks below. His thinning, gray-black hair contrasted sharply with the wan complexion of his face. But his heavy, glowering eyebrows and steel-gray eyes so dominated the judge's physiognomy that one overlooked its lack of floridity.

"Last Friday," said Sammons turning to Henry, "counsel for the district attorneys *ex parte* requested a temporary restraining order concerning your Office's recent indictment of certain political figures."

Henry bolted upright. Temporary restraining order? Recent indictment of political figures? Obviously, he was referring to last Thursday's indictment of the politicians who fixed pollution summonses. But why?

"Your adversaries," Sammons went on, "asked me to halt prosecution of that matter until the issues raised by their own action were resolved."

"Excuse me, Your Honor," Henry said. "I'm not sure I understand. I thought we were here for a conference in the lawsuit the district attorneys brought against the Special Prosecutor's Office. Why are we talking about the pollution-fixing case?"

Justice Sammons's eyes shifted to Max Olman. Some communication passed between the two men that Henry missed. Then he heard the judge sigh. "I'll spell it out for you, Mr. Perkins."

The judge's long fingers entwined. "Mr. Olman has raised a simple, but persuasive argument. If the Special Prosecutor is not constitutionally authorized to act, he should not be permitted to prosecute presumably innocent persons such as the defendants in last week's indictments. Why, he asks, shouldn't the prosecution of these persons be enjoined until the issue of the constitutionality of the Special Prosecutor's Office is resolved?"

Henry's mouth went dry.

"I felt," Sammons continued, "that a representative of the Special Prosecutor's Office ought to be present when I made my decision. Hence"—Sammons swept his hand to take in both lawyers—"this meeting."

What Justice Sammons was saying was that he was prepared to stop Howard Matlin from prosecuting the pollution fixers. Such a bizarre possibility, no one had even considered it. He started to protest but the judge silenced him with a hand.

"There was a second reason for my delay in acting on the district attorneys' request. There was, on Friday, some uncertainty as to my status with respect to this matter."

Now Henry was confused again. What did the judge's "status" have to do with his enjoining the pollution prosecution?

"That status," Sammons went on, "has now been clarified and I must inform you, it is my intention to act. I intend to issue the order requested, enjoining your Office from prosecuting the matter in question." The judge's steel eyes fixed on Henry. "Not only that, but, in the absence of more compelling arguments than I have seen in your papers or have heard from your Mr. Matlin, I intend to go further than Mr. Olman requests and enjoin your Office from proceeding in *any* matters."

Henry reeled back in his chair. The judge was going to close the Special Prosecutor's Office! Henry felt like he was having a nightmare.

"I will, of course, permit further filing of papers before I make my injunction permanent. But I shall conclude the matter before I leave the court next month."

"Leave the co–?"

"Apparently," interjected Max Olman, turning toward Henry with a chilling smile, "counsel for the Special Prosecutor is unaware of the fact that Justice Sammons has been appointed by the Governor to a seat on the Court of Appeals."

Oh, my God, thought Henry. *That's what Sammons meant by his "status."* The judge is on his way to the state's highest court. And in a month.

"Uh, congratulations," he stammered.

"I thank you."

Suddenly Henry felt sick as the situation sank in. Sammons was about to issue an order that would temporarily bar the Special Prosecutor's Office from prosecuting any cases at all. Then he was going to make the order permanent within a month. The Office would have to close and appeal the decision. But the only court to which the decision could be appealed was the Court of Appeals—the court on which Justice Sammons was going to be sitting in a month. Dan Nelligan had said that the district attorneys were up to something unusual. But not even Dan could have imagined anything this bad. This wasn't just a nightmare. This was a nightmare come true.

He heard Sammons talking again. "There is one chance that I may change my mind concerning the injunction."

Henry looked at the judge.

"I have reason to believe," Sammons continued, "that the district attorneys would be amenable to a compromise. A compromise I will outline for your consideration."

My consideration? Henry took a breath. How could this be happening? What should he do? What would Howard Matlin do? If only Matlin were here...

And what will the people of New York do if the Special Prosecutor's Office is shut down just as it's beginning to function? What will the Governor, who opened the Office less than three months ago, say when it's suddenly closed? And the press? What will they say? Especially when he, Henry Perkins, the man entrusted with defending the Special Prosecutor's Office, in less than two weeks permitted it to be eliminated?

Henry could feel his fingernails pressing into his palms. His breakfast was gathering in a small part of his stomach, threatening to re-emerge.

"What kind of compromise?" he asked.

CHAPTER 7

"Howie, it's not that bad," Nat Perlman was insistent.

Matlin's eyes told nothing of his reaction to Henry's recounting of the proposal given that morning by Justice Arthur Sammons. Nor did they reveal his opinion of Perlman's recommendation.

"I have no real problem," Perlman continued. "We could live with it."

Matlin continued to look at Perlman, masking whatever he was feeling or thinking.

Perlman went on. "All we would have to do is to submit a list of our investigations to the district attorney in whose county the matter arose. We wouldn't have to turn over any cases or stop investigating anything. We wouldn't even have to give details—names of witnesses, sources—nothing. If the DA wants to question any of our matters, he must make a formal application to Sammons or his replacement on the Appellate Division to review the case. And it would be the district attorney who has the burden of showing why he ought to get the case. If he can't show that, we keep the case. Even if we don't, it still gets prosecuted by the DA—something we'd certainly make sure happened."

Matlin said nothing, so Perlman went on.

"Look at the benefits, Howie. Instead of five powerful enemies in the district attorneys' offices, you'll have five allies. And Sammons, who I've heard is already in line to become Chief Judge of the Court of Appeals next year, will be one hundred percent in our corner. Why? Because we're operating according to his rules. We'll be stronger than we are now because we'll have Sammons behind us. Also, we won't be using so much of our energy bucking the powers-that-be."

Henry felt his stomach relax slightly. Perlman was at least making some sense. Henry didn't like the idea of someone outside the Office reviewing the Special Prosecutor's investigations before they were concluded. But, given the harsh choice Justice Sammons had presented, maybe Perlman was right, and they could somehow live with it. Sammons wasn't asking the Special Prosecutor to go out of business. Only to co-ordinate his activities with the district attorneys, under judicial supervision. At least, they wouldn't lose everything. And losing the district attorneys' lawsuit seemed a certainty, now that the judge overseeing the case had taken sides.

Matlin looked at Henry. So did Matt Corey, the chief investigator.

Was Henry expected to comment? Should he say that Perlman made a certain amount of sense? He glanced at Matt Corey and immediately decided against it. The chief investigator's burly six-foot-three frame was still. But his eyes were full of anger, and his large mouth was drawn downward, causing his heavy jowls to hang like powder pouches. There was no doubt what the chief investigator thought about the offer. Henry had heard stories about Corey's temper.

Matlin's eyes flicked back to Perlman. "No," Matlin said at last.

"But..." It was Perlman.

"Arthur Sammons is not going to hogtie this office." As he spoke, Matlin leaned over and pressed a button.

"Yes?" said the intercom.

"Harriet, get me the Governor." He released the button and looked back at Perlman. "The Governor likes to take credit for establishing this Office; now he's going to earn his credit."

"Howie," Perlman protested, "what in the world do you think the Governor can do? He can't overrule a judge. And even if he could, he's certainly not going smear egg on the face of someone he's just appointed to the Court of Appeals."

"Let me worry about the Governor, Nat."

"But…"

"Nat, I've said it before," Matlin broke in, "and I'll say it again. There's no compromising with corruption. The only way this Office can investigate effectively is by ourselves. I don't want any elected officials peering over our shoulders, telling us what we can and can't do. Or any judge, either. I want them ignorant of what we're up to. I want them scared. And that can happen only if we're independent and can go after whomever we want, whenever we want. Unimpeded."

As soon as he heard Matlin say it, Henry felt better. The whole idea of a Special Prosecutor's Office was to be independent of the "powers-that-be," as Perlman had called them. Not to play ball with them.

But wait. How could Matlin simply reject a compromise proposed by a judge as powerful as Sammons? And Perlman was right—what could the Governor do? And why, in any case, would he allow himself, as Matlin seem to be suggesting, to be used as a weapon against someone he had just appointed to the State's highest court? Did Matlin realize how bad things really were? Henry glanced out the window. The sky was darkening as if to storm.

The buzzer sounded. "The Governor," said Harriet.

Matlin picked up the phone. "Governor? Yes. Governor, I'd like to see you. Is four o'clock today convenient?"

"Hello, Howard. It's good to see you." The Governor strode around his mahogany desk with his massive hand outstretched. His frame seemed even larger in person than on television or the front pages of the newspaper. "Big Jim" Whelan was big indeed.

"You know my counsel, Harry Weinstein." Whelan nodded toward a cadaverous figure who had risen from a chair near Whelan's desk.

"Yes," said Matlin, shaking hands with Weinstein. "And this is Henry Perkins, one of my assistants."

The Governor shook Henry's hand, fixing Henry's eye and flashing a smile. The same quick direct eye and smile which he must have bestowed upon millions of voters in his years in politics. Friendly enough to make you like him. But bestowed briefly, so that you would never dream of asking such an important man to linger over your own insignificance. It worked. Though he knew Whelan to be a politician, Henry was impressed.

"Sit down," said Whelan heartily, pointing to a cluster of small fabric-covered chairs gathered around a coffee table near one of the windows. "We'll be more comfortable here." He strode over to one of the chairs and sat down, his back to the window.

Henry waited until Matlin had selected the chair opposite the Governor, then he took the one to the Governor's left. He still had no idea what Matlin was planning to say to the Governor—the Special Prosecutor hadn't discussed it during the short ride over to the World Trade Center, where the Governor had his city office. But how Matlin was going to convince the Governor to keep Justice Sammons from closing down the Special Prosecutor's Office was beyond Henry's imagination.

His eyes swept briefly about the large office. It was elegantly furnished, he noticed. He asked himself if the Albany office was as nice. Or if the antique bookcase in the corner was real. Of course, what he was really doing was the old dentist's chair trick. Focus on something else so he wouldn't have to think of what was about to happen.

"Been stirring up a bit of controversy, I see," said the Governor as soon everyone was seated. He looked pointedly at Matlin.

"It comes with the job," responded Matlin offhandedly. Then he changed tones. "I want to…"

"Doesn't help, though, does it?"

Matlin didn't hesitate. "It doesn't surprise me. Or get in the way of doing our job."

"Your job or mine?" the Governor persisted. He eyed Matlin closely.

Without flinching, Matlin returned the Governor's gaze. "I can only speak about my job."

"That's a luxury you have, Howard. And one I don't." Whelan folded his arms and leaned against the back of his chair, as though he were relaxing. But the hardness in his eyes and mouth told the truth. "Your job reflects on my job. And you haven't made my job any easier."

Matlin calmly folded his fingers together. His eyes never left the Governor's. "Then I have a solution for you."

"The solution I suggest," interjected the Governor, "is for you to be a bit more discrete."

Matlin didn't move. He still held the Governor's eyes.

Whelan matched him for a moment. Then he leaned back a few inches in his chair. He tilted his head slightly to one side. "All right, what kind of solution?"

"I want you to tell the district attorneys to drop their suit." Matlin's voice was placid, his eyes steady.

Weinstein lurched forward and started to speak. The Governor silenced him with a raised palm. "And just why should I do that?" he asked Matlin.

"Because your credibility is at stake."

Governor Whelan's face reddened. "*My* credibility?" His eyes narrowed. "Perhaps I ought to remind you that I'm not the one who's been saying that the courts are full of maggots. With no proof."

Matlin made no effort to respond. Instead, he placed his folded hands on one of his thighs and looked directly at the Governor. The Governor sat still, as well, eyeing Matlin in return. Neither man seemed ready to back off.

There was a twitch in Henry's leg. He wanted to change positions, but he didn't dare move a muscle while the drama played out in front of him. He shifted his eyes to the Governor, then to the Special Prosecutor. Neither moved.

Suddenly he understood Matlin's point. Brilliant! He hadn't even thought of that. The Governor's credibility *was* at stake. He had made an appointment—a well-publicized appointment—that was now being challenged by five district attorneys. The Governor, they were saying, was legally mistaken—even stupid—to have made that appointment. But Governor Whelan couldn't afford to look stupid, or even mistaken and still maintain his credibility.

Henry looked back at the Governor without moving his head. The Governor's lips parted.

"What makes you think that any of them would listen to me?"

Matlin moved his folded hands to the table in front of him. Otherwise, he remained still, his dark eyes fixed on the Governor, his mouth sealed. It was the Governor who spoke again.

"I know," he said answering himself, "I'm the governor." He leaned forward, toward Matlin. "You know, Howard, I didn't put you in that job to splash mud in my face."

"You know where the mud is coming from, Governor."

Once again, for what seemed to Henry a very long time, the two men locked eyes. Henry had thought Matlin had won. Now he wasn't certain. Would the Governor refuse Matlin's request, despite the risk? He almost forgot to breathe.

Then Whelan moved. In fact, he rose from his chair.

"All right, I'll see what I can do," he said, turning toward his desk. Weinstein, too, was on his feet.

Matlin rose and nodded.

"But, Howard," added the Governor as he stepped behind his desk. "From now on, please behave yourself a little better."

It was shortly after five o'clock in the afternoon a few days later, and the Office of the Special Prosecutor was having its first Christmas party. Henry glanced around the room he had just entered. The library, as it was optimistically called, had a set of books reporting state cases, along with the basic criminal statutes. They were in shelves on one wall. There was little else adorning the large windowless room except two long tables which had been pushed up against one wall and a handful of straight-backed chairs, also against a wall. Someone had strung a few rolls of red and green crepe paper on the ceiling and there was a small artificial Christmas tree on a desk near the door. Ice, glasses, and a few bottles of liquor were set out on one of the tables and some pretzels, potato chips, and a coffee urn were on the other.

"Hey, Perk, congratulations." It was Angie Palumbo, one of the senior investigators, these were retired cops or FBI who were leading the younger investigators in the Office's investigations. "You deserve a drink."

"Thanks, Angie. I could use one." He walked over to the table. No beer. So, he poured himself a scotch and water. Palumbo followed, but waited until Henry had his drink.

"Sometime," Palumbo said quietly, once Henry had stepped away from the bar, "you gotta tell me how you got those fuckin' DAs to fold so quickly."

Henry nodded. "Amazing, wasn't it?"

"Well, my man," Palumbo continued, "whatever you did, I thank you. Now Tim O'Leary 'n' me don't have to go job shoppin' again."

"It was Howie, not me."

"Bullshit. That's not what Howie said. Don't be so modest." He waved his hand around the room. "Especially in a joint like this." Palumbo took a gulp of his drink, a clear drink on the rocks.

"What's that?" asked Henry.

"Vodka on the rocks. Only thing I drink."

"Hey," said Henry, anxious to change the subject, "I hear you and Tim almost snagged a lawyer. Right on top of the pollution case."

Palumbo laughed. "'Almost' isn't the word I'd pick." Friggin' skel of an informant we had."

"Why? What happened?"

"Ah, this scumbag, he and his buddy got arrested for posin' as cops and shakin' down some poor fag. A couple days later, the creep claims his buddy that got locked up with him has a lawyer that's supposta fix the case. Bullshitted poor Hal Baker into gettin' a wiretap on a lawyer that didn't even exist."

"Huh?"

"The lawyer that was supposed to be fixin' the case? Doesn't even exist."

"Jeez. Why would the guy do something like that?"

Palumbo waved a hand. "Who knows? Probably figured he'd confuse the guys who're prosecutin' him for the shakedown. You wait'll you're here a while. You'll see what floats up onto the doorstep with some information." He looked up. "Hey, there's O'Leary. I better see he gets a drink."

After Palumbo had gone, Pat Dixon, the press secretary, added his congratulations. Others, too, congratulated Henry on helping rid the Office of the district attorneys' suit. Henry smiled and accepted their congratulations gracefully. He knew that it was Howard Matlin, not he, who had disrupted the litigation and saved the Office. But he did have a part in it, and he was as happy as everyone else about the result. The truth was, he enjoyed the limelight. And the scotch, as well.

He looked up to see Howard Matlin walking into the now well-filled room with a short, elderly woman, who from her physiognomy was clearly his mother. Someone intercepted Matlin and, at once, he was surrounded by people greeting him and his mother. Henry went to the bar and poured himself another scotch. Then, spotting his group chief, Pete Flannery, he headed in his direction.

Henry had expected the party to be one of those one-quick-drink-and-go-home types. He was surprised when, over two hours later, no one had left. On the contrary, the makeshift party had turned into a very spirited affair, in every sense of the word. Somehow, new bottles of liquor kept replacing the empty ones and ice, mixer, and the dishes of pretzels and potato chips were constantly being replenished. He had just poured himself another scotch and water, the effects of which he was beginning to feel, when he noticed Matlin's mother, or, since he had not been introduced, the woman he had assumed to be Matlin's mother, standing next to him without a glass in her hand.

"Can I get you something?" he asked.

"Thank you, no. Unless…" she peered toward the far end of the second table, "there's some coffee?"

"Certainly." Henry started toward the coffee urn, then turned back. "Anything in it?"

"Just black, thank you."

Henry handed her the coffee then extended his hand. "I'm Henry Perkins."

"I'm Rose Matlin. Howard's mother." Her head bobbed, causing her white curls to jiggle, almost girlishly. "Nice to meet you."

Henry nodded but didn't speak. He wasn't sure what to say next.

"Are you a lawyer or an investigator?" she asked.

"I'm a lawyer. I'm in my third week with the Office."

"Have you worked before with my son?"

Henry was relieved that she seemed able to lead the conversation. "No, I haven't." What do you say? He wasn't sure what to say. "I'm quite impressed with him," he added. That was true.

"Yes. He's a very special person." She looked Henry in the eye. "He has a force inside that makes him very…different."

It wasn't hard to see where Matlin had learned to get to the point quickly.

"Sometimes I'm surprised he's my son. I often wonder where that force comes from. As if it came from somewhere beyond." She gave out a tiny laugh and blinked. "He was that way even as a boy."

Henry shifted his weight. Were it not for the scotches, he knew that he would feel uncomfortable. He took another sip.

"Some of it he gets from his father. But most comes from, I don't know where." Rose Matlin shrugged her shoulders, then leaned closer to her new confidant. "When he was thirteen, or fourteen maybe, he took on the whole police department."

Henry lifted his head sharply. "What? How?"

Rose Matlin smiled and shook her head. Her curls jiggled again, as did the tiny bags under her chin. She leaned back toward Henry. "Howard wouldn't like me telling you this."

"Oh, I won't say anything," replied Henry quickly.

She smiled conspiratorially. "Well, the sergeant had tried to get money from Herman—that was Howard's father. He's gone many years now."

"I'm sorry." For an instant Henry felt foolish. Then he came back to her story.

"The sergeant, he wanted money to protect the store—Herman's butcher shop. That's what the sergeant said, but Herman threw him out of the store. Then someone tried to start a fire in the store. It would have burned our house down—we lived over the store—only Howard and his father put it out. Howard said it was the police who started the fire. He said he saw a squad car drive away just before. So, he went to the captain to complain. He even went to the local district leader and our assemblyman. We couldn't stop Howard." She shook her head. "I don't think anyone can." A smile crossed her face. "He certainly made a lot of trouble." She stepped back, apparently finished with her story.

"What happened?" asked Henry.

"To the police? Nothing. And the District Leader, he told us that we made too much trouble." She shrugged. "Herman wanted to move anyway, so we went out to the Island. Much nicer there." She was smiling again.

Henry was picturing Howard Matlin as a young boy taking on the whole establishment. Then he remembered the woman standing in front of him.

"It's nice that your son is able to bring you here."

"Yes," she agreed. "Especially since he's alone now."

"What do you mean?"

Mrs. Matlin looked at him. "You don't know about his wife?"

"No. Is she here?" At once he realized that was a dumb question.

"Gone, too. Passed away over a year ago. Cancer. But Howard still misses her terribly."

"Did they have children?"

She looked sadly at him. "No. Perhaps God was saving him for something else."

Henry shifted uncomfortably. He tried to think of something to say but was suddenly saved by the subject of the conversation.

"Is my mother boring you with Howard Matlin stories?" Henry had not seen Matlin approach.

"Now Howard, I was just meeting this nice young attorney. He is in his third week here and is enjoying his work."

"You see," said Matlin smiling at Henry, "my mother is the best investigator of us all." He turned to her. "If I'm going to drive you home, we'd better get started."

After Howard Matlin and his mother had left, Henry decided to have another drink. He didn't want to compare mothers with Matlin or think about mothers in general. Scotch would be better.

He walked a bit unsteadily to the bar and half-filled his plastic cup with amber. He forgot the water.

She was right. Howard Matlin *was* special. He was obviously a fighter; he'd just proven that. But there was something about Matlin that seemed almost spiritual, as though his guidance came directly from a source that others could only grope to imagine.

"Hey, Perk."

Henry jumped. It was Hal Baker, one of his fellow assistants.

"Oh, hi, Hal." Henry shook his head to clear his eyes.

"Wantcha ta meet my wife, Kim." Baker's words, like Henry's, were a bit slurred.

Henry's head cleared enough to see a very pretty woman. But he wasn't really looking at her. Or thinking about her. He was thinking about Howard Matlin. Even with the scotches he had consumed, Henry knew one thing: He was where he wanted to be. His old colleague Jerry could scoff. His friend George could try to discourage him. But things were clear to him now. Howard Matlin was a strong force for the things Henry really believed in. The rotten roots that undermined society could be pulled out of the ground. And Howard Matlin was the one who could do it.

He put down his drink and headed home.

CHAPTER 8

Henry stepped into his office, took off his suit coat and hung it on the back of his door. He still felt the energy of his walk across Chambers Street from the subway in the clear early May air. He dropped into his chair with the two morning papers he had bought at the East 77th Street kiosk, where he boarded the train.

This morning, each paper had a story on the Special Prosecutor's Office and its latest investigation into a group of police officers in Brooklyn who had been taking money to protect a house of prostitution. In fact, in the seven and a half months the Office had been in operation, the stream of indictments was enough to keep the Office on or near the front page regularly, sometimes pushing the latest developments in Watergate to the second page. There was Lou Morotti's indictment of the two commissioners and two other politicians for taking bribes to fix pollution summonses. It was now being prepared for trial, as was an indictment of a bureau chief in the Bronx District Attorney's Office who had been caught by the Blinn Commission discussing the fixing of heroin cases. Among the significant matters involving police officers, in addition to the Brooklyn prostitution protection, were the arrest of a deputy inspector and two sergeants for lying about their knowledge of organized gambling "pads" in the twenty-eighth precinct and the recent arrest of two Narcotics detectives for taking a bribe to let a drug dealer go (who happened to be an undercover Internal Affairs cop). There were smaller cases, too, such as a recent charge involving two traffic patrolmen who were accepting gratuities from Park Avenue doormen to overlook double-parked cars. And the Office's present investigations promised much bigger things.

"There is an atmosphere inside the Special Prosecutor's Office," wrote Mike Welling of the *Daily News,* "that seems purer, cleaner than the smoggy air that darkens the precincts and clouds the courthouses of our city. It makes one believe that maybe something is finally being done to clean up the soot that has lain too long around our town."

And Sabrina Wilcox, of the more sedate *Times,* in one article crooned, "Edmund Burke has said that 'corrupt influence…is itself the perennial spring…of all disorder.' Howard Matlin seems to have listened, since he is moving with unprecedented boldness to cap that spring."

Of course, the Office had its critics. Like the Patrolmen's Benevolent Association, or P.B.A., the largest union of police officers. Every time the Office indicted a police officer, it encountered angry attacks from the P.B.A., which then sent batteries of lawyers to the officers' defense.

Nor was the P.B.A. alone. Although he had agreed to drop the lawsuit against the Special Prosecutor's Office, along with the other district attorneys, Queens District Attorney Martin Ross kept up a barrage of criticism of Howard Matlin. Perhaps to avoid stepping on Governor Whelan's toes, Ross aimed most of his barbs directly at Matlin personally, calling him such things as "a bungling intruder in New York's justice system."

Ross had two staunch allies in the press. Toby Copin, the political reporter for the *Times* who had confronted Matlin at his very first press conference, hadn't let up on the Special Prosecutor since then. "A threat to the civil liberties of all New Yorkers," he had called Matlin after the Office had used an eavesdropping device to catch three Narcotics detectives selling cocaine. When the Special Prosecutor's Office used an unsavory informant to catch a bribe-taking court officer, he wailed: "The ear trembles at the sound of the jackboot stomping over the Bill of Rights."

Copin had recently been joined in his campaign against Matlin by Johnny Donegan. A popular columnist who billed himself a "man of the people," Donegan was a man of the bottle, often seen in bars bumming drinks from certain politicians and judges who always seemed to escape the javelin thrusts he directed at most public officials. One of the commissioners indicted for fixing pollution summonses in Lou Morotti's case had been a drink-buying friend of Donegan. "Big deal," thumped the columnist, after the indictment had been announced: "All this taxpayer money spent on a Lord High Special Prosecutor, and the best he can come up with is a phony claim about fixing a few tickets. I know junkies who spend their money better than the Special Prosecutor spends ours."

A friend of District Attorney Ross as well, Donegan didn't miss the opportunity to attack Matlin in an article complaining about the settlement of the District Attorneys' lawsuit: "So now we have to watch while this ferret from some hick county goes nosing around our city until somebody finally notices that the only thing he knows how to do is to spend the taxpayers' money for nothing."

It was obvious from the columns that Howard Matlin had never bought Johnny Donegan a drink.

Henry put down the newspapers and scanned the legal papers on his desk. The top paper was a copy of an indictment of a detective lieutenant in the Safe and Loft Squad, who had masterminded several burglaries committed by police officers under his command. He and Pete Flannery, Henry's group chief and an experienced prosecutor, had received some information from a regular informant for the Waterfront Commission and the F.B.I. that a group of cops was planning to steal a shipment of new television sets and deliver them to a fence the informant knew. A team of investigators led by Tim O'Leary and Angie Palumbo had staked out the warehouse where the sets were while Henry, Flannery, and Dan Nelligan waited in the office. It was Henry's first all-nighter, but it had paid off: The cops were caught loading the sets onto a truck. A sergeant and two patrolmen on the Safe and Loft Squad had been brought into the Office at about three in the morning and, after a long night, one of them gave up their lieutenant, who had planned the operation. The participants had been indicted and the preparation for trying the officers was already underway.

An hour later, as Henry was working on trial preparation, his door opened, and Barry Conlon walked in.

"Hey, lover boy," beamed Conlon as he dropped into a chair across the desk. "D'ja get any action last night?"

"Not too much."

"How come?"

"Well, the first problem was that I didn't have a date. And the second was that I was here, closing out some old Internal Affairs cases."

Conlon shook his head. "You gotta stop that stuff, man. You're workin' too hard."

"Not really." Henry *had* spent several evenings in the office working instead of socializing or dating. But he liked to work. At least, he liked *this* work. The real reason he hadn't been dating, though, was that he had no one to date. Henry had met few women of interest since he had joined the Special Prosecutor's Office. In February, a girlfriend of his college buddy Gary had introduced him to one woman—a stockbroker—whom Henry had liked. She was bright and pretty and liked to play tennis. They had played twice at an indoor club to which she belonged and had had dinner a few times. Henry was just becoming encouraged with the relationship when she announced that she was getting engaged to an investment banker.

"So have you got something going this weekend?" Conlon asked.

"Not too much. I'm meeting a couple of guys uptown for a few beers Friday night. You're welcome to join us."

"Not a chance." Conlon's eyes twinkled. "I've got a date with a ballet dancer."

"A ballet dancer? Is this a new one?"

"Yup."

"I don't know how you do it, man."

"I eat my oatmeal in the morning. Gives me energy. Hey, d'you want me to see if she has a friend?"

Henry swallowed. A ballet dancer. Taut and trim and... "Aw, nuts. I promised these guys..."

"These *guys*?" Conlon's eyes opened wide.

"Well, it's sort of a celebration. One of my buddies is getting married."

"Oh. Well, I'll ask her anyway. For the next time."

The telephone rang.

"Perkins here."

"Perk? Dan Nelligan. Got something interesting for you."

As the third-ranking investigator in the Office, Dan Nelligan didn't trifle with small cases or minor allegations. He had also been friendly with Henry since the beginning of Henry's tenure, and Henry could always rely on Nelligan for advice when he had a difficult problem.

"Great." He sat up and signaled Conlon, who took the hint and left.

"I'm in Matt Corey's office," continued Nelligan. "Can you come down right away?"

"You bet."

Henry's blood raced. Matt Corey was the chief investigator. If Matt Corey and Dan Nelligan were working together on a case, it must be important.

Henry grabbed a pen and a yellow pad and left his office.

Matt Corey was both a cynic and a curmudgeon. His bursts of anger at foolish actions by lawyers and investigators alike were legendary. He intimidated Henry, as he did most of the other employees of the Special Prosecutor's Office. The effect was probably intended, Henry knew, but that didn't prevent

Henry's stomach from contracting whenever the heavy eyebrows lowered or the steely gray-blue eyes flashed in anger. Still, Henry knew the other side of Corey's reputation, too. That he was one of the best investigators anywhere in law enforcement, and that he hated corruption.

Corey's office was a corner one. But rather than entering it from the hallway, one had to go through the large area containing the investigators' desks to get there. It always made Henry feel as though he had to pass some kind of inspection before he could visit Matt Corey.

A glance told Henry that Corey's mood was no cheerier than usual. He was seated behind his desk with a scowl imprinted on his large face, making him look like an irritated bloodhound. It was Nelligan who began.

"We've been going through some of the tapes made by the Blinn Commission's undercover agent, Oley Skinner. You remember him from the television hearings?"

"Yes." Henry recalled a slender man sporting slick blond hair whose stories of organized corruption spreading throughout the whole criminal justice system had made Henry's own hair bristle.

"Well, if you know about Skinner," said Nelligan, "then you know he dug up some good stuff."

Henry nodded.

"One of the conversations Skinner taped was with another cop, who told Skinner about four Narcotics detectives that stole a pile of money from a major drug dealer named Bermudez."

"Did Skinner know who the four Narcotics cops were?"

"No. The other guy didn't say. But I did a little checking around and I came up with some 'fives' from a Narcotics investigation about three years ago that led to the arrest of a major heroin dealer named Arnaldo Bermudez and a partner."

"Fives?" asked Henry. "What are they?"

Corey winced.

"DD-5s," responded Nelligan. "They're the routine reports kept by detectives on their activities. Anyway, there were four cops in on this Bermudez investigation, so that much fits. And with the mention of an unidentified C.I...."

"In case," Corey interjected, looking at Henry, "you also don't know what a 'C.I.' means…"

"I do," Henry said. "Confidential informant."

"Good," murmured Corey.

Henry was aware how little he knew of the terms and techniques of prosecutors. But he was trying.

"Anyway," Nelligan went on, "the 'fives' say that the cops were led to Bermudez by a C.I. who's neither identified nor registered. And that's all."

"Can we find out who the confidential informant was?"

"Ha!" barked Corey. He leaned forward and picked up his telephone receiver and shoved it at Henry. "Here. Meet him."

"What?"

"A wiretap," explained Nelligan quietly.

Henry still didn't understand.

"An illegal wiretap," Nelligan went on. "That's the way the bad guys on the Narcotics teams operated. They'd hear about a big operation from some source or another. Then they'd set up a file on the operation and mention their source as a C.I., probably a non-existent one. For the record. But what they'd really do is put in a wiretap—no warrant or anything—on the ring-leader's phone and gather enough information to find out when and where a big deal was goin' down. Then they'd hit the deal, knowing that there'd be a lot of cash on hand. Only they'd take the money and put it in their pockets."

"So that's the way they worked," said Henry, shaking his head. "Nice guys."

Corey looked up. "Welcome to the real world."

"At any rate," said Nelligan, "there's a good chance that's what happened here. Because, when the cops arrested Bermudez and his partner, they turned in four kilos of pure heroin and only twenty thousand dollars."

"They turned the money in?"

"Yes."

"But if they turned in the money…" Henry saw Corey shake his head.

"Twenty grand," Corey said, "is peanuts for dealers carrying four keys of pure shit. That's almost a million bucks' worth of the stuff. They'd have had a lot more'n twenty grand on 'em."

Henry thought for a moment. "So, you think the cops here took some of the money?"

"Sure," growled Corey. "Three years ago. When it happened. The friggin' thing's got mold on it now, with mold on the mold."

Nelligan smiled.

"But do you think," Henry asked them both, "that *your* case—the one in these reports—is the same case that Skinner heard about on the tape?"

It was Corey who responded. "Correction, it's *your* case now. And if you want to know the answer, go find out."

As the first step in his new investigation, Henry and Dan Nelligan interviewed Patrolman Skinner, the policeman who had gathered the evidence for the Blinn Commission. Together they listened to Skinner's conversation with another cop, a Patrolman Osterow.

Osterow: Hey, I'll tell ya a good one. These fuckin' four cops I know. Lucky fucks. Over in the one-fourteen. Took down some big Cuban dealer. Name of Bermudez, I think it was. Took him for a pile. I mean a *big* pile. Had to split it four ways. But, from what I hear, there was plenty to go around. I mean *plenty*.

Skinner: Oh yeah? Lucky bastards. Who were they?

Osterow: Ja…ahhh…some guys. You know how it is. I mean, it wasn't me, anyway. Shitty fuckin' luck.

Unfortunately, that was all Skinner knew.

As the next move Henry had sent Jock Zabiskie and Pat Mallon, the two young investigators Matt Corey had assigned to work with him, to talk with Osterow. The investigators had struck out when Osterow told them to get lost. At Nelligan's suggestion, Henry then reviewed some notes from the Blinn Commission, where he found a handwritten note that read, "Osterow's partner listened but took no part in the conversation." This note gave some hope. Dan Nelligan said that he would approach Osterow's partner at the time, Patrolman Alfred Hanley.

"What makes you think he will cooperate?" Henry asked.

"I figure he was a grass eater, not a meat eater."

Henry looked perplexed. "Grass eater?"

"Guys who went along with the rotten system so they wouldn't be ostracized. Most of the grass eaters are really good cops at heart. And if the system wasn't rotten, they wouldn't be, either."

"Well, good luck," Henry said as Nelligan opened his door to leave.

No sooner had Nelligan left than Barry Conlon stuck his head in. "Hey, man. Lunch time."

Across the street from the New State Office Building was a German restaurant called the Rathskeller, run by a towering Munich native with a booming voice whose ever-present figure was its most notable adornment. It didn't strive for ambience like some German restaurants with a zither player in the corner or waiters in lederhosen. But the good German food and, more importantly, Dortmunder Union and Spaten on draft, assured that Henry would become a regular customer. Convincing Barry Conlon to go there took no more effort than convincing himself.

"Hey," said Conlon as they took their seats, "I had a run-in with Sergeant Pelton." They were sitting at a table in the middle of the room, where the noise was greatest, so Conlon had to lean forward to speak.

Henry laughed. "You mean the Sherlock Holmes of Internal Affairs?" Henry had worked with Sergeant Pelton while looking into some minor allegations received by Internal Affairs. Each time, Pelton had bungled the case through some stupid move, such as asking the target himself if he was corrupt

"The very guy. Listen to this one. Internal Affairs gets a blip that some bartender was overheard telling some other guy that a cop named Hogie was shakin' down bars in the one-three-o precinct. The informant's some off-duty housing cop who insists he heard the conversation. Pelton gets the case."

"That's the end of it right there."

"Just about. Guess what he does? He goes right over to the place, plops a tape recorder on the bar, and asks the bartender if he's been payin' off the cops. Guess the answer."

Henry laughed.

"Then he asks the bartender if he knows of any other bartenders who are payin' bribes. Same answer. Case closed."

"So how did you get stuck with Pelton?"

"Bad luck." Conlon perked up suddenly." Hey, by the way, did I tell you about this new woman I met, Sally?"

"Another one?" Henry paused as the waiter set two steins of Dortmunder Union beer on the table. He took a sip and smiled. "No, I don't think so."

"Oooohh. Talk about a workout. She's a gym instructor in some midtown sports club, with a body that'd give a priest a hard-on."

"Ha! With some of the priests I knew, that wouldn't be too difficult."

"Yeah. Anyway, this one's something else."

"Where did you meet her?"

"In a bar. On Second Avenue. And how about you? You got anything new?"

"Not really." Henry wondered how Conlon had the time to meet as many women as he did. Of course, it didn't take Barry Conlon long to meet a woman. Perhaps if Matlin hired some single women, Henry might be able to meet one at work. Like the one yesterday. "I did see one that I sure wish worked for us."

"Oh, yeah?"

Henry took a sip of beer. "In court yesterday. She's an assistant with the Manhattan DA's office, I think. Maybe you know her."

"Describe her."

"Well, she's sort of tall. Slender. With dark hair. About to here." Henry pointed to a point just below his shoulder. "Gorgeous skin. Like transparent, but almost olive, too. Not really dark, but smooth and sexy. And green eyes—like the sea."

"Boy, you really checked her out."

Henry laughed.

Conlon's eyes focused. "Oh, oh, wait a minute. Was she all business? Pushin' the judge. Organized. That kind of thing?"

"Yeah, actually." Her apparent competence was one of the things Henry had noticed. And admired. "You're right. She was really put together. I was kind of wishing Matlin would hire somebody like her."

"Well, wish no more. At least about that one. Sara Leventhal. She's about as warm as the iceberg the Titanic hit. And a little more dangerous, I think."

Henry smiled. "Why? Did you try to take her out, or something?"

"Are you kiddin'? Miss Ice Cube? Freeze your fingers off. I wouldn't get near her with the far end of a twenty-foot pole."

"Well," Henry said, lifting his beer as in a salute, "I would." He looked back at Conlon, who just shook his head.

Two days later Nelligan came through. Patrolman Hanley had told Nelligan that he knew Osterow's source. It was a Narcotics detective named Jack Keene, who had bragged to Osterow and himself about how he, Keene, and three other Narcotics detectives had taken a pile of money from a Cuban drug dealer named Bermudez.

As follow up, Nelligan dug up some more records on the arrest where the four cops arrested drug dealers Arnaldo Bermudez and Felix Aguilar and then turned in only twenty thousand dollars. The papers included write-ups on the detectives involved in the arrest of Bermudez and Aguilar. Henry looked at the first report. Detective John F. Keene, it said. Special Narcotics Unit, ten years. Before that, Manhattan South Precinct Investigative Unit, two years, preceded by four years on patrol. Henry's eyes moved down the page. "Commendations," said one heading atop a long list of awards and commendations which Jack Keene had received. "Discipline: None," said another entry. Henry flipped to the other sheets. The other detectives— Ramon Olivera, Neil O'Brien, and Harley Fulton—had similar reports.

He looked up. "These guys have impressive records."

Nelligan nodded. "You don't take down major drug dealers if you're a half-assed cop." He shrugged. "That's the tragedy of these guys. If they were honest, they'd be among the best cops in the Department." He stepped to the door. "Gotta go. I'll see you later."

After the door closed, Henry looked again at the material he had. What he needed was a witness. But who was present when the theft occurred? Six people: two drug dealers and the four cops.

What a choice for witnesses. Two major drug dealers and four crooked cops. *Well,* he decided, *I'd rather be in a room with a cop than a drug dealer.*

CHAPTER 9

Detective Jack Keene looked anything but scared. Lounging in a chair across from Henry, he wore on his face a look that hovered between amusement and boredom. Nothing Henry had said seemed to intimidate Keene. Not Henry's claim that they knew Keene had taken money from the drug dealer Bermudez. Not Henry's threat that Keene would be tossed out of the Department without his pension. Not even Henry's white lie that Patrolman Osterow had given him up and could be forced to testify against him.

"Cop talk," Keene had called Osterow's story. "So what? Cops like to sling bullshit, just like everyone else."

Detective Keene had been so much in control that he had totally ignored the P.B.A. lawyer at his side, who hadn't even spoken once introductions had been made. Keene himself batted away every question Henry posed, more often than not with a wisecrack and a laugh. Now Henry felt his back against the wall. He had shown his own hand and gotten nothing in return. Nothing at all. And he was convinced by now that he wasn't going to get anything. Still, he didn't want to give up, so he tried once more.

"Detective, you had an illegal wiretap on Bermudez. We know it."

Keene's eyes opened wide. "What? What is this, amateur hour?" He shifted in his chair slightly, crossing a leg. His open-necked floral shirt made him look like he was relaxing at the beach. He looked hard at Henry. "How long have you been a prosecutor?"

"What does that matter?"

"How long?" Keene's voice was calm, almost gentle.

"This isn't about me. It's about you."

Keene tipped his head. Like a friend would do in conversation. "Come on. Tell me. You know I can find it out in two minutes."

Henry paused. Keene was right. "Six months." Actually, it was a little more than five, but six sounded better.

"I thought so," said Keene. "That explains it."

"Explains what?"

"Your approach."

"What do you mean, 'my approach?'"

The detective uncrossed his legs and sat slightly forward in his chair. "You know, I've been a cop for many, many years."

Sixteen, Henry seemed to recall from Keene's file. "So?"

"I've met a lot of prosecutors. Good ones and lousy ones. But one thing I can always tell is a new one. By the way he goes about it."

Henry wanted to say something...

"Look at today," Keene continued. "First you call me in here. With a subpoena." He shrugged. "You didn't need a subpoena. All you needed was a phone call."

"Or a call to me," injected the P.B.A. lawyer. Keene gave the lawyer a look that silenced him.

"Then there were your questions. You say somebody took money from some drug dealer named Bermudez. A guy, for all I know, I might have locked up sometime. The truth is, I don't remember all the drug dealers I've arrested in the ten years I've been in Narcotics." Keene shrugged. "But let's assume you've got a reason to investigate this Bermudez and his money. Now let's also say that Osterow...was that the guy?"

Henry sat still.

"Is that who you say got you started on this thing? Osterow?"

Henry nodded. "Yes."

"Okay. Say Osterow told you that I took money from this Bermudez person. Now you've got a crime and a suspect. But then look how you went about it. The very first thing, you call me in here and accuse me right up front of stealing this Bermudez's money. Then you tell me I'm lying because I don't know what you're talking about. When that doesn't get you anywhere, you start talking illegal wiretaps, or whatever. All without an ounce of proof. And what's worse for an investigator—and don't forget, that's what you are now, an investigator—you do this without having any kind of ace up your sleeve. Just hoping, I guess, I'd fall on the floor and confess whatever it is you think I did." He pursed his lips. "And you wonder why I think you're new at this game?"

Henry didn't know what to say.

"Hey," added Keene. "Don't take offense. You might turn out to be a very good prosecutor. You look pretty smart. And you're real earnest. You might get to be a real pro. But everybody's gotta start sometime. Even me." He smiled. "I don't want to think about the blunders I probably made when I was starting out."

"Look, I..."

Keene cut him off. "Is there anymore? Because, the truth is, I've got an informant in a big case I'm suppose'ta meet in a half an hour." He raised a hand. "If you're done, of course."

Henry didn't have any more questions, or, as Keene had put it, any ace up his sleeve. So, he let Keene go.

An hour later Howard Matlin was sitting behind his desk, his hands folded on its surface. He had asked to meet with Henry to update him on the progress on the Bermudez matter.

Progress, Henry had laughed to himself. *If only.*

The late afternoon sun over New Jersey filled Matlin's office with a peach-pink glow that softened the fluorescence of the overhead lights. Even Matt Corey's visage was tempered by the light, although his eyes remained uncharmed.

Henry relayed to Matlin his meeting with Keene.

"Jesus," grumbled Corey.

Matlin looked at the Chief Investigator. So did Dan Nelligan, the fourth person in the room.

"What is this, friggin' amateur hour?" Corey growled.

Henry felt a jolt. Almost the exact words of Detective Keene.

"I mean, what kind of bullshit is this? I never heard so many fuck-ups piled on top of each other. First, you send our investigators out to walk up cold to a goddamned old-time hard-ass cop—what the hell's his name?" Corey looked at Nelligan.

"Osterow."

"Yeah, Osterow." He looked back at Henry. "Did you do any background work on the guy? See if he's been in Narcotics himself, or maybe worked with Keene? Find out if he's got problems in the Department—somethin' you could hang over his head? At least get an idea of how the guy'd react before you approach him?"

Henry said nothing.

"You don't have to answer. 'Cause if you did, you wouldn't've sent our guys out there to look like assholes beggin' the guy for help. All right, then you got smart. You did a little spade work on the other guy, whatever's his name."

"Hanley," said Nelligan.

"...and you got something. But then..." Corey's eyes lifted in their sockets, then fell back on Henry. "Jesus Kee-reist." He shook his heavy head, causing his jowls to ripple. "You call in one of the toughest, shrewdest sons of bitches ever to stuff his pockets with drug money...I mean, did you find out before you got Jack Keene in here that he blew away two guys on two separate occasions in the back of his squad car?"

"What? He did? No. When?"

"Doesn't matter. A few years ago." The intimidating blue-gray eyes bore in on Henry. "But what does matter is the fact that you didn't know that. Or anything else about this guy. What the fuck did you think you were going to do? Call him in and listen to his confession? Like a friggin' priest?" He shook his big head. "You were talkin' to a goddamned legend in the Department. One of the hungriest guys out there. And all you accomplished with your stupid move was to tell him everything you knew so far. For Christ's sake, you even told him we knew about the wire. Not that he gives a shit or is gonna worry. But at least he knows now exactly what we know, and even what we suspect. And what did you get in return? Dicksweat."

Henry could feel his heart beating. It was pounding hard enough that he assumed that both Matlin and Nelligan could hear it, too. But he could think of nothing to say.

"Look," Corey continued, "you fucked up the case. That's bad enough. But look at the rest of what you did. To the Office. To him." Corey gestured in Matlin's direction. "You know, every time somebody here fucks up—makes us look stupid—we give the P.B.A. and the politicians and those dirtbag assholes in the press just what they want: a nice sharp knife to skin us with. A way to knock our credibility to shit—dump crap all over us and make us look bad to the rest of law enforcement. And with informants and potential informants. And that's what really hurts. Because the only damned thing that keeps a law enforcement agency in business is credibility."

Henry swallowed.

"And look what it does to Howie." Corey glanced at Matlin. Henry did not. He didn't need to note his disapproval, too.

"The only guy with the balls to take on all these scumbag judges and politicians and guys like Keene, and you make him look like some two-bit amateur in a…"

Matlin held up a hand. "Matt."

Corey stopped talking at once. He sat back in his chair.

Now Matlin turned to Henry. Henry forced himself to look at the Special Prosecutor. He settled first on the close-cropped black hair, then on the unlined forehead and dark eyebrows, and finally he approached the deep brown eyes, which were looking right into his own eyes. The eyes surprised him. There was no sign of anger, no glowering contempt. Instead, they seemed firm and relaxed at the same time, like a soldier standing at ease.

"It's not easy, is it?" Matlin asked.

Henry took a few seconds to absorb the question and the change of mood. "No," he answered at last.

"No, it isn't. And it never will be."

Henry swallowed. His head was a whirlpool of thoughts. He was grateful to Matlin for taking the heat off him and wished he could say so without looking foolish. But he also knew that Matt Corey wasn't wrong; he *had* made the Special Prosecutor's Office, and Matlin as well, seem bumbling, at least with Keene and Osterow. There was no answer to that.

Matlin spoke again. "Have you given any thought to the other three cops involved here?"

"Well…" He looked at Dan Nelligan, who gave him what looked like a half-wink. "Dan thinks that I'd get the same treatment. At least at this point."

Matlin nodded. "I think Dan's right. I think your time could be better spent. Why don't you take a look at the DA's records? There'll be a file in

Ross's office on the arrest of the two drug dealers. If you subpoena that file, you might learn something more. Maybe find a new lead."

Henry sat up. The DA's file. Of course. "Thanks. I'll do that."

Matlin gestured that the meeting was over.

As Henry got up to go, Corey spoke. "Check with Dan before you do anything."

Henry looked at Corey, feeling the sting again. He looked at Matlin, but the Special Prosecutor was already reading some papers on his desk. So, he left the room.

As he walked back to his office, Henry tried to cast off the humiliation. He'd been put down by Matt Corey. Badly. And it stung. But he wasn't going to let it stop him. He still had a lot to learn about being a prosecutor. But that was it—he would learn and do better.

A hand on his shoulder made him jump. It was Dan Nelligan, who had come up beside him.

"Wha…? Oh, it's you, Dan."

"Are you interested in a drink?" Nelligan asked.

"A drink? Sure. I could use one. Just let me drop these papers on my desk."

The bar at the Japanese restaurant where they sat was a popular watering hole for the Special Prosecutor's Office. On Friday nights, when everyone felt like letting off the powerful heads of steam they built up on the job, investigators and attorneys would crowd into the "Lion's Roar" around the corner. But this was the place they went for talk. Talk and perfect martinis.

Nelligan had suggested the Japanese place, so Henry thought he might want to talk to him about something, maybe some advice on what to look for in the District Attorney's file. As he took a seat at the bar, Henry was about to order a cold Asahi, a routine Japanese beer which, for some reason, always tasted good in this place. But Nelligan had just asked for a very dry martini on the rocks, and Henry succumbed.

They both watched while the slender, slick-haired man mixed their drinks, knowing that they didn't have to worry about too heavy a hand with the vermouth. As expected, with a broad smile and a slight bow from the waist, the bartender came through with a flawless result.

"Ahh," said Henry as he sipped his drink.

"Yeah," said Nelligan quickly, then he put his head down and spoke softly. "Look, Perk. I hope you don't take Matt Corey in the wrong way."

Henry stiffened. He didn't feel like discussing someone who had just made a fool of him in front of his boss.

Nelligan went on. "He comes on a little strong sometimes."

Henry let out a short, not humorous laugh.

"I know he can hurt feelings," continued Nelligan. "But you gotta understand him, and the boss, too. They go back a long way."

Henry listened.

"Matt's one of the best, maybe the best cop I ever worked with, an' he's solved some of the toughest cases I've seen. He was on the DA's squad when Howie was there. That's where they met. And they got to be friends. And a lot of respect, too. That's when I met 'em. Then Howie went into private practice. But when he left that and went up to Fuller County as chief assistant, he got Matt to put in his papers and go to work for him in Fuller. They've been together ever since."

Nelligan stopped to take a sip of his drink. His eyes lifted and met Henry's for an instant. Then they returned to the drink.

Henry toyed unconsciously with a small wooden bowl of pastel rice puffs. He pushed it away. "You worked with them at the DA's office?"

"Yeah," said Nelligan.

"Matt's always seen things the same way Howie does. Fact is, Matt screwed himself more than once with the DA—the old one, not this present guy—because he stood up for Howie. Like the time the DA wanted to indict this guy Howie and Matt had been investigating, but Howie wouldn't do it. Political case. Lots of press. It would've made the DA look really good. The DA put all kinds of pressure on Howie. Only Howie knew the guy hadn't done what the DA wanted to say he did. And Matt knew it, too, and he backed Howie.

"The DA was mad as hell, and he wanted to fire Howie. But he knew that if he did, the whole mess'd come out in the papers, and he'd get egg on his face. After that, though, the DA 'n' Howie never spoke a friendly word. And Howie never got another raise or promotion, either."

Nelligan rolled his drink between his fingers and glanced at Henry. "See, that's the kinda guy you work for. And the guy who stood right by him and took the same shit was Matt Corey. He never got promoted again, either. Never had a good word put in for him with the Department. And he ended up with all the shit work in the DA's squad. But he never once—and I got to know him really well—he never once complained about anything he'd done."

Nelligan took a drink. Henry shook his head slowly, then took a sip of his own drink. Just then the door to the restaurant opened and a tall, statuesque blonde woman stepped in. She was followed by a large, totally bald man stuffed into an expensive looking double-breasted blue suit.

Nelligan eyed the couple. "He's into somethin' illegal," he murmured as the pair headed for a table.

Henry smiled.

Nelligan emptied his drink. "Another round," he said to the bartender.

Henry finished his drink and slid his empty glass toward the hand reaching for Nelligan's glass. "Is that why Matlin left the DA's office?" he asked.

"No."

The two men sat without speaking while the bartender went through his ritual again. The fresh drinks were set in front of them.

"Thanks," said Henry.

Nelligan nodded to the bartender and went on, looking at his hands and his drink. "Naw, it was somethin' else that did him in. It had to do with a judge."

Henry looked up.

Nelligan took a sip of his fresh drink before he went on.

"It started with an old pickpocket who'd just gotten busted for the umpteenth time. The guy'd told Corey he fixed a judge once. Matt didn't believe him until he said the judge's name was Platz.

"Judge Platz, see, was an old timer on the bench. Been a judge so long that no one really knew who'd made him a judge in the first place. An' he was a real hack. An idiot who used to fly off the handle and yell at the cops or the lawyers or the witnesses, whoever pissed him off at the moment. But everybody knew he took money, too. Small change. He wasn't a big, connected judge. Nobody was gonna pay him a lot of money to fix a case 'cause the administrative judge knew he was so bad that he wouldn't let him handle anything serious. So, he got nickel-and-dime cases. And if the right lawyers were involved, who knew how to approach the judge, he was for sale for a few bucks.

"Everybody knew the guy was takin'. But nobody'd do anything. They all stuck together, and pretended nothin' was wrong. Including the DA himself, even though he used to complain about old Judge Platz all the time, sayin' things like he was collectin' his lunch money by lettin' some street dealer off in the morning.

"Anyway, Corey brings this guy to Howie and me—I was workin' with them regular then—and he tells us the story. Platz had given him time twice, and the last time he sent him up, he said if he saw him again, he'd give him the max. So, when he gets busted again and finds himself in front of Platz, instead of waitin' for assigned counsel and takin' a plea like he usually did, the old guy picks one of the criminal lawyers he'd heard knew the right people. The lawyer asks him if he has any money and, when the old guy says yes, he tells him he can reach the judge. The lawyer takes the money and, the next day, the old guy gets a walk." Nelligan looked at Henry. "He gets a walk from the same judge who said he was gonna give him the maximum next time he saw him."

"Interesting," said Henry. He took a sip of his drink.

"Yeah." Nelligan's eyes returned to his drink. "Anyway, we go over and over it with the guy, until we're sure he's tellin' the truth. Then we set the old guy up with a wire and send him back to the same lawyer, this time on the case he's just gotten busted on. It's in front of some other judge, but we figured the lawyer'd take his money, say he was gonna fix the case, and then we'd bust the lawyer for larceny and use him to get Platz."

Nelligan took a few peanuts, chewed them, then took another sip of his martini.

"But this lawyer really fools us. Instead of takin' the money like we figured he would, he tells the old guy that he can't help him on this case, except in the regular manner, 'cause this judge doesn't take money like Platz." Nelligan smiled and glanced up at Henry. "I mean, if we were writin' a script for a TV play, we couldn't've gotten anything better outta the guy. Here's this crooked lawyer, but he's honest enough to tell our guy that he can't fix this case like he fixed the last one.

"So, Howie gets the tape and, like the rules of the office say, he goes to the DA to get permission to turn the lawyer and go after the judge. But the DA turns him down flat. He says the witness is no good, and all of a sudden Judge Platz is an esteemed member of the bench, or some horseshit like that. He won't let Howie go ahead. So, Howie quits. Right there and then." Nelligan glanced at Henry, then turned away again. "That's why he went into private practice."

"Wow." It was all Henry knew to say. He shook his head, then took a drink. "Did he ever do anything with the tape he had?"

"Nope. He gave it to Matt. Told him that since he wasn't an assistant district attorney anymore, he couldn't act on the case. Matt wanted to quit, too, but Howie told him not to. He had a family, and bein' a cop was all he could do, unlike Howie. So, Matt stayed."

"And you, too."

"Yeah, for a little while."

"Shit. No wonder Howie feels the way he does."

For a moment or two, Nelligan said nothing. He just stared at his drink, rolling it back and forth between his fingers. Then he spoke.

"No. That's not why he's the way he is. If you think that, you don't understand the guy. I've never heard him mention Judge Platz again. And I really don't think he ever thinks of it. Somethin' else pushes him. I see it and I sorta understand it. But he's the only guy who really knows what it is. He's like someone comin' from a place no one else comes from. Where the air's cleaner than the air anywhere else. Where there's no crime and no cheatin' and no lying. And no one else lives there, only everybody wishes they did."

Henry was stilled. He didn't know how to respond. So, he said nothing. Just lifted his eyes and stared at his drink.

"I gotta get goin'," said Nelligan, breaking in. "My wife's waitin' for me."

Henry reached for the tab, but Nelligan beat him to it. "Nah," he said, "this one's on me."

CHAPTER 10

It was Friday noon and Henry was sitting with his feet up on his desk eating a ham and cheese sandwich when the door opened and Dan Nelligan entered followed by Jock Zabiskie and Pat Mallon, the two investigators working with Henry on the Bermudez matter.

"Did you get it? asked Henry as he swallowed his last bite of sandwich. Henry had followed Howard Matlin's advice and subpoenaed the Queens District Attorney's file on the arrest of the two drug dealers, Arnaldo Bermudez and Felix Aguilar.

"We got it," said Zabiskie, holding a manila folder in the air. He and Mallon took seats. Nelligan remained standing.

"Great!" Henry exclaimed, crumpling, and throwing the sandwich paper into his wastebasket The pickle went too.

"Damn."

"What's the matter?" asked Nelligan.

He had wanted the pickle. "Nothing."

Zabiskie handed him a manila brief holder with the words "QUEENS DISTRICT ATTORNEY'S OFFICE" printed in capital letters. As he took the file, he noticed Nelligan still standing. "Sit down," he offered.

"Nah, I gotta get goin'. Just stopped by to say goodbye."

"Goodbye? Where're you going?"

Nelligan smiled. "The Bahamas. Hard duty," he said laughing. "Actually, it will be." He dropped the laugh. "I'm trackin' down a secret bank account for one of Paul Meade's cases. And the guy who belongs to the money is no dummy."

As Nelligan left, Henry untied the ribbon and extracted the sheets of paper.

"Not too much, is there?" Zabiskie said, leaning forward. In the light, Henry could see the gleam of the polyester threads in Zabiskie's plaid shirt. Short and stocky, with dark hair cut in a genuine brush cut from the fifties. Zabiskie and his polyester plaids seemed well-matched.

"Well, let's see." Henry picked up the top sheet, one labeled "Intake." "It just says that the defendants were seized in an apartment in possession of four kilograms of a substance believed to be pure heroin. Also seized was $20,200 in United States currency. Charged with possession with intent to sell."

"They're big-time dealers, according to Matt," said Mallon. "Bad characters." Pat Mallon was a Norman Rockwell vision of the all-American boy. Tall, with clean, light-brown hair, bright blue eyes, and shiny cheeks, he looked as though he had just showered up after a high school basketball game.

Henry nodded. "Well, these are heavy felonies. Four kilos of pure heroin ought to have been good for some serious time."

Henry flipped to the next sheet of paper. As he did, something fell out and fluttered to his desk. "What's this?"

"Looks like a newspaper article," said Mallon.

Henry spread it out on his desk so that the investigators could see it as well. The headline said, "Big Drug Arrest." Next to the headline was a photograph. District Attorney Martin Ross was standing closest to the camera, smiling, and pointing to a table to his right. Behind the table stood Detective Jack Keene and another man who looked like Detective Ramon Olivera, one of Keene's team. On the table was a pile of clear plastic bags, filled with what was apparently the seized heroin, along with a stack of bills and two pistols. To Ross's left was a figure Henry didn't recognize. He was a large man, with thinning dark hair. He did not look like a detective.

"I wonder who that is," said Henry.

"No idea," said Zabiskie and Mallon.

Henry picked up the photo and looked closely. "The caption says, 'Chief Assistant Bert Donner.' I've heard of him; he's Ross's right-hand man." He flipped on through the file.

"What?" Henry exclaimed as he read one of the entries. "It says, 'Pleaded to Crim. Pos. 5-D. Cond. Dis.' If I understand this, these guys pleaded guilty to criminal possession of drugs as a felony, and then they got a conditional discharge. That's a walk."

"A walk?" Mallon and Zabiskie spoke together.

Henry picked up the phone. "Barry? Henry. If a couple of drug dealers pleaded guilty to criminal possession of narcotics—heroin…" Henry looked at the file again. "…in the fifth degree—a D felony—would it be normal for them to get a conditional discharge? No jail time?"

Zabiskie and Mallon both sat up.

"Thanks." He hung up and turned to the investigators. "Conlon says that it *could* happen, maybe. But only if the defendants were cooperating or something like that. Not normally." Henry sat back and rubbed his chin. "You know," he said after a few seconds, "we need a closer look."

It was a typical Friday evening in the Lion's Roar, the raucous bar that drew the Special Prosecutor's staff at the end of each pressured week and packed them in tightly together with the Wall Street contingent. The bar itself sprung from the wall at one side of the room, near the entrance into the dining area. It poked out into the room, turned left, turned again in a wide "U," returned almost to the wall in the center of the room, then bent around and did the same thing to create a second bay, completing its journey by the door to the restrooms. A lot of bar space. But hardly an empty inch as Henry entered the "Roar" for the end-of-week ritual. Spotting Senior Investigator Tim O'Leary, he squeezed through the crowd to the place where Tim stood.

"Hey, Tim."

O'Leary turned to greet him. "Howya doin', Perk?"

"Good. Any word on Angie?"

O'Leary's partner, Angie Palumbo, had been in the hospital for a gall bladder operation. Henry missed his droll perspective on the criminal world.

O'Leary nodded. "Yeah. He's better. Be comin' back soon. Ya know, I miss the bastard."

"Me, too," said Henry, waving a hand at the bartender. "A draft," he called out. "And a…"

"Dewars and soda," said O'Leary loud enough for the bartender to hear.

Both men had to shout. The noise level in the Lion's Roar immediately explained its name to anyone entering at cocktail hour. With the clinking and banging of glassware, the raw-voiced exclamations, and the blaring jukebox, the volume in the bar approached air hammer level. Some might wonder why this kind of chaos was called relief. But they probably weren't prosecutors or investigators on a Friday night after work.

Henry had squeezed in next to O'Leary at the bar.

"So what'ya workin' on these days?" O'Leary asked.

"I'm looking into an old case from the Blinn Commission tapes. It looks like some cops stole a bunch of money from a couple of drug dealers."

"What unit?"

"Special Narcotics."

"Forget it. You won't get anything outta those guys."

"I know. But what's weird is what happened in court."

O'Leary looked with surprise at Henry. "Whattaya mean, the cops arrested the mutts after they'd ripped 'em off?"

"Looks that way. Charged 'em with four kilograms of pure heroin."

"Holy shit, they musta been crazy."

"Well, someone's crazy, 'cause the dealers took a plea and got a walk."

"What? Four keys and they got a walk?" O'Leary shook his head. "Looks like you got a real doozie this time." He looked up. "Hey, John. How ya doin'?" The lilt returned to O'Leary's voice.

Henry turned to see John Cappelli, another senior investigator, who had just carried his drink into the same bay of the bar. Then his heart skipped a beat.

"Hiya Tim. Hey, Perk. How's it going?" Cappelli looked at Henry, then followed his gaze to its object. "Oh," he said, "have you met Sara Leventhal? She's just joined us, starting Monday."

It was the Assistant from the Manhattan District Attorney's Office Henry had seen in court recently. The one he'd talked about with Barry Conlon. The one who had made his heart flutter.

Sara turned and faced him. When her limpid green eyes landed on his, something inside Henry melted.

"Hello. I'm Henry Perkins," he managed to say. He leaned forward and extended his hand, giving her his best smile.

"Hello," she said firmly shaking his hand, but not returning the smile. An inch or two taller than Cappelli, she was almost as tall as Henry himself. She held herself erect, like a dancer, and appeared to be comfortable dominating her surroundings. Her face was long, with dark hair falling free to her shoulders. Well-defined dark eyebrows, a strong, straight nose and lightly rouged lips framing white teeth gave her a classic, almost formal look. Henry was suddenly reminded of a painting he had seen in a museum in France, one he had stood in front of admiring for a long time. It had featured a Florentine princess with dark tresses flowing around her regal face. She was surrounded by courtiers, to whom she was paying no attention. Instead, she gazed past the artist at something apparently more significant than her surroundings. Henry had wished then that the princess were real.

And now she was.

He started to say something when she turned to Cappelli. "Thanks for the drink, John. I've got to get going."

"Won't you have another?" Henry said quickly. He looked into her eyes and felt like his knees would buckle. Speckled green surrounded by pure white. The thinnest rim of dusty gray separated the green irises from the white, giving her a slightly astonished look. Long dark lashes swept upward to protect her eyes from the elements above. Whatever warmth her eyes might have lacked went unnoticed by Henry.

"No. But thank you." Finally, a smile. It melted what was left of Henry's manpower. To Cappelli she said, "I'll talk to you Monday," and left.

"Nice work, Romeo," said O'Leary. Cappelli laughed.

"Thanks a bunch," said Henry, trying to shake off his failed gesture. "For all the help you two guys were, the least you could do is to buy me a beer."

"Done," said Cappelli, and he signaled for a refill for all of them.

Early the next week Henry met with the young Assistant District Attorney whose name was in the DA's file. The Assistant recalled that he had been told by the Chief Assistant District Attorney that Bermudez and Aguilar were cooperating with the police on an important narcotics investigation and that the cops wanted them back on the street right away. That was the reason for the "walk."

If they cooperated then, Henry thought, perhaps they would cooperate now. Especially against the four cops who arrested them and then stole their money. In the file Henry had found the name of the attorney who represented Bermudez and Aguilar. Immediately he had called the number.

"Paul Grassi's office," the voice had said.

"May I speak to him, please?"

"Who may I say is calling?"

"Henry Perkins. From the Special Prosecutor's Office."

"Just a moment, please."

Henry waited several minutes, drumming on the desk with his fingers. He was trying to figure out what kind of a deal he could offer for the dealers' cooperation when a voice said, "Yeah? Grassi here." The voice was cold.

"Mr. Grassi, my name is Henry Perkins. I'm an assistant with the Office of the Special Prosecutor. Mr. Matlin's office."

"I know who the Special Prosecutor is. What do you want?"

Henry was taken aback by the hostility in Grassi's voice. But he went on. "According to some records I have, you represented two drug dealers…"

"Were they convicted?"

"Huh?"

"You heard me. Were they convicted of sale or possession of narcotics?"

"Well, as a matter of fact, they pleaded guilty."

"Go ahead."

"Your clients' names were Arnaldo Bermudez and Felix Aguilar." He gave the date of their arrest, the names of the arresting officers, and the charges. "As I said they pleaded guilty to possession of a controlled substance with intent to sell in the fifth degree."

"Go on."

"At the time of the plea, your clients were cooperating with law enforcement. In fact, they were permitted to plead to a lesser charge and were given probation because of that cooperation."

"Get to the point. What do you want?"

"I want their cooperation again. I have reason to believe that the officers who arrested them also robbed them. Took their money. I would like your clients to cooperate with our Office against those police officers."

There was silence on the other end. Henry's hopes rose. Perhaps Grassi was trying to figure out what kind of a deal he could make with the Special Prosecutor's Office.

"Go on."

Huh? Henry had been waiting for Grassi to respond.

"What do you want from *me?*"

"Well, you're their attorney. I presume you would know where they are. And, I was hoping, you could arrange to produce them as witnesses for my Office."

This time the pause was only a few seconds. Then Grassi spoke again. His voice was venomous. "I won't say where you can go because you're probably taping the conversation. But it's a hot place. And it's down." The dial tone followed immediately.

Henry was stunned. For a moment he wondered if a mechanical problem had terminated his conversation, but that clearly was not the case. Then he got angry. Angry that Grassi had hung up on him. Angry that Grassi was hindering his investigation. He reached for the phone again to have it out with Grassi but stopped himself. *Maybe Grassi's not their lawyer anymore. That case is over.* Perhaps Bermudez and Aguilar would help if the Special Prosecutor's Office approached them directly. If he could find them.

After the phone call, Henry gave Zabiskie and Mallon the job of trying to find the two drug dealers. A day later the investigators returned. "We have good news and bad news," they reported. The good news, Zabiskie began, was that they found the drug dealers. They were in Atlanta Federal Prison sentenced to fifteen to twenty years.

"Fifteen years? But if they're cooperating?"

"Obviously," said Mallon, "they're not. At least with the feds."

"What's the bad news?" Henry asked.

Mallon answered. "D.E.A. They're the guys who locked 'em up."

"What did they say?"

"Forget it. No way." Zabiskie shook his head. "Bermudez is a real king-pin in the heroin business. A major dealer. And a killer, too. Apparently blew away at least two of his rivals they know of..."

"Yeah," Mallon broke in, "and a girlfriend who'd talked to the wrong people once. Cut her into pieces and dumped them in the harbor. He's bad news."

Zabiskie went on. "So, they say, there's no way Bermudez or anyone connected with him cooperated. And there's no way they will let us try."

Just then Henry's telephone rang.

"Perkins here."

"Just a moment for Mr. Grassi."

"Paul Grassi, Bermudez's lawyer," Henry said to the investigators.

"I thought I was clear the other day," Grassi began without salutation. "Obviously I was talking to another stupid prosecutor."

Henry scowled.

"This time I'll make myself clearer. And I don't give a shit if you're tap-ing it. You stay the fuck away from my clients. You got that, Mr. Prosecutor?"

Henry was wondering who in the law enforcement grapevine had told Grassi that he was checking up on his clients.

"I said, have you got that?"

Henry took a deep breath. He was so angry that he didn't know what to say. "I don't need your permission for..."

"Listen here, Mr. Prosecutor," Grassi cut in. "I represent those men and if I hear one word that you've gone around me to contact my clients, I'll have your pimply ass up before the Bar Association. Have you got that through your stupid head?"

Henry started to say, "Fuck you," but realized that it was probably Grassi who was taping the conversation.

"I don't want to hear from you again," Grassi continued, "or even *about* you." The dial tone followed.

"Shit," said Henry. "Shit."

"Who was that?" asked Zabiskie.

"Paul Grassi. Bermudez's lawyer."

"I've heard about him," volunteered Mallon. "He's part of the white powder bar."

Henry looked quizzically at Mallon.

"Lawyers who represent mostly drug dealers."

"Anyway, he's not going to let us talk to Bermudez." Henry shook his head. "We'll have to figure out another angle."

"Well," said Mallon with a chuckle, "we have some time. Bermudez and Aguilar aren't going anywhere soon."

As the two investigators left, Henry looked at his watch. Five thirty. Friday evening. Time to forget the Bermudez case and hit the Roar for a few beers. And then, maybe, he might pay a visit to his buddy Gene's bar in Greenwich Village.

A translucent haze clouded Henry's eyes and a smile lingered on his lips as he finished his beer. Perched on a barstool in Gene's Village Tavern, he had reached that mellow point when dreams begin weaving their way into reality.

He had begun his hegira in the clamorous exuberance of the Lion's Roar, where cases were hashed out, and the week's adventures shared. Then he and Barry Conlon had grabbed a quick dinner in an East Side pub, before Conlon went off to a party in Queens. Turning down Conlon's invitation to crash the party, Henry had boarded the subway and headed down to Greenwich Village and the bar his friend Gene had opened, after leaving Henry's last law firm and a promising legal career.

At the moment, Henry was thinking about Sara, the woman he had just met. But his beer glass was empty.

"How about another one, Perk?"

Henry re-entered the present. He looked at his friend, then at his glass. "Sure, why not?"

Gene moved toward the taps.

"Wait a minute," Henry said, holding up a hand. "I think I'll pass. It's late. I'd better get going."

Gene looked at Henry closely. "You sick, man?"

"Huh?"

He smiled. "You in love, or something?"

Henry grunted. "You never know," he said, lifting himself off the barstool.

Outside in the warm air, he breathed deeply. The air almost smelled good by New York standards. Such a beautiful June night. It was very late, but Friday, and he didn't have to work the next day. He wasn't ready to go home yet. Not tonight.

Henry started to stroll along West 11th Street until, incongruously, it crossed West 4th Street. He didn't know much about the Village, or where he was exactly, so he turned the corner onto West 4th Street because it looked interesting.

The June night was like a child's kiss. The warm air lightly bussed him on the cheek, delicate and precious in its immaturity. Tiny pliant fingers touched and stroked him, luring him gently along the street, enticing him into the pleasures of what passes for nature in New York City. Willingly, he succumbed.

He walked past comfortable brick townhouses that lined the quiet street. Angular Victorian homes in reddish purple, joined together with those in the truer red of the gentle Federal style. Groups of houses, themselves interspersed between tiny shops which, in the daytime, dispensed fresh pastries or door locks, or repaired shoes. Black iron balustrades mounted the stoops to the houses, drawing the eye to well-groomed doors and darkened transom windows.

Just above the level of his head, as he passed by, flower boxes full of geraniums and petunias and morning glories graced the windowsills, their floral statements spoken joyfully, even into the dark of night. Climbing up the side of one house was a hefty vine of wisteria, to which clung tenaciously a few lingering blossoms, lending their fading perfume to the air nearby.

There was a magic to the deserted street—an enchantment of half-light on brick facades and mullioned and latticed windows and tiny beds of flowers. A charm in the air itself. Air that was warm, but not too warm. Not really perfumed, but clear enough of any intrusive scent to let imagination provide the fragrance nature omitted. A night with just enough suggestion of romance to turn a city street into a meandering pathway. A night that offered a brief moment of elation, made all the sweeter because soon summer would come and hammer the city into sweat-soaked surrender.

As he strolled along the street, he felt himself dissolving into the warm night. The harsh intentions of daylight had dissipated into disengagement—a drifting through spaces cleared of the commanding and directing signposts that shape and define so much of a day.

A cat scurried across the street, but he didn't take notice of it. Someone somewhere was playing a radio, but its notes mushed like breaking wavelets into the muffled hum of the evening. It was the magic that had caught his senses now, numbing each one individually, so that impressions blended together into dream.

He was interrupted briefly as he crossed Sheridan Square, where avenues and streets converge from all directions. Then, once again, he was back on a single street.

From behind him, the sounds of traffic still jangled. Busy avenues never slept. Past the intersection, back on a quiet side street, the discord dissolved again, and the muted undertone of the nocturnal city re-emerged.

He glanced up. Above him, the moon was a large lemon pie, struggling, almost successfully, to dominate the night-dimmed lights of the city.

As he crossed Sixth Avenue and continued toward Washington Square, he slipped imperceptibly into reflection. The warm night air was an ethereal Siren, tempting his mind to wander over ground untrampled for many busy years. No longer was he in New York City on a certain night in June after a day wrestling with crime and corruption. He was free. Free of the confining space of the city. Free of the constraints of time that pressed upon him by day. Free to let thoughts and feelings surrender to the bewitchment of the night. Free enough that the rusty doors of his mind creaked open, and imprisoned thoughts blinked their eyes and tested the freedom.

Then rude trumpets blared. And the wrong thoughts charged. Old disappointments. Past mistakes. Unfinished programs. Half-done tasks, with tools left unattended on the ground beside.

The sweetness of the night turned sour.

Why do I screw things up? Why can't I just do things right?

He kicked a stone on the sidewalk, half-watching it skitter across the street and under a parked car.

And what about a woman? How come he'd never been able find someone to share his life instead of merely a night of grappling and sweat and one more regretful breakfast?

So many things that hadn't worked out. Right from the beginning. With two doctors for parents who paid more attention to their patients than they did to him.

If only…if only…

He stopped. He had reached Washington Square, the center of New York University. Being surrounded by university buildings prompted his mind to flow back in time and space to another campus. He pictured a dome: the bright white dome of the Rotunda. The most perfect of buildings. Nights like this looking up at a white dome on top of elegant red brick. The epicenter of the University of Virginia. Thomas Jefferson's final achievement.

It must have looked like that already in Jefferson's mind, as he conceived it, standing in his window at Monticello and looking down at Charlottesville, planning the University. His university. That's what he had put on his own tombstone. Founder of the University of Virginia. Nothing about being President of the United States. He was above that.

He, too, would dedicate his life to the kind of ideals that drove Jefferson. To justice. To fairness. To seeking ways to enhance the nobility of the human spirit. As Jefferson had, with his timeless prose, with his improvement of nature and his far-seeing public projects. And with elegant structures like the lacy-windowed brick edifice that commanded Henry's vision. Jefferson never compromised with mediocrity. Nor would Henry. He wouldn't settle for some humdrum job, with a wife and kids and two cars and a grease spot on the concrete garage floor where the station wagon usually sat.

There were things that needed to be done out there in the world. Things that needed someone to do them. There was injustice and unfairness and, what made him the sickest of all, cesspools of corruption. Not the likes of Thomas Jefferson, but Boss Tweeds and Jimmy Walkers and Richard Daleys. Congressmen with their fat hands out, filling their pockets with loot while they aimed plastic smiles at the public from under blow-dried hair. Judges pontificating from the bench about the majesty of the law while they felt the size of the envelope one of the parties had given them, making sure it was all there. Campaign breakfasts with millionaires who then received big government contracts. Weapons that didn't shoot and planes that can't fly, all forgotten with a contribution to some politician's child's college education or his new swimming pool. No wonder Jefferson hadn't wanted his eternal resting place to be polluted by a reference to political office.

The air was warm then, too. So many nights. With the scent of magnolias in the air and the ever-present chirping of the cicadas. A tapestry of sound and scent and warmth of the Virginia mountain nights that draped itself like a satin shawl around his shoulders. Sitting in the grass, in front of the statue of Homer at the end of the Lawn, looking up the long rows of delicate columns of the arcade, interspersed between the elegant brick houses, letting white pedestals in the moonlight draw his unresisting eyes, just as Jefferson had planned, up to the domed Rotunda in the center of it all.

What couldn't he do? What forces of destruction could stop a young man in his third year of law school, who had fallen under the spell of the long-deceased accomplisher of such noble perfections? What limits could confine the gaze of two starry eyes that knew that dreams lay somewhere out there, just past the pool of moonlight, where the hand can reach beyond the length of the arm.

And where was that place now? When could he reach his arm up like this and touch the sky?

A screech in the street gave Henry a start and blew away his dream. An empty cab had seen his raised arm and outstretched hand.

Well, it *was* late. He stepped toward the cab.

CHAPTER 11

What a miserable change. Two pleasant weeks in Scandinavia and now, here he was immersed in the quagmire of a New York summer enduring the IRT Lexington Avenue line on a steamy August Monday morning. August, when the heat rolls into the City and lingers like an unwelcome relative. Immense clouds of it, almost visible, clogging the streets and subways, democratically draining the energy from doormen and dowagers alike. When crisp clean shirts turn into limp shrouds in a short subway ride to work, and gritty air dissolves expensive hairdos and befouls just-scrubbed skin. August, when New York settles uncomfortably into hell's hottest hole.

Henry struggled up the subway steps, wondering if he had the energy to make it all the way across Chambers Street to his office. Reaching the sidewalk, he loosened his tie and pushed off.

Fifteen minutes later he flopped into his desk chair, wet and exhausted. Immediately he began to recover. For one thing, the air conditioning in the New State Office Building had elected to function properly. More importantly, he was back at his battle station, ready to fight. Settling into his desk chair, Henry ignored the clammy chill brought on by the rapid cooling of his wet shirt and reached for his pile of mail. He was interrupted immediately.

"Aha!" exclaimed a grinning Barry Conlon as he sauntered in. Conlon scrutinized Henry's face closely. "Definitely. Satisfaction. Evidence of friendly Scandinavia."

"You're right," Henry laughed, returning Conlon's greeting. "You ought to try it. Everything they say is true."

"Oooh, I don't know if I'd survive two weeks of Scandinavian women."

"Well, if your actions in New York are any indication, I'd say you might need a rest home afterward."

"Yeah, but what a way to go." Conlon sighed dramatically and dropped into a chair.

"So, what's been going on?" asked Henry.

"A couple of things. For one thing, I met a new woman. Whooo! This one is too much. She used to be a Rockette, but now she gives massages at a Swedish men's club."

Henry shook his head. "I don't believe you, Conlon. Where *do* you come up with these women?"

Conlon grinned.

"Actually, I meant what's been going on in the Office. Any hot news?"

"The Office?" Conlon mocked a look of disappointment. "Hey," he said brightening. "Did you hear about that bitch's case?"

"What are you talking about?"

"That ice ball you think is so pretty, Sara Leventhal."

Henry could feel a little thump in his chest as Barry said her name. He had tried not to think of her. But one night, wandering by the harbor in Copenhagen and staring into the swirling fog, her image snuck into his mind and for a moment he forgot the beautiful women of Scandinavia.

He pulled himself back to the present. "What did she do?" he asked Conlon.

"Nailed some heavy guys in the Auto Squad. A detective lieutenant and another detective. A couple other cops, too. Even scooped up the guy who ran a chop shop in the Bronx."

"Chop shop?"

"Yeah, the place where they cut up stolen cars to sell the parts."

"Well, I'm impressed." He eyed Conlon. "How come you say such bad things about her all the time?"

"I don't. Not as a lawyer. I admit she's a good prosecutor. But so're some *guys* I know, and I wouldn't wanta go out with them, either. Hey!" Conlon sat up sharply. "I forgot. You made the *Daily News*."

"What?"

"Well, not by name. But your case did. In Johnny Donegan's column. Last Friday."

Henry's throat tightened. Donegan? What was that son of a bitch saying? "Which case?"

"Weren't you investigating some case from the Blinn Commission files? Some cops that were supposta've ripped off some drug dealers?"

"Yes, I was." He had put aside the case for a while until after his vacation, hoping a bit of time would help him decide what to do next. But he hadn't expected it to make the newspapers. "What did he say?"

Conlon got up. "Wait a minute. I think I've still got it in my office."

Henry didn't wait. He followed Conlon into his office. In a moment, he had Friday's *Daily News* in his hand, open to Johnny Donegan's column entitled "I Get a Pain." Donegan had listed several matters that bothered him, a kind of potpourri of grievances. Halfway down the page, Henry found what he was looking for.

"It boggles the mind to see how our mighty Special Prosecutor continues to throw our money into the breeze. Now he's 'investigating' an old claim by a convicted drug dealer that four highly decorated policemen stole some money from him. Three or four years ago! The next thing you know, the Special Prosecutor will be looking into cost overruns on building the Brooklyn Bridge. That's after he's tried to buy it. With our money."

"Goddamn." Henry slapped the paper back onto Conlon's desk. "Fuck him."

Conlon laughed. "You oughtta buy him a drink. Get on his right side."

Henry rose, ignoring Conlon's jest. "Was there any reaction to this?"

"I don't know. I was in the grand jury all day Friday."

Shaking his head, Henry returned to his office. As he entered, his phone rang. "Perkins," he answered.

"Hi, Henry. It's Harriet Winsor. Could you come down to Mr. Matlin's office?"

By the time he had reached the western corridor, Henry had reviewed the possible reasons that he was being summoned to Matlin's office and concluded that it had to be the Bermudez case.

He passed Harriet Winsor's desk with a nod and opened Matlin's door.

"Welcome back," said Matlin as Henry entered. "I hope you had a good trip."

"Yes, I did. Thanks." He nodded to Chief Assistant Nat Perlman, who was seated in a chair next to the western window, looking plump and scholarly. It always surprised Henry that Perlman had become a prosecutor. With his wire-rimmed glasses and baggy suits, he looked much more like a professor. Beyond Perlman, across the river, was New Jersey, already cloaked in haze and heat.

Henry sat down.

"Is anything happening with that case you started a couple of months ago?" Matlin was leaning back in his chair, his arms folded in front. His shirt sleeves were rolled nearly to his elbows. He did not look angry, Henry decided.

"I assume you mean the Bermudez thing, from the Blinn Commission—where I was investigating the theft of some money from drug dealers."

Matlin nodded.

"Well, actually, I ran into a few roadblocks in June. But I'm ready to take another crack at it."

"Good," said Matlin. "We'd like you to."

Perlman jumped in. "With a little experience to guide you."

Henry looked quizzically at Perlman.

Matlin responded. "What Nat is referring to is you're working on the case with another assistant. Someone with more prosecutorial experience. An assistant Nat worked with at the DA's office. Someone he has confidence can help push the case in the right direction."

Perlman resumed. "We got the file from your office on Friday and gave it to her for review."

"Her?"

"Yes. It's a young lady. I'm sure you've seen her around. Her name is Sara Leventhal."

Henry nearly choked.

"She's very smart and a very experienced prosecutor. And she's just finished a successful investigation and has some time. I'm sure that you'll learn from her. Do you know where her office is?"

"Well..."

"It's right here, on the west side of the building."

Henry acknowledged the assignment and rose from his chair, a bit unsteadily, he thought, and exited. Outside in the hall, he stopped and leaned against the wall. Here he was, having daydreamed for weeks about a woman who barely acknowledged his existence, and suddenly he was assigned to work with her. On his own case.

"Hey, Perk."

Henry jumped. Then he saw who it was. Larry Santarella. One of the other assistants. A buddy.

"Hi, Larry."

"Whatsamatter? You look terrible."

Henry shook his head. "I'm okay. Just a stomachache, I guess."

"Ha! Been eatin' in the State cafeteria again. Oh, no. That's right. Sweden. All those Swedish meatballs. Or the blondes. Hey?"

Henry had to smile. He nodded his head. "Tough life."

"I'll bet. See you at lunch?"

"Sure."

Okay, he said to himself. *On with my case.* And he headed for Sara's door.

The door was closed, so he had to knock.

"Come in," he heard, and he entered.

Sara was sitting behind her desk with papers spread out in front of her.

Out of the corner of his eye, Henry could see the gleam of the Hudson River, forty-four floors below Sara's window. A cruise liner, a large white sliver with a pale blue smokestack ringed in yellow, was sliding smoothly down the river toward the harbor, heading out to the open sea to battle the waves and the currents, maybe even a tempest. The sight of the boat heading resolutely on its way made him feel good. He stepped forward and took a chair.

"Hello, Sara. I understand we're going to work together on the Bermudez matter."

She looked up. "How could you be so dumb as to call Jack Keene in here and tell him what we had on him?"

Henry stiffened.

"Never mind." She sat back, folded her arms, then looked right at him with her dusty green eyes. "What did you have in mind to do next?"

Henry avoided her eyes. Her skin. Clear, almost pellucid, with subtle undertones of burnished gold and red. Too healthy to be sallow, but not dark enough to be olive. Her smooth brown hair. Falling casually from a loosely defined part to splash onto her shoulders.

"I just got back from vacation and was going to go over the case to see what might be done."

"That's what I thought. So, I've already done something. We're going after the only witnesses we have."

"The drug dealers?"

"Who else?" Her hair swung free of her shoulder, reflecting in ripples the light from above. Henry tried to ignore it.

"I already tried that," he said.

"I know. But you didn't do it the right way."

He sat up. "The right way? What's the *right* way, as you put it?"

"Through the United States Attorney's Office. Both Bermudez and Aguilar are in Federal prison. In Atlanta. Doing long terms."

"I know that."

"But do you know that they're both in re-sentencing?"

"What's re-sentencing?"

He saw her eyes roll up for an instant, and he reacted. "Damn it, I wasn't a prosecutor for five years, like you were. So, stop playing games."

She sat up and looked at him. Then she nodded. "Fair enough."

She began more gently. "Under federal law prisoners can be re-sentenced during a certain period of time after the initial sentence. In Bermudez and Aguilar's case, that period hasn't expired. If the United States Attorney demonstrates that they've cooperated with law enforcement, they could be given shorter sentences."

"Would that include cooperation with us?"

"We're part of law enforcement, aren't we?"

"But I already asked the feds…"

"D.E.A., you asked. They don't owe us anything or care a damn what we're up to. And they spent a lot of time catching these two dealers. Of course, they'd say no. But we have cases with the U.S. Attorney. We can help him, and he can help us." As she spoke, she brushed back hair that had fallen forward of her left shoulder. Henry caught himself watching her hand sweep through her dark tresses. Then he pulled his eyes away.

"I've already spoken to the U.S. Attorney," she continued. "He's agreed that if the two dealers cooperate with us, he'll apply for re-sentencing. And I've sent Harry Rood and John Cappelli to Atlanta to speak with the two prisoners."

"You *sent* Harry Rood?"

Haaken Rood, known to everyone as Harry, was the deputy chief investigator, the Office's number two investigator and its expert on organized crime, as well. He oversaw only the most important investigations. He wasn't someone an assistant special prosecutor "sent" somewhere. But apparently, Sara had.

"When did you do all this?"

"Friday. Rood and Cappelli left early this morning."

Henry sat back in his chair. What could he say? He was stunned at the speed with which Sara had taken over his case and got it moving again.

"Wait a minute," he said. "What about their lawyer?"

"What do you mean?"

"Their lawyer said I couldn't speak to them."

"And you believed him?"

"Why not? He's, their lawyer."

"And they're witnesses, not defendants or suspects. He can't stop us from talking to them."

"He can't?"

"He can't. You know, you were right."

"About what?"

"About not having been a prosecutor. You've spent too much time in the white shoe world of corporate law and not enough time down in the pits. It shows." There was a hint of a smile on Sara's lips. She went on. "You ought to know something about Felix Aguilar, Bermudez's partner."

"What?" He sat up.

She picked up a sheet of paper. Henry recognized it as a rap sheet—a copy of a criminal record. "This is Aguilar's sheet. Updated Friday. He's just been charged in Miami, by the feds again. With sale. Serious enough to guarantee life. Without parole."

"You mean in addition to the crime he's in jail on?"

"Yes."

"Do you think that's enough weight to get him to cooperate?"

She sat back. "We'll have to wait and see, of course. But if you ask me, I'd say yes."

CHAPTER 12

Rood and Cappelli were successful in their trip to Atlanta. Bermudez would not speak to them. But Aguilar, facing life in prison, was more accommodating. In fact, he was due the next day in the Office.

"Good work," Henry said to Harry Rood.

"Thanks," he responded. "By the way," Rood said to Sara, "I spoke to Patrolman Hanley, and Jack Keene has some connection with a big defense attorney. Maybe a drug connection."

"Who's the lawyer?" asked Sara.

"Paul Grassi."

"Paul Grassi?" Henry nearly shouted the name.

Sara looked puzzled. "What's wrong? I know Grassi." She wrinkled her nose. "He's scum. But why are you so upset?"

"Because Paul Grassi was Bermudez's lawyer. And Aguilar's. He's the guy who wouldn't let me talk to them."

Genuine surprise showed on Sara's face, and she sat up sharply. "Wait a minute," she said to Henry. "You mean Paul Grassi is the guy who told you to keep away from Bermudez and Aguilar?"

"Yes. Paul Grassi."

Sara whistled. "I love it." She smiled and looked at Harry Rood, who was shaking his head. "It's beautiful. The cops steal the drugs…"

Henry broke in. "Drugs?"

She looked at Henry. "Of course. You don't think they just took money, do you?"

"Well, yes."

"Well, no. These kinds of cops steal drugs, too. And then they sell the drugs themselves."

Henry shook his head in wonder.

Sara looked back at Rood. "So Grassi represents dealers the cops arrest and then he arranges to sell the drugs the cops steal through his other clients." She looked at Henry. "I presume now you understand why he didn't want you talking to his so-called clients?"

The air in Sara Leventhal's office crackled like a high-tension wire as the man sitting across the desk from her finished speaking. He was small and wiry. His sharp black eyes, set in a deep olive complexion, were underscored with dark, rocker-like shadows, and his thin lips were accented with a pencil-thin moustache. He had been speaking in Spanish.

Sara sat unmoving, waiting until the interpreter, seated to the man's left, had translated the answer from Spanish to English.

"Nine kilograms of pure heroin. On the table."

Now she moved. Her eyes opened wider. "Nine?" she said incredulously.

"*Nueve?*" repeated the interpreter.

"*Si,*" came the answer.

Sara looked sharply at Harry Rood, who was sitting at the man's right. The muscles of her neck tightened. She turned back to the speaker.

"You're certain about that?"

She waited for the translation.

In his seat near the window, Henry leaned forward as the import of the answer sunk in. In his matter-of-fact way, Felix Aguilar, the drug dealer-turned-witness, was delivering even more than Henry and Sara had hoped. Aguilar had begun his story with himself and his partner, Arnaldo Bermudez, seated one afternoon at a kitchen table in the house Bermudez had rented in the Corona section of Queens. They had just finished counting a bagful of cash which had been turned in that morning by their dealers. They had placed the cash back in its paper bag on the floor next to the table. Three hundred and ninety-seven-thousand dollars. Then Bermudez placed on the table a large package of heroin, a recent shipment which they were going to cut and divide up for distribution to their dealers. They had just opened the package when four detectives burst through the door with guns out and arrested them both. During the arrest, the detectives seized both the drugs and the cash in the paper bag on the floor.

"How much heroin was on the table when the cops arrived?" Sara had asked.

Nine kilograms of pure heroin. Henry repeated Aguilar's answer to himself. Four had been vouchered. Five were missing. Just like the cash. Nearly four hundred thousand dollars in the paper bag and twenty thousand turned in. Over three hundred and seventy thousand dollars missing. Clearly stolen by the arresting officers. Yet Aguilar and Bermudez could do nothing about it. Any complaint would have been an admission of what they were doing. And who would have believed them? Or cared?

Henry could feel the anger rising inside as he began to appreciate the cruel cynicism of the detectives, able to steal such sums safely. Almost four hundred thousand dollars. And five kilograms of heroin. Five kilos of pure heroin, Henry recalled, was worth over a million dollars.

"And so, altogether," said Sara, appearing to read Henry's thoughts, "the police got five kilos of heroin and about three hundred and eighty thousand dollars. Is that correct?"

Henry fixed his eyes on Aguilar as the interpreter began to translate Sara's question. Aguilar, he expected, would wait quietly until he understood the question and then respond in his accustomed reportorial manner. But this time, as the interpreter spoke, Aguilar's face darkened with anger. A torrent of Spanish followed.

"What did he say?" Sara asked the interpreter.

"Exactly?"

"Of course."

"The dirty pigs of sons of whores, they took our drugs and our money and then we had to pay again."

"Pay again? What does he mean?"

The interpreter made the communication.

"We had to pay one hundred thousand dollars after the arrest to get out of jail."

Sara registered surprise. "And that got you out of jail?"

"*Si,*" responded Aguilar.

"Pay whom?"

Again, a delay for the translation.

"I paid my share to Arnaldo and Arnaldo told me that the money went to the same policeman who took the first money. The one who gave the orders to the others when they arrested them."

She looked at Rood. "That has to be Keene."

Rood nodded in agreement.

"That was in addition to the money the cops took when they made the arrest?"

The translator spoke to Aguilar and received his response.

"Yes."

Sara shook her head and exhaled audibly. She glanced at Henry, but her eyes slid by. She seemed absorbed by the new information.

For almost an hour more, Sara debriefed Aguilar, retracing his story, gleaning more details, filling in blanks. At one point, she showed photographs of several Narcotics officers to the witness. While Aguilar failed to pick out Keene, he was able to identify one of the detectives who had stolen his money and drugs: Detective Harley Fulton, one of Keene's team and the only Black officer of the four.

At last John Cappelli left with Aguilar to return him to federal custody and Henry spoke up. "Sara, that was great. You've broken it open."

Sara didn't answer him immediately. "What I want to know," she continued, "is how Keene got them out of jail after they'd paid him that extra hundred thousand. How did he kill the case?"

"Keene told the DA that Bermudez and Aguilar were cooperating," Henry said. "And the DA told the sentencing court. That's why they got a walk."

"What?" Sara's eyes widened.

"I mentioned this earlier. You didn't seem interested. The DA's office said that Bermudez and Aguilar were cooperating and were needed back on the street. That's what Bert Donner told the sentencing judge and that's why the judge let them go. And that's why I called their lawyer, Paul Grassi. I assumed he was the one who'd advised them to cooperate and that he'd do it again, with us."

Sara eyed him sharply. "Why didn't you ask Aguilar if he'd cooperated so we could eliminate the possibility?"

"Because you were doing the questioning. And I assumed you remembered what I'd told you and that you had some reason not to bring it up."

He looked at Sara, but she was staring past him and Harry Rood, as though at some object behind them, although there was nothing there but the wall. Then Henry noticed her eyes. They seemed to have softened. There was even the hint of fear in them. For an instant, she seemed vulnerable. And so pretty.

And then it clicked off. "Harry, go see Aguilar this afternoon and check out that cooperation story. I'm sure that he'll deny any cooperation with Keene."

Rood nodded. "I will. By the way," he went on, "I've been looking at the files on the four detectives."

"And?"

"Fulton's got some problems."

"What do you mean?"

"I think Fulton—the guy he identified—is vulnerable. He's got a daughter with some kind of disability. Goes to a special school. Mostly taken care of by the medical plan. But if he were dismissed and lost his pension and benefits, he'd have problems."

Sara eyed Rood intently.

"Also," Rood continued, "I checked around. Fulton's very wrapped up in the girl. Spends a lot of time with her. She obviously means a great deal to him."

"Hmmm." Sara leaned backwards in her reclining desk chair until its back touched the wall. She pursed her lips, then spoke. "Very interesting." She sat up again, glanced at Henry, then fixed on Rood. "Get him in here, Harry. Get him in here."

Detective Harley Fulton's face was like a carefully carved block of deep brown mahogany. There was no fear apparent in his eyes or in the set of his mouth. Indeed, there was no expression at all as the detective faced Sara across her desk in the afternoon. He was sitting in the same spot where a few days earlier Felix Aguilar had put the finger on him as one of the four detectives who had stolen money and drugs. But if he felt any lingering vibrations, he didn't show it.

Sara, too, was a study in resolution. She was sitting straight in her desk chair, looking directly at Detective Fulton. Her features were rigid, her eyes unyielding as she faced the detective. The only movement by either of them was Sara's right hand, which was resting on the desk, rolling a pencil slowly back and forth between her fingers.

From his chair to Fulton's left, half turned in, Henry was looking at the detective. Fulton had a poster face for a cop. Virile, sculpted jowls and cheeks. Black curly hair cut short and neat, jutting forward confidently at the temples and back on top to outline a smooth forehead. Under a full, slightly flaring nose, a thick, well-trimmed mustache sitting atop unsmiling lips. When he had entered, Henry had briefly wondered why a handsome man like that had spoiled his life by stealing drugs. Now he was merely waiting for Sara to begin.

"I want you to know where we're coming from and where you stand," said Sara at last.

With Henry on one side of Detective Fulton and Harry Rood on the other, each with their chairs turned slightly inward, there were three pairs of eyes on Fulton, watching for a response.

There was none.

"As I'm sure you know by now, my Office is looking into the old Bermudez-Aguilar arrest." She paused. "You remember the Bermudez arrest undoubtedly."

Fulton made no acknowledgment.

"Putting it simply, Detective, you've been put four-square in the middle of what really happened there."

Still no reaction.

Dark brown irises surrounded by clear white looked back at Sara. They took no cognizance of the others. Nor did the eyes gave any hint of the workings of the mind behind them.

"You helped Jack Keene take three hundred and eighty thousand dollars in cash and five keys of pure shit," Sara said.

Fulton's face was stony, the eyes, as well.

Sara leaned forward across the desk. She pressed the point of the pencil into the blotter in front of her. "What I'm trying to say, Detective, is that you're going down on this one." She sat back and looked the detective in the eyes. He held his ground.

"You've been identified. Your role in the theft has been spelled out. And your friends aren't going to help you." She narrowed her eyes. "You, Detective Fulton, are going to go down for all of them." She paused. "You take the fall. They walk."

Fulton made no response.

Henry began to wonder if they were wrong about Fulton. He hoped not.

Sara persisted. "On April 21, at about 2:30 in the afternoon, you, along with Detectives Keene, O'Brien, and Olivera raided a home on 182nd Street, where you found two men sitting at a kitchen table about to package bulk heroin."

Fulton moved slightly. To Henry he seemed to relax. What Sara had just told him was all in the police report—a report with which Fulton was certainly familiar. His movement gave him away.

He knew about the theft, Henry said to himself. And he was part of it. That's why he relaxed when he heard Sara say only what was in the police report. Now, Henry feared, Sara's plan wasn't going to work even if Fulton *was* guilty. Because knowing Fulton was involved wasn't enough to force him to admit it. Look at himself and Jack Keene—his own frustration, knowing Keene was guilty but unable to do anything about it.

Sara went on. "You lined both men up against the wall. Detective Keene handed you a large shopping bag with money in it. You counted out twenty thousand two hundred dollars and put it on the table while Keene removed five keys of the heroin and put it in another shopping bag lying on the floor."

That wasn't in the police report; that had come from Aguilar. Henry detected in Fulton a slight tensing. Perhaps the detective was trying to figure out who had told Sara these things: the drug dealers or a fellow officer who had turned. Whatever he was feeling, Fulton kept it off his face. It was as wooden as ever.

"After that, you all left," Sara continued calmly. "You brought in your prisoners and turned in twenty thousand odd dollars and four of the nine kilos of heroin. And you kept the rest."

Nothing.

"Then, when all the hoopla was over, you divvied up the loot. And Keene let you have your nut."

She was speculating now, Henry knew. On very dangerous ground. It amazed Henry how unworried Sara seemed. Especially since she was almost out of ammunition.

Fulton appeared unfazed. Henry looked at Sara again, expecting to detect some evidence of concern. Certainly, Henry was worrying now that their efforts with Detective Fulton might fail. Why wasn't Sara worried? They'd played most of their hand. What could she do now? For a moment, he was relieved that it wasn't he who was asking the questions. It wasn't he who was going to have to face Howard Matlin and Nat Perlman and Matt Corey and explain why he had again missed making the case. Then he heard her again.

"After you got your share of that three hundred eighty thousand, and after Keene had disposed of the drugs you and he stole, you got lucky again. You got your share of the next hundred thousand that Keene got from Bermudez after the arrest."

"What?" Fulton's eyes opened wide as the question popped out.

For a split second, Sara looked as surprised as Fulton. Henry was confused, too. What was happening? Perhaps there was no hundred thousand dollars. Perhaps Aguilar had lied to them.

But Sara was ahead of him, already on the attack.

"That's right, he stiffed you." She smiled coldly. "He put your share in his own pocket and never told you about the hundred thousand dollars. The money Bermudez and Aguilar paid to get out of jail. Remember," she added with a lilt in her voice, "how quickly they walked?" Then she shook her head, still smiling. "And you're sitting here protecting him."

Henry could now see what had happened. Sara was correct; Fulton had been cheated by Keene, and Sara's question about the hundred thousand dollars was the first he had heard about it. He had reacted accordingly. Now Fulton seemed to be desperately trying to figure a way to get himself back together and recoup his loss. He obviously wanted to ask Sara about the hundred thousand, but he couldn't do it without admitting the rest. For the first time, he seemed on the defensive. And Sara was taking advantage of it.

"While you sit here protecting Jack Keene, he's off spending your money. Meanwhile, you're the one who's going to take a trip into the Commissioner's hearing room and get yourself booted out of the Department." Pausing, she eyed him directly. "No pension. No medical. No more benefits." She leaned back slowly, almost languorously, in her chair, keeping her eye on the detective. Then, just as slowly, she came forward. She spoke very deliberately.

"What, Detective Fulton, will happen to Maridee when her daddy can't give her medical care anymore?"

Fulton bolted upright. "You fucking cunt!"

"No, Detective," Sara replied deliberately. "I'm not a fucking cunt. You're a fucking idiot. You're going to lose your job, lose your pension, lose your medical benefits, jeopardize your daughter's health, and leave her behind while you go sit in a jail cell for several years and rot, just so that you can stand up like a big macho cock and know that good old Irish Jack Keene, who stiffed you out of twenty-five thousand dollars, and who'd just as soon see you ground up for black dogmeat, is still smiling over how smart he is as he pours himself another glass of Johnny Walker Black Label. Neat, like he always drinks it."

Harley Fulton seemed ready to burst. He glared at Sara. Pure poison. Then his eyes closed, and his lower lip disappeared between his teeth. His eyes opened again. He adjusted his position on his chair and looked at Sara.

"What do you want to know?"

Two hours later, Henry watched Sara lean back in her chair and let out a sigh. She wiped her eyes, perhaps to clear away the smoke from Fulton's cigarettes. She appeared as exhausted as Henry felt, and he hadn't even opened his mouth.

But Fulton was gone, in more ways than one. They had their evidence. Keene was the ringleader, with O'Brien, Olivera, and Fulton as associates. They had split $350,000—Keene had kept the rest for his organizational work. Only Keene had wanted any part of the drugs, so Keene had taken them as well. He had probably sold them through attorney Paul Grassi, with whom Keene had a close relationship.

"What happens to Fulton now?" asked Henry. "And his kid?"

"If he keeps cooperating? He sort of becomes part of the team. Until it's over. And then it's up to the Commissioner. We'll put in a good word for him and at least he'll keep his pension. And the medical. So, his daughter will be okay. And if he really does well, maybe he'll even keep his job. Pay a big fine and stay on the payroll."

"I hope so."

Sara looked at Henry curiously. "Yes, you do, don't you? Anyway," she went on before he could respond, "there's still one big question left." She sat up and folded her hands. "That other hundred thousand. Fulton never heard about it, and I'm willing to bet neither did O'Brien or Olivera."

"Keene probably pocketed it himself," suggested Henry. "He told the DA that Bermudez and Aguilar were cooperating and just kept the money."

Sara shook her head. "No. It doesn't work that way. It'd take more than one cop's word for a district attorney to let two big dealers like that out on the street. Especially with a heavy charge. Don't forget, they turned in four kilos, and that's enough for a long time in jail." Sara leaned forward in her chair and began to rise. "There's something more here," she said as she headed for the door. "And I think I know what it is."

CHAPTER 13

It was early the next morning when Henry emerged from the investigators'
area with a cup of black coffee in his hand. Although still sleepy, Henry's spirits were high. The night before, he and a few friends from his old law firm had
met for dinner at Gallagher's and then gone to a tennis match at the Garden.
Afterward, they had stopped in at a new bar called Lizardskin for a nightcap
and a look at the attractive women the place was known to draw. But it didn't
hurt that the Bermudez case was working out.

"Hi, Mike," Henry said, greeting one of the investigators who was leaving. He glanced down the long hall ahead of him that would take him back
to his office, but he decided instead to stop by and see how Scoop Dixon, the
press secretary, was doing. Strolling to the end of the corridor and past the
door to Howard Matlin's office, he turned right and walked two doors up to
Dixon's door. He knocked.

"Yeah, come on in."

Behind his desk, Scoop Dixon was reclining in his chair, his back to the
window, clutching an unfiltered cigarette in his nicotine-stained fingers. His
small office was cluttered as usual with books piled to toppling on the win-
dowsill and old newspapers heaped on the floor. As the door closed behind
Henry, Dixon exhaled a lungful of smoke and pointed Henry to a chair with
two books on it.

Behind Dixon, through the smoke, Henry could see the blue sky above the Hudson River. The first time he had visited Dixon, Henry had wondered why anyone would obscure such a panoramic view of the Hudson River and New Jersey by facing away from the window. Having witnessed Dixon's preoccupation with his work, Henry decided that the desk was in originally in that position and Dixon never gave it a thought.

"What's going on?" asked Henry, removing the books and taking a seat. He took a swallow of his coffee.

"I might ask *you* that question."

"What do you mean?"

"Well, from what I hear, you and the lady are about to make some of New York's finest not so happy."

Henry smiled. "You know about that, do you?"

"It's my business." Dixon took a drag on his cigarette. Henry sipped his coffee.

"Well," Henry responded, "it's starting to look good."

"So, keep at it. We could use a good indictment. Especially after the Bronx fiasco."

"Fiasco?" Henry sat up. "You mean the thing in the papers yesterday about the Bronx politician we indicted?"

"Yeah."

"How's that a fiasco? The papers said Howie nailed the guy. A treasurer for some political organization. In fact, one of my lawyer buddies was talking about it last night."

"Well, that's what the public thinks. But the truth is Galligan outmaneuvered us."

"Galligan?"

"Yeah. Erin Galligan." Dixon leaned forward and snuffed out his cigarette. The ashtray had several butts in it already, even though it was only ten

137

in the morning. "Officially, he's the party chairman of the Bronx. But he's a big enchilada in the whole city. And in the State, too, since he's a buddy of Whelan. Even has his hand on Washington's nuts. There's at least a half dozen congressmen who squeak whenever he squeezes because he's the guy who put 'em in Congress. But this time we almost had him nailed."

"How?"

"There was a bribe set up. This little bank had a lawsuit against it that it thought it was gonna lose. So, the president of the bank used some connections and arranged to pay fifty grand to Galligan to influence the judge who had the case. Judge named Dennis. State Supreme Court. Galligan put him on the bench a few years ago so he owed his ass to Galligan. Of course, then the bank won."

Dixon took a deep breath and let it out. Probably to clean out his lungs. "We had an informant who heard about it. Knew that the money had been paid to a city councilman named Scammett who Galligan controls, who acts as Galligan's bagman."

"Bagman? I thought just crooked cops had bagmen who collected the loot for them."

"Nope. Anyway, we were close to making a case when Galligan got wind of us. He threw us a baby—you remember the story about the Russian family in the sled throwing the baby to the wolves?"

Henry nodded.

"He got his party treasurer to come in and admit to a violation about recording the fifty grand the wrong way. It was bullshit, but it could be twisted around to explain about half the evidence we had. So, we had to give up on Galligan himself and settle for the bullshit indictment your buddy heard about."

Henry shook his head. "I guess the system's pretty bad."

Dixon laughed. "I hope you're not just discovering that."

Henry gave a humorless laugh. "And I thought four cops stealing drugs was a big thing."

"Hey, it is." Dixon took another cigarette from the pack lying on his desk. He lit it slowly, taking a deep drag before he spoke. "Because maybe you can send 'em to jail. See, cops are vulnerable. But politicians are like cats. Except they've got even *more* than nine lives."

"I can't say you've lifted my spirits," Henry said as he rose to leave. He opened the door. "But maybe at least we can put *these* guys away."

Henry left Dixon's office and walked down the hall to Sara's office for a brief meeting with Sara and Harry Rood. Once he and Harry sat down, Sara began.

"We're not there," she said, shaking her head. "Even if Aguilar testified that four cops stole his and his partner's money and drugs, he can only identify one of the cops. And anyway, he's just a drug dealer whose word is going to be weighed against the word of three decorated policemen. And Detective Fulton is no help yet. Because he is an accomplice and, as I assume you know..." she looked at Henry, "...under the brilliant law of the State of New York, you can't even offer the testimony of an accomplice unless you can corroborate it with some independent evidence. Like a little old lady who happened to overhear the four cops planning the rip-off." Her upper lip curled distastefully. "A law put in by politicians," she added, "for obvious reasons—to protect themselves. Anyway, we need more."

"And what I still want to know," Sara continued, "is about that extra hundred thousand they paid to get out of jail."

"Does it matter?" asked Henry. "We've almost got Keene and the other two cops on the theft. So why worry about that?"

"Because" said Sara, "it matters to me."

The sudden change of tone in Sara's voice caught Henry's attention. It was almost pleading. He looked at her more closely. As he half-expected, her face had softened.

Henry took over. "According to Aguilar, Bermudez paid the hundred thousand to Keene."

"And I'm sure Keene kept *some* of the money." The iron was back in Sara's voice. "But Keene couldn't have gotten two major drug dealers out of jail on *his* word alone." She looked at Henry. "You know where this case was prosecuted," she said.

"Of course. Martin Ross's office."

"Right," Sara nodded. "And what do you know about that office?"

"Other than that he's a nasty son-of-a-bitch, I don't know too much."

"Well, a lot of good people in law enforcement *do* know. Things happen in that office. Bad things." She looked at Harry Rood.

Henry also glanced at Rood and saw him nod in agreement.

"Deals," Sara went on. "And not legitimate plea bargains, either."

"Well," said Henry, shaking his head. "By now, nothing surprises me." After his talk with Dixon this morning, it was true. "Is Ross part of it?"

Sara shrugged. "Who knows? But it's his office."

"Well," said Henry, "it wasn't Ross who appeared in court to tell the judge the dealers were cooperating. It was Bert Donner, Ross's chief assistant."

"That doesn't surprise me," Sara responded. "Did you happen to see who the judge was?"

"Let me think." Henry wiped his eyes. "Yes. It was an unusual name. Pfister, I think his name was."

"Interesting," Sara said. She looked at Rood. "From what I've heard, he's one of the few honest judges out there."

Rood nodded his head. "He has a good reputation."

"So now I know what happened to that hundred thousand dollars." Sara sat back in her chair. "Bert Donner got it, or some of it, and, who knows, he probably gave the rest to Ross."

"Whew." Henry shook his head. His mind went back to Martin Ross sitting in Max Olman's office glaring at him.

It was Sunday afternoon and Henry was at his desk catching up on some matters he had put aside during the past week. He was also reviewing material the investigators had gathered on Bert Donner during the week. There were, of course, several newspaper clippings, all featuring District Attorney Ross, along with Donner, announcing some arrest or indictment, and all shimmering with praise for the "tough-talking" district attorney.

But there were also confidential reports of the police department's organized crime experts, noting that both men had been spotted in the company of known mobsters. According to one source, both Ross and Donner had attended a private luncheon in Little Italy for Savario Tutino, the nephew of the late Franco ("Big Frenchy") Tutino, founder of the Tutino family of organized crime. Another memorandum quoted underworld sources to the effect that someone in the DA's office had been protecting Ralph ("the Shark") Casteggio, a Tutino family capo, in a waste-disposal company that had repeatedly violated environmental restrictions in Queens and Nassau Counties but had always escaped prosecution. There were other allegations indicating that several good cases against the mob had somehow sputtered out once in Ross's office.

At last Henry stood and stretched. He stepped to his window and looked out. The afternoon sun still filled the China-blue sky while below, between stretches of concrete and asphalt, patches of luxuriant green were tinged with red and gold. It was late September, almost October, and to Henry, it was the sweetest time of year in New York City.

Henry had often challenged friends from Cleveland or from college or law school, who held the city in low esteem, that they should see New York in

October. October, when sunlight still warms the air but no longer bakes the sidewalks and streets. When New York begins to sparkle and come alive, even as leaves begin to die. Indeed, the air then seems to absorb the vital spirits that pass from the leaves, as they turn color and flutter in sere sprinklings to the ground. The air vibrates with enthusiasm, begging the battered and bruised residents of the world's most complicated city to get up and do it, whatever *it* is. Or at least to try. Nowhere, poets and songwriters have attested, does the blood run as vigorously, nowhere do skin and brain tingle with such anticipation, as they do in the evanescent, magically purified atmosphere of New York City in autumn.

Especially on Sunday. Sundays are the best of the best. Clear bright Sundays that draw the apartment-dwelling New Yorkers to the street, where they spend the day walking in the safety of daylight in the parks, smelling the roasting chestnuts in the vendors' carts, watching the boats drifting along in the Hudson and East Rivers. Such a day looks down on laughing children crowding onto a small, street-bound machine valiantly doing urban service as a country carnival ride or gathering around a Good Humor truck. It smiles on elderly couples leaving home well before the matinee at Lincoln Center so they can stroll comfortably along Broadway or Columbus Avenue, watching the antics of the young, and filling them with tender recollections before they must enter dark halls and listen to Wagner.

For Henry Perkins, looking down from the forty-fourth floor of the New State Office Building, it was no longer a day for work. It was time to join the rest of New York in the celebration.

As he passed by Sara's office, he saw that her door was open, and she was at her desk.

"Hi, Sara," he said, stepping in.

"Oh, hello. I didn't know you were here."

"Been here since morning. Incidentally, I've been reading about Ross and Donner. It looks like your instincts are right on target about them."

"What have you been reading?"

"Police reports and the like."

She smiled. "Nice to know that Queens law enforcement is in such good hands, isn't it?"

"Sure is. Well, I'll see you tomorrow." He turned to leave.

"Wait a second." Sara got up. "I'll go out with you."

Henry descended the forty-four floors with Sara. Having stowed away his feelings for her, he was beginning to get along with her better. By sticking to business. But he was through with business today, and he was looking forward to a late Sunday afternoon of relaxation. He was relieved as they signed out in the Sunday log and passed through the revolving door to the street.

Outside, Sara looked up at the clear, blue sky. "My goodness, what a beautiful day!"

"I know," said Henry. "That's why I'm heading up to Central Park to take a walk."

Sara turned toward him. "You are?" There was a note of request in her voice that Henry didn't miss, and it unnerved him. Just then the sun caught Sara's eyes and she raised a hand. Her hair fluttered casually against her cheek.

Damn it, she's beautiful, sighed Henry to himself, and he felt a tug in his gut. But he resisted the temptation to ask her to accompany him.

It was Sara who spoke. "You know, it's too nice to waste time on the subway. Would you be interested in taking a walk down here?"

His mind spun for a second. "Sure," he said at last.

Sara pointed south, toward Battery Park and the World Trade Center. "Let's go this way."

They crossed the street and headed south. It was still warm enough for them to be comfortable, despite the breeze, and they loped briskly along the sidewalk. Henry liked the fact that Sara walked as energetically as he.

"You know," Sara said, "I don't know how we can do it, but I really want to prove that someone in the D.A.'s office took part of that money."

"So do I," Henry responded. "But I don't want to forget what we've already got: some major cops we *know* took money and drugs."

"Don't worry, I'm not forgetting that. Anyway," she added, "it's too nice a day to talk business."

They walked along Church Street toward the World Trade Center. Discount stores and shoddy fabric outlets lined most of the way. At one corner, Henry pointed to a sterile institutional building they were passing. "Internal Revenue Service is in there," he said with a laugh. "Did you ever try to get help from them?"

"It's got to be better than in there," Sara responded, pointing to the post office building in the next block.

Reaching the World Trade Center, they entered the plaza that lay between the two towers. The plaza was a wide plane, over a hundred yards in all directions, punctuated in two places by the spiky silver pillars of the principal towers and bounded elsewhere by the forms of lesser auxiliary buildings, mostly still under construction. The wind was brisk, snagged high above by the tall towers and channeled downward. Although the sun had passed to the west, it still shone brightly, except where the North Tower cast its long shadow across the center of the plaza. They walked toward the center, which was dominated by a round fountain with no water. A handful of people sat on the rim, even though the sun was gone. In the center of the fountain was perched an eccentric brass ball-like sculpture.

"That thing looks like it fell off one of the towers and landed here," Henry laughed. "Speaking of which…" he glanced up at the North Tower, "do you remember when some guy climbed right up the side of the building?"

Sara turned abruptly. "Don't talk about that," she snapped. "Let's go."

Henry's mouth dropped open. "Whaat?"

"I'm sorry," she said less harshly. "Can we go?"

"Well, sure." He shrugged. But he was trying to imagine what had pre-cipitated Sara's response. He wanted to press her on it, but when he looked at her, he held his tongue. She was gliding along the sidewalk, unseeing. Her eyes had drifted off, away from the world around her, the world on which she usually had so firm a grip. The usual set was gone from her mouth. Instead of a tough, determined prosecutor, Sara looked suddenly like a lost little girl.

And then, as quickly, she was herself again. "Let's go this way," she said, indicating with her head.

They walked south to the Staten Island ferry, then northeast, past the tall buildings of the Wall Street district. Their conversation stayed away from Office matters, and they talked of what they saw as they walked. Tourists, with eager faces, who gaped at the tall buildings of the financial district. Stress-laden bankers and stockbrokers, wandering out of these same buildings where they had spent their Sunday afternoons.

Three earnest, slick-haired men emerged from one tower. "I'll bet they were in there counting the money they make," remarked Henry.

"Or playing cards and losing some of it," Sara laughed.

They passed the South Street Seaport, with its tired eighteenth century buildings and a few sailing ships badly in need of care. Turning inland, they came to the Brooklyn Bridge.

"Come on," suggested Sara, pointing to a set of stairs leading up to the pedestrian walk that crossed the bridge. "Let's walk across."

Watching Sara bounding up the old stairs ahead of him, Henry felt a pang of desire. She usually seemed so sure of herself, so capable of carrying out her wishes. And yet there was sometimes an awkward coltishness about her, or a profound sadness such as he had witnessed a short while before, that made him believe that inside Sara was a spirit, trapped, arrested, wanting to get out. He was aware, too, of the odd conflict in his attraction. What he wanted most in her—her vulnerability and her freshness—was what she least wanted to reveal. She fought that part of herself with determination, declaring her independence over and over, and reinforcing the walls around her as an army might under siege. Henry knew that Sara could hurt him. So, to avoid that, as they started across the bridge toward Brooklyn, he assured himself that he wouldn't allow his feelings to get the best of him.

They emerged onto the walkway, where Sunday strollers walked in both directions, to and from Brooklyn. On either side of them, below a network of girders and electrical cables, cars whished by, going, and coming in a steady stream, their tires humming and bumping over the uneven surface of the roadway. Ahead loomed the first of the two gothic towers that supported the suspension cables. Behind them, the fading sun still shone, glimmering on the spider web of cables, celebrating the great conception of John Roebling.

Crossing bridges was special for Henry. He always relished that fleeting instant exactly halfway, when he was suspended between two definite points, connected to both, but committed to neither. It was an exquisite, nearly impossible moment of freedom, when all that mattered was that he was.

As they reached the center of the bridge, he stopped. They were above the cables now, with an unobstructed view in both directions. He looked north up the river, flowing under the Manhattan and Williamsburg bridges. Then he turned to the south, toward Governors Island and beyond it, the Statue of Liberty, and the broad expanse of New York Harbor. He felt good.

"What's wrong?" Sara asked.

"Nothing. I just want to stand here in the middle of the bridge for a minute."

"What for?"

He tried to tell her about the halfway thing. About the suspension between disparate points.

"That's sort of silly, isn't it? A bridge is a means of crossing to go somewhere, not a place to linger in limbo."

Despite her words, Sara stopped and turned into the brisk breeze blowing from the harbor to the south. Her hair crossed her face, then billowed out behind her as her eyes gazed into the distance. Then she turned to Henry.

"Come on," she said brightly, "let's go to Brooklyn Heights and have some dinner."

"Dinner?"

"Of course," she responded. "It's getting late and I'm hungry."

Henry felt he should take charge at this point, so on Montague Street, when he spotted a small French restaurant, he suggested they try it.

"Yes, it's quite good," Sara agreed.

"You know it?"

"Sure. I've even eaten there before."

So much for taking charge.

"Actually, it's a famous place," she went on. "All the politicians and judges eat here during the week. I'll bet more cases have been fixed here than any other place in Brooklyn.

Henry frowned. "Maybe we shouldn't eat there."

"Don't be silly. The food's good. And I'm hungry." She laughed. "You can think of it as research."

He smiled. "On that note, how can I resist?" He opened the door for her.

They sat near the rear of the single room. As he looked around, Henry was reminded of a small family-run restaurant he had frequented during his year in Strasbourg, France. It, too, had light pink walls hung with simple country scenes, and brass wall lamps that added their light to chandeliers hanging from wood-beamed ceilings. Even the napkins on the white tablecloths were similar—red and white stripes folded in simple rectangles. Perhaps the proprietors were related. At any rate, the familiarity allowed Henry to forget the restaurant's unsavory clientele and settle in comfortably.

Henry ordered a Kronenbourg beer and Sara a glass of white wine as they took menus from the waiter. Glancing at the bill of fare, the anomaly of the situation suddenly amused him. Henry had wanted a date with Sara since the first time he had seen her in court, even before he had met her. But he had never asked her. Yet here they were, about to enjoy dinner together in a cozy French restaurant, and it was Sara's idea, not his.

"The fish is good," Sara said. "And the *choucroute*."

"That's for me," Henry responded, picturing the savory dish of sausages, ham, potatoes, and sauerkraut he had enjoyed frequently during his stay in Strasbourg.

"Somehow, now that I'm getting to know you, I expected that," she said. She was smiling.

Henry's face prickled as he returned her smile. "And how about you?"

"Dover sole. It's not very French, but it's terrific here."

"Should we order a bottle of wine?"

She shook her head. "Not for me. One glass is enough. I've got some work to do at home."

Work again. It reminded Henry of why they were here. But it was better than nothing.

The waiter returned with their drinks, and they placed their orders.

"Cheers," Henry said, lifting his beer. As she picked up her glass, he added a thought. "To all the politicians and judges and everyone else who's sat here fixing cases, but who we're about to send to jail."

"That I can drink to, happily," she said, and clinked glasses with him.

He learned that Sara had gone to Wellesley and then to Columbia Law School, where her father had once taught.

"What did he teach?"

"Criminal law and criminal procedure. And torts."

"Ugh."

"Criminal law?" she asked with surprise.

"No, torts."

They talked about her experience in the District Attorney's Office.

"The last case I worked on was an investigation into a group of car thieves. They were stealing cars in Manhattan and then cutting them up at a chop shop in the Bronx."

"A chop shop, where they cut up stolen cars, right?"

"Yes," she nodded. "Anyway, I was working with the police department's Auto Squad, and I had a good case going. The cutters had organized crime connections and everything. I set up a series of raids on the chop shops at times when I knew they'd be dirty. But whenever we raided, somehow the stolen stuff wouldn't be there. I suspected a leak, but it wasn't until I got to our Office that I knew what was happening."

"What?"

"Well, the lieutenant and two of his sergeants had a whole string of chop shops on a pad, protecting them. When the assignment sergeant would learn of an upcoming raid, he'd tell the lieutenant and then they'd tip off the chop shop to clear out the stolen stuff until after the raid."

"And these are the guys you arrested?"

Sara nodded. "Yes. And after what happened to me before, it felt awfully good."

For a moment there was silence. He loved to talk about catching crooked cops. But this was the first chance he'd had to get Sara talking about herself. So, he tried to change the subject.

"What do you do when you're not putting cops in jail?"

"Not much. You know, Jack Keene had a brother on the Auto Squad."

No luck, he thought.

"…he worked on one of my investigations that got sold out. I guess it runs in the family."

Their dinner came, and he dived into his *choucroute*, washing it down with another beer. At one point, she put a piece of her fish on his plate.

"Here, try it."

He was surprised at her gesture. But he ate the sole. "Delicious." He tried again. "I never got down to Wellesley when I was at Dartmouth. Did you like it?"

She shrugged. "Did you ever have a case fixed right out from under you?"

Damn. "Not really," he said.

"I had a trial fixed right in front of me. A landlord who had a tenant organizer beaten up. I had the guy six ways to Sunday for assault and conspiracy. Four eyewitnesses. The case was before this political hack judge. So just before trial, the landlord changes lawyers. Hires this political lawyer who's part of the same organization as the judge. Suddenly, my witnesses are found incompetent to testify. All four of them. Then the judge lets it go to the jury and, of course, they acquit."

These were stories Henry wanted to hear. Almost any time. But not just now.

A few minutes later he tried again. "You're an only child?"

"Yes."

"So am I. Did you ever want brothers or sisters?"

"No."

Henry wanted to follow up, but she cut him off.

"Have you had a run in with Matt Corey yet?"

Henry almost sighed aloud. "Sort of."

"I thought he just didn't like women lawyers when I started. But now I just think he sees *all* lawyers as jerks. Except Matlin, of course."

Henry shrugged. How could he get her off the Office?

"The problem," she persisted, "is that he's a good investigator. He's damned good."

"That's what I've heard."

The waiter picked up their plates, and they ordered coffee. Then he tried another tack. "This place reminds me of a little restaurant I used to eat in in France."

"Oh? When were you in France?"

It worked! "For a year. After law school. One of my professors arranged a job for me with the early European Parliament in Strasbourg. I wasn't much more than a glorified messenger, but I had fun and got to practice my French."

"That's nice. I lived in France, too. For a summer. At the Sorbonne."

"What did you study?"

"Art. What else did women study then?" She was holding her coffee cup in one hand, the other resting on the table. Her eyes looked down at her coffee for a moment as though she were gathering her thoughts. Then she put her coffee back on the table and lifted her eyes to his.

"My father was killed mountain climbing in Europe. That's why I didn't want to talk about it earlier when you mentioned the climber on the World Trade Center. I'm sorry if I was rude."

He was stunned. Not just by the information, but by her sudden change in subjects. All evening, she had talked about little else but her work. Then, in a flash, she had revealed something as intimate as he could imagine her revealing. It took him a moment to respond. "I'm sorry. Really. And I'm sorry for reminding you of it."

She shrugged. "Before he died, he climbed all kinds of things. Big mountains, rock cliffs, hills. Whatever. And sometimes he took me with him. One time, in particular, I remember, I was about thirteen then. We were climbing a rock face in the Catskills. Right near the top."

She was speaking softly now, with a rhythm, leaning slightly forward. Like someone telling a story late at night around a campfire.

"My father had just gone over the top. Next in line was me and, below me, a friend of my father's. A real veteran climber. I had one more toehold to find and then I could go over the top, too."

A picture of Sara flashed into his mind—a vision of her spread out on the side of a rock face in boots and climbing clothes, searching for a toehold.

"...when I spotted a slight crevice to my right that was just big enough for the foothold I needed. I started to shift my weight and move my foot when the man below me said 'over there, to your left.'

"I'd already begun my move, but I heard his suggestion. He was a very experienced climber. He'd been up Dhaulagiri, and the Eiger. So, I listened to him. I stopped myself in mid-movement and changed directions and went for the suggested spot. But the shift threw off my balance, and I started to fall."

Henry inhaled sharply.

"Both my feet slipped. I felt them go and I began dropping. I knew that I was going down the mountain, maybe to die."

"Good God." Involuntarily, Henry's hand moved toward Sara's. He had to pull it back. "What happened?"

"My father was able to grab my arm at the last second, and he held me up until I found another foothold so I could finish the climb."

"And that was it?"

"Yes."

"Amazing."

"I'm telling you that story for a reason."

"What do you mean?"

Their eyes met.

"The other day, I told you that I like to make my own decisions. And to follow through on them. On my own. Without anyone else's interference."

Henry nodded, remembering the brief conversation they had.

"Well, that, Henry, is what happens when I don't."

CHAPTER 14

The city was definitely going downhill. As he walked along the western end of Chambers Street toward his office, Henry glanced at the shabby, tawdry string of commercial establishments that rimmed the broken sidewalks. The once-attractive buildings in this part of old New York reminded him that once, New York City had been attractive and even charming. But these modern times, with the City running out of money, with inflation threatening to cheapen the dollar even in the face of the new price controls President Nixon had put in place, with the stock market languishing in the doldrums, all New Yorkers could do was watch their once-lovely city slide down the hill toward decay and maybe even bankruptcy.

On that cheerful note, Henry tried to think of something more pleasant. Like Sara at dinner the night before.

After she had opened up to him, Sara had avoided talking business until they were in a cab uptown. "You know, Henry," she had finally said, "I was dead serious when I told you I wanted to get whoever in Ross's office took that money."

"I believe you."

"I don't think you know what it means to me." She looked at him. "Someday I'll tell you why."

At that point the cab arrived at Sara's brownstone on West 75th Street. Henry started to get out to see her to her door.

"Don't get out. Keep the cab. I'll see you in the morning—I'll be in a little after nine—and then we'll figure out a way to make our case."

By 9:30 a.m., Henry was looking across the desk at Sara, seated and ready for business. This morning she was wearing a chocolate brown blouse with puffy shoulders and a bow at the neck, all of the same hue. The color of the blouse highlighted the buttery undertone of her skin and enriched the nut brown of her hair. She reminded him of chocolate chip cookies. But her expression was rock candy.

"I've decided what to do," she announced. "I'm going to hit Donner— the guy who misled Judge Pfister—with a subpoena."

"A subpoena?" Henry gave her a puzzled look. "Why not just call him and ask to meet?"

"No, I want him scared. I want him upset. And I want his boss to worry, too."

"Sara, I know you've got more experience than I do, but isn't it kind of risky, tipping your hand? Like I did with Jack Keene."

"Who said anything about tipping my hand? I don't plan to give anything away. Just ask some questions."

"What does Matlin say?"

"I haven't asked him."

Henry sat up sharply. "You're going to, aren't you?"

"I hadn't planned to."

"Sara, that's a chief assistant district attorney you want to subpoena. And he works for the most well-known DA in New York. Don't you think you should clear it with Howie?"

He saw her mouth and her eyes harden. "Henry, I don't need anyone's oversight."

"That's nonsense, Sara. We're part of a team and Howie's the boss." Henry shook his head. "You know, there's a difference between acting on your own and acting recklessly."

Sara's eyed Henry directly. "And how we define that difference may be the difference between you and me."

"What happens if Ross raises hell over your summoning his chief assistant in here like a criminal? He's caused trouble before."

Sara laughed. "Now you sound like Nat Perlman. Worrying about offending someone. I'll tell you one thing I wouldn't have to ask Howie about—whether I should worry about offending the 'establishment.' That's why I respect him. Because he does what's right. And screw anyone who doesn't like it."

"No. No." Nat Perlman slapped his desk with the palm of his hand, keeping his eyes on Sara. It wasn't long after their conversation that Sara and Henry were called into Perlman's office. Perlman didn't raise his voice; he rarely did. But his feeling on the subject was clear.

"For any number of reasons, Sara, you should have known better than to subpoena the chief assistant of a major district attorney's office without clearing it through the front office first."

Immediately after Sara had issued her subpoena, Chief Assistant Donner's boss, District Attorney Ross, had reacted. He had called Perlman and told him off in no uncertain terms.

"It's not just a question of protocol, Sara." Perlman shook his head. "Calling someone like Donner in here is bound to set off fireworks, just as it did. But letting the front office be hit blind, like we were, is dead wrong. In any case, when you call someone of that stature, you've got to have evidence to back you up. Something more than a theory that the person took a bribe. And, as far as I can see, that's all you have."

Sara started to say something, but Perlman continued.

"The way it stands, the only good thing I can point to is that nothing has hit the press. But knowing Ross, that's a distinct possibility, too. And if that happens, you'd better have something to back it up."

He paused a moment. "My point is that we have to be more careful, Sara." Perlman was still looking at Sara, but his voice had lost its angry edge. His hands were neatly folded again on his desk in front of him. "We can't afford risks like this. The Office isn't invulnerable."

Perlman paused for a moment, allowing this information to sink in. "You know," he went on, "enough of these kinds of mistakes and, come funding time, we'll find ourselves in serious trouble. Or worse."

"Are you done, Nat?"

"Basically."

"Okay." Sara folded her arms decisively. "You say that all I have is a theory. Maybe as to whether Ross himself received part of the bribe, that's true. But not as to what happened. His chief assistant lied to one of the few decent judges in Queens, so that two major drug dealers could walk out of court."

Perlman started to speak.

"Wait a minute. It's my turn," she said, raising a hand.

Perlman sat back to listen.

"Donner told the judge that the drug dealers were cooperating with law enforcement and were needed on the street. But there was no cooperation from those two drug dealers."

Perlman nodded. He'd undoubtedly spoken to Harry Rood.

"So, Donner lied to the judge." She shook her head once. "Isn't that something the Special Prosecutor's Office should concern itself with?"

She sat forward. "And as far as this thing hitting the press, why do you think it hasn't?"

She sat back and answered herself. "Because Donner knows, and Ross probably knows, that we're on to something they'd rather keep to themselves."

Perlman nodded his head and sighed. "Okay. So maybe Donner lied and maybe he didn't. You know, it's also possible that he was misinformed himself..."

Sara started to interject a response, but Perlman raised his hand to silence her.

"All right, Sara. I'll let Howie decide." He shook his head. "But my point is still the same. We're a team here. We all have the same objective. But if we keep putting obstacles in each other's paths, we'll never reach it."

As they rose, Henry couldn't see Sara's reaction.

"Perlman was a little rough on you," Henry said, as he finished his beer at lunch that day.

Sara dismissed Henry's remark with a wave of her hand. "Donner's coming in. That's what counts."

"I guess," Henry responded. He glanced up at the waitress, who was removing his plate. "Coffee for me."

"And for me, please," added Sara.

They were finishing lunch at a restaurant located in the interior plaza of the World Trade Center. The place was filled with denizens of the two massive towers that soared above the mall outside the restaurant. Inside, dark wood-paneled walls surrounded them, hung with hunting scenes in gilded frames, turn-of-the-century etched mirrors, and brass lamps sporting green glass shades. Cane-backed chairs and checkered tablecloths completed the composition, along with the expected ordinary food. It was a comfortable, if ersatz, environment and, to Henry, it was far preferable to the coffee shop Sara favored. Henry had wanted to go to his favorite lunch spot, the Rathskeller, where he could have a German beer, but Sara disliked German food. So, they had compromised on the pub, where Henry could at least order a draft beer.

Silently they waited while the waitress poured the coffee. When she had departed, Henry spoke.

"I hope we're not getting so far off track that we forget about the other guys—Keene and his partners. They stole drugs and money. And their lawyer, Grassi, probably sold the drugs. I'd love to get him, as well."

Sara took a sip of her coffee. "I haven't forgotten," she responded. Her eyes met Henry's. "But I want to get into Ross's office. And Donner is our path."

Henry was about to reply when Sara's eyes floated away, and her thoughts seemed to drift off. Henry put his hands on the table and waited for her to return.

"In the cab the other night I told you that there was a reason I wanted to go after Ross's office."

He nodded.

"Okay, I'll tell you. Not many people know this. I'm not even sure Matlin does." Her hands dropped to her lap. "My father worked for that office once."

"For Ross?"

"No. Ross was just a junior lawyer then. For his predecessor. Logan, his name was."

"Oh."

"Anyway, my father left teaching because he wanted to do something about organized crime. He had a thing about it, and he felt teaching was kind of hiding out from the problem. So, he got a chance to work with Logan's office as head of their organized crime bureau."

"That's a big job," said Henry, impressed.

She laughed humorlessly. "Not in Logan's office it wasn't. Logan didn't give a damn about organized crime, or any other crime, really. He was an employer for the clubhouses. A couple of years with District Attorney Logan was part of the game for the hack lawyers from the political clubs before they went into politics. The organized crime bureau had exactly two attorneys in it. Daddy and a young assistant named Martin Ross."

"Aha."

"My father worked there for almost two years. I was young then, but I remember him being the happiest I ever saw him. He loved going after the mob."

"Was he successful?"

"At first, he was, I guess. The police were so surprised to have a serious prosecutor going after organized crime that they gave him all the help he could ask for. He made several good cases and was beginning to make a name for himself as a crime buster. I really don't remember details. As I said, I was young."

"How young?"

"Oh, maybe thirteen or fourteen."

"What happened? Why didn't he stay longer?"

"I'm getting to that. He had a big investigation at one point. With a couple of good informants, I think. Anyway, he was beginning to get some real dirt on the Tutino family." She lifted her eyes. "You know the Tutino crime family?"

"Sure."

"Well, he put over a year into that investigation. With very little support from District Attorney Logan. And then things suddenly went bad. His sources of information dried up and, finally, one of his informants was murdered. Everything went wrong."

"A leak, it sounds like."

"That's what he found out. Another informant told him where it came from, too, but there was no way Daddy could prove it."

"Who was it? Ross?"

She shook her head. "No. It was District Attorney Logan himself. He met with the head of the Tutino family and gave him the whole picture." Her eyes hardened as she spoke. "Ross probably knew what Logan was doing. At least I assume. But the result was that Daddy's informant was killed and Daddy's case was ruined. And that was it for his career as a prosecutor."

"Jesus." Henry shook his head. "I had no idea. What did your father do?"

"Quit and went back to teaching. Until he died."

"Geez, Sara. I'm sorry. I didn't know."

She didn't respond.

Henry took a sip of his coffee. It was already cold, so he set the cup back on the table. He was trying to think of something else to say.

"I think what your father did was great, Sara. Even though he didn't make it."

She shrugged.

"Wait a minute." He lowered his eyebrows. "Don't you think so?"

"Not the way he did it."

"What do you mean?"

"He shared what he knew with Logan and Ross. And he let them help him out. That's how they learned about the informant and that's how they learned how to wreck Daddy's investigation."

"Don't be ridiculous, Sara. He worked for Logan. He worked with Ross. He couldn't do it alone."

Sara looked Henry in the eye as she stood up. "That's exactly what he should have done." She picked up the bill as she rose and opened her purse. "I'll get this," she said.

"Hold on," persisted Henry. He hadn't risen. "You can't do everything by yourself. Sometimes, you have to rely on others."

Sara placed some money on the table along with the bill. "Oh, yes? Look what it got him," she responded angrily, and turned to leave. "Let's go."

Henry rose and joined Sara.

"By the way," Henry asked, as they left the restaurant. "What ever happened to Logan?"

Sara turned to him, this time with a thin smile on her lips. "The same thing that normally happens to crooked politicians. They made him a judge."

Henry was not sure what to expect as he waited in Howard Matlin's office two days later for Bert Donner to arrive. After the confrontation between Perlman and District Attorney Ross, it had been agreed that Donner would appear at the Special Prosecutor's Office but that he would be questioned by Matlin himself, not by Sara. Sara had expressed disappointment that she wouldn't be asking the questions. "But I don't think," she had said, "Donner is going to be too happy with Howie."

Henry looked across the big desk at the Special Prosecutor. If he was preparing for some kind of confrontation, he wasn't showing it. He was smiling as he and Nat Perlman chatted about something. Sara was talking with Harry Rood, who sat at the corner of Matlin's desk, where Matt Corey usually sat. It suddenly seemed as though they were a group of actors, about to go on stage, having a moment of relaxation before the play.

But they weren't going on stage. They were about to confront the Chief Assistant District Attorney of Queens County, who, if Sara's theory was correct, had received a large sum of money from Detective Jack Keene to let two major drug dealers out of jail.

Matlin's buzzer sounded.

"Yes," he said.

"Mr. Matlin, Mr. Donner is here."

"Show him in, Harriet."

Bert Donner entered, trying to look jovial. He was a heavyset man in his mid-forties. Across his balding dome lay strands of heavy dark hair, vainly trying to obscure the shine underneath. Although it was morning, Donner's eyes peered out from shadow—those under his eyes and the five o'clock shadow that already darkened his puffy cheeks. If Henry had seen him on the street, he might have picked him out as a lawyer, but the kind who made his money defending slum lords, rather than a major New York prosecutor.

Donner shook hands with Matlin, who failed to return his smile. Then he greeted Perlman, Henry, and Harry Rood with the same cheer, but ignored Sara and sat down across the desk from Matlin. "Now what's this all about?" he asked, settling into his seat.

There was silence. Matlin simply looked at Donner.

Donner adjusted himself in his seat.

No one spoke.

Then Matlin began, his voice cold and stern.

"You've got some explaining to do. And this is your chance."

Donner was clearly taken aback.

"The arrest of Arnaldo Bermudez and Felix Aguilar," continued Matlin. "I want to hear why it was handled the way it was." There was no camaraderie in Matlin's voice.

A flush appeared on Donner's face. "In what respect?"

"You tell us."

"But…"

"Tell us of all the personal contact you had with the defendants."

"Oh." Donner seemed to relax a bit. "I handled the arraignment." He smiled. "Slow day in the office." He didn't say anything about the fact that he had also gotten his picture in the paper with Ross in front of the four kilos of heroin.

"You never saw them again?"

Donner's face reddened. "I, uh, saw them when Judge Pfister accepted the plea. And he wanted me to confirm something."

"What?" Matlin's voice was cold.

"Let me see…can I see the file?" He smiled weakly. "You people have it, you know. You subpoenaed it some time ago."

Either he's delaying, thought Henry, or he's afraid there's something there that will contradict him.

"If I could…"

Matlin's eyes continued boring into Donner.

"Well, uh. If I can remember…" He looked at Nat Perlman as though he would help him. But Perlman's face was a blank. "Without help from my own records…" He looked back at Matlin but saw no relief. Donner closed his eyes, as though searching his memory.

"I think that these two…" He paused. His words were coming out very slowly, as though they were drops squeezed by great effort out of a dry memory. "They were the drug dealers who had given the police a very valuable lead on a major heroin ring." He looked up.

"What heroin ring?"

This answer came quickly. "I couldn't remember. If I ever knew."

Matlin's voice cut like a razor. "You talked a tough judge like Pfister into walking two major narcotics dealers and you can't remember why? I want names, dates, and arrests resulting from their cooperation."

"What?"

"I want to know precisely what cooperation you received from Bermudez and Aguilar. When, where, and to what effect."

Donner appeared nonplused. "I can't tell you that."

"You told a judge on the record that Bermudez and Aguilar had cooperated and that you were personally aware of the cooperation. That representation put them back on the street. Now you're going to tell us what that cooperation was."

Donner sighed deeply and seemed to come to a decision. "I can't. I don't know."

"Then you lied to Judge Pfister."

"Yes," he said at last. "I did. But only by saying I knew personally of the cooperation. I didn't. I took the word of a very experienced and capable police officer." He looked at Nat Perlman, then back at Matlin. "I was wrong."

"What police officer?"

"Detective Keene. Jack Keene." Donner glanced over at Rood. "You must know of him."

Rood didn't move or respond.

Donner's eyes returned to Matlin. "He'd handled a lot of matters with our office. Everybody knew him. And everybody knew he was good. One of the best. So, I, uh, let down my guard." Donner's head dropped slightly. Then it lifted again. "I figured that these two were so cold cocked by Keene's case, that it was logical that they'd cooperate in order to avoid a long stretch in jail. It made perfect sense to me." He was almost pleading now.

Matlin's eyes offered Donner no relief. "What did Keene tell you?"

"He said Bermudez and Aguilar were helping in a big operation in another borough—he wouldn't say which one."

"How could they have been cooperating with Keene, if they were in jail?"

Donner reddened and swallowed. "They must have been cooperating before the arrest."

"Did you ask Keene why he arrested them, if they were cooperating?"

Donner cleared his throat. His eyes scanned the others in the room, but he didn't really seem to see them. "I, ah, really don't remember."

"Did you make any effort to check out Keene's statement?"

"Well, uh, no. I guess, maybe, I didn't exactly check. I don't really remember."

"So, on uncorroborated, untested, self-contradictory information, you arranged to put two major heroin dealers back on the street?"

Henry saw Donner swallow again.

"Well, when you put it that way..."

"The answer is 'yes.'"

Donner lifted his hands, then let them drop.

Matlin continued questioning Donner for almost an hour, but the Chief Assistant stuck to his story. When he had left, Matlin turned to Sara. "You were right about him."

"Well, to some extent," ventured Perlman. "She was right that he didn't know about any cooperation when he told the judge. But it's at least conceivable that he took Jack Keene's word."

Matlin was shaking his head.

"What are you saying, Howie?" asked Perlman.

Matlin looked at Perlman. "He took money."

"Who, Donner or Keene?"

"Donner."

Henry felt a rush. The Special Prosecutor had just forced a chief assistant district attorney to admit to lying to a court. Now he was dubbing him a bribe-receiver, as well. Henry had never seen Matlin work on someone before, but he was beginning to understand his reputation.

Perlman spoke again. "If you think he was involved, why did you let him walk out of here?"

"Because without Keene, we can't prove a thing."

"But he admitted he lied to a judge about an important case. You could at least get his job taken away."

Matlin laid both hands, palm down, on his desk. He shook his head. "Not in *that* office." Then Matlin almost smiled. "Don't worry, Nat. We won't forget him. He's in our sights."

CHAPTER 15

Fifteen minutes later, Henry dropped into a chair in front of Sara's desk as Sara seated herself behind it. "I guess you were right about him taking money. But I'm afraid we can't nail him or Ross on this one."

"You may be right." Sara looked directly at Henry. "But I want to try."

"But..."

"The other day, you said we shouldn't forget the cops. And I'm not. We're going to set a trap for Jack Keene and his friends. Nail them cold enough that just maybe Keene will give up Donner."

For the tiniest fraction of an instant, their eyes engaged. Not just met, but engaged, melded. Then Sara was speaking again.

"...here's the way our little trap will work."

Henry wondered if maybe it was he who was falling into a trap.

"Jeez, Perk, what's that crap?" Larry Santarella pointed to a dish of pudding on Henry's cafeteria tray.

"I'm not sure," Henry laughed, glancing down at the bowl of gooey, yellowish mass. "Looks good, though, doesn't it?"

"Yecht."

Henry was having lunch with three of his buddies from the Office in the State employees' cafeteria. The cafeteria, with its long, stainless-steel food service counters and over a hundred Formica-topped tables, took up more than half the 48th floor of the New State Office Building. Its food aside, it was crowded, noisy, and plastic ugly. But it was four floors away from the Special Prosecutor's Office and it was cheap.

"Wait a minute, Larry," said Hal Baker, another assistant. "You talk about Perk's pudding. What about those meatballs on *your* plate. They look like they were mined in West Virginia. And that broccoli musta been cooked for the Union Army and kept warm."

Santarella spoke up. "Oh yeah? It's no worse'n your mystery meat. That stuff was probably pullin' people through Central Park yesterday."

Henry glanced down at his own meal. "'Chicken Divan,' they call this." It was brown and hard around the edges. "Looks like somebody forgot the chicken and just cooked the divan."

"Hey, will you guys quit bitchin' about the food here," injected Steve Wonderman, an assistant in Sara's group. "If you guys had a mother who cooked like mine used to, you'd appreciate this stuff."

"How 'bout your wife?" queried Santarella. "I hope she cooks better'n this."

Wonderman shook his head. "Are you kiddin'? I gotta do the cookin'."

"How come?"

"Self-defense. Her mother never even taught her to boil water."

"Well," said Santarella pointing to Baker, "Hal here's the lucky guy. Best lookin' woman in New York, his wife. *And* can she cook!"

Baker smiled broadly. "You got it, guys. Eat your hearts out. Cooks like Escoffier."

"Like who?"

Baker made a face. "Escoffier, you clod, Santarella. He was a famous chef." He looked at the others and pointed to Santarella. "His idea of a chef is the guy down at the corner who slaps tomato sauce and cheese on a pizza and sticks it in the oven."

"Oh, yeah?" Santarella retorted. "Just for that, I'm not gonna invite you n' Kim over for my special lasagna."

"Whew," said Baker, pretending to wipe his brow. "Safe. Hey, Perk," he turned to Henry. "Rumor has it you got a hot case on the fire."

"Cross your fingers."

"Can't talk about it?"

"Not yet. We're setting up a little trap. But if it works..."

"Who?" It was Steve Wonderman. "You and Miss Ice Cube?"

Henry made himself smile. "Why? You don't like Sara?"

"What's there to like? She never talks to anyone unless she's actually workin' with them, so who knows her? Not me."

"Perk, here, must know her," Santarella offered.

"In the biblical sense?" laughed Wonderman.

Henry could feel himself blushing. He tried to cover it up with bluster. "Listen you blowhards, she's a damned smart lady. As a prosecutor, she can run circles around me. I'm not ashamed to admit it. Maybe even you, too."

"Oh, oh," laughed Santarella. "I detect something developing."

"Me, too," added Wonderman. "Is our old buddy Perkins going soft on us now?"

Hal Baker came to the rescue. "Come on, give the guy a break. All he said was she's smart. Probably is." He looked around the cafeteria. "You don't see her eatin' here, do you?"

It had taken some serious arm-twisting to convince Detective Harley Fulton to go along with Sara's plan. But, in the end, he had no choice; if he wanted to save his pension and his medical benefits, he had had to cooperate. That was why, a week later, Henry and Sara were sitting nervously in Sara's office, waiting for word on their operation.

After a discussion with Sara, Fulton had contacted Detective Keene and told him that he had heard the Special Prosecutor's office was closing in on the four of them. He wanted the four participants to meet to get their story straight, preferably with the help of an attorney. Sara was confident that Keene would pick attorney Paul Grassi.

To lend credence to Fulton's story, the Special Prosecutor's Office had caused Detective Neal O'Brien to be subpoenaed to the grand jury investigating the matter and, to protect Fulton's cover, they had subpoenaed him as well. The next day, Keene told Fulton that the four detectives were to meet the following day with the lawyer Grassi to work out their story.

Sara had wanted to record the meeting. She had suggested sending Fulton in with a body tape, but Fulton himself dissuaded her.

"You can't do it with this guy," he insisted.

"Why? Do you think that he'd frisk you for a tape?"

"Listen, counsellor." Fulton flashed a knowing smile. "Frisking is old fashioned. From what Keene tells me, this guy sweeps his lines and his office for wiretaps and bugs no less than once a week. He has some machine in his desk that detects any transmissions from the office, from a Kell transmitter or whatever. And, to go into his office, you gotta go through a metal detector. Like a goddamned airport."

Sara had smiled and turned to Henry. "Your typical honest lawyer."

"Anyway, taping's impossible," Fulton had concluded.

But it wasn't. Sammy Parisi, the head of the Office's technical staff, had assured them that he could plant a bug in Grassi's office that would escape detection, at least for the day or two they needed it. So that was what had been done. Sara had obtained a court order, based on Fulton's information and police intelligence files, and Parisi had planted the bug.

Now came the wait.

The phone rang. Sara grabbed it. "Hello." A pause. Sara's face brightened. "Great. We'll be here." She hung up and looked at Henry. "They got it."

"So, the meeting took place?"

"And it was taped. The tape's on its way in."

They sat silently for several minutes. Sara had turned her desk chair away from the window and seemed to be focusing on her hands in the light from the window behind her. Her thoughts, Henry knew, were elsewhere, probably with the car wending its way through New York traffic with the tape.

Henry looked at Sara's hands. They were sensuous hands, he thought, strong but smooth and flexible. The skin, like that of her face, was dark and light at the same time, as though light tan tissue paper wrapped around ivory. Her fingers were long and straight and supple, and at the tips, clear nails extended slightly, just enough to be decorous, without being noticeable or garish. When her hands moved, they flowed like seaweed undulating in a current. She could have played the piano beautifully with those hands.

Abruptly Sara broke into his thoughts. "I appreciate your putting up with me, Henry."

Henry sat back sharply in his chair. "What?"

"I know I'm difficult. But you've been there, anyway. Not many people would be." She turned to him, and her sea-green eyes met his.

He held her gaze for a few seconds, wanting to prolong the contact. But he didn't want to push too far so he looked away. "I just want to make this case," he said, looking back at her.

Now it was Sara who looked away. "Let's get Sammy in here to set up the tape player before they get here with the tape."

They had just plugged in the machine when Sara's door opened and Harry Rood entered, along with Jock Zabiskie and Pat Mallon, who had helped Rood by monitoring the plant during the meeting.

"It's a bull's-eye," said Mallon, holding up a tape cassette.

And it was.

They all gathered around Sara's desk as they listened to the drama unfold.

Grassi had met with the cops, but one at a time, keeping the others waiting outside his office.

"The guy's smart," admitted Sara. "This way, it's one-on-one. If any of the cops ever turned against him, it's just that guy's word against Grassi's. And since you need two witnesses for a perjury charge, there'd never be two guys to say Grassi was lying. Smart. Except for one little problem." She smiled and patted the tape player. "This witness."

They listened as Keene and Grassi concocted a story for O'Brien and Fulton to tell.

"The key guy who's gotta get it straight is Neal," said Keene. "He ain't too smart. So, make it simple."

"Okay," Grassi replied. "You want a simple story? The simplest one is to stick close to the original story. That's what you found. That's what you turned in. Who the fuck's gonna refute it. Who's gonna say there was more? Two drug dealers? No, one drug dealer. Bermudez told them to go fuck themselves."

Henry glanced at Sara, but she was smiling as they listened to Paul Grassi and the three detectives hang themselves.

"So, it's just Aguilar who spilled the beans?" Keene asked.

"You got it. And believe you me, he's not gonna live five minutes after he hits general population again."

Jesus, thought Henry. A lawyer putting out a contract on his own client.

"Good," responded Keene. "Now let's go over the story."

After Keene left, Olivera and Fulton followed separately, each being told by Grassi the same story to tell if they should have to testify before a grand jury.

"It's a good thing we didn't use Fulton and a body wire," said Rood. "We'd have missed most of this."

Sara nodded.

Now it was O'Brien's turn. "Hey. What the fuck is this one-at-a-time shit? A fuckin' barbershop?"

Everyone in Sara's office laughed.

"Siddown, Neal."

Like a schoolteacher, Grassi then instructed Detective O'Brien on the false story he was to tell the grand jury should the Special Prosecutor's office grant him immunity and compel his testimony. Sara nodded as Grassi spoke the words that would indict him. She was smiling.

Amid Formica, stainless steel, and the usual noisy crowd, Henry and Sara were lunching in the coffee shop in the lobby of the New State Office Building. In their two-person booth near the rear corner of the restaurant, Sara was chewing unhappily on the last of her tuna fish sandwich. She and Henry had just completed an unsuccessful interview of Detective Jack Keene. The detective, despite his indictment, had made it very clear that he was not going to cooperate with the Special Prosecutor and help Sara catch anyone else.

After the taping in attorney Grassi's office, the case had flowed to conclusion without a hitch. Detective O'Brien had testified in the grand jury, telling the story concocted for him by Paul Grassi and Jack Keene. After O'Brien's sworn testimony, the grand jury heard the Grassi tape, which proved that O'Brien's testimony was fabricated. On the tape, the grand jury also heard the detectives admit that they had stolen the money and narcotics. The tape now substantiated the earlier testimony of Detective Fulton and the drug dealer, Felix Aguilar, and the grand jury quickly indicted Detectives Keene and Olivera for grand larceny and possession of the stolen narcotics. Detective O'Brien was charged with perjury and attorney Paul Grassi was indicted for suborning the perjury.

The lawyers had no role in the arrest—it was handled by the investigators. But on the day the three detectives were brought into the office to be taken to the nearby precinct for booking, Henry couldn't resist stepping briefly into the room where they were being held, and glancing at Jack Keene, the man who had been the cause of his own embarrassment in the interview weeks before. Instead of acknowledging Henry, though, Detective Keene had met his glance with steely, defiant eyes. No way, Henry had said to himself then, is Jack Keene going to cooperate.

"You didn't really think Keene would cave in and give up Donner, did you, Sara?"

Sara shrugged.

"Look," Henry went on, "as Matlin said, they'll do it again. And next time, maybe you'll get whoever." He waved a hand. "Meanwhile we got five bad guys and some great headlines." He smiled. "How about 'Drug Busters Busted' in the good old *Daily News*? And the *Post* with 'Mouthpiece Slammed Shut.' Not bad."

This time Sara smiled. "No, I guess not." She started to get up.

"Uh, Sara." He caught her eye. "Could you wait a second?"

"What for? Aren't you finished?"

"Just sit down for a minute. I want to ask you something."

She eyed him oddly but dropped into her seat again. Her hair rippled like deep water. She was wearing a light tan blouse open at the neck so he could see the smooth curve that swept up from her shoulder to her neck. Her skin was smooth and creamy; he could almost feel it.

"What is it?"

His eyes lifted to her mouth, where her lips touched each other, waiting for him to speak. He hesitated. Was he falling into a trap? Was he about to make a mistake?

"What is it?" she urged again.

He leaned forward. "You know about the Office dinner dance Saturday night, I assume. 'The First Annual,' they're calling it."

She looked quizzically at him. "What about it? You're not planning to go, I hope."

"Well, uh, actually, I thought it might be nice."

"A dinner dance? With a bunch of people from work? At some creepy, mob-owned catering joint?" She shook her head. "You're joking."

"No, I'm not joking. I think it might be fun. At least if you went with me."

"No way." Sara laughed. "You didn't really think I'd agree, did you?"

"Actually, I kind of hoped you would," he said starting to get up. "Otherwise, I wouldn't have asked you."

"But you didn't think I'd agree?" she repeated without moving.

He looked at her. Her eyes were smiling. "What do you mean?" he asked, sitting down again.

"I mean you didn't think I'd agree that Office dinner dances are fun?" She was definitely fighting a smile.

"Okay, what are you up to?"

"I'm just trying to respond to your statement specifically. Like a lawyer. You said that the Office dinner dance would be fun if I went with you."

"Well then, let me be more specific." He looked in her eyes. "Will you go to the dinner dance with me?"

"Now that's better. Yes."

CHAPTER 16

"Hiya, Tim. Hey, Manny."

"Attababy, Perk."

What a great party. The first annual dinner dance of the Office of the Special Prosecutor. Sara had been right about one thing: the party was held in one of those glitzy halls in Queens where Rosalies marry Dominics while the godfathers look on, or Patty stands meekly in the background while Stosh and his groomsmen throw beer on each other. Ersatz brocaded wall coverings, mirrors everywhere, chandeliers dripping with glass beads, and surly waistcoated waiters who looked as though they were on work-release programs from prison.

But so what? He was with his friends. A team of lawyers and investigators who were on a mission together. A mission to do something no one had ever done before. To clean up law enforcement, the courts, and maybe even the government of New York City. To Henry Perkins, it was better than going to the moon in a Rolls Royce. And best of all, Sara Leventhal was his date.

"Hey there, Angie. Vodka on the rocks, I bet."

"Bread of life, my boy," said Palumbo.

He liked everybody in the office.

"Frieda, great to see you." Lou Morotti's secretary. "Hi, Hal. Your wife looks super tonight." She really did. He almost envied Baker.

Cocktail hour lasted a lot longer than an hour. With this group, it had to. Long before dinner was served, Henry was soaring. Not just on the beers he had consumed. But he was lifted aloft by the sheer joy of being with so many people who already meant as much to him as family. In his case, a hell of a lot more.

He frowned. But then he felt an arm around his shoulder.

"Hey, Lou."

Lou Morotti was standing with a drink in his hand. Next to him stood a man Henry had never seen before. He was tall and movie-star handsome. Swarthy skinned, but with features that spoke of a long line of aristocrats. The impression was reinforced by the erect way he held his head. Confident and elegant. Smooth. A straight nose between high cheekbones, and sleek black hair that fell gracefully to one side, just forward of the temple.

"Perk, this is Justin Cole. Justin, Henry Perkins."

The two men shook hands.

"He's just joined us. Starting Monday. Gonna be with my group. You guys have something in common. You both came from the civil side."

"Oh. Where did you work?" asked Henry.

"Coddington, Wilkins."

Holy shit. Probably the best firm on Wall Street. Law review guys only, and you still just about had to be in the Social Register to get an interview. What was he doing here?

"And you?" Cole asked.

"Uh, Blakeman, Olins, and Green," Henry said, a bit indistinctly. He was embarrassed. A guy at Coddington wouldn't have heard of the little firm he'd worked for.

"Oh, yes. I think I've heard of them."

He lies well, at least, thought Henry.

Just then Morotti's wife called him, and Cole left with Morotti.

Maybe he did something wrong at Coddington, thought Henry. Maybe that's why he left a place like that to come prosecute. Or it could be, he's like the rest of us. Wants to clean up the system.

Somehow that thought didn't seem to ring true.

A bell sounded, announcing dinner.

Henry looked around quickly. Where was Sara? He'd forgotten about her, talking to the guys.

A moment of panic. No. She wouldn't leave, even though she didn't like office parties.

"Henry?"

"Oh, hi, Sara," Henry tried to disguise his relief. Just in the ladies room.

Then his heart nearly stopped. She was passing under an oversized chandelier, which cast a sheen on her plain black dress, creating, for an instant, the illusion of translucency. Beneath the dress, Henry imagined he perceived the lines of her lean body. He could see, below the narrow waist, full hips and long, slender thighs gliding toward him. There was an animal grace in her movement tonight, as though she were a lioness, pursuing her prey. He felt a tingling all over until the sudden glitter of a single diamond hanging from her necklace drew his eye up to her neck and prevented him from making a fool of himself.

"Time to eat," he said hoarsely.

At the table, he was still reveling in the companionship of his fellow corruption fighters. Especially when Matlin said a few inspiring words. But his attention was never far from the figure in black, sitting next to him and making him feel higher than the champagne they were now drinking.

Indeed, she was drinking—keeping up with him, drink for drink. And beginning to show it.

"Henry," she said at one point, leaning close to him. "You're missing a button on your shirt." She turned and, as she did, some of her hair brushed against his cheek. "You need someone to take care of you."

"Got anyone in mind?" he whispered. He breathed in the fresh smell of her hair and her skin and closed his eyes. He could feel a fluttering in his chest.

"You're silly," she murmured with the slightest slurring of the tongue.

"Only when you're around," he whispered.

She sat up abruptly. "That's not true," she protested. "I think it's my being around that keeps you unsilly."

Her eyes lifted to his. He could see the tiny speckles in her sea-green irises, surrounded by the distinctive wispy gray fringe. There seemed to be a slight gloss over her eyeballs, undoubtedly a product of the champagne, but it only enhanced their beauty for him. For the first time, it seemed, he was able to look as long and as deeply into those eyes as he wished. He didn't care how much he might be saying with his own eyes. It was a moment of victory and a moment of surrender. Both of which felt too good to curtail.

Then her eyes dropped, and he followed them to their landing place.

It couldn't be. He swallowed and tried to think of something to say but, under the table, her hand followed her eyes and made his blood race to his head.

"Can we go?" she asked.

"Now?" Even his scalp tingled.

"Now," she whispered.

In Sara's brownstone on West 75th Street, they were sitting on the couch in front of the fireplace. A small fire, which he had managed to start while Sara found some brandy, was crackling.

She was sitting next to him, still in her black dress, holding a brandy snifter. She had kicked off her shoes, and her stockinged feet were propped up on the coffee table in front of her. He was sitting in the same way holding his glass.

He hadn't tried to kiss her yet, although he ached to do so. But he still wasn't sure what was happening.

In the cab back into Manhattan from the party, she had changed moods several times, rather dramatically.

"Do you think I'm awful?" she had asked Henry as she settled into the back of the cab.

"Awful? Now where would you get an idea like that?" he had laughed as he felt her slender body press against his arm.

Then she had pulled away and sat up, almost facing him. "I'm serious."

"Well, no, then, Miss Serious. I don't think you're awful."

"Maybe you should."

"Why?"

She didn't answer him right away, but turned around in her seat and leaned her head against the window. Then she began to sing, almost under her breath.

"… 'a bird and saw it fly, as it soared alone through a lonely sky. The sky was dark…'" Her singing faded away. She lifted her head and stared out the window in silence.

He said nothing. But he could feel her hips pressed against his and he could smell her perfume. Her skin and her hair, redolent always with that same compelling scent: not exactly perfume, not exactly somatic. But distinctly Sara. Overpoweringly Sara. Seductively drawing him to her like a bee is led unerringly to its favorite flower.

He leaned closer, breathing in her scent. Tentatively, he let his hand brush her shoulder as the cab slipped into the Midtown Tunnel.

Abruptly, she turned to him again.

"My mother was sick all the time. All the time. Nobody could tell what was wrong. Just that she was always sick. And so, my father was always helping her. Helping her and helping her and helping her." She shook her head and looked at him. "I don't think that's right, do you?"

He tried to think of how to answer her. It was the first time she had mentioned her mother. He knew nothing about her mother, except that she also had died.

"It's hard to say," he said, trying to sidestep a reply.

"Oh, plosh," she protested. "That's no answer." She turned away from him.

"Sara, is that what you want to talk about tonight?"

She twisted around to face him again. "What's wrong, you don't like to talk about mothers?" She almost sounded angry.

"As a matter of fact, I don't. But if you really want to talk about *your* mother, I will."

She sighed deeply and faced the front again. Then she turned back again. Her mouth was rigid.

"I want to nail that shit Ross somehow."

She was slurring words now. Despite his own consumption, he could tell. He was afraid he'd encouraged her to have too much champagne.

"And you know who else is a shit? That pompous ass judge that Whelan just made Chief Judge—Arthur Sammons. He's a clubhouse sleazeball. Everybody thinks he's such a big intellectual, but he's just a rat out of the sewer."

Henry recalled his only confrontation with Justice Sammons when Sammons almost closed down the Special Prosecutor's Office during the district attorney's suit. "What in the world made you think of Sammons?"

"Because you know what Sammons said to me once? When I was just starting with the DA's office?"

"What?" he asked. He didn't let his inquiry sound enthusiastic. He really wished Sara could forget work.

"He asked me if I was a witch hunter. Like my father was. The scumbag." She looked in his eyes. "Do you think I'm a witch hunter?"

"A hunter? Yes. Not a witch."

She smiled. "How diplomatic of you." Then she sighed and settled onto his arm again. "I think I'm a little drunk, Henry Perkins. And I think you made me this way."

He started to protest, but she twisted her neck so that she could see him. "Did you do this? Do you have designs on me?"

He swallowed. "Yup."

Settling back against him in the rear seat of the cab she had sighed. "Good."

"It's nice," he was saying in her apartment, "having a fireplace." He wiggled his toes to feel the lingering heat.

She turned to face him. As she did, her hand dropped into his lap and opened. That does it, he thought.

He leaned over and brought his mouth to hers. At first their lips just touched; then they pressed together. They stayed together for a long time, their heads bobbing and swiveling rhythmically around their union. He snatched at air as he could, unwilling to disturb the kiss. At one point, he wanted to stop and lift his head and look at her, so that he could see her mouth and verify that the soft fleshy surfaces so deliciously mashed against his mouth were the same two lips at which he had gazed so often wondering how they would feel pressed against his own. But he didn't. Instead, he continued crushing his mouth into hers, telling himself that he was really there. Kissing her at last.

Then her mouth opened and admitted his tongue.

The kiss lasted a long time. As it went on, fingers began to move, first up to faces and necks, and then down along arms and shoulders and backs. Touching, stroking, squeezing, continuing to tour. Emphasizing and expanding on the kiss. Communicating. And then, finally, straying. Wandering beyond propriety into intimate places.

Henry was breathing heavily now as their mouths parted. Inside he could feel a fire burning, hotter than the crackling embers in the fireplace. He leaned forward to kiss her again. But she backed away.

"Not here."

She rose from the couch and took his hand, pulling him up with her. They crossed the living room and entered her small bedroom. With one quick motion, she unzipped her dress and let it fall to the floor. She reached for his trousers, but he had already begun lowering them and they were sliding over his hips when her hands arrived. With a few quick finger twists, he disposed of his shirt as he stepped out of his fallen trousers. Then, with Sara in his hands, he dropped onto the bed.

They kissed. This time he let his hands slide slowly up over her now exposed rib cage, up to her chest and around her back. In a single deft motion, his fingers released the snap of her bra. His hands drifted up and down her sides, and his head bent slowly toward her exposed breasts. She arched her back.

The tip of his tongue touched one of her rigid nipples and began to tease it. She sighed. Already enflamed, the nipple became even more rigid. Then it slipped past his lips and entered his mouth. Almost at once he released it, allowing it to scrape along the roughness of the tip of his tongue as it emerged.

She moaned. "Please."

He shifted slightly, and as he did, his leg brushed across her thighs at the place where they met. Even through her pantyhose he could feel the wetness against his leg. She was soaking.

He pulled himself up slightly and began to tease her nipple again. His tongue traced around and around it. Then he dropped down. Opening his mouth, he sucked in her breast. Gently. Sucking and releasing, sucking, and releasing. Sucking and releasing. So gently.

"For God's sake," she cried, "take off my pantyhose and fuck me."

He did.

CHAPTER 17

The elevator door opened on the 44th floor of the New State Office Building and two men emerged. They stepped into a small vestibule that opened on one end into the reception area for the Office of the Special Prosecutor. A few short steps across the vestibule Howard Matlin and Henry Perkins entered the reception area.

"Good morning, Mr. Matlin, Henry," said the young investigator tending the desk at the door to the inner offices. Neither had the opportunity to reply. Like a sudden explosion, up from one of the chairs in the waiting room jumped a scrawny figure who rushed toward the two startled men. "Here's someone I can talk to," she screeched.

The young investigator leaped to his feet and started around his desk, but Matlin put up a hand. "That's all right, Brian. I'll handle it."

The woman wore a long winter coat, even though it was quite warm in the room. The coat was frayed and worn, as was the wearer. Her thin, wrinkled face had something of a chicken about it, while perched atop her head was a coil of steel wool-like hair covered in part by a greasy kerchief that passed over it, knotting under her pointed chin. On her feet was a brand new-looking pair of red running shoes while swinging from her hand was a webbed reticule crammed with what appeared to be old newspapers and other documents.

"There's a conspiracy," she began. "You have to listen. You have to do something…"

Matlin's quiet voice stopped her. "Yes?" he said with concern.

She went silent.

"We'd be happy to hear what you have to tell us," Matlin continued. He looked at Henry, a request in his eyes.

Henry nodded.

"This gentleman will speak to you but…" He lifted a finger of caution. "You mustn't take too much of his time; he's very busy today."

The woman listened intently, seemingly bewitched by Matlin's voice. "No, sir. I won't. Thank you."

Matlin glanced at Henry. He might even have winked. Then he disappeared through the door to the inner office.

Henry watched Matlin's receding figure, then turned to the woman staring up expectantly at him. He beckoned her to follow.

They passed around the reception desk and entered the door that spilled into the interior hallway—the one that crossed from the western corridor to the eastern one. Halfway down the hall to the left was a small windowless room with a desk, two chairs, and a coat rack in the corner. Nothing else. The room was used by the investigators to speak with confidential informants who didn't want to be seen walking around the office. Occasionally it also served as a place to listen to people who came off the street with complaints or information.

"Sit down, won't you, ma'am?" Henry said as he seated himself behind the desk. He opened the desk drawer and took out a yellow pad and a pen. "Now tell me the problem."

"The door," she whispered.

"The door?" he queried. Then he saw what she meant. "Of course," he said, reassuringly. He rose and closed the door, then seated himself again. "Now you can talk."

"They are after me."

"Who are they?"

"The CIA and the FBI and the KGB."

For the next several minutes the lady confirmed what one of his colleagues had told him: that one of the problems prosecutors often face is obviously disturbed individuals popping in with bizarre stories, paranoid and clearly troubling to the teller, taking up the lawyer's time with no reward or information.

Henry had plans for this morning other than sitting with an elderly, obviously disturbed lady, listening to her story of how someone was after her. He wanted to leave. Then he looked at the worried face fixing him with trusting eyes. He settled back into his chair. His work could wait. "I see," he said. "And why are they after you?"

"I don't know, but they are."

"And what are they doing?"

"Watching me. Very clever. Very vicious," she announced with a whistle, and her eyes widened further.

"That's serious," he agreed. He almost succumbed to the power of suggestion and whistled his own "s." "Tell me, how do they spy on you?"

She looked furtively at the door again.

"Now," he said, growing serious, "what is their *modus operandi*? You know what that means? Their method of operation."

"Yes." The sibilant made a tea kettle sound. "I've heard the term."

"So how do they watch you?"

She whispered softly. "The privy."

"The privy?" he said.

"How do they operate in the privy?" he asked, lowering his voice to her level.

"They look up the...thing. You know, the seat."

"The bowl, you mean?"

"Yes," she hissed in the tiniest of voices.

"They look up the potty, is that it?"

She looked terrified, but he gestured for her to relax, pointing to the walls, and shaking his head.

"There's nothing to worry about. We're safe here," he said again.

"Yes," she finally hissed. "That's what they do."

Several seconds passed, during which Henry surreptitiously checked his watch. Or at least, he thought it was surreptitiously.

"What are you looking at?" she demanded.

He started to say his watch but stopped himself. "I need to check the date so we can be certain when this matter came to our attention." *Good thinking,* he thought.

"October eight."

She was correct. It startled him, the incongruity of her awareness of the date and the nature of her problem. But he only nodded wisely.

Then he had an idea. "I thought so," he said seriously. "The sneaky devils." He shook his head. "But we'll outsmart them."

Her eyes opened wider. "How?"

"With their nemesis. The one thing they can't deal with."

"What? What?"

"Blue Bowl Flush."

She looked confused.

"You know what that is, don't you?"

"No," she said, her mouth turning down.

"Well, there you are. That's the source of your problem. You don't know about Blue Bowl Flush."

She looked as though she might cry, so he went on quickly.

"Blue Bowl Flush. You can buy it in the grocery store. It comes in a little package that you hang in the water reservoir behind the bowl. Once a month you put it there. Change it every month." He raised a finger for emphasis as he went on. "You ask 'what does it do?' It turns the water in your bowl blue." He leaned forward and paused for effect. "And blue is the one color they can't see through. Can't see a single thing. Not even a shadow."

Her face lighted up. "Not a thing?"

"Nothing. If you put Blue Bowl Flush in your bowl, they won't be able to tell whether you're in the room or not. Won't even know whether the light's on. Then, after a day or two of that, they'll give up completely and go after someone else who hasn't heard of Blue Bowl Flush."

"Do you mean that?" she asked excitedly.

"You have my word for it," he pronounced.

Suddenly her face clouded over. "But where will I get it?"

"Where do you buy your groceries?"

"At the A and P just down the street."

"Well, you're in luck then, because I am certain that the A and P would carry Blue Bowl Flush." He ripped a sheet from the yellow pad and wrote the words "Blue Bowl Flush" in capital letters. "Here it is."

She took the paper, looking around to see whether anyone else was observing her. Then she stuffed the paper quickly into her reticule. Instead of getting up, though, she stayed in her chair, looking uncertain about what to do next. So, Henry spoke.

"If you want my advice, I'd go to that A and P as quickly as possible and buy the Blue Bowl Flush and go home and put it into your bowl. The sooner you do, the sooner they're going to give up on you and go after someone else."

It worked. She jumped from her chair and, without a word, scurried out the door. Henry hurried after her to make sure that she got to the elevator, but his caution was unnecessary. She went through the waiting room like an aimed dart, popping onto an elevator whose door had just opened. And then she was gone.

With a sigh of relief Henry turned and started back through the waiting room. As he did, he nearly bumped into Tim O'Leary, who had just stepped off the elevator. "Oh, hi, Tim."

O'Leary smiled. "Who was that, Perk, your mother?"

"Huh? Oh, no. Actually, she tried to tell me she was yours. But don't worry, I didn't believe a word she said."

"You're learning, son," O'Leary concluded, patting Henry on the back as they headed for the door into the office.

At his desk later that day Henry was reviewing some Internal Affairs reports. But his mind kept returning to that special night a few weeks ago.

Sara's lithesome body, moved like a dancer, almost in rhythm, as he held her tightly. Then like a leopard suddenly uncaged, she had exploded into arms and legs that grasped and held him with such amazing strength.

"You're very good in bed, Mr. Perkins. Do you know that?"

He cleared his throat. "It's the company I keep."

"Oh, you mean before you met me?"

He laughed. "No. Present company."

She leaned her head against his shoulder. He could tell she was still feeling the effects of the champagne. "Why would someone like you want to keep company with someone like me?"

The question took him by surprise. "I..."

She continued. "What I am is difficult. And where I am is all alone at the top of an icy mountain."

He started. The Ice Queen. Suddenly Barry Conlon's pejorative description of Sara took on a new poignancy. He pictured Sara sitting alone on a high peak, surrounded by barren fields of ice. Lonely. Isolated. Afraid.

"You don't want to climb an icy mountain," she went on. "No one should. That's how my father got killed."

Trying to think of a response, he reached out and stroked her cheek. As he did, her eyes met his and held him. Inside her eyes he could see pain, as though it were made of tangible, visible particles. His earlier restraint dissolved. "I know where you are, Sara. And I know the risk. But I think I'll climb that mountain. Maybe reach you..."

"Hey, we got a judge!"

Henry's office door burst open, and his group chief Pete Flannery stepped in.

"Wha...?"

"We got a judge."

"A judge?" He sat up, struggling to recover from his reverie.

"Yup," said Flannery. "Our first judge. Indicted."

Henry pulled himself together as the news sunk in. "Hey, that's great! What's the story?"

"I don't have the details. Lou Morotti just yelled it in my door. But the charge is bribe receiving and conspiracy."

"All right!" Henry slapped a hand on the desk. "That'll shut that scumbag Donegan up. Who got him?" he asked Flannery. "Lou?"

"I don't know any more than that." Flannery started out. "I gotta go. See you."

"Okay, thanks." Henry rose from his desk. "Great," he said aloud to himself. Which judge, he wondered. He opened his door. I know who can tell me, he thought as he went out.

He reached Scoop Dixon's office in time to find the press secretary tearing through a pile of paper on his disordered desk, a look of near panic on his face.

"Scoop?"

"Can't talk, Perk. Got to find…ahh." He relaxed. "Here it is." Dixon retrieved a piece of paper from one of several piles and sighed.

"I hear we nailed a judge."

Dixon smiled. "We sure did."

"Who is it?"

"Name's Crocker. Criminal court in Brooklyn." Dixon slipped by Henry, who was standing in the doorway. "I gotta go. Press conference in half an hour."

"You can spare a minute for a buddy."

Dixon stopped just outside his door. "Five seconds."

"What'd the guy do?"

"Aha," Dixon said, smiling. Then he lowered his voice, although no one was nearby. "He took a bribe from a guy to give the guy's son a walk in a rape case."

"Hey. Hot stuff."

"You bet. Now, I gotta go." Dixon started in the direction of Matlin's office.

"Scoop."

Dixon turned. "I gotta go, Perk."

"Who got him?"

Dixon smiled. "The new guy. Justin Cole. A real hotshot."

It was lunchtime the following day and the noise in the State employees' cafeteria was at its daily peak. Henry had once commented that whatever architect designed the cafeteria had probably skipped the course on acoustical engineering. The bare painted walls, the glass windows, the steel serving counters, and the pale orange, white, and blue tiled floors all reflected noise as a mirror does light. At the moment, though, the animation at the table of four assistant special prosecutors overrode the clamor.

"Boy, d'j'you see the *Times* today?" asked Steve Wonderman.

"Sure did," replied Hal Baker.

"And Howie's name's all over the front page," added Larry Santarella. "And how about that new guy, Cole, who got the fucker? They showed him on channel five and eleven last night."

"Oh, yeah?" It was Steve Wonderman. "I didn't see that. But he's a piece of work. The guy's here two weeks and already he bags a judge."

Hal Baker chimed in. "I'm told he left some fancy Wall Street firm after they'd offered him a partnership."

"That's gotta be bullshit. No one'd do that."

"I only know what I heard. But I'll tell you, the guy's smart. Nat Perlman told me the guy was Law Review. At Harvard no less. And for college, he went to some other big school. Yale, I think."

"Then what the fuck's he doin' down in the pit with us?" retorted Larry Santarella. "Talkin' to junkies who got flaked. Or skels like I'm workin' with in that Corrections Department case?"

"Who knows?" Baker laughed. "Maybe he wants to go into politics or something."

Henry chewed on his corned beef, saying nothing. He was happy for the Office and for Howard Matlin. Their first judge. But he couldn't help wondering how someone who had no more background in criminal law than he had could catch a crooked judge only two weeks after he'd arrived. A judge. All by himself. While Henry was assigned to work with Sara to catch a few cops.

He stopped himself. Why would he complain about working with Sara? That's how he'd gotten to know her. Not just gotten to know her. He'd fallen in love with her.

He hadn't seen Sara yet today and he missed her already. Especially because yesterday she was so tied up that she'd only had time for a quick "hello."

It was getting bad. He thought of her all the time. In the office. At night in bed. On the subway. Reading Internal Affairs memos. Even at lunch. In fact, the only thing that could take his mind off her for a few minutes was a new development in the Office—like the indictment of a judge. And even then, his first thought had been to go to her office and discuss it with her.

But being with Sara wasn't as easy as thinking about her. She had been too busy to spend time with him except for one movie, and one evening when he'd let Sara drag him to City Center to see some modern dance troupe writhe about the stage. It was frustrating.

He sighed.

"Whatsa matter, Perk? Stomach again?"

"Huh?" He looked at Larry Santarella. "Nah." He got up with his tray. "Come on. Let's get back to work."

CHAPTER 18

Henry had just sat down at his desk, having hung his suit coat on the back of his door, when he received a call asking him to come right down to Howard Matlin's office. He put his coat back on and headed out the door. As he entered Matlin's office, he saw the Special Prosecutor himself seated with his hands on his desk, looking businesslike. Chief Investigator Matt Corey was in his customary seat at the side of Matlin's desk with his arms folded in front of his chest. Across from Matlin was Group Chief Lou Morotti and the group chief investigator in Morotti's group, Sid Wise. In a chair next to Morotti sat Justin Cole.

"Gentlemen," Matlin began once Henry was seated, "we may have something interesting." He nodded to Cole and to Henry. "Last week, Lou and Sid were looking into allegations that stolen items were being fenced by some off-duty court clerks. They encountered a man who was trying to pass some stolen bonds—a valise full of them—and they arrested him. Once he realized that he was caught, and who had caught him, he offered to cooperate with us and help us out. It was clear that this man was a lot smarter than most crooks handling stolen goods, and that he knew his way around. Lou and Sid called me, and we talked it over and we decided that we might be able to use him in our investigation. But then we came up with a better idea."

Matlin looked at Henry, then at Justin Cole. Then he continued.

"We decided to peek into the judicial system and see what would turn up. For openers, we sent this fellow—by the way, his name is Moe, Hubert Moe—we sent Moe back onto the street with the stolen bonds to be arrested again. We gave an anonymous tip to the police about the bonds, and, within an hour, our man was in police custody.

Matlin paused a moment, then continued. "Before we sent him out to be arrested, we instructed Moe that, as soon as he was booked, he should let it be known—to bail bondsmen and the like—that he was looking for help. For someone with the right contacts.

"So, our man put out the bait and a fish bit right away. A bail bondsman named Victor Stanzak approached Moe and agreed to arrange his bail and then to meet Moe later to talk about his problem. So once Moe was out on bail, we sent him, wearing a tape recorder, to meet in a bar near the courthouse in Brooklyn Heights. You'll hear the tape later. It's quite good, although parts of it are obscured by music in the background."

Everyone was listening very closely.

Matlin went on. "Stanzak agreed to help Moe fix his case. For a few thousand dollars. He says he knows the right people who can get things taken care of."

"How?" asked Cole.

"We aren't sure yet. Stanzak wants Moe to use a certain attorney who's apparently a fixer. But we don't like it. Because for us to know what's happening, Moe obviously must know what the attorney is doing, and no crooked lawyer is going to let someone see how he operates."

Henry looked at Morotti, who was nodding.

"But we gave it a shot," Matlin continued, "and had Moe tell Stanzak that he wanted to keep on top of everything."

"Wouldn't that tip off Stanzak and the attorney that something was fishy?" Henry asked.

Out of the corner of his eye, Henry saw Corey nod. "Good question," Corey mouthed silently.

"You're right," Matlin responded. "So, we had Moe tell him he'd been double-crossed once, and he didn't trust anyone without knowing first-hand what was being done."

"You have to see this guy," Morotti added. "He's a real con man. He makes his living that way. He had no problem convincing Stanzak."

"According to Stanzak," Matlin went on, "he has good contacts in the criminal court, where the case is now, so he'll be the one making the overtures. The attorney will just be part of the team, so to speak."

Matlin sat back in his chair. "That's where things stand now. We're waiting to hear from Moe on Stanzak's attempts to reach out for someone. As soon as we do, we'll decide on our next move."

"What can I do?" asked Henry.

Matlin smiled. "Can you oversee the transcription of the tape of the meeting between Moe and Stanzak?" He nodded in Henry's direction. "If I recall, you have an ear for music. There's a lot of it on the tape. Perhaps you can hear through it and decipher more of the conversation than the investigators have been able to do so far."

"And what can I do?" asked Cole.

"Nothing just yet," Matlin responded. "But we should hear from Moe by tonight or tomorrow at the latest. Then we'll all have our roles."

It was already mid-afternoon, and Henry was still struggling with the background noise of a jukebox. "Boy, Matlin wasn't kidding," he said aloud, referring to the amount of music he had to hear through. He had ascertained most of what Stanzak and Moe had said and had made some improvements in the rough transcript the technical staff had prepared. It was time for a break.

He knocked on Sara's door and entered. "Yes," she said with a scowl, looking up from her desk. Then she saw who it was, and her expression softened. "Sorry. I was concentrating."

"Well, don't let me get in your way." Henry said pretending to leave.

"I'm sorry," she said again. "Sit down a minute." She put down her pencil and pointed to a chair. Then she leaned back in her own chair and gestured with her head at the papers on her desk. "I can use a little break."

"What are you working on?"

"The motions to dismiss the indictments in my Auto Squad case."

"Ugh."

She smiled and nodded. Absently she picked up her pencil again and began rolling it between her fingers.

"How are you, Sara? I haven't seen much of you lately."

"True. As you can see, I'm pretty busy."

"Too busy to see me?"

She shook her head. "Don't do that, Henry. We're both overworked. Let me get out from under this mess."

Henry shrugged. "Okay." Then he decided to stretch the Office rules and tell Sara a little of what he was doing. "I'm not supposed to talk about it, but it's us. So, keep it quiet."

"Of course, I will."

"We may be setting up a sort-of sting operation. This guy was caught with some stolen bonds and now he's working for us. We had him arrested again and now he's working with this crooked bail bondsman who's trying to arrange to get his case fixed."

She sat up. "That's very good."

"Yeah, and confidential."

"Henry," she scowled.

"I know. But I've seen so little of you that I'm thinking of you like one of the guys. Like Larry Santarella or Steve Wonderman."

"Now I'm insulted," she laughed. "The next thing, you'll expect me to have lunch with you in the State cafeteria."

"Well, speaking of eating, how about dinner with me tonight?"

"Henry, you know I can't." She motioned to the papers in front of her. "My response is due the day after tomorrow and, as Robert Frost said, I have miles to go before I sleep."

He got up, shaking his head. "Well, Sara, if you don't watch out, it'll be the State cafeteria."

She laughed. "Okay. I get the message." She looked at Henry as she picked up her pencil. "Soon."

"There's a new development," Matlin said as Henry and Cole took seats in front of him." He was smiling. "Moe has been indicted."

The District Attorney's Office had gone ahead in the normal course of business and caused Moe to be indicted by a grand jury for possession of the stolen bonds. That meant that the case would no longer be heard in the lower criminal court but would move up into the State Supreme Court.

"Is that good?" Henry asked.

Matlin gave him a puzzled look.

Henry continued. "Doesn't an indictment mean we're out of criminal court, where Stanzak's contacts are?"

"Yes," Matlin responded. "But it puts us in a better playing field. The indictment will come before a Supreme Court judge. And they're a part of the political clubhouse system. Criminal court judges are at least reviewed by the bar associations." He turned to the others. "Anyway, Moe and Stanzak have already discussed reaching someone who can help."

Matlin turned to Justin Cole. "What I'd like you to do is work with Sid," gesturing toward the Group Chief Investigator, "as Moe reports on Stanzak's progress." He turned back toward Henry. "Lou Morotti is tied up on another matter now, so you two," nodding at Cole and then Henry, "will work directly with me as we move along."

"Any progress?" asked Henry as he opened Justin Cole's office door. A meeting had been scheduled by Matlin in his office and Henry was picking up Cole on the way there.

Justin was behind his desk, writing. "Hold on for just a minute," he said, continuing to write without looking up.

Henry glanced around the room. On the credenza was a valuable looking vase and on top of the bookcase sat a bronze horse that looked like it belonged in a museum. A gold embroidered desk set graced the top of Justin's desk, while on the inner wall hung an original hunting scene in an ornamental frame. Henry looked out the window. Cole's office faced east, across lower Manhattan. From it, one could see part of the Municipal Building and the Brooklyn Bridge. Otherwise, the view was of the dingy buildings of Chambers Steet and factories and apartments in Brooklyn. At least Henry had a better view.

At last Cole finished writing and stood up. "Stanzak's made a contact," he said. "Let's get down to Howie's office."

"Stanzak told Moe he'll have something lined up in a couple of days," Cole reported as everyone took a seat in Matlin's office. "He told Moe that he has someone specific in mind."

"That's good," said Matlin. "Henry," he said turning to him, "I'd like you to start familiarizing yourself with the standards for a court order to plant a bug. I have a feeling we may need one sometime here."

After a discussion of possible next steps, the group broke up and Henry and Justin Cole headed out the door.

Cole turned to Henry. "I hear you play tennis."

Henry started at the unexpected change of subject. "I played in college. On the team. But not much lately. Why?"

"Well, we have a couple of indoor courts at my club on Long Island. And the clay courts are still in use when the weather's good, which it still is. So, I thought perhaps you'd like to come out this Saturday and play a bit of tennis."

"That's very nice of you. I'd love to do that."

"Bring a date, too. I have one. And we'll make it a dinner there too."

Henry nodded. "That's very kind of you. Just let me know directions and time."

The Mattawanis Club was probably the most exclusive club on Long Island. Henry had heard of it several times, although he'd never been there. Now he was on his way there to play tennis with Justin Cole.

The best part was that he was on his way there with Sara, who had finally agreed to have dinner with him. She was sitting next to him in the front seat of her car, driving to Justin's club for the tennis game and dinner.

Henry glanced at Sara as she concentrated on the winding streets approaching the entrance to the club. She wore glasses when she drove. It was the first time he had seen her wearing glasses. Simple horned rimmed frames that perched on her nose and, by contrast, made her skin look creamy.

He felt a thump in his chest. It happened just about every time he looked at her now. Regardless of the fact that she seemed to be standing off, whenever he looked at Sara, he wanted to dissolve into her, the way an object would if it flew into the sun. Suddenly he spotted the gate to the club, and he pointed to it. "That looks like it up ahead."

"I don't need…" she began.

But he cut her off. "Grruump."

Immediately she turned to him, an apologetic smile on her lips. Then she wrinkled her nose and he melted.

Justin met them as they started up the walk toward the clubhouse from the parking area. He directed Henry to the men's locker room and then took Sara to join his date, who would show her the way to a group of courtside seats where they could watch the tennis.

Within fifteen minutes, the two men were warming up, and a few minutes later they began to play.

Wham. Henry could feel the ball blast off the sweet spot in his racket and streak over the net.

"Nice shot," said Justin as he watched it evade his racket.

Henry couldn't believe it. He was leading five-love in games. He could tell by the way Justin moved that he was a good tennis player. Probably very good, when he was at his best. But Henry had amazed himself. Despite his lack of practice for over a year, he was serving well, and his backhand was as good as he ever remembered it. He felt strong and virile. Dominating the court.

It was Justin's serve now. One more game, if Henry won this one.

He looked over at the two women. They were sitting near the court, coats buttoned against the chill, chatting comfortably. Unfortunately, they had been paying little attention to the tennis. Sara probably didn't realize how well he was playing. He wished that, at least while he played what might be the last game, Sara would watch so that she could see how good he was today.

Blam. Shit. An ace. He'd better pay attention.

He dropped to his crouch just behind the baseline, waiting for Justin's serve. Justin usually served the ball in the center of the service court, so Henry readied his forehand.

Whissss. My God. The ball had hit the tape and passed by his backhand side so fast that he hadn't even seen it. Another ace.

He walked back to the forehand court and readied himself.

Bam. Ouch.

Henry's hand stung as his attempted return plopped lamely into the net. Jesus, what was happening?

He poised himself in the backhand court and took a deep breath. Where were these serves coming from?

Wham. Clunk. Shit.

The ball came right at him, so hard that Henry barely had time to protect himself with his racket. It struck the handle of his racket and bounced out of bounds. Game, Cole.

Twenty minutes later, Henry was jelly. In the last six and a half games, he had successfully returned only about a dozen shots, at most. And each of those had been returned by Justin with new fire, to die on Henry's now-ineffectual racket. He was down thirty-love in the twelfth game, with Justin leading six games to five.

He calmed himself, waiting for Justin's serve. He was beginning to anticipate them now. Maybe he could still recover.

Blam. Henry connected solidly with the rocket served him and watched his return skim across the net heading for the tape. Good shot!

Zzzzzz. Jesus! How the hell could Justin put the ball there after that return of his?

"Set point."

Thanks, Justin. It was the first time Cole had said anything in several games.

Henry decided to return Justin's next serve to his forehand since his last two shots to the backhand had been returned without a chance for Henry to respond. Justin tossed and swung.

Smack. Henry felt the sting in his hand as Justin's serve bounced off his racket. But he'd gotten the ball back across the net.

Ohmygod. The ball bulleted across the net to Henry's backhand side and touched the tape, before disappearing into the neighboring back court. Justin was already across the net and offering his hand.

What a bummer. Seven games straight, he'd lost.

He looked up and noticed that the women were gone. Thank goodness for that. At least Sara hadn't witnessed his humiliation.

Showered and dressed, Henry was beginning to forget the match. One reason he didn't feel so bad about losing to Justin hung near the entrance to the men's locker room. Six times, Justin Cole's name appeared as Club champion. The last four years as singles champion and the last two as doubles champion, as well. So, he hadn't done badly winning five games, though he did wonder whether Justin had tried as hard in the first five as he had in the next seven.

At the moment, they were seated in the dining room of the club and Henry was sipping on a cold beer. To Henry's left, sat Sara in a dark green velvet dress, looking more beautiful than he'd ever seen her. Across from him was Justin Cole in his double-breasted blue blazer and club tie, while Justin's beautiful blonde date sat to Henry's right.

The dining room bespoke the understated elegance of the upper classes. Two of the room's walls were taken up by a wraparound mural of fox hunting, while one end of the room looked out on a putting green and the other featured a large fireplace framed by white pilasters. The rug was a hunter's green, picking up the greens in the mural, while the drapes at the several windows were muted red, echoing the jackets of the hunters in the scene on the wall. Brass sconces shed most of the light, assisted by two small brass chandeliers above.

Henry glanced at the beer mug in his hand. Sterling silver, with the initials of the club etched on the side. On the plain white linen tablecloth in front of him sat four settings of simple but elegant china. Unassuming but intimidating, nonetheless.

They each had a second drink and then six chilled and gleaming oysters, before launching into their main courses. The club's cooking was, as in most good clubs, acceptable, but not overwhelming. By this point though, Henry was past noticing the food. He was too uneasy.

Justin was just finishing another of his several stories, looking at Sara. "'No, not Shakespeare,' I said to him. 'Lenny Bruce. But you're close.'"

Sara laughed. Not for the first time that evening. Indeed, Henry had never seen Sara laugh this much. She seemed to be having a very good time. The problem was that it wasn't he who was entertaining her. Sara and Justin had hardly stopped talking since they had sat down.

He glanced at Justin's date, Muffie. Muffie—a popular girls prep school nickname—Muffie Swensen. He hadn't met a Muffie since college. Blonde hair hanging to just above the shoulders, where it ended in a razor straight line. A royal blue ribbon over her crown, holding the straight tresses precisely in place so they wouldn't detract from the soft, picture-perfect face that flashed deep blue eyes at whoever came near.

Right now, though, the eyes were not happy. Muffie seemed to be as troubled by Justin's lack of attention as Henry ached over Sara's. Henry decided that it was time to force himself back into the conversation. But even so, he knew it could be a long meal.

CHAPTER 19

It was a few minutes after seven o'clock in the morning the following Wednesday and Henry was already at the office. He was seated in the conference room with several colleagues from the Office, watching the television set mounted in one corner of the room. They were waiting for the appearance on the screen of Howard Matlin, who was about to be interviewed on the "Today" show.

Henry sipped his coffee and nodded to Hal Baker as his friend entered and took a seat across the table next to Arnold Gurwitz, an assistant in Sara's group. Sara, he knew, had worked late the night before and was probably watching at home. He had had a chat with her before he left himself, as she settled in for another night of work.

The bad taste of the dinner at Justin Cole's club last Saturday still lingered. Although Henry had managed to reassert himself and Cole's date into the conversation, he had not been able to shed the discomfort Justin Cole provoked. Not only was Cole intelligent, clever, handsome, rich, successful, and a great tennis player, but he had been able, with no effort, to amuse Sara and put her at ease—something Henry had been trying to do since he'd met her but had not mastered.

Yet the dinner *had* come to an end, and afterward, Sara had apologized on the drive back to the City. They had gone for a nightcap at a quiet

East Side bar Henry knew. As they nestled into a small back table with two brandies, Sara took a sip of her drink and turned to him with her dusty green eyes. "Henry," she said, taking his hands in hers. "I'm seriously sorry about the dinner. Justin's very amusing, but I don't think it was much fun for you. You deserve better."

He shrugged and smiled. "It's forgotten."

She smiled back. "You know, you *really* are sweet. I want you to know how much I appreciate you. Especially the way you're concerned about me. I haven't had much of that in my life. At least since my father died." And then, before he could respond, she leaned forward and kissed him firmly on the mouth.

"Morning, Perk." Henry's head snapped up to take in Ed Scanlon, the new chief of appeals, as he bounced into the conference room and dropped into a seat across the table.

"Hey, Ed," he responded, mentally rejoining his colleagues.

Scanlon nodded, his tousled red hair moving with him. The Appeals Chief's hair usually made him look as though he had just emerged from a wind tunnel, an effect that was enhanced by his unpressed, double-knit suit.

To his left, Henry could hear Harry Rood chatting with Angie Palumbo. On his other side sat Lou Morotti, Justin Cole's group chief, drinking coffee and perusing the *Times*. There was no sign of Cole.

Someone got up and adjusted the volume on the set. It was the chief of technical services, Sammy Parisi. "Can everybody hear okay?" he asked.

"Yeah," answered Steve Wonderman from the far end of the table. A few others voiced agreement, but everyone quieted down quickly as the "Today" show's host began.

"Corruption, it seems, has been with us as long as government. Yet there is one man here in New York who insists that corruption's days are numbered—that he is going to change history and eliminate graft. He is New York State's special anti-corruption prosecutor, appointed a little over a year ago by Governor James Whelan, to follow up on evidence of extensive corruption in New York City's police department and its justice system. The Special Prosecutor's name is Howard Matlin, and he is with us this morning. Good morning, Mr. Matlin."

The cameras took in the Special Prosecutor sitting next to the host.

"Good morning," responded Matlin.

"You've stated several times, Mr. Matlin, that corruption is endemic to New York City's judiciary and to its government as well as to its police department. Yet, to date, a year after your appointment, you've indicted only one judge and four or five minor political figures. If corruption is as bad as you say it is, why haven't you done more to clean it up?"

The camera shifted to Matlin. "We *are* cleaning it up. As you know, we've indicted and convicted dozens of police officers, some as high as Inspectors. We've exposed whole detective squads on the take from drug dealers and gamblers and prostitutes. We've arrested attorneys for paying bribes, and recently, we arrested one well-known defense lawyer along with a group of Narcotics policemen for participating in a scheme that kept both drug dealers and their drugs on the street."

Henry smiled broadly as Hal Baker saluted him.

Matlin continued. "As to the 'minor' politicians you mentioned, they weren't involved in such minor crimes. In one case, they were helping keep New York's air polluted by taking bribes from polluters and in the other case they appeared to have been part of a conspiracy to bribe a judge."

"But if corruption is as widespread as you claim, even these accomplishments are at best a small part of the solution."

"Yes, they are. But they're a beginning—of an attack on a system that's bad from top to bottom. For too long, New York's been sold the 'rotten apple' theory—the idea that the police department and the court system and so forth are basically honest with only a few 'rotten apples' to spoil it. What I'm saying is that the system itself is rotten from the roots up."

The host smiled. "You mean the Big Apple's a rotten apple?"

Matlin didn't return the smile or acknowledge the pun. "The point is we're finally penetrating and exposing the system itself. First the police department and, in time, the courts and the rest of the system."

"But when? You've had a year."

"And we're going to need even more time." Matlin eyed his questioner sternly. "But don't worry, we'll get there."

"With what? Not with one indictment of one judge."

"Of course not. There will be more." Matlin paused a moment, sitting back a few inches. "Perhaps sooner than you think," he said.

Henry's face tingled. He wondered if Matlin was referring to his and Justin Cole's new investigation.

"And don't underestimate the effect of one indictment," Matlin continued. "The fact that we caught one judge means we *might* catch others. An indictment like that sends shock waves through the system. It scares others—makes them think twice before taking bribes." At this point, the Special Prosecutor turned and eyed the camera sternly. "You see," he said with an edge to his voice, "if we can't have honest public officials, at least we'll have scared public officials."

"Whew," said someone in the room with Henry.

Two hours later, everybody involved in the Moe case was gathered in Howard Matlin's office. Except Howard Matlin, who was on his way downtown from the television studio. Matt Corey was slouched comfortably in his usual chair. Justin Cole and Sid Wise sat next to each other. Nat Perlman was reading Johnny Donegan's column in the *News*, where the columnist had managed to write a whole piece without attacking Howard Matlin or anyone else in law enforcement. And Henry was standing by the window near Perlman, gazing down on the Hudson River.

The river sparkled in the morning sun. Light splashed across the surface, making the water shine. Wavelets twinkled, emitting a coruscation of bright flashes on the black surface, blinking as though with an audible tinkle of wind chimes. The effervescence below matched Henry's mood. They were tackling corruption, led by a man of strength and courage and moral honor who had just reaffirmed his own commitment publicly. Being on Howard Matlin's team filled Henry with hope and made him feel like the river, shimmering below him. It was something of a transcendent moment.

The door opened.

"Good morning," said Howard Matlin as he entered. "Sorry I'm late."

"You were great!" exclaimed Henry.

Perlman rose and shook Matlin's hand vigorously. "Nice job, Howie."

"Is everything ready?" Matlin asked as he seated himself.

Henry took his own seat and looked across the desk at Matlin, as the Special Prosecutor launched into the business of the day. His jaw was set, his eyes trenchant. The same face Henry had just seen two hours earlier on television talking about corruption. Now it was here, doing something about it.

"Okay, where are we?" asked Matlin.

Sid Wise responded. "Stanzak met with his contact, who turned out to be Richard Delaney, the law secretary to a state supreme court judge named Morris Bentzel. The price, Stanzak told Moe, was forty thousand dollars, the first twenty of which was to be paid the beginning of the next week."

"Marked, of course. And observed," said Matlin.

"Of course," Wise assured him.

Corey nodded.

"And then the case will be transferred to Bentzel. When that's accomplished, Moe's lawyer will be told to make a motion to dismiss which, after the second twenty thousand is paid, will be granted. Then we move in."

"Wait a minute." It was Nat Perlman.

Everyone turned to the Chief Assistant. He looked at Matlin.

"You say Moe is really guilty of possession of those stolen bonds—that this case is for real." Perlman looked back at Cole. "Then how is Bentzel supposed to dismiss the case?"

This time it was Justin Cole who answered. "We've worked that out."

"How?" asked Perlman.

"When Moe was arrested the second time, there was built in a little search and seizure problem with the evidence. Not serious enough to justify dismissal if the case were decided by an honest judge. But enough for a lawyer to make a motion about and a dishonest judge to grab onto."

Perlman sat back, seeming to ponder Cole's information. "No," he said after a moment. "This is going too far."

"What do you mean, Nat?" Matlin turned toward Perlman, who sat forward anxiously in his chair.

"This isn't monitoring. We're making the crime. Bentzel's being set up."

"Nat, I'm sorry, but you're wrong," Matlin said softly. He seemed neither angry nor upset. "We didn't make this crime. Those stolen bonds are really stolen. All Moe said is that he was interested in getting some help. And out of the woodwork came Stanzak and then Delaney. And Delaney asked for money. And named the price." Matlin raised a hand from his desk and gestured. "This isn't any different from an undercover purchase of narcotics." He smiled faintly. "You aren't suggesting that undercover narcotics buys are improper, are you?"

"Of course not. But Bentzel isn't a drug dealer. He hasn't done anything to justify the attempt on him."

Henry looked back at Matlin.

"Nat, this isn't an 'attempt' on Bentzel, as you call it. He came to us from out of the blue. Or at least his law secretary did. And if Bentzel never gets involved in this thing—if, for example, Delaney uses some other judge, Bentzel won't be touched."

Perlman's eyes wrinkled in thought.

"I know what's bothering you, Nat."

"Oh?" Perlman sat up.

"It's the fact that it's Bentzel. His reputation."

Henry had heard of Morris Bentzel. He was a favorite of liberal journalists, including the *Times'* Toby Copin, for his "humane" approach to crime and punishment. Which meant not sending convicted criminals to jail.

Perlman shrugged, perhaps in agreement.

Suddenly Matlin's voice was icy. "Well, let me tell you something, Nat. Something you know as well as I do. Too many judges in this city can be compromised. I don't care if they're liberal or conservative. Respected or laughed at. Dumb or smart. They have one thing in common. They got to the bench by way of the sewer. Galligan's club. Tonetti's club. Melish's club. It doesn't matter. They earned their way onto the bench with favors or with money."

For a moment no one moved. Nat Perlman sat silently, staring at the window to his right. At last, he turned back to Matlin. "Howie, will you grant one concession?"

"What?"

"Will you inform Chief Judge Sammons of this thing before it goes any further?"

Matlin was silent for a moment. Then he spoke. "Why?"

"Because, whatever you say about narcotics buys and the like, what you're doing here is fiddling with the justice system. You've got honest assistant district attorneys prosecuting a case they think is straightforward. You're planning to have a defense attorney make a motion he doesn't know is fixed…"

Matlin's eyebrows dropped.

"I know," said Perlman, responding to Matlin's gesture. "If he has half a brain, he'll know something's rotten in Denmark when his client tells him how and when to make his motion. But my point is there *is* deceit here. And it's in court. So, I'd feel a lot better if the top judicial officer in the state had at least tacitly given his approval to the operation."

Matlin looked at his chief assistant, saying nothing, apparently considering Perlman's words. Finally, he spoke. "I'll think about it, Nat. I'll think about it."

Henry was at his desk reading the investigators' reports on the morning's activities. Stanzak had been given the $20,000 by Moe and, afterward, had transferred it to Richard Delaney in a coffee shop near the Brooklyn courthouse. The investigators then followed Delaney to the courthouse and to Justice Bentzel's chambers.

Henry smiled. A bribe was being arranged for a member of the judicial establishment to fix a criminal case. Only this time, the Special Prosecutor's Office was watching.

He glanced at his watch. Five twenty-five. Enough time for a quick drop-in on Sara before his meeting with Barry Conlon.

Henry waited for Sara to get off the phone. At last, she hung up. "Hi," she said, shaking her head. "Did you have as bad a day as I did?"

"No. As a matter of fact we've had a pretty good day. Our little operation seems to be moving along."

"Good. At least one of us is getting somewhere." She pushed a large red file folder aside with a disgusted look.

"Why, what's wrong?"

"What isn't?" She pointed to the files. "A new case they want me to investigate. Records missing. Witnesses no one seems to recall." She shrugged. "You name it. Horrible case."

He followed her eyes to the window.

"At least I have something promising. I told you about the Queens attorney—Harold Remelt—who said he can get things done in the Queens district attorney's office. I think we're going to have a wire on the lawyer soon."

"Dark already," Sara said with a sigh, looking out the window. "Winter's coming, and shorter days." She laughed. "Not that it makes a difference here in the office."

Suddenly Henry had an idea. The heck with Barry Conlon. "Listen, Sara, since it's dark already, how about leaving now and skipping uptown with me for an early dinner?"

For a minute, Henry thought that Sara might do it. She even looked like she would. Then she disappointed him again.

"I really can't." She shook her head slowly. "Our moods would be too different. I think, Henry, you could be upbeat at a funeral..."

"Depends on whose funeral," he laughed.

She smiled sadly. "But I, I can't be at ease when I feel this out of control. And this horrible new case makes me feel that way." Then she brightened a bit. "Soon. I promise."

Henry started to get up. Then he stopped. "Sara, I just remembered. I've got subscription tickets to 'Traviata' next Friday. How about that for 'soon?'"

"Friday?" She thought for a moment. "Yes," she smiled. "Friday would be nice."

The bittersweet music of *La Traviata* always moved Henry. It spoke of deep sadness with sublime beauty. But tonight, it seemed to have an ominous overtone and Henry barely heard the pleas of Alfredo and his father as they watched Violetta die.

From the moment he had met Sara in front of the opera house, he felt something was wrong. And the feeling had not gone away. Indeed, it seemed to resonate in the tragic tones of Verdi. With the opera finally over, he and Sara were heading for a nearby saloon for a post-performance drink.

It was nothing she had done or said. In fact, he had not seen her more pleasant and friendly than she was tonight. She had greeted him warmly with a kiss. During the performance, she had complimented the singers and expressed delight with the guest conductor. When Henry had suggested a drink afterward, instead of noting the lateness of the hour, as he thought she might do, she had quickly consented, and was walking briskly beside him, still chatting about the production they had just left behind.

They crossed Broadway and headed toward a pub which Henry liked. Once there, they ordered their drinks, which now sat on the table in front of them. Yet instead of feeling comfortable, for some reason Henry felt like a prisoner who has been led to the guillotine, facing nothing but a violent and final moment of truth.

"Henry," Sara looked in his eyes. "I don't think we should date each other anymore."

Thump. The blade fell. Surprisingly, a surge of something like relief swept through him. Here it was at last. This must be what the prisoner felt when finally, the blade passed through his neck bone and severed his head. The horrors of expectation were over. Now only death had to be dealt with.

Fate had taken over and removed choice from his hands. His head was falling into the basket, and there was nothing he could do but let it fall.

Unfortunately, he had rather expected it to happen. He almost saw it as an affirmation of what he feared about himself. That this was his way. The almost. The heady touch of the hems of goddesses strolling just above his head. A pinch of celestial silk, for a moment soft and sensuous to his touch, until it passed beyond his fingertips, leaving him with an arm outstretched, reaching for what he could never really have.

"I guess I should ask why," he said at last.

"I think you know."

"Well, let me hear it anyway."

"I've said it before, Henry. But I'll say it again if you insist."

He said nothing. Just nodded for her to continue.

"You and I, we're just too different."

"How?" He was on autopilot now. Probably headed for the side of a mountain. But he didn't care.

"How? Henry, we've talked this about many times. Look at you. You've got friends you have fun with. You play tennis and ski. People like you right away. And like to be with you."

He did not move.

She continued. "Look, you're very dear, Henry. I really mean that. You're bright, attractive. And you're a completely moral person. As moral a person as I've ever known. Like Howard Matlin. And like my father. That's what's most wonderful about you. You're an inspiration. And I value that most about you."

Sara looked down, then back at Henry. "If my mother were alive, or even my father, God rest his soul, they would tell me that I should marry you."

A ball of wet fur formed in his throat. He said nothing.

"But I don't need an inspiration. I don't want guidance, or support, or help." She looked into his eyes and leaned slightly forward, across the table. "I'm too prickly, too independent. As a woman, I'm probably out of character, I just want to go my own way, on my own terms."

She shook her head slowly. "I don't know why I'm that way. But I am what I am. Despite the thousands of dollars I've flushed down the drains of shrinks talking about my mother's helplessness and my resentment of it and blah, blah, blah."

That's the first time she's ever mentioned going to a shrink, he thought.

She went on. "Henry, I know who I am. I know what I want. And what I don't want. I don't want someone helping me." Sara placed a hand on Henry's hand. The one wrapped about his now warm mug of beer. "And I don't want someone looking for help from me."

Henry sat up and started to speak, but Sara continued. "I don't mean you *need* my help. And certainly, you don't need to go to a shrink and waste as much time and money as I have." She shook her head. "But there's a part of you, Henry, that's somehow incomplete. A part that needs something more in order to function properly." She eyed Henry directly. "And I can't be that something."

Sara took a deep breath and let it out. But she went on before Henry could respond. "You need other people, Henry. You do. But I don't. I stand by myself, and I make my own decisions and I aim for my own goals. And most of the time, I reach them. And when I don't, I figure out why I didn't, and then I do better next time."

Sara stopped talking and looked into Henry's eyes.

He had no response. There was nothing to say. He took a sip of his beer. "Ugh. Warm," he said and smiled at Sara. He turned around and signaled the waitress for a cold one.

Henry didn't sleep much that night. Or the next night either. He kept replaying his times with Sara, from the first time he saw her until the final goodbye in front of Sara's brownstone.

Sara's last few words, before they left the pub, stood out in his mind. "Henry, I know that I've hurt you. And that fact hurts me, too. But I meant it when I said how much I value you as a person. And I really hope you can understand this, and that somehow, we can still be friends. It would mean a lot to me."

Henry didn't respond. He wasn't sure what to say. And, as he lay in bed thinking of Sara, he didn't know what he would do. All he knew was that the relationship he had hoped for was over.

"It ain't over till it's over," the great Yogi Berra had once said. "Well, Yogi," Henry sighed, "this time, it's over."

CHAPTER 20

Henry wasn't one to take pleasure in another's misfortune. But as he settled into his desk Monday morning, he had to say that Larry Santarella couldn't have picked a better time to have an emergency hernia operation. It was early Sunday afternoon, while he was lounging in a chair trying to clear his sleepless head with a third cup of coffee, when Santarella called.

"Hey, buddy," he began. "I need a favor. A big one."

"Sure," Henry had responded. "What is it?"

"Well, I'm out here in Queens General Hospital. They ran me in last night when my old hernia acted up. I'm goin' into the operating room tomorrow and I need some coverage for a hearing in that Corrections Department case."

"Gee, sorry to hear that. Are you okay?"

"Yeah. At least they say I'm gonna be. But I won't be doin' any hearings for a while."

"When is it—the hearing?"

"Tomorrow morning at eleven. The witnesses are ready but someone's gotta show up and question 'em. There's some other stuff scheduled for later in the week, too—it was gonna be my big week. But I can probably get most of it postponed if the hearing goes okay."

At the moment the Moe case was on hold. Henry had learned Friday that Moe's motion to dismiss had been filed and that the District Attorney's Office had a week, until next Monday, to submit its responding papers. That meant that nothing would be likely to happen until then, at which time Moe would be notified about arrangements to deliver the second $20,000 of the bribe.

Even more importantly at the moment, Santarella was offering him the chance to involve himself in a project that would take his mind off Sara.

"I'm on for the hearing at the least," he told his buddy. "Just tell me what I should do tomorrow and where the papers are now so I can go down to the office now and get ready."

Monday afternoon, a week later, Henry was on his way to Howard Matlin's office. He had genuinely enjoyed the previous week. He had worked very hard, seeing Larry Santarella's Corrections Department investigation through its final stages: attending the hearing, meeting with other witnesses, compiling the results of undercover work, sorting out subpoenaed records, and conferring with the Office brass overseeing the investigation. Santarella had done a great job combing the dregs of the city's criminal element to compile evidence of widespread bribe-taking by Corrections personnel to give special treatment to favored prisoners. On Santarella's return that morning, Henry's friend found himself ready for a major grand jury presentation. Santarella was delighted, thanking Henry repeatedly. In truth, though, it was Henry who was grateful. This unexpected assignment had allowed him for over a week to avoid almost all thoughts of Sara.

Matlin was settled in his chair, facing Henry and Justin Cole. Next to Cole sat Group Chief Investigator Sid Wise, humorless as usual, who had taken over the responsibilities for the investigation. Matlin was wearing a simple white shirt and brown challis tie, with his sleeves rolled up to mid-fore-arm. He glanced at Henry and Cole. Then his eyes traveled back to Nat Perlman, in a chair next to Henry.

"No, I'm not going to do it, Nat. That's final."

Chief Assistant Nat Perlman had just renewed his earlier entreaty to Howard Matlin that Matlin inform the state's Chief Judge about the under-cover investigation they were conducting in the courthouse.

Perlman shook his head. "You're making a big mistake, Howie."

"The mistake would be if I did tell him."

Perlman started to respond, but Matlin cut him off.

"Nat, he may be the chief judge now. But that's now. A few years ago, Arthur Sammons was just another supreme court judge who came out of Vince Tonetti's organization. The same place Bentzel came from."

"Howie..."

"No."

"But..."

"Nat, use your head. We're not here to act like politicians. To make friends and influence people. Garner votes or support for some political deal. We're here to fight corruption. Wherever and however we find it. And it appears we've found some. Right there in Tonetti's borough. Sammons's home turf. His original court. If I tell Arthur Sammons we've already passed marked bribe money to Judge Bentzel's law secretary to get Bentzel to dismiss a case, how long do you honestly think it would be before Bentzel suddenly dumped this case? Either that or tried to put our man Moe in jail so we'd have to surface and admit to a botched investigation and get egg all over our face, the way we almost did in that mess with Galligan and Judge Dennis?"

Perlman sighed. "Howie. You're talking about the Chief Judge. Like it or not, Arthur Sammons is the top judge in the state. And ultimately, if he wants to, he can hurt you—us—very badly. We can't afford to have him as an enemy."

"And we can't afford to have him in possession of information he can use to wreck the best investigation we've had yet."

"But…"

"For the last time, no."

Perlman gave up and sat back, shaking his head.

Now Matlin's features relaxed and he looked again at his chief assistant. "I'll tell you what, Nat," he said quietly. "As soon as I believe it's safe, I'll inform Sammons of everything."

Perlman shrugged his shoulders. "You're the boss," he sighed.

Matlin looked at Sid Wise. "Has the case actually gone to Bentzel?" he asked.

"Yes," responded Wise as everyone's eyes turned to him. "We were able to get someone inside the clerk's office to confirm that."

"Without raising suspicions, I assume," Justin Cole interjected.

"Of course," Wise responded.

"But even if the case was transferred to Bentzel's calendar," said Nat Perlman, looking at Matlin, "you still haven't connected it directly to Bentzel."

"Not yet," admitted Matlin. "But if Bentzel dismisses the case, or takes the money, that's when we can connect it to him." He gestured with a hand toward his chief assistant. "And, Nat, I promise you, if there's no connection to Bentzel, he will be dropped off the radar immediately and only the law secretary will be on the hook." He nodded as he went on. "And Sammons will be told everything."

At the next team meeting, Justin Cole was speaking. Like Matlin, Cole was without a jacket, revealing bright red suspenders. The sleeves of his expensive red-and-white-striped shirt were buttoned, allowing Henry to see the monogram just above the left cuff.

Cole was talking. "So Stanzak told Moe to deliver the second twenty thousand Friday morning. He said that Delaney promised him the dismissal would be issued immediately. At which time we can make our arrests."

Matlin leaned back in his chair and looked at the ceiling. He sat that way for almost a minute. At last, he sat up again. "I don't like it," he announced.

"Don't like what?"

"I don't like the fact that we're giving Delaney another twenty thousand dollars that we might not be able to connect to Bentzel."

Henry nodded. "That's right, what if it got lost?"

Justin Cole scowled at Henry.

Matlin went on. "I didn't like doing it with the first twenty, but it's a risk we had to take. Because there was a second installment. But this *is* the second installment. And the last one. It's the only chance to connect Bentzel to the bribe money. If we can't show he got the money, he can wiggle out of this thing even if he *is* involved."

"But we've got Delaney cold," Justin argued. "And we can use Delaney to get Bentzel."

"Not good enough. In the first place, we don't know that Delaney will cooperate. He might take the rap for himself. But even if Delaney *does* cooperate, Bentzel could say his law secretary was lying about sharing any money with him, and that he'd convinced him to dismiss the case with legitimate legal arguments."

Matlin looked at Justin. "When is the next installment due?"

"Friday."

"Well, there's going to be a delay."

For a moment, there was silence.

Then Justin Cole spoke. "Do you think they will do the same thing?"

"I'm counting on it."

Matlin turned to Henry. "Based on the way the first installment went, we know that Delaney took the money to chambers immediately. If there is a delay, Delaney will have to explain it. In chambers."

Now Henry understood. "So, we will want a bug in the chambers."

"We will," Matlin responded.

"So, I should begin preparing an application."

Justin Cole broke in. "I have a draft of an application already done. All I need to do is add a few specific facts. So, I'll do it." He smiled, without humor, at Henry.

"Okay, thank you," Matlin had said. "Let me see it today." He ended the meeting.

"He was so mad; smoke was comin' out his ears." The diminutive speaker smiled gleefully at his audience: Justin Cole, Henry Perkins, and Sid Wise, all gathered in Cole's office.

"So, I turned on the beamers," he said, pointing to his eyes, "lookin' so sad, and said I was gonna make sure he was rewarded well for his part. And the fish was back on the line." A high-pitched giggle followed, full of joy as though it had come from one of Santa's elves.

Hubert Moe was a charmer. He had a funny little nose that seemed to make an angled turn halfway down its abbreviated length, so that it wouldn't cast a shadow on the wryly grinning mouth. The cheeks looked like they had been borrowed from Santa himself, resembling little rubber balls that bounced as Moe laughed. Underneath black hair that always seemed to be falling down over his forehead, his eyes laughed, too. But Henry could see that they were not naive or gullible eyes. Indeed, the eyes were the principal clue that Moe was more dangerous than the grin or chubby cheeks would suggest.

It was late Friday morning and Moe had just come from his scheduled meeting with Victor Stanzak—the one at which he was supposed to deliver the second half of the bribe money for transmission to Bentzel's law secretary, Richard Delaney. Moe had met Stanzak at the same coffee shop in Brooklyn where he had delivered the first installment. But this time, he hadn't delivered the money.

Moe, of course, was not privy to the reason for the delay, but he went along with the plan cheerfully. He liked a challenge, he said. And telling the middleman in a bribe that the bribe money was late was a challenge.

"So now you're supposed to deliver the money..." Cole began.

"Tuesday."

Cole seemed to be considering saying something more when his phone rang. He listened for a moment and then hung up.

"As I was about to say," Cole continued, addressing Moe. "I want you to call me Monday noon for your final instructions for Tuesday's meeting."

Moe nodded, rose from his chair, and stepped to the door. Paul Ahern, a junior investigator, was there waiting to escort him out of the Office.

Once the door closed, Cole spoke. "Howie wants us all in his office."

They entered Matlin's office and sat down. The Special Prosecutor set aside some papers he had been reading.

Matlin began. "Our friends did just as we expected. Stanzak met with Delaney and presumably told him about the delay. He then actually walked to the chambers with Delaney. And then Delaney went in, again, presumably to explain things to the judge." He looked at Perlman. "Or to whoever it is that is going to throw the case."

"Anyway, based on everything we have to date, an eavesdropping warrant will be in order."

"For the delivery Tuesday?" Henry asked.

"No," said Matlin. "For when Moe tells Stanzak on Tuesday that he needs more time."

"But..." Henry sat up quickly.

"That's the kind of response I expect Stanzak to have," said Matlin, nodding toward Henry.

"And Delaney also." Matlin looked at the assembled team. "Last time there was a delay, Delaney went right to chambers. This time, we expect that he will do so again." He nodded. "And we will be listening."

That afternoon Henry stood up and walked to his window. It was one of those bad days in New York. The leading edge of winter. With fog and drizzle and clouds hanging low, capturing the gritty effluents of the city as they drifted skyward, then spitting them back into the streets below. As he gazed into the dull gray Manhattan sky, Henry felt like the sky. Gray. And useless now that Justin Cole appeared to have taken over the Bentzel investigation and squeezed him out.

He turned away from the window and glanced at his watch. Almost lunch time. Maybe Barry Conlon would be up to lunch at the German restaurant. He could use a Dortmunder or two.

Opening his door, he stepped into the hall to go next door to Conlon's office.

"Oh, Henry," Sara said with surprise as he nearly knocked her down.

She stopped.

He stopped.

She looked at him.

He looked back at her.

"How are you?" she asked.

"I am fine," he lied. "And you?"

Now what?

"Well, I'm off to a meeting," she said, turning to leave. "I'll see you."

He stood watching her slim figure stride down the hallway toward the corner.

"Hey, man!" It was Barry Conlon, popping out of his office. "Just the guy I was lookin' for. Feel like a little Dortmunder with lunch?"

Henry turned. He looked at his friend for a moment, then smiled. "Conlon, you read my very mind. Let's go."

After the eavesdropping warrant was signed, Technical Services Chief Sammy Parisi himself had planted the bug in Richard Delaney's office, which was just outside the judge's personal chambers. Then, after Stanzak had been told by Moe that he needed another day, and Stanzak had met with the judge's law secretary, investigators followed Delaney to chambers where the bug picked up a conversation between Delaney and someone who could have been no one else but the judge. "Tell that guy that he has one more chance, one day," said the voice. Following that conversation, Stanzak had met with Moe and told him that Delaney had given him "one more chance, one day."

Howard Matlin assembled the team to discuss the next step. Matlin's door opened and Justin Cole strode in. He was wearing a sky-blue shirt with a paisley bow tie and his red suspenders. He looked expensive.

"I think we're ready to go ahead," Matlin began. "It looks like the judge is involved." He looked at Nat Perlman. "And if it turns out that he's not, Nat, I'll do exactly as you want me to do." He turned to Sid Wise. "The money's ready?"

"Already prepared. Except dusting. Serial numbers recorded and photographed. Just before it goes to Moe, we'll dust it with telltale powder."

Matlin thought for a moment then nodded. "Okay. Let's go for it. Just be sure we have enough men there to cover anything unexpected."

Late that afternoon, Henry dropped into a chair in front of Justin Cole's desk. "Is everything set?"

Justin lifted his eyes from some paperwork. "What do you think?"

"If I knew the answer, I wouldn't have asked you."

Justin took a sip from his coffee mug. It looked like an antique. Probably worth a lot more than the cups Henry drank from. But Henry reflected with satisfaction, it was the same bad coffee.

"Well, the answer is yes."

"So, Moe's giving Stanzak the money at noon tomorrow in the coffee shop?"

"Yes."

"Then we follow Stanzak to meet Delaney."

Justin folded his arms and looked at Henry. "Yes," he said with a sigh.

"Listen here," Henry snapped. "This happens to be an important investigation and whether you like it or not, I'm part of it."

"Sadly."

Henry sat up and glared at Justin. "Fuck you."

Justin smiled.

"Where are the investigators going to be?"

"It's being handled."

"How many men will be there?"

Cole sighed deeply. "Two. Enough."

"Howie said to be sure we have enough men there. I think we ought to have more than two." He paused. "At least a back-up team in case something goes wrong."

Justin looked up with obvious disdain. "Henry, I'm running this part. I don't need you or anyone else to tell me what to do."

Henry almost choked. These were almost the very words Sara had said to him once.

"Matlin brought you into the case. But as far as I'm concerned, you're irrelevant."

Henry was up from his chair and on his way to the door. As he reached it, he turned. "Justin, you are a class-A shit."

He stepped out the door, but behind him he could hear Justin Cole laughing.

As Henry rounded the corner, he nearly bumped into his buddy Barry Conlon.

"Hey," said Conlon, coming to a stop. "Why the dagger-in-the-eye?"

Henry stopped and looked at Conlon. "I just had a few words with Justin Cole."

"Aha. Our class pet. What does Mister Blue Blood have to say today? Was he reading you his references from the Social Register?"

Henry couldn't help himself. He smiled. "Not much more than that."

Conlon shrugged. Then he looked at his watch. "Hey, I've had a busy day today. Worked up a real thirst. How about checking out a few pubs up on the East Side?"

Henry thought a minute. There was nothing left for him to do. The next stage of the case was in the hands of the investigators now. So why not?

"Yeah, why not?"

Henry pushed his empty mug toward the bartender along with that of Barry Conlon.

"So, anyway, this guy…"

"Yeah?" said Henry.

"Shit, man, are you listening?"

"Yeah, yeah," Henry assured him. "I'm listening. Jus' wanted to get our beers."

They each took a couple of gulps from the refilled mugs. Then Henry nodded for Conlon to go on.

"Oh, yeah. So, this cop—Spanke, his name is."

Henry laughed. "Don't tell me that's what he's into."

Conlon bent forward, as if speaking in confidence. "Listen, this guy is into everything." He sat back again. "I mean he's tellin' me about one time. The friggin' guy's in uniform, no less. He's checkin' out this joint where alotta hookers hang out. And see, they're behind for the month. So, he's there pickin' up the joint's payment—two hundred a month—from the owner. She's a broad named Tina." He smiled and licked his lips. "I had her in the grand jury, too." He laughed once. "You shudda seen the grand jurors. They loved old Tina."

Henry leaned forward, hoping that putting himself closer to Conlon would help him listen to the story through the beery haze. And the image that kept intruding. Sara.

Conlon chuckled to himself. "Let's see, where was I?" He took a swig. "Oh, yeah." Another gulp of his beer and he went on.

"So, Tina's daughter comes out. Her daughter comes toolin' out and, before you know it, ol' Spanke's screwin' her in a booth in the back room. Hadn't even taken his uniform off." He guffawed. "He musta been screwin' her with his friggin' handcuffs bangin' against her ass." He laughed again. "So then what happens?" His wet eyes looked at Henry. "Aha. The old lady comes in and catches Spanke with his pants down, doin' her daughter."

Again, Conlon took a mug-emptying gulp. They had been at it, in a Third Avenue saloon known as Mulligan's, for several hours, and the beer was beginning to enter its air phase. The time when it seems to slide inside at the same rate, and with the same resistance, as the air breathed between swallows.

"Hey, Rusty. A couple more here."

Henry wasn't finished with his. But what the heck. He drained his mug.

"So, anyway, Tina walks in on Spanke and the daughter. *In flagrante.* But good old Spanke. He just looks up at her and tells her she's late with the monthly deuce. And he gets it from her."

Conlon concluded his story with a roar of laughter. When Henry failed to join him, he ceased abruptly. "What's the matter, man. You didn't even hear the story."

"Huh? Oh, sure I did. Spanke. Your key cop you turned for your sharg-sergeants' club case." He tried to remember more.

"And?"

"And, uh. He was bangin' somebody's daughter."

"Jeeesus." Conlon shook his head. "You gotta be in love, or somethin'." Then his reddened eyes lit up. "Hey, you aren't still takin' out the Ice Queen, are you?"

Henry felt as though Conlon had punched him. "Nah."

"You're not still thinkin' about her, I hope."

Henry said nothing.

"Hey, man!" Two late-night diners at a nearby table looked up. He lowered his voice. "Forget her. That broad's got ice cubes up her cunt. If she has a cunt."

Henry opened his mouth to argue. But through the haze, discretion placed a hand over his mouth, and he said nothing.

"Ya didn't answer me, buddy." Conlon lowered his head and peered up at Henry, perched on the next barstool. "Are you still tryin' with her?"

"She gave me the leg."

"She did?" Conlon's eyes opened wide.

"Yeah," Henry sighed.

Conlon reached over and grabbed Henry's hand. "Hey, put'er there, buddy. You just dodged a heap of flyin' shit. Take my word for it."

Henry shrugged. Then Conlon's eyes suddenly shifted away, and Henry followed them. Two women were strolling into the pub. They had already removed their overcoats.

"Hey, look at that, Perkins. Look at that."

Henry did look. Conlon was right. At least, half right. One of the women was short, with curly brown hair and an ordinary face and figure. But her companion was a long-haired blonde with unusually large mammaries barely contained in a gray sweater meant for a smaller person. Her wool skirt likewise was stretched to the limit where it counted. The effect drew Conlon from his seat. Henry got up as well.

"The blonde is dynamite," said Conlon as they started toward the women. "And yours isn't too bad, either."

CHAPTER 21

Fire! It had to be a fire alarm. That gonging. The place was on fire!

Eventually, like two pieces of old rubber which had been stuck together for a hot summer in a cellar, his eyelids managed to part. The "fire alarm" was, in fact, the small clock next to his bed. Ringing.

Eventually he comprehended the problem and put together its solution. Tentatively, he reached out a hand and found the button on the back of the clock and pressed it into silence.

Whew.

He worked his legs around until they were out of the bed. Slowly he lowered them to the floor and sat up.

"Ouch." Then it hit.

Bikini Atoll reenacted in his head. An agonizing explosion that began somewhere in the back of his eyes and rolled outward, sending shock waves to slam painfully against his eyelids, only to rock back through his head and ram into the top of his neck.

"Aaarrggguugg."

He reeled backward but caught himself with an arm down and regained his sitting position.

It was then that he became aware of his mouth. At first it was just sour. Until he tried to open it and his tongue stuck to the roof. It wouldn't come loose by itself, so, with a hand, he forcibly pulled down on his lower jaw, until his tongue broke free. Then he closed his mouth again.

Old socks. Old socks and cat litter. He must have had a bowl of it before he went to bed, since his mouth still tasted of it. He wasn't exactly certain since his tongue couldn't move around to sample the residue. Once again, it was nailed in place by some gluey mass that had accumulated during the night.

He tried standing up. Big mistake. Like an eruption of Old Faithful, a wave of dizziness swept upward from his unstable feet to his now-throbbing head. He sat down on the bed quickly, before he might experience a second, and undesired, viewing of whatever he had consumed the night before.

He leaned back against the headboard of his bed. *Shit.* And today was the day their guy—he couldn't even think of his name—was delivering the final bribe payment to the law secretary. Delaney. He remembered his name all right. Goddamn Irishman. Not Delaney, either. His buddy Conlon. It was his idea to take those two women to that place that stays open until 4 a.m.

Oooohh. Just a thought about what he had done the night before caused a surge of pain to rush through his head. Better forget it, have some aspirin, and try to make it to the office. For the big day.

Sid Wise was sitting at Justin Cole's desk when Henry entered. Justin was not there.

"Where've you been?" Wise asked Henry.

Henry, still moving gingerly, took a step into the room.

Then Wise took a second look at Henry, apparently recognizing the symptoms. He did not smile.

"Is the money gone?" Henry asked.

"Long ago."

Henry was disappointed. He had wanted to watch the investigators apply the "telltale" powder to the money. The powder, invisible in ordinary light, adheres not only to the money, but also to the skin and clothing of anyone handling it. Under ultraviolet light the powder glows, telling the tale of the money's path.

"Who's watching the pass?" asked Henry.

"Kaplan and Cooper." Two good young investigators.

"Oh."

"And Cole's there, too. In case something goes wrong."

Justin there? Watching the transaction? Now Henry, if possible, felt worse. His best case to date and he'd missed the chance to be right in the middle of it by going out and getting drunk. *Damn*, he swore at himself. Then a wave of nausea ended his reflections on the night before.

"Moe's still meeting Stanzak at Arlie's at noon?"

Wise nodded.

"And then Stanzak passes the money to Delaney?"

"Yes."

So, the pass was definitely going down today. "Is the plan still to arrest Delaney and the judge in chambers?"

Wise looked at Henry as though he were an outsider, asking a lot of stupid questions. Then he seemed to relent. "Yes. It's basically the same. As soon as Cooper and Kaplan see Delaney go back into chambers with the money, they'll join the guys in the plant and listen in on the bug. When they hear Delaney give the money to the judge, they'll go arrest them." He stopped. "You should know all that. I don't have to tell you."

In Henry's condition, it wasn't a bad idea to tell him where his office was. He wasn't sure he could remember.

"Well," Henry said as he opened the door to go, "I'll be in my office. Buzz me the minute anything happens."

Buzzzzztt.

"Ooh!" Henry was startled. It was his intercom buzzing him awake after he had dozed off, his head on some papers on his desk.

"Yes?" he answered, after locating and picking up his phone. His neck hurt from the angle at which it had lain while he slept.

"Sid Wise wants you to come to Matt Corey's office."

"Thanks, Flora."

Oh, crap. Matt Corey. That was all he needed today. He still felt terrible. He looked at his watch. Forty minutes of sleep. If anything, it had made him feel even shakier, he realized, as he began to stand up. Never mind. It had to help. And once he had some coffee in him, things would improve. He hoped.

Matt Corey's office was off the investigators' room. Henry walked shakily down the hall toward the large room in which the investigators sat. Once there, he poured himself a cup of black coffee but in the few steps to Corey's door, he spilled half of the coffee. "Damn," he said. He stopped long enough to take a gulp of the coffee, then placed the paper container in a wastebasket. It would be messy when the cleaning people came, but he was in a hurry.

He knocked on Corey's door.

"Come in," someone said.

Henry opened the door. Wise, Corey, and Harry Rood were gathered around Corey's desk. "Jeeesus fuckin' Christ!" yelled Matt Corey suddenly. Corey slammed down the phone and looked at the others. "They missed 'em."

"What?" It was Sid Wise.

"Had a goddam flat tire. Hit a fuckin' pothole and flattened the goddam tire. Lost Delaney."

Corey looked at Harry Rood. "You gotta get a team there. Now."

Rood stood up. "I'll arrange it, Matt. I'll go with them myself. Sid knows the case; he should stay with you."

238

Corey looked relieved. "Thanks, Harry." It was the first time ever Henry had heard Matt Corey say thank you. "Just get there pronto," Corey concluded.

"I will," said Rood, and he departed.

"May I ask what's happened?" Henry ventured.

"The judge isn't there," Wise informed him. "He's not coming in today."

"The judge isn't? How do you know?"

"The bug. Delancy called someone, undoubtedly the judge, and told him that he had it."

"The money, obviously," added Corey.

"Then Delaney told somebody who stopped in to see the judge that he wasn't coming in today."

"How's Delaney getting the money to the judge?"

Wise looked at Henry as though he had asked a stupid question. "We have no idea. We don't have a wiretap, as I assume you know. So, we didn't hear the conversation."

They sure found the right investigator for Justin Cole, thought Henry. "Sometimes people speak to whomever they're calling," he responded. The hangover made him feisty. It felt good.

Wise retreated. "Anyway, Delaney told the judge that he had it and arranged to meet the judge right away with it."

Corey cut in. "And our team tried to follow him but, you heard it, they crapped out." He looked at Wise. "We shoulda had two teams in cars. One team's like a rubber dick. It can get lost up there."

Henry suppressed a smile. He remembered his last conversation with Justin Cole where he'd said that they ought to have another team covering the situation. Maybe Cole wasn't as perfect as he thought he was.

Howard Matlin shook his head slowly. "Not good," he said, voicing the obvious.

Matlin looked at Matt Corey. "They've gone by the judge's house?"

"Right. No one there. And no one at Delaney's place. Harry's team checked that out. We've even checked the judge's club. It's not far from his home. But his car's not there, either." Corey tightened his lips, then released them again. "There's no sign of either of them."

"They checked the chambers?"

"Yeah. The team on the plant did."

Matlin looked up at the ceiling, his jaw tight. Then he addressed Corey again.

"Have the law secretary's place staked out. Arrest him tonight."

"But…" It was Justin Cole, who had come back by subway.

Matlin looked at Justin. "We have to move tonight. We don't have enough to arrest the judge. But the law secretary's covered with powder. And he may still have the money."

"But what about the judge?" asked Justin.

"The judge will have to wait. If we're lucky, we can tie him in through the law secretary. Or the powder. Or both. But we can't wait until the law secretary's washed his hands or taken a shower and washed off the powder. Because then we'll have nothing."

Henry was sitting in the investigators' area, drinking coffee, and waiting for developments.

"It looks like a long night," said Harry Rood, as he prepared to leave. Rood had returned to the office in the early afternoon, helping Matt Corey deploy the teams of investigators to their various locations.

It was almost eleven o'clock and Delaney had not yet returned to his bachelor apartment. Two teams were parked outside of the apartment, waiting to arrest him as soon as he did. Another team was sitting on the judge's house in case they got lucky, and Delaney showed up there. They even had another team watching the courthouse in case one or the other of the men turned up.

"Good night, Harry."

"Good night. And good luck."

Henry felt terrible. His misconduct of the night before and his lack of sleep, exacerbated by the tension of the day's events, were making him nauseous. Almost lightheaded.

Justin, he knew, was in his office, working on some motion papers relating to his earlier indictment of Judge Crocker. But Henry felt too bad to do any productive work. So, he sat, reading the *Daily News* for the third time, and drinking the investigators' coffee.

At last, he made up his mind. He had to get some sleep, or he'd end up in the hospital, the way he felt. He walked down the east hall to Justin's office.

"Any news?" he asked Cole as he opened his door.

"Not yet," he responded without lifting his head.

"How long're you staying here?"

"Until Delaney comes home."

"What if he doesn't come home?"

"Then we'll do what Howie wants and arrest him at the office." Cole looked up with a distasteful scowl. "Obviously."

Henry decided not to ask Justin if he was prepared to stay up all night. The answer was too obvious.

"Look. I don't feel too well right now."

Justin shrugged his shoulders. Undoubtedly, he'd heard about Henry's hangover that morning.

"I'm going to grab a couple hours of shuteye."

"Suit yourself."

"Will you have someone call me if Delaney's arrested?"

Justin looked up again from his papers. "You can tell the night opera-tor. He or she will call you if you want."

Henry ignored Justin's tone and left. It was too late at night, and he had no fight left in him.

CHAPTER 22

At nine o'clock the following morning, Henry went to Sid Wise's desk, but he was out. He was glad that no one had called, since he had slept like a dead dog. He was still less than perfect, but he felt incomparably better than he had the previous day. He was even able to enjoy the cup of investigators' coffee he had grabbed as he entered the room.

He decided to risk it and ask Matt Corey, whose door was open. "No arrest?" Henry asked the Chief Investigator.

Corey looked up. He obviously had not gotten much sleep. "No. He never came home."

"When's Delaney due at the office, do you know?"

"We hope it'll be soon. At any rate, we have a team in the judge's chambers now. Searchin' the joint. With a warrant." He smiled. "Woke our own judge up to get it signed."

Just then Corey's phone rang. "Okay, right away," he said. He turned to Henry. "We're all wanted in Howie's office.

"Good morning, Henry," said Matlin as Henry entered. Henry scanned the room, spotting Harry Rood, Justin Cole, and Nat Perlman sitting across the desk from the Special Prosecutor. Cole was wearing the same shirt and tie he had on the day before, telling Henry that Justin had been in the office all night. But to look at his face, one would think he had just arrived. Sid Wise, he noticed, was missing.

Matlin spoke. "The law secretary has been arrested. On his way to his office. But it appears he spotted something wrong in the hall outside and, before they could grab him, he rushed downstairs and got off a phone call from a booth in the hall. We're assuming it was to the judge. So, the team assigned to watch the judge has been alerted."

"Where was the judge? Wasn't he on his way to work?"

"No. He went to his club this morning. Apparently took another day off." Matlin smiled. The dimples at the edges of his cheeks appeared. "Perhaps to celebrate." Then he became serious again. "Shortly after they were alerted, the team reported that the judge had left the club in a hurry and had driven off in his car. They're following him. That's what we're waiting for."

"What about the law secretary?"

"Clammed up tight," said Nat Perlman, who was sitting next to Henry. "Asked for his lawyer."

"Did they find anything in the search?"

"Nothing but a draft of the opinion dismissing the case. No money, or other evidence," responded Matlin.

"But Delaney's finished, anyway," said Justin, apparently wanting to correct the impression, if such were the impression, that the morning's events had been less than successful so far.

After that, no one said anything. They all sat in their seats, looking at the phone on Matlin's desk and wondering what it would reveal when it rang next.

Nothing happened. But the tension around Matlin's desk inhibited conversation. Matt Corey rose and walked to the couch across the room and dropped onto it. Harry Rood rose and followed him, taking a chair next to the couch, where the two investigators began to talk in tones that couldn't be heard clearly by the people waiting around the desk.

Justin was looking at the ceiling. Then his eyes dropped to the window. He did not look nervous.

But Henry was. And he was wondering where the judge was going in such a hurry.

"Uh, Howie." It was Nat Perlman who broke the silence at the desk.

Matlin looked at his chief assistant.

"Have you told Sammons yet?"

Matlin shook his head in the negative.

"Howie…"

Matlin said nothing.

"I don't want to lecture you…"

"But you will," said Matlin with a hint of a smile. He laid one hand on top of the other as he looked at Perlman. His eyes showed no anger.

"I will," said Perlman with conviction, "because I think you're going to get hurt if you don't. We're setting up a judge for a fall." He raised a hand to forestall any protest.

There was none.

"Whatever you call it, we're manipulating the court system to catch a judge."

"If we catch him," interjected Matlin.

"Yes," agreed Perlman. "But the point is that, from the judiciary's point of view, we're deceiving the whole criminal justice system. From the District Attorney to the original criminal court judges, to the grand jury and even the court clerks. This case is a ruse. And Chief Judge Sammons isn't going to like it. Even if he knew about it, he wouldn't like it. But if he finds out about it after the fact, he's going to be very, very angry." Perlman looked directly at Matlin. "At you," he concluded.

"Nat, I can't take the chance. I don't trust Sammons, or anyone else in the system, not to try giving a quick bit of offhand helpful advice to their friends. At our expense." He sat forward. "I'll tell Sammons when I think…"

Matlin's words were interrupted by the telephone on his credenza. He picked it up as everyone else tuned in.

"Hello." There was a long pause while someone talked to Matlin.

Rood and Corey returned silently to their chairs.

"We could," Matlin said at last. "But ask for his consent. Maybe he'll give it and save us the trouble."

Again, there was a pause, but no voice could be heard.

"They got him," said Matlin to the others, as he held a hand over the mouthpiece, speaking softly.

"Who, the judge?" asked Justin urgently.

Matlin nodded.

"What happened?"

"They followed him to a bank. He went inside to the safe deposit box area. They came in a minute later and caught him red-handed stashing the money—our twenty thousand dollars. All there."

"Hooray," said Henry. "Good work, boys." He pictured the investigators in the bank, putting the cuffs on the judge.

"What were you talking about to whomever called?" asked Justin.

"Searching the judge's house. For clothes or other items with the powder on them. To show that he had the money before he'd gone to the bank in case he tries to say that someone else put the money there, or that we flaked him, or whatever. I suggested trying to get his consent instead of waiting to get a warrant."

"Who thought of the search?" asked Perlman.

"Sid Wise," responded Matlin.

"Good thinking," said Perlman.

Corey nodded. "Wise's a good man."

Wise, too, Henry thought with a chuckle.

"Yes?" Someone was speaking to Matlin over the phone. "He did? Good. Go right now before he changes his mind."

It was much more festive this time. Last Christmas, they had made do with a fledgling library and some crepe paper and half-gallons of booze. This time, the Christmas party was in a reception hall on the Executive Floor of the New State Office Building, and it was catered. They were having it there because it avoided the security problem of having so many guests in the office, Harry Rood had told Henry. But it also gave the now nearly sixty members of the Special Prosecutor's Office and their guests a much nicer celebration.

Which, combined with the recent arrest of Justice Bentzel and his law secretary, made it a very pleasant occasion for all.

"It was a smacker of a pinch," said Angie Palumbo.

"Sticking to your vodka, I see," said Henry, to whom Palumbo was speaking.

"It sure was," agreed Tim O'Leary. Then he lowered his voice. "I hear the chief judge was mightily pissed off that he hadn't been told about the set-up." He laughed aloud.

"How did you hear that?" asked Henry.

O'Leary patted Henry on the back. "Come on, me boy," said O'Leary, putting on the brogue. "It'll be a dark day in Dublin when an O'Leary misses a trick."

Henry smiled.

"It's around," O'Leary said quietly, in his normal voice.

"Well, it's true," said Henry nodding. "Sammons was pretty unhappy when Howie finally called and told him that we had caught one of his own."

"Sure," added Palumbo enthusiastically. "With the money in his hot little hands."

"Way to go," said George Reed, who had joined the group while they were talking.

"Fuck him," said O'Leary.

"Who?" asked Reed.

"All the fuckin' judges."

"Amen," said Palumbo.

The group broke up. Then Henry felt a hand on his shoulder.

"Nice work, Perk." It was Scoop Dixon.

"Thanks. And you got some great coverage for us."

"Great cases make for great coverage," responded Dixon.

Dixon was on the mark. The coverage had been good. The investigation had been hailed in the newspapers and on television as the most important achievement of the Office to date.

"Howard Matlin has turned the corner," read an editorial in the *Daily News*. "As he has been promising us for over a year, Howard Matlin has finally struck a blow at the soft underbelly of the justice system: the courthouses. He has nabbed a crooked judge with his hand right in the cookie jar. And he slapped handcuffs on him before he could pull it out. Bravo. May he keep up the good work."

The rest of the coverage had a similar cast. Mike Welling had written a long story for the *News*, spelling out the achievements of the Special Prosecutor's Office to date, culminating with a colorful description of the arrest of Justice Bentzel in the safe deposit area of the bank. Sabrina Wilcox had featured the investigation in her front-page story in the *Times*. It was full of details, some of which Henry had thought were not known publicly. There was a photo of Howard Matlin walking toward the office. Somehow Justin Cole had gotten himself squeezed into the picture, walking with Matlin to the office in the winter cold, wearing only his business suit.

Of course, Johnny Donegan and Toby Copin had presented another side. Donegan, it seems, was a drinking buddy of Bentzel's and was horrified that Howard Matlin had "set him up." And in a column the day after the arrest, Toby Copin attacked Matlin for putting a false case in the judicial system and for using fraud, deception, and lies to entrap the Honorable Justice Bentzel. "There is about Howard Matlin," Copin had written, "the smell of the Gestapo. His methods should provoke chills in all those who value our sacred civil liberties."

Henry glanced across the room to where Justin Cole was standing, conversing with animation. Cole seemed to be holding court, surrounded by curious and admiring fans. Henry didn't care. The conclusion of the case satisfied him enough.

"Mr. Perkins," a woman's voice. Sabrina Wilcox of the *Times*.

"It's Henry," he said. "That was a nice article you wrote."

"Thank you, Henry. I'm Sabrina." She was facing him. "I hope that is just a beginning."

"What do you mean?"

"I mean that you people have barely scratched the surface yet."

"Oh?"

"Of the political system. And that's what's at the root of the problem, as Mr. Matlin puts it."

Henry laughed. "You sound like Howie."

"Maybe so." Sabrina had a serious look on her face. "But if you're really going to make a difference, you have to get into the political stuff." She paused a moment. "And that will be much rougher going."

Henry continued to look at her.

"It will," she went on, "make what you've done already look easy."

Henry shook his head and smiled. "Boy, you're sure laying it on us."

"What I am doing is hoping," she said. "I'm hoping that you're going to make the effort." She turned to speak to someone else.

Just then someone began clanking a glass for silence. When the talking had died down, Howard Matlin stepped up on a chair and looked out over the crowd.

"This is a time for celebrating and enjoying ourselves and not for speeches. So, I'll be very brief. This week, our office turned a very important corner. A corner some in our city hoped we would never turn. We began our assault on the courts."

Henry glanced at Sabrina Wilcox, but she was facing Matlin.

"That was the first step. A beginning. And, most importantly, it was the beginning for *all* of us."

Applause interrupted Matlin.

"I have faith," Matlin continued, "that, before long, every one of you who is with our Office will be working on cases like this. Cases that penetrate the district attorneys' offices, that peer into the courts, and finally, cases that strip away the thick insulation around the political clubhouses that are the source of so much of the problem."

Sounds like something I just heard, Henry mused.

"...that it won't be easy. We'll make enemies every time we strike. And those enemies will strike back. We'll be opposed by those who are corrupt, and by those who benefit from corruption. We'll be criticized by their friends in public service. Attacked in the media and thrashed about in other parts of the establishment.

"It won't be easy," Matlin repeated. Now his dark eyes began to glow again, the way they had on that television screen in that midtown bar Henry had watched those many months before. "But, together, we will do it. Because…because that's what's right."

Applause broke out. But this time, Matlin waved a hand and persisted in finishing. The applause quickly ceased.

"As I said before, today is for us a beginning. But for corruption in the city of New York, it's the beginning of the end."

As the applause died and Matlin climbed down from his chair, Henry still gazed at the place where the special prosecutor had stood. The chatter and the clanking of glasses commenced again, but Henry was still seeing Matlin standing on the chair. Standing and, with a few words, soothing his hurt, reviving his confidence, and giving him a reason to go on.

He looked up at the ceiling as though it had disappeared, and through it imagined he saw a lighted dome in a perfumed night.

A burst of laughter brought him back to the room. He saw Justin Cole talking to two others, amusing them with some story. As Justin finished his point, his listeners nodded fervently in agreement. Then one of them, apparently adding a further gesture of approval, reached out her hand. As Sara placed her hand on Justin Cole's, Henry Perkins felt as though a sword had been rammed into his gut.

PART II

CHAPTER 23

Henry strode across Chambers Street with a big smile on his face. He had just spent two vibrant weeks in Austria, spring skiing with two of his college buddies, partying, and thinking of nothing but fun and good beer. And the pretty Austrian women. The snow had been excellent, and Austria was so much cheaper than the U.S., he had almost forgotten how little he made as a prosecutor.

But now he was on his way back into battle. In the year and three months since the arrest of Justice Bentzel, many investigations had been brought to fruition, or at least were making significant progress. And the public support for the effort Howard Matlin was making had not wavered. Even with the cheap shots regularly emanating from the pens of Johnny Donegan and Toby Copin, the Office's efforts were well-received by the public.

Henry's buddy Barry Conlon had made headlines with his year-and-a-half investigation into the sergeants' club in the 130th precinct. A sergeants' club, Henry had learned, was not some social organization where policemen played poker together. It was a group of sergeants and other officers who systematically shook down businesspeople, legal and illegal, in their precinct. Barry's investigation had implicated just about every officer in the 130th precinct above the rank of patrolman. They were either taking money or protecting or ignoring those who did. So much for the idea there were only a few "rotten apples."

The Office's record against errant police officers was spectacular. As Matlin had noted on a recent television appearance, the conviction rate of the Office was 92 percent—an astonishing achievement.

The Office was making progress in other areas as well. Lou Morotti's team had been especially effective in probing the criminal courts. His group had been responsible for the indictment of three assistant district attorneys— one in the Bronx and two in Staten Island—who had taken cash or in one case a new car to let a case be dismissed or plea bargained improperly. And Lou himself had overseen the indictment of a criminal court judge in Queens who quietly sidetracked a drug prosecution of the son of a good friend of his.

As for himself, he had assisted Howard Matlin at the trial of Justice Bentzel, compiling and organizing exhibits, doing legal research, and sitting proudly next to the Special Prosecutor's chair as Matlin had mesmerized the jury with the story of Bentzel's bribe-taking and of his being caught in a bank with fistfuls of marked bills. The judge had finally resigned after his conviction late last year.

It was exhilarating being part of this important mission. But Henry couldn't shed a sense of incompleteness. He had helped out in several interesting cases. At one point he had looked into allegations concerning a judge who was rumored to be on the take, but the case had gone nowhere. He did catch a pair of cops who were helping a crooked doctor sell methadone illegally. But the matter extended no further. At one point, he tried to start his own sergeants' club investigation in another precinct, but the investigation had never uncovered any solid witnesses and thus had not gotten off the ground.

Nevertheless, Henry's enthusiasm for the Special Prosecutor's Office had not waned and he was anxious to return to action and to make a serious case.

As soon as Henry got off the elevator on the 44th floor he was met with a crowd, including several reporters. He spotted Angie Palumbo at the edge of the crowd.

"Hey, Angie. What's the commotion?"

"Press conference. Ferrante's indictment. Today."

"Ferrante?"

Palumbo looked at him oddly. "Where've you been?"

"Huh? Oh, Austria. Just got back last night."

"Oh. It's a good one. Meade's case. A couple-a wiseguys were up for dumpin' waste illegally. They bribed this hack judge named Ferrante, out in Queens. Got him to throw out the case."

The crowd had filtered into the grand jury room, which doubled as an auditorium, and Palumbo left to join them. Henry considered slipping in and watching, but he was to meet with Chief of Appeals Ed Scanlon. They were going to begin preparing the response to Justice Bentzel's appeal of his conviction.

A week later, the floor of Ed Scanlon's office looked like a blizzard had swept through it. There were piles of paper along the ledges underneath the windows, on the floor, and on most of Scanlon's desk. The piles included photocopies of cases copied from law reports, copies of law review articles and other research material, and even copies of newspaper articles. There were pages of notes in three different scrawls, some on yellow legal paper, some on white Xerox paper, some on rough-torn scraps of paper. In several places, the floor was occupied by stacks of law books, with strips of paper sticking out, marking the location of cases or statutory sections to be cited in the brief. Finally, there were prior drafts of the brief itself, which Justin Cole had just removed from a chair in which he was about to sit.

"For Christ's sake, Henry, what do you need all these old drafts for? Are they some kind of security blanket?"

"Just put them on the floor," Henry responded coldly and returned to reading his latest draft.

Justin spoke again, this time to Scanlon. "What about this argument that the judge's clothes we seized weren't admissible as evidence? I don't think we're strong enough here."

The appeals chief leaned back in his reclining chair, looking at the two other lawyers across his desk. His tousled red hair seemed to glow in the artificial light from the ceiling. "We've said enough, I think." He passed a hand through his hair. "Look, we had the judge's consent to search his house. And we also had enough evidence to convict even without the clothes. We had the marked money in the safe deposit box. We had traces of powder on the judge's hands and on the steering wheel of his car when he took the money to his safe deposit box. We had all those conversations with Delaney and Stanzak, and the conversation in chambers which is clearly the judge's voice. So telltale powder on a few pieces of clothing in the judge's house was just window dressing. Even if the search wasn't done right, it was harmless error."

Scanlon leaned forward and clasped his freckled hands together on the desk. "What I'm a lot more worried about is the way the case was conducted. I don't think the Appellate Division is going to like our little undercover foray into the courthouse."

"You sound like Nat Perlman," said Henry.

Scanlon shook his head. "What I am is a lawyer who's spent over fifteen years in appeals work, watching judges, talking with judges, trying to think like judges. And I'm telling you this much: The judges on the Appellate Division and the Court of Appeals are not going to like the fact you sent a phony case into court..."

"It was a real case, Ed," protested Henry.

"Semantics," responded Scanlon. "The problem is that neither the District Attorney nor any supervising judge knew what we were doing. And the appellate judges are going to seize on that to rip us apart unless we can improve our argument."

"The real problem the judges have" Henry responded, "is that we invaded their domain and caught one of them red-handed."

Scanlon shrugged. "Sure. But try to tell that to the Appellate Division. Don't forget, *they're* judges and we're not."

"Hey, come on," Cole broke in roughly. "Cut the law school seminar. I want to get this next draft done and go home."

"Hey, Scoop, what's new?" Henry asked as he walked by Scoop Dixon's office early Monday morning a couple of weeks later.

As usual, a cloud of smoke hovered about Dixon's head. Dixon smiled through it, brushing a hand as though to clear the air. But the air didn't clear, it only moved, swirling in visible disorder. "Aha. We've got a big one to announce this morning," Dixon responded.

"Which one?"

"The Brooklyn County Clerk and two of his assistants. They were operating a regular bazaar, taking money from lawyers to assign cases to the judges the lawyers wanted."

"Nice work. Who got 'em?"

"Justin Cole." Dixon smiled through the smoke. Behind his thick glasses, his eyes seemed to bug. "He's a one-man show."

This wasn't what Henry had stopped in to hear.

Dixon went on. "The guy's gotten three judges and convicted two of 'em already himself. And the other one you and Howie convicted. He's nailed lawyers and law secretaries and cops and you-name-it."

"Yeah, he's impressive." Henry didn't have to share his real feelings with Dixon. But he didn't have to keep up the conversation, either.

"So, how's the campaign going?" Henry said jokingly. He was referring to a movement in some corners to push Howard Matlin for governor of New York. With the oil embargo causing long lines at the gas pumps, and inflation eating into everyone's wallet while the moribund stock market made everyone feel poor, President Ford was given little chance by the media of winning election the following year. The talk was that Governor Whelan might run for President or as was more likely, that he would be a natural selection for Vice President on the Democratic ticket.

"You laugh," said Dixon. "J'you know there's already an ad hoc committee out there sounding out some big donors. If—I mean, when Whelan goes to Washington, that ancient hack he's got as Lieutenant Governor is done, too. So, who's the big cheese? Howie."

Dixon took a deep drag on his cigarette. Immediately he began to cough, dark, gurgling evacuations from tortured lungs that hacked their way past his larynx. When he had finished, he took a few quick breaths, probably trying to restore oxygen to his system. "Sorry," he said. He looked at the cigarette still smoldering in his right hand. "Gotta quit someday," he said, snuffing out the offending instrument. "What were we saying?"

"I was just saying hello," said Henry. He really didn't want to talk about the Matlin-for-Governor campaign, either. Not only was the whole notion of politics distasteful to Henry, but he knew that one of the people most active in trying to convince Matlin to run was Justin Cole. "I gotta get to work."

Could he squeeze in a new matter that might prove interesting? That was Howard Matlin's question to Henry as he sat down in front of Matlin's desk a few days later. Matt Corey was seated in his usual chair to one side of the desk.

Henry sat straight in his chair. He fought back a smile and nodded seriously across the big desk. "Yes. I could spare some time."

"Good," Matlin said with a nod. "Here it is briefly. The police department has been investigating organized crime's infiltration of the franchised towing business."

Organized crime. Henry sat up straighter.

"The investigators set up a phony towing company and went into the business. Apparently, they've already made some progress with some of their targets." He waved a hand. "But that's their business, not ours."

Henry glanced at Matt Corey, who nodded. Matlin's voice brought his eyes back to the Special Prosecutor.

"What *is* our business," Matlin was saying, "or might be our business, is some contact the undercover officers had with an attorney they retained who apparently represents a number of shady companies. This lawyer claims he has a number of City officials in his pocket so he can get permits and do other favors. Now it seems he's preparing to bribe someone..."

Henry was listening closely now.

"...actually, some police officials who oversee the towing business to obtain some permits that we're told wouldn't be issued if things were on the up and up. That's why they came to us. To ask us for a wiretap on the lawyer to intercept the calls to the police."

"How come they came here for a wiretap?" Henry asked, breaking in on Matlin. "Why didn't they just go to the District Attorney?"

Matlin nodded. "That's a very good question. And there's an equally good answer."

The Special Prosecutor sat back in his chair. "At some point the lawyer..." Matlin turned to Corey. "What's his name? Robert Black?"

"That's right."

Matlin looked back at Henry. "At some point, Black bragged to the undercover agents about his political connections. He said he was close to Erin Galligan and several other politicians in Galligan's organization." Matlin lifted a hand. "You know who Galligan is, don't you?"

"Sure," responded Henry. "He's one of the county leaders."

Henry recalled Scoop Dixon telling him about Erin Galligan. He ran Bronx County like a feudal kingdom, leaving his stamp on the courthouses, on the city and state agencies, on virtually every public project or licensed business in his borough, to say nothing of the rest of the city. He was also a good friend of Governor Whelan, making him a force in the state as well as the city. Henry also remembered that Erin Galligan had outsmarted the Special Prosecutor's Office, turning aside an investigation into the fix of a case and outmaneuvering Howard Matlin.

"Galligan's the boss of the Bronx," said Matlin. "And Black's office is in the Bronx. Mike Lanigan, the Bronx district attorney is one of Galligan's people. So, the police are worried that if Black has the connections he claims to have, and Lanigan were to obtain the wiretap on Black, all it would take is a word to Black about being careful on the phone and the department's investigation would be history. They don't want to take that chance."

"So, I should get them a wiretap?"

Matlin nodded again. "And supervise it."

"Supervise?"

"Yes. As I was starting to say, if we get the wiretap, we run it." Matlin looked directly at Henry. "And we'll use it if we can. Which means, you'll keep a close watch for something that might give us another shot at Erin Galligan."

Involuntarily, Henry took a breath. This might even be a chance to go after a political clubhouse.

"I mean am I working alone?"

Damn, he thought, *why did he ask?* He might be told he was working with someone like Justin Cole.

"You'll be the lawyer. But I've asked Dan Nelligan to give you a hand. And Matt's available, if you need him." Matlin paused. "And I'll be here," he concluded.

Henry looked at Matlin, feeling relief from the Special Prosecutor's last words. Then something in Matlin's eyes caught Henry's attention. Something he had never seen before. Matlin was leaning forward, arms on his desk, face solemn, almost stern. Yet the determination, the fire he'd seen so often was muted. If Henry didn't know Matlin to be all business, he would have said the eyes looking across the big desk at him were almost bemused.

"I'll get started right away," Henry said, as he got up from the chair.

Henry had gone right to his group chief, Pete Flannery, and asked him for a wiretap application Flannery had done recently. As a model. While he'd worked on an eavesdropping application when they bugged Justice Bentzel's chambers, Henry had never done one for a wiretap. Now he was working on, and had almost finished, his draft of an application for a wiretap and a bug in the office of attorney Robert Black.

A knock on the door interrupted him. Dan Nelligan opened the door.

"Oh, hi, Dan. Come on in."

Dan Nelligan closed the door and sat down. He looked at the papers now spread across Henry's desk and smiled. "Getting started already, I see."

"Yeah," he said with a grin. "And I hear you're going to be helping me on this one."

Nelligan nodded. "Yeah." Then he looked out the window for a moment.

"What is it?" Henry asked. Nelligan seemed preoccupied by some thought. Henry felt a twinge of concern. Then Nelligan turned back to him.

"Look, I don't want to get you worried. But I don't want you to stub your toe in the dark either." Nelligan's hands lay quietly on the wooden arms of his chair in which he had seated himself.

Henry waited for his friend to go on.

"Perk," Nelligan looked directly at Henry. "You didn't get this thing by accident."

"What do you mean?"

"I mean that…how should I put it?" Nelligan's eyes dropped, then looked back at Henry.

"Some people up front didn't want you to have this one. When the request came in, your name was raised as someone who had some time. Nat Perlman didn't want you involved. Corey didn't, either."

"Why?"

Nelligan did not respond.

"I'm sorry to hear that," Henry said.

Nelligan shrugged. "Well, it's nothing personal. But they're both afraid you might slip up and embarrass the Office. But I know you won't," Nelligan went on. "I thought you ought to know where things stood, so you won't make a mistake." He folded his arms. "Don't forget, it was Howie's choice, and he didn't let anything stop him."

"What do you mean?"

"I mean Howie insisted on giving you this chance." Nelligan paused and looked at Henry before he spoke. "I think he really believes in you."

CHAPTER 24

"It's in."

Two days later Technical Services Chief Sammy Parisi flopped into a chair in front of Henry's desk, a broad smile on his face. "He even helped us." Parisi's smile widened, making his face resemble a child's drawing of a grin.

"What'd you mean, 'helped?'"

Parisi scratched his head, apparently pursuing some itch. "I mean he actually helped me install the bug."

Henry's face showed his confusion. Parisi relented.

"We went in as electricians, supposedly looking for a short circuit. I'd already put in the tap, and I was working on the bug when the attorney— what's his name, Black?—came in. He saw me trying to get to a ceiling light with a ladder his secretary had given us, but the ladder was too short. So, the guy goes to a closet and gets a longer ladder and gives it to me so I can get up to the light fixture and install the bug over his desk. And then he watches for a few minutes until he gets a phone call." Once again Parisi's grin divided his face in half. "I figure maybe we owe him for a quarter hour's work." He looked at Henry. "Maybe you should send him a check from the Special Prosecutor's outside labor fund."

Before Henry could respond, Parisi was out of his seat and at the office door. He looked back. "You should start getting stuff tomorrow."

He did get some "stuff," as Parisi had called it. But nothing very useful. Most of the day, Black was out of his office, apparently in court. During the two hours he had been in his office, he had spent most of the time working on some papers, producing on the bug only scratching noises and a few instructions to his secretary. The one call not immediately identifiable as a legitimate client was from someone who called himself "Cavaliere." As soon as he said hello, Cavaliere informed Black that "we got the information and we're working on the modifications." Black replied that he was glad, and the conversation ended.

But it was only the first day. Henry had twenty-nine more days on his eavesdropping order in which to obtain evidence against Black and the police he was supposed to be bribing. What Henry and Matlin were hoping for was that the bug or the wiretap would pick up a conversation about some other illegal activity within the Office's jurisdiction. Then they could not only renew the eavesdropping order for another thirty days but they could also expand the investigation into other areas of interest.

Three weeks later, Henry's great hopes seemed dashed. "I don't know what to say," he reported to Howard Matlin.

"It isn't your fault, Henry," responded Matlin. "I know that."

It wasn't. How could Henry have known that two days after Parisi had installed the wiretap and bug, Robert Black would take a vacation? Three weeks, he'd been gone. Twenty-one of the thirty days permitted by the warrant, and not a single useful conversation recorded. Still, he remembered what Nelligan had said of Howard Matlin: "He believes in you." He couldn't shed the feeling that he had let Matlin down.

"When's he due back?" asked Matlin.

"Monday."

"Well, let's see what Monday gives."

Monday gave nothing, as far as Henry could see.

Tuesday he finally picked up something. Black had agreed to "try his luck" with a building inspector. From the rest of the conversation, it was clear that Black meant to offer the inspector a bribe. But building inspectors weren't part of the justice system, to which the Special Prosecutor's jurisdiction was limited. So, the call was useless.

Wednesday, Black got another call from the person his secretary called "Mr. Cavaliere." Cavaliere told Black, "The financing is lined up. And I'm sure we'll deal with the waiver, so you don't need to worry." He said that he'd talk to Black later "about the next step." But there was nothing in the conversation to indicate what they were talking about or that it had anything to do with corruption.

The day had produced one interesting call, this time relating to the justice system. Black had agreed to help a friend "reach" a judge in upstate New York. But since the call pertained to matters outside the territorial jurisdiction of the Office, for Henry's purposes it was useless.

Now it was Thursday. And nothing. In fact, worse than nothing. Henry received a call from one of the police officials overseeing the towing investigation that had led to the wiretap. Black had just informed the police official that he had turned over the towing matter to another lawyer when he went on vacation and would no longer be involved. Thus, no calls to the police about bribes would be forthcoming. The period of the wiretap and bug was running out and Henry's big chance was turning into a dead end.

"What a bum break," he moaned, leaning back in his desk chair.

Dan Nelligan, sitting across the desk from Henry, shook his head and smiled. "You haven't exactly been showered with good luck," he agreed. "As I told you, though, my instincts tell me that this Cavaliere thing is something we ought to be interested in."

"I don't see how we can find out," Henry protested. "The guy calls twice. Once he says something about modifications. And then yesterday he talks about financing and waivers. Sounds corporate, not corrupt." Henry picked up a sheet of paper lying on his desk. "That's all that's here," he grumbled, pointing to the "line sheets," or daily written descriptions of conversations intercepted by the bug or the wiretap.

Nelligan didn't give up. "He said that Black didn't have to worry. Worry about what? I'm telling you, it smells funny."

"Well, I don't see it," Henry responded. "It could mean anything."

"When are you getting today's line sheets?" asked Nelligan, changing the subject.

"I'll get 'em tomorrow. Probably with nothing again."

Nelligan started to respond when the door suddenly opened, and investigator George Reed entered.

"We just got somethin' that might be interesting," said Reed, holding a tape cassette in his hand. "Thought you'd want to hear it right away, so we made a cassette."

Henry sat up sharply. He had almost forgotten that conversations could be recorded from the original tape onto cassettes and brought right into the office. In fact, cassettes were normally made only when a conversation seemed important enough to be heard immediately. So far, none of the Black wire conversations had fallen into that category.

As he put the cassette on a small player on his desk, he prayed that the conversation would give him something useful. Anything.

When Reed was seated, Henry started the machine.

"Sssssss."

"Tape hiss. Don't worry, it's coming." Reed nodded his head.

"Who?" asked a voice on the tape.

"That's Black," Reed said.

"He is?" There was surprise in the voice on the tape. *"Show him in."*

The noise of a chair moving preceded the voice of Robert Black speaking again.

"*Hey, Al. Nice to see you. What're you doin' here?*"

"*I got a little thing I wanna talk to ya about.*"

The voice was gruff and gravely, like a soft-spoken Jimmy Durante.

"*Somethin' I don' wanna talk about on the phone. Know what I mean?*"

"*Skkrtch.*"

"Must be moving a chair or somethin'," offered Nelligan.

"Yeah," said Henry.

"*I got a little legal matter I wantchya to handle.*"

The speaker was the person Black had called Al.

"*It's somethin' Erin's interested in.*"

Henry perked up. "Erin" had to be Erin Galligan, the county leader.

"*Sure, Al. What've you got?*"

"*You ever heard of an outfit called 'Ben-Evans?'*"

"*Repair contractor, aren't they? Do a lot of City work on machines and stuff?*"

Pause, perhaps for a nod from Al.

"*I think I met the president—whatever his name is...*"

"*Hammer. Saul Hammer.*"

"*Yeah. I met him at the club dinner last year.*"

"*That's right, he was there. Anyway, he's got a little problem you can help with.*"

Again, there was a pause, but none of the three men moved or spoke. Finally, Al's voice broke the silence.

"*Some asshole group of troublemakers've gone after an injunction. They wanna stop Ben-Evans from usin' their new facilities. They just moved into some*" *new garages and these turds are grumblin' because they say that the trucks and the machines and stuff are runnin' all night and keepin' everyone awake."*

"Are they?"

"Who gives a shit? This is business."

"If it's a commercial area, they don't have any problem."

Pause.

"Oh."

"Yeah, it's residential."

"How'd they get in there? Past the zoning rules?"

Pause.

"Oh. Okay, I get it. Go on."

"Erin wants you to get rid of the thing. However, you gotta do it."

Pause.

"It's real important."

Pause.

"'Cause Hammer's a big help at election time."

"Where're the papers? Have they been served?"

"Yeah. Hammer's got 'em."

A scraping noise indicated a chair moving.

"And he's expectin' your call."

Noises of persons moving, probably toward the door, followed. Then Black's voice was heard faintly, across the room from his desk.

"Thanks."

"Right. Call Hammer right away. He's there now."

"Okay."

Pause.

"Al?"

269

"Yeah?"

The response was faint, as though Al was leaving the room.

"Is there a fee in it?"

Another pause was followed by the sound of a door shutting. Al's voice spoke in a hoarse whisper, barely audible.

"Hmoo…wang…k a judgeship eryh…nn…ashey?"

In a moment, the door closed again and there was silence, except for the noise of someone walking.

"What'd he say?" asked Henry, stopping the machine.

"Something about a judgeship," Nelligan responded.

"Play it again," suggested Reed.

Henry rewound the tape a few rotations and pushed play again.

". . .expectin' your call."

The men sat, listening again to the noise of Black and Al crossing Black's office. Henry leaned forward and increased the volume. The two subjects went through their parting remarks. Then Black spoke again.

"Is there a fee in it?"

Three pairs of ears moved closer to the machine.

"Hairy kw. are…ker judgeship arwhea…nns k free?"

"Shit." Henry rewound it again and began to replay the parting scene. This time the volume was increased to its maximum which, for a small desk machine, was surprisingly loud. As Al spoke, the door opened.

"What the fuck is the noise?" It was Barry Conlon, his next-door neighbor.

Nelligan scowled darkly. Henry spoke as he stopped the machine.

"Sorry, Barry. It's a tape."

"Oh, yeah? What's it about?"

Nelligan opened his mouth, but Henry spoke first.

"We're not quite sure, man. But we gotta get back to it. Sorry."

Conlon looked surprised. Even hurt.

Now Henry wanted to say something. He wasn't in the habit of brushing his friends off. He didn't want Conlon to think he was trying to be a hotshot, or something. Then he glanced at Nelligan and Reed, who were obviously impatient to continue.

Conlon bailed him out. He smiled and shrugged his shoulders. "Sure," he said. "I'll get back to my sergeants." And he left.

"Try it again," said Nelligan.

Once again, the three men listened as Al spoke.

"*Whewyew anna...ake a judgeship arhwa...nna may kewphe?*"

"Screw," said Henry reaching for the rewind button again.

"I got it," said Nelligan.

"You know what he said?"

"Yeah. He said 'Hey, you wanna make a judgeship, or you wanna make a fee?'"

Henry sat for a moment, absorbing what Nelligan had said. Without a word, he replayed the remarks in question.

That was it! Nelligan was correct.

Henry's heart thumped. His throat tightened. He didn't know exactly what was going on, but he was certain that, whatever it was, he had stumbled onto something not only unexpected, but something that could be important.

"I think you're right," he said, clearing his throat.

"Yup." Nelligan turned to Reed. "Is there more?"

Reed nodded affirmatively. "Yeah, the phone call to Hammer to make an appointment."

Henry turned on the set again.

At six fifteen that afternoon, Henry was pacing back and forth in front of his desk, impatient for the investigators to arrive from the plant with the conversations recorded that afternoon. He looked out the window, down onto the buildings of Lower Manhattan, and the early blue shadows they cast in the fading light of the late summer evening. Picking out Hudson Street, he began to follow it up from what he figured had to be Canal Street. Tiny specks of red light moved in disorderly columns up the street, marking the many commuters, sitting in their cars, stereos alive, finally leaving their work behind on this Friday evening and heading home for the weekend. At intervals, the red specks paused to permit other red or yellow lights to cross their paths, before resuming their crawl northward through Greenwich Village.

From the 44th floor of the New State Office Building, the Village looked like an old movie being shown on a small screen. Appearing as a gap in the tall buildings spotting the rest of Manhattan, the crazy-quilt pattern of the Village's streets, with the low buildings and tiny chimneys, seemed like a last holdout, a dying voice of reason from the past, about to be absorbed and lost in metal and glass conformity. He wondered if that's what would happen to the ideas of the past, too. Would the sophistication of the great political thinkers—from Plato through Locke and Burke and Mill—would they all be superseded by the kind of minds that thought up one-size-fits-all?

Behind him, the door opened, and Henry started. Dan Nelligan entered, joined by Paul Ahern, who had been manning the plant.

"I got it," said Ahern. He stepped to the tape machine on Henry's desk as Henry returned to his seat. Inserting the cassette, he pushed the play button. "Take a listen to this."

The three men dropped into seats.

The sound of dialing.

"Supreme," said someone answering the phone.

"Is Mike there?" asked Black.

After a pause, a new voice answered. *"Pasco."*

"Mike? Bob Black."

"Hey, how ya' doin', Bob. What's up?"

"Mike, I got a case that they tell me has been assigned to Culligan. Defendant's name's Ben-Evans. Plaintiff's something called Good Nei…"

"Good Neighbors' Association." Mike laughed. *"Yeah, I know the case. I just got the papers."*

"Uh, um, who's available if Culligan doesn't get it?"

"But he already has…"

He stopped himself.

"What'd'ya mean?"

Mike lowered his voice.

"I mean if, uh, somthin' was, uh, real important to, uh, Erin, and, uh, Judge Culligan, uh…"

"Oh."

There was a long pause, as though Mike was thinking. Then he was heard again, his voice low.

"Well, actually, Culligan's been sick this week. So, er, maybe I could do somethin'."

"Like, who's available?"

Again, there was a pause, apparently this time because Mike had left the phone. In a minute, he spoke again.

"Hurd's available."

"Hurd? Oh, great! Fantastic! You can arrange it?"

"Uh, sure, uh…Erin knows?"

"I promise."

"Done."

"Thanks, Mike."

Pause.

"And Mike?"

"Yeah?"

"Don't worry, I'll take care of you, too."

The phone was hung up.

Nelligan and Perkins looked at each other.

"There's your renewal," said Nelligan. He was referring to the need to have gathered some evidence of criminality on which to base a renewal of the eavesdropping warrant. Then Paul Ahern forestalled further conversation by raising his hand as the tape continued with the sound of dialing.

"Brrrnng. Brrrnng. Justice Hurd's chambers."

"Hello, Sam?"

"Yeah, who's this?"

The speaker's manner was brusque.

"It's Bob. Bob Black."

"Oh. Howya doin', Bob? What can I do for ya?"

"Uh, Sam. Uh, you, uh, are gonna get a case that's being transferred over from Culligan."

"Whaddya mean?"

Sam was still curt.

"I, uh, just, uh, heard from Mike. It's comin' to you."

"So?"

"*Well, it's an injunction matter. The plaintiff's some group called Good Neighbors' Association and the defendant's the Ben-Evans Company. You know Ben-Evans, don't you?*"

"*I've heard of 'em somewhere.*"

"*Saul Hammer, he's the president.*"

"*Oh, yeah. I know Hammer. Wasn't he the guy who bought all those tickets to Erin's dinner last year?*"

"*Yeah. That's the guy.*"

"*And you're representing, what's it, Ben...?*"

"*Ben-Evans. Yeah, I'm representing them. And, uh, the thing I want to let you know is, uh, that, ah, well, this one's real important to Erin. You know what I mean?*"

Silence followed for a moment before Sam spoke.

"*I read you. I'll let his Honor know.*"

"*Thanks, Sam. And I hope I'll see you around the club soon.*"

"*Right. See you.*"

After the parties had hung up, the three men sat still. Henry's hands were on his desk, and he was looking at them. He could feel them beginning to tingle as the import of what he had just heard started to sink in. But it was Nelligan who spoke. Softly.

"That's the way it's done."

"Huh?" Ahern looked at Nelligan quizzically.

"That's the way a case really gets fixed."

CHAPTER 25

Now they were cooking. Henry was sitting next to Dan Nelligan in Howard Matlin's office, waiting for Matlin to get off the phone. Three days had passed since the investigators had intercepted the phone calls that saved his wiretap of Robert Black and launched him into an investigation that touched on the powerful political leader Erin Galligan. For two of the days, Henry had scanned the line sheets from the previous day's eavesdropping, only to be disappointed by the series of interrupted conversations. The law required that the investigators manning the plant discontinue recording any non-criminal attorney-client conversations, or personal calls as soon as they were identified as such. There had been one call from the mysterious Cavaliere. This time Cavaliere had told Black that "the specs are out, and things are moving again." Nelligan had again expressed his opinion that the Cavaliere calls were important. But Henry didn't see how they might help. Cavaliere might be fixing Black's car, for all they knew.

Then today, only a half hour ago, two events had propelled the investigation ahead and raised the stakes even higher. The first event was Dan Nelligan popping into his office with a piece of information.

"Good news, Henry," Nelligan said as he dropped into a chair. "We confirmed who Al is."

Henry sat up. "Who?"

"It's Della Bove."

It had been Matlin's theory, based on what he knew of the political scene, that the person called Al, who had met with Robert Black about the Ben-Evans case, was State Senator Alphonso Della Bove. Della Bove was the number two man in Erin Galligan's organization and, himself, a power in state and city politics.

"How'd you confirm it?" Henry asked.

"I got ahold of a tape of him speaking at some public hearing. There's no doubt. Listen."

There wasn't.

The second break came fifteen minutes later. Paul Ahern arrived from the plant with two cassettes of conversations intercepted over the wire that day. The first cassette began with a call from Justice Hurd to Robert Black intercepted that morning, and it was that cassette which was waiting to be played on the tape machine sitting on Howard Matlin's desk as soon as the Special Prosecutor got off the phone.

Matlin hung up and turned to Henry. "You have something you want me to hear?"

"Yes. Listen." Henry pressed the play button, and the sound began.

"Bob? Sam Lorraine."

"Hurd's law secretary," said Henry.

Matlin nodded.

"Hey, Sam," responded the now-familiar voice of Robert Black.

"The judge wants to speak to you."

A pause while Black waited.

"Bob. How are ya?"

"Judge, nice to hear your voice. To what do I owe the honor? Har, har."

"I understand you've got a client in the construction business."

"A couple of 'em, Judge."

"I mean home construction. Like building additions to homes, and so on."

"Oh, yeah? That would be Salerno Brothers. Louie and Sal. Why?"

"Well, I need a little favor."

A momentary silence.

"Sure. What?"

Caution appeared in Black's voice.

"Well, I'm fixing up a new room in my house. A sort of family room, I guess they call it. Nothing too big. But I've been getting estimates of eighty or ninety thousand for the job." He chuckled. *"That's a bit steep on a judge's salary, you know."*

Black joined in the laughter. It sounded forced now.

"So, I thought maybe you could help me out."

"Ah, ah..."

"You know. Maybe give the Salerno boys a call. I know who they are. They're good people. See if you can jiggle something out of them."

"Well, uh...sure, Judge. Uh, I, uh'll give 'em a call right now. Where are you? Oh."

He laughed nervously.

"In chambers, of course. I'll get right back to you."

After the conversation terminated, Henry looked at Matlin. The Special Prosecutor's jaw was tight, his eyes angry as he appeared to consider the significance of the conversation.

"Is there more?" Matlin asked.

Henry nodded. He pressed the play button again and sat back.

Matlin listened intently to the taped call of Black to his client. The lawyer spoke to "Louie" and informed him of the judge's request. Louie grunted a few times and said that he would speak to "Sal," presumably his brother, and would call Black afterward.

Now Matlin's lips were pursed. He was thinking hard.

"There's still more," Henry said, inserting the second cassette into the machine. He watched Matlin lean toward the machine.

"Hello, Louie?"

It was Black, receiving Salerno's promised call.

"Yeah. I talked to Sal. He agrees."

"Terrific."

"We'll take a look and giv'm an estimate. You find out when we can call'm at home."

"An estimate?"

"Of course, an estimate. We ain't payin' for the fuckin' materials. I don't care if the fucker's on the Supreme Court!"

Black chuckled.

"He is."

"What?"

"Never mind. Tell Sal that it's okay."

"But listen, counsellor."

There was warning in the voice.

"What?" asked Black.

"If we're gonna go a mile for this guy, you'd better make sure fuckin' Galligan comes through for us this time. No more nickel and dime shit for the fuckin' borough. Somethin' real big. A whole project, or somethin'. For the City. And with some real gravy in it. You hear?"

"I promise, Louie. Erin'll hear about it. And you won't be sorry."

After the parties hung up, Matlin reached for the button.

"Wait," said Henry. "There's more."

They listened to Black call Hurd's chambers and ask for him.

"Uh, Judge, it's Bob Black."

"Hey, Bob. You got something?"

"Yeah. But they wanna see the job first. And, uh, you, uh, you're gonna have to pay for, ah, materials, and that kind of stuff. You understand?"

There was a pause.

"You say materials?"

The judge's voice reflected a touch of annoyance.

"How much is that gonna be?"

"I don't know. They want to make an estimate. But I'm sure it won't be too much. Listen, they want to call you at home. Is tonight all right?"

"Tonight? Uh, no. I'm speaking at the County Bar Association tonight. Have 'em call tomorrow morning or, if I'm already gone, on Saturday. I'll be out Friday night, too. But I'll be home in the morning Saturday."

"Good. I'll tell 'em."

Pause.

"And, uh, um..."

"I've got the papers. It'll be okay."

A sigh of relief was audible on the phone.

"Great, Judge. See you."

They hung up.

"Is there more?" asked Matlin grimly.

"Just Black calling Louie Salerno and telling him when to call the judge."

At Matlin's signal Henry turned off the machine.

Matlin folded his hands. His lips were pressed tightly together. "There's your *quid pro quo*," he said at last.

"I know," agreed Henry. "The judge decides the Ben-Evans case Black's way and Black gets the judge a deal on his new family room."

"Ball breakers, aren't they?" laughed Nelligan.

"Huh?" Henry looked at him quizzically.

"The Organization. Galligan. They really squeeze it outta their people. Not only has Black gotta figure out how to put in the fix for Galligan's buddy, but then he's gotta pay for it himself by usin' up his own credit card with his client." He shook his head and laughed again. "Hard life, bein' a crooked pol."

Matlin broke in. "Salerno's calling the judge tomorrow or Saturday, right?"

"Yes," responded Henry. "I sure wish we had the judge's phone tapped so we could hear the call."

"You will," pronounced Matlin decisively. "I'll alert the Attorney General to stand by to sign the application and I'll tell our judge that it's coming. Can you have the application ready in an hour?"

The next morning, Friday, Henry was sitting at his desk, disappointed. The wiretap had been in since the night before but there had been no call from the Salernos before the judge had gone to work. Nor would there be that evening. The one intercepted conversation had revealed the judge's plan to go out to dinner directly from his office. If there was any call, it seemed, the call would come Saturday.

His door opened. It was Dan Nelligan, carrying two Styrofoam cups of coffee, obviously from the investigators' pot.

"Good morning," said Nelligan. "Any news?"

"Nope. The judge's gone to work, but no call."

"Too bad. Here," he said setting one of the cups on Henry's desk, "I brought you some coffee."

Henry eyed Nelligan closely. "You didn't make this stuff, did you?"

"Naw," Nelligan laughed, and sat down. "No call, huh?"

Henry shook his head.

"Well, it'll come."

"I hope so." Henry took a sip of coffee. *"Ough.* You sure you didn't make this?"

"Ah, come on. It'll put hair on your teeth."

"Yeah, I've heard that one before."

"I hear you had a tough time with the new judge."

Henry frowned. "Yeah."

It had been Henry's first meeting with Justice Albert Winerude, Governor Whelan's replacement for the retiring Justice Foster. Winerude had been a professor at NYU Law School and had become a judge only a year earlier. On the wall near his desk was a certificate showing him to have been Managing Editor of the *Yale Law Journal* and a photograph of some scholarly looking man who Henry assumed was one of the judge's own professors.

"The guy's still living in an ivory tower," said Henry, setting his coffee on the desk.

"Figures." Nelligan sipped his coffee.

"He can't believe that a member of the bar or, heaven forbid, an esteemed member of the judiciary could do something naughty." Henry leaned forward. "You know what he asked me about three minutes into our first conversation? He asked if I *really* believed what Matlin said—that there was corruption in the courts. Jesus!" He slapped the desk. "This is the judge who's going to sit on our cases and review our wiretap applications, and he doesn't believe there's any corruption?"

"But he gave you the warrant."

"Sure. For five days. Not thirty. Five. Including yesterday. If we don't get something by Monday, it's all over."

Nelligan shrugged. "Doesn't bode well for the future, does it?"

"No, I can't say it does."

Nelligan stood up. "Hey, are you goin' to the racket tonight," he asked.

"Racket?"

"Yeah. For Will Campbell."

"Oh, that's right. I'd forgotten." Henry remembered the retirement party or, as the cops called it, the racket, for Senior Investigator Will Campbell, who had suffered a mild heart attack and was retiring and moving to Florida.

"If you gotta work…"

"Nah," said Henry. "There won't be anything until tomorrow. I'll go."

"Hey, Perk."

"Hi, Barry."

Conlon leaned over and spoke *sotto voce*. "You want to come with Tony and me after this thing?"

"What's doing?"

"Tony DeLeon's girl—she's got a couple of nurses she works with coming over to her place later." Conlon's eyes wiggled as he spoke. "Might be interesting."

"Yeah, sure. Sounds good." Henry wasn't planning anything else. And maybe he'd get lucky.

Then, across the room, talking with Harry Rood, he spotted Sara Leventhal.

It was just a few months' short of two years since that bad night after the opera. But he still remembered.

Since then, though, Sara and Justin Cole had become an item. They were careful not to let it show in the office. But Henry knew that outside the office—which was still rare for Sara—they were together much of the time.

Of course, he was over Sara, he insisted. In fact, now he talked with her frequently in the office. About Office matters. The fact that every time he saw her, he still felt a little jolt in his stomach was something he had learned to ignore.

He turned away and took a swallow of his beer.

"Hey, Perk. What's goin' on?"

He started. "Oh, hi, Tim." Tim O'Leary. "Not too much. How about you?"

O'Leary grinned. "You wanna know?" he asked, a twinkle in his eye.

"Sure."

"You're gonna love this one."

Henry always enjoyed O'Leary's stories.

"The other day, we get a tip on this City official," O'Leary began. "Some guy named Muscio. He's some kind of bigwig in the License Bureau."

Henry turned away from Sara.

"Anyway, Paul Meade—it's his case—Meade decides we start with a tail. Like the guy's supposta be meetin' the wrong kinda people for lunch."

Angie Palumbo joined them. Hearing O'Leary's story, he smiled and nodded his assent.

"So, Angie 'n' me, we pick the guy up as he comes outta his office this noon. You get the picture. Big Commissioner or whatever, and he's goin' off to some important lunch."

Palumbo laughed. Then he took a gulp of his drink. Vodka on the rocks, Henry noticed.

"So, we pick him up and start the tail." O'Leary gestured with his glass for emphasis. "Now remember, this guy's some big public official for the City."

"Right," Henry nodded.

"Anyway, we figure the guy's a politician so followin' him's gonna be a lark. Like how many politicians get tailed when they're goin' to lunch?"

Henry laughed. "In this city...?"

"Anyway, this guy Muscio. The commissioner. Guess where he goes first?"

"I give up."

"Around a revolving door. All the way."

"A revolving door?" Henry pictured a man in a suit whirling around a revolving door, emerging where he had just entered. He chuckled.

"Sure," explained O'Leary. "It's an old trick when you're tryin' to shake a tail."

"You mean he spotted you?"

"Nah. The mutt never spotted us. But the guy's as tail-wise as any wise-guy I ever ran into."

"Where'd he go?"

"That's the bad part," O'Leary laughed. "We don't know. He does this dance—shake the tail—for about fifteen minutes. Then, *shazam,* he disappears like a flash into a crowd near City Hall and we never see him come out the other side." O'Leary pursed his lips. "Lemme tell you, this guy's good."

"Yeah," said Palumbo. "A good, honest public servant. Spendin' his lunch hour duckin' law enforcement."

Henry laughed. "Sounds like you're onto a good one."

"You betcha."

They really were really getting a look at the other side of government, Henry mused. The side that the television cameras missed. Then he noticed that his beer was gone, and he excused himself to get another.

He saw Barry Conlon signal him. "Ten minutes," Conlon said.

Henry bent over and reached in the bucket for a beer. As he did, he spotted a familiar pair of legs. Long, shapely limbs, in sheer stockings.

He stood up, a dripping can of beer in his right hand.

"Hi, Sara."

"Still drinking beer, I see." She smiled.

"You want one?"

"No, Henry. You know I don't drink beer. But thank you."

He hesitated, trying to decide what to say.

Sara saved him the trouble. "I may have something going," she smiled. "And it might even lead to my—our—favorite district attorney's office."

Henry nodded. "That's good. What is it?"

She lowered her voice. The Office rules were still formally in place about not sharing confidential investigations. But Sara didn't seem to mind breaking them.

"Well," she began, "OCCB—the organized crime cops—have an undercover investigation into a Tutino family capo." She lowered her voice a bit. "Remember, that's the crime family my father was after when he got sold out."

"I remember."

"Anyway, this guy's name is Ralph 'the Shark' Castegglio. I love these names."

Henry laughed and nodded.

"Anyway, Ralphie has a lawyer out in Queens by the name of Remmelt, Harold Remmelt, who, our undercover guy tells us, was bragging to his client about his connections in the DA's office. Sounding interesting?"

Henry had to agree. "It does. Might lead to something."

"Well, it's a long story, but it looks like we are going to try getting a wire on this Remmelt lawyer." Sara smiled. "And it might get very interesting."

"Sure, sounds like it, Sara," Henry said. And then he looked into her dusty green eyes. But Barry Conlon saved him.

"Hey, buddy." Barry pointed to his watch. "We gotta get going." He wiggled his eyebrows. Then, hidden from Sara's view, he made a face at her back. "Come on."

Henry went.

CHAPTER 26

Henry stepped off the elevator on the 44th floor at exactly eight o'clock the next morning. It was Saturday and there would be few people in the office. Few people to see the dark circles under his eyes from his late night in the pubs with Barry Conlon after the nurses turned out to be on duty after midnight. But it was also the morning that he expected one of the Salerno brothers to call Justice John Hurd and discuss construction of the judge's new family room and he wanted to be there when the investigators called in or arrived with results.

His first stop was the investigators' area, where he made some coffee. In a cabinet above the table where the coffee maker sat, he located a fresh packet of coffee and a filter. With a potful of water from the fountain outside the door, he went about brewing a pot of coffee. *Why,* he had always wondered, *did the investigators always manage to make such terrible coffee.* Perhaps it had something to do with the inky brown substance packing the crevices of the filter holder or with the smudges in the pot itself. Or maybe the unlabeled packets of coffee.

When the coffee was made, Henry poured himself a cup and set out for his office. He took the long way down the hall to the west corridor and passed by an open door where Scoop Dixon, the press secretary, was planted behind his desk, puffing on a cigarette.

"Scoop. What're you doing here on Saturday? Looking into Jimmy Hoffa's disappearance?"

"Hey, Perk. Hoffa? Nah, they'll find him soon in the off-ramp of some freeway. I'm here fighting our own fires."

Henry stepped inside. Dixon was wearing a burgundy short-sleeved polo shirt. His thick glasses sat on top of his small nose. At the moment, they were partly obscured by a cloud of smoke that hovered about his head. Seeing the smoke begin drifting toward him, Henry fanned it away. "Fighting fires? It looks more like you're starting one."

The press aide laughed and waved his hand through the smoke.

"So, other than your desk, what's on fire?" Henry asked.

The press secretary's grin disappeared. "Right now, it's a few brush piles." Dixon snuffed out his cigarette. "But maybe soon the whole Office of the Special Prosecutor."

"What are you talking about?" Henry removed some papers from a chair and dropped them to the floor. He sat down.

"The backlash. It's likely to happen soon."

"Backlash?"

Dixon nodded. "For now, a few potshots. Like Toby Copin saying that we're setting up judges we don't like and violating their rights. Like your Judge Bentzel. And Ferrante last April. And that judge on Staten Island we just indicted. He complains we use wiretaps."

"Well, we do," Henry laughed. "Anyway, Copin's full of bullshit."

"Of course, it's bullshit, but we have to reply. And every time we have to deny something, it gives the lies a little more credence."

"Oh, I don't know. Copin's been after us since Howie's first press conference. And we're still here."

"I know. But it's chip, chip, chip away at our image. That's the way it works. And Copin's not all. There's Donegan, too."

"Another asshole."

"Yeah, but also another chip. And I learned yesterday that the *Daily News* is doing an overview of the Office. They're gonna take the opposite tack—that we're not doing enough, like going after the big guys, the politicians. That we spend too much time on cops and the little stuff."

"You mean, they say we *should* go after politicians?"

"Yeah. And then when we do, guys like Copin jump in and say we're being political or targeting people we don't like."

Henry shook his head with a laugh. "We can't win."

Dixon's face turned grim. "Unfortunately, you may be right."

Henry didn't respond. He started to pull himself up from the chair. "Just tell them all to go fuck themselves."

Dixon smiled. "That's what I'm doing this morning." He sat forward and pulled another cigarette from the pack on his desk. He lit it, leaned back in his chair, and took a deep drag. Immediately he began to cough, exhaling the smoke in short blasts.

Henry waited for the coughing to subside.

"Sorry," said Dixon, exhaling sharply to clean out his lungs.

"I don't see it, Scoop," Henry began. "We're making real progress. The police department's already a different place. And we've bagged two crooked judges, some crooked assistant district attorneys, some court clerks, and a bunch of others." He paused. "And this case I'm working on now might even involve Erin Galligan himself."

Dixon nodded. "I know. But take my word. The counterattack's going to start getting under way."

Henry watched Dixon take another drag on his cigarette, though more gingerly this time. "It's enemy country out there, Perk. And the enemy outnumbers us. And they've got more guns."

Henry stood up. He didn't want to listen to any more of this. "Scoop, I've got to get to work." He stepped to the door. "I just think you're wrong." What he meant was, he *hoped* Dixon was wrong.

When he reached his office, Henry spotted a handwritten note someone had left on his desk. The conversation. It must have happened.

"George called," the note said. "They got part of one."

He dropped into his chair, holding the note. What in the world did that mean—"part of one?" He assumed that "George" meant George Reed, who was covering the plant for the wiretap on Hurd's telephone. But part of what? A conversation? Was it the anticipated but elusive conversation between the Salernos and Justice Hurd? And, if so, why only part?

A half hour later, his answer arrived. George Reed rushed into his office with a cassette fresh from the plant. He was wearing a blue work shirt and heavy green pants with a toolbelt around them. In the hand that wasn't holding the cassette was a blue cap. Henry could see the logo of Con Edison, the local power company, on the front.

After a brief hello, Reed placed the cassette into the tape player on Henry's desk. "Listen to it first and then I'll tell you what happened," he said.

"What is it?"

"It's a phone call. From the judge's house."

"Brrrnng. Brrrnng."

"Salerno."

"Hey, Sal?"

The voice was restrained, as though the speaker was trying not to be overheard.

"Louie?"

"Yeah. I'm here. And I looked it over."

"Oh yeah? How much, you figure?"

"Shit, Sal. The fuckin' guy wants like a whole new room and half a basement. I figure it'd be eighty, ninety grand, regular."

"Fuck."

There was a pause.

"So what'd'ya figure..."

A click was followed by silence.

Henry watched the tape continue to run without producing any sound. "What happened?" he asked after a few seconds.

"We got interrupted."

Henry saw the muscles around Reed's mouth suppress a smile. Henry's blood surged.

"What the hell's funny about that. That conversation was important. And how'd Salerno get to the judge's house without setting up the meeting in the first place?"

Reed's smile disappeared. "I don't know. They must've arranged it earlier, before we got set up. Or over another phone."

"But what about this conversation? Why was it cut off?"

Once again Reed fought a smile. "I know it isn't funny, to miss an important conversation..."

"What the hell happened?"

"Well, we got to the truck about seven-thirty this morning."

"Truck?"

"Yeah. You know about the plant, don't you?"

"No."

"We're usin' a Con Ed truck. A repair truck. We've been there for a day and a half. We dug a hole in the road near the judge's house and we're sittin' out there next to it."

"Oh." A Con Ed truck. And a hole in the ground. Sammy Parisi was good.

"So, me 'n' Pat Mallon were on for the morning. We're in the truck. About nine or so, this van comes up in front of the judge's house. It says, 'Salerno Brothers.' A guy gets out and goes into the judge's house." Reed reached into the pocket of his shirt and pulled out a pack of gum. He offered a stick to Henry. "Want some?"

"No, thanks. So, what happened?"

Reed unfolded the paper on the gum. He removed the foil, rolling the gum as he did. Placing the gum in his mouth, he began to chew. Then he resumed his narration.

"Well, *slurmph*, about fifteen minutes, *tchrulpp*, after the Salerno guy, *gmmumph*, goes in…"

"George, could you chew the gum later—after you tell me what happened?"

"Sorry. *Gumlp.*"

Henry sat up with a start. "Jesus, did you just swallow it?"

"Sure. Why not?"

Henry made a face. *"Argh."*

Reed shrugged. "Anyway," he went on, "Pat's sittin' on the equipment when the light comes on. That's what tells you someone's picked up the phone and we can monitor."

Henry nodded.

"So, we flip on the machine. And you heard the call."

"But it was interrupted. How come?"

"While we were listenin', there's, all of a sudden, a knockin' on the truck. Like wood bangin' on the door. So, I had to open it."

"Who the hell was it?"

Reed started to smile but caught himself. "It was the cops."

"The cops?"

"Yeah. Somebody'd got suspicious. I figure because the truck was there a couple days, and no one was doin' any work after that first day. At least that's what the sergeant said."

"Sergeant?"

"Yeah, there was a sergeant and a patrolman."

"So, what'd you do?" Henry was beginning to picture the scene. Two guys in a Con Ed truck, pretending to be workers, but actually manning a wiretap. Two cops drive up in a patrol car... "They were in a squad car?"

"Yup."

"And the cop was banging on the door with his nightstick?"

"You got it."

"So, what happened?"

"Well, the sergeant, right off, he asks us for identification. So, we show 'em our phony Con Ed ID."

"What'd he say?"

"He seemed to buy it. Then he asks us what we're doin'. Only just then his patrolman looks into the truck and sees the equipment."

"The recording equipment? Shit. What'd he say?"

"Not really the recording equipment. Pat'd thrown a sheet we had over the tape recorder. But he can see that there's some kind of electronic equipment. Probably not what's in the usual repair trucks."

"So, what'd he do?"

"Nothin'." Reed smiled. "I threw 'em off."

"How?"

"Well, they asked what the equipment was, and I told 'em we were doin' some measuring of the static electricity in the ground. That's why we had the hole there. To measure."

"Holy shit. And they bought it?"

"Seemed to."

Jesus, Henry thought to himself. The cops must be dumber than he thought. Or, more likely, smarter than his investigator thought they were. And right now, there's probably a squad of them preparing to raid this obviously phony operation.

"What if they come back and check?"

"We're gone."

"Gone?"

"Yeah. I called Sammy. He arranged for another location. So, there's nothin' but a filled-in hole."

Henry reflected on the bizarre encounter for a moment. Then he remembered the interrupted conversation. He frowned. "Why didn't you turn the machine back on?" he asked.

"We did, but Salerno'd gone and, a few minutes later, the judge went out. With golf clubs."

"Shit." Henry shook his head. "Well, why didn't you leave the recorder on while you talked to the cops?"

Reed looked shocked. "It's not legal. You can't record if you don't monitor."

What could he say? It wasn't easy fighting guys who didn't play by the rules when you did.

Henry had to wait until Monday afternoon to report the truncated conversation between the Salerno brothers to Howard Matlin. By that time, Justice Hurd had called Robert Black so Henry was able to follow the interrupted conversation with a complete one.

Chief Assistant Nat Perlman was sitting with the Special Prosecutor when Henry arrived with his cassette player. Henry took a seat in front of Matlin's desk, next to Perlman and handed each a copy of a transcript he had had his group's secretary type. He played Saturday's interrupted conversation, then continued with the conversation intercepted that morning.

BLACK: Yes?

BLACK'S SECRETARY: Judge Hurd on the line for you.

BLACK: Thanks. [PAUSE] [CLICK OF CONNECTION] Good morning, Judge. Nice to hear from you.

HURD: Morning, Bob. Your friend was at my place on Saturday.

BLACK: He was? That's great. Glad to hear it.

HURD: Yes. Except they were a little steep in what they wanted.

BLACK: You mean in the price?

HURD: Yes.

BLACK: Oh. Gee. That's too bad.

HURD: Yes, it is.

BLACK: Well, uh, I think I'm going to see Sal today. If you want me to, I'll ask him about it.

HURD: I'd like that, Bob.

BLACK: You would. Sure. Okay. [PAUSE] Say, Judge, I was wondering…

HURD: It's all right. Don't worry.

BLACK: [SIGHS] That's great! Okay. And I'll talk to Sal.

HURD: Good. I'd appreciate that. I'll see you.

BLACK: Sure, Judge. See you around.

Henry turned off the machine. "What do you think?" he asked Matlin.

It was Perlman who responded. "You haven't got a case yet, if that's what you're asking."

Henry looked at Perlman, then back at Matlin. The Special Prosecutor leaned back in his chair, saying nothing. Henry's eyes flicked back to Perlman.

Behind Perlman, the windows were streaked with rain, spilling down the side of the building. Occasionally, the wind would whip against the panes, sending little rivulets of water sidewise across the face of the glass. Hurricane Esther, it had been called as it had driven furiously across Haiti and the Dominican Republic. By now, though, it was just another wet, unpleasant fall storm.

"You don't think so?" Henry was afraid this would be the response. Because he knew it was probably true.

"Look at what we've got so far," he ventured anyway. "We have Black representing someone who's a big contributor to the Galligan organization. He maneuvers the case to a judge who's part of the same organization, saying that the case is important to Galligan. Then the judge asks Black for a big favor—the new room—which Black agrees to do and puts pressure on his client to do the favor, promising that Galligan will reward his client with some city contracts."

Henry glanced at Perlman. Behind his steel-rimmed spectacles, the Chief Assistant's eyes were trained on Henry.

"Then," Henry went on, "you have Black telling the judge that he's done the favor the judge asked him to do—that Salerno will give him an estimate for materials only..."

"Not exactly," said Perlman. "Only that he'd have to pay for materials. He didn't say that he wouldn't have to pay for labor, too."

"Come on, do you really think the judge is supposed to pay for labor?"

"It doesn't matter what I think," Perlman retorted sharply. "It's what a properly charged jury would find was proven. Beyond a reasonable doubt."

Henry shrugged. He glanced at Matlin, but Matlin wasn't disagreeing with his chief assistant.

"But in the conversation that got cut off," Henry continued, "Salerno implied that it was a reduced-price job."

"Implied?" Perlman asked. "Who's going to testify to what Salerno implied? And how do you explain the judge's complaining in that conversation you just played that the price is too steep."

"Because the judge wanted it cheap. That doesn't mean he isn't getting a favor."

Perlman eyed Henry. Behind him the rain still streaked across the windows.

"Henry, you can't build a case on surmise and speculation. And your own opinion. That won't work." Perlman shook his head. "Even if you had the proof that Hurd got the job at cost, you still don't have a case of bribery. Because to prove bribery you have to prove that Black did what he did for the judge in return for Hurd's deciding the case in favor of Black's client."

Henry sat up. He turned to Matlin, who looked back at Henry.

"Nat's right," the Special Prosecutor said. "There's no doubt about what's actually happening here. But what you have so far is too diffuse. You need some firmer evidence to tie it down. "Matlin lifted his hands from his desk. "My advice is for you to go and get it."

Henry rose to leave.

"Oh," Matlin added. "Isn't your wiretap on Hurd over today?"

Henry nodded. "Unfortunately, yes."

"Get it extended."

"You think I can?"

Matlin smiled. "You filled in the blanks for us here. Do it in an application for Judge Winerude and, yes, I think he'll extend it."

CHAPTER 27

"What do you think about this Bregner thing?" asked Henry as he dropped into a chair in front of Dan Nelligan's desk. Although he was the number three investigator in the Office, Nelligan, by his own insistence, had a tiny office, just off the Special Prosecutor's office, away from the other investigators. It was unadorned by pictures or any other decor. "I assume you saw it." He pointed to the *Post* in Nelligan's hand.

"It means we take on another case," said Nelligan.

A little over a week earlier, an article in the *Village Voice* had claimed that a City Commissioner of Purchasing named Arthur Bregner had arranged to purchase an expensive and unnecessary fleet of cars from a company owned by a political colleague. The article suggested that a bribe may have influenced the purchase. No sooner had the story broken, than the media began demanding that Matlin investigate the matter.

Matlin responded that his jurisdiction was limited to the justice system and the law enforcement agencies. It didn't include the actions of city commissioners unless they had something to do with law enforcement or the courts.

The press took the hint and began openly calling on the Governor to sign a new executive order expanding the Special Prosecutor's powers by superseding the District Attorney's in more types of corruption. Faced with growing demand, Governor Whelan finally agreed to have his counsel draft an order so that Matlin could look into the Bregner matter. Now the superseder had been signed, narrowly restricting the expansion of jurisdiction to matters of City government already under investigation by the Special Prosecutor at the time of the superseder. Thus, the Governor avoided stepping on too many toes.

"Whelan's a good politician," Nelligan said. "He knows how to avoid problems. So, he made sure that the superseder he signed would apply to nothing much beyond this Bregner matter."

The new case was assigned to Justin Cole, who enthusiastically undertook it.

"MATLIN INDICTS POLITICIAN, COMMISSIONER."

The story was in the *Times* under the byline of Toby Copin. It told of the new case involving Commissioner Bregner.

"How did this get in the paper?" Henry asked as he squeezed into Scoop Dixon's office where Larry Santarella and Steve Wonderman were already standing. "And what's this about an indictment?"

"Yes," said Dixon. "Bregner was indicted yesterday."

"But it hasn't been announced. I didn't even know it. So how did it get into the newspaper?"

Dixon nodded. "That's what Larry and Steve were just asking."

"So, it was a leak?"

"Not exactly," said Dixon.

"Then what was it?" queried Steve Wonderman.

"It's pretty obvious," Dixon responded. "Max Olman represents Bregner. And he knew about the indictment."

Henry winced. The ubiquitous Max Olman, who was now chairman of the Criminal Courts Committee of the Bar Association.

"But why would he tell on his client?" Henry asked. "Especially if we could trace it back to him?"

"And what if we do?" responded Dixon. "He'll simply deny it. And the reporter isn't going to reveal his source. Especially this one."

"So why did he do it?" asked Santarella.

"Because it gives Olman a weapon to attack us. It's an old defense law-yer trick. The attorney leaks the story, then, when the indictment at issue is announced, he attacks the prosecutor for leaking the story and asks the court to dismiss the indictment for prosecutorial misconduct."

"You really think he'll do that?"

He did. All the papers, reporting on the Special Prosecutor's indict-ment of Bregner, gave space to the attack by Bregner's attorney, Max Olman, on Howard Matlin for leaking the story of the indictment before the arrests.

"Prosecutorial misconduct of the most irresponsible sort," Olman had dubbed it. "The Special Prosecutor should be punished for his misguided and heinous actions. And the indictment immediately dismissed."

The next day, Dixon told Henry, as they met in the hall, the City Bar Association President, Potter Wilberton III, had called Matlin to bawl him out for leaking the Bregner story. And Chief Judge Sammons did the same.

Henry merely shook his head and walked on.

Henry slid into the small two-person booth in the coffee shop off the lobby of the New State Office building. He intended to have a quick sand-wich by himself and read the *Post*. But then someone slid into the other seat.

"Mind if I join you?" asked Sara.

"No," said Henry, putting down his newspaper.

The waiter arrived and took their order.

"How are your political things going?" Sara asked.

"Okay. But more importantly, how is your wiretap on the mob lawyer going?"

Sara smiled. "We've heard some juicy stuff. Two things happened recently. This guy seems to be a trading floor for dirty deals." Then she scowled. "We're not onto anyone in the DA's office yet. But I might have been if it weren't for Howie Matlin."

"What the heck do you mean?"

"Remmelt was going to have dinner with someone from the DA's office—it might have been Ross himself—about one of Remmelt's cases."

"And..."

Sara took a breath. "Howie stopped me from bugging the table."

"Why?"

"Because..." She lowered her eyes, then looked back. "Oh, it doesn't matter."

"Yes, it does. What happened?"

Sara's jaw firmed.

"Sara, what happened?"

"Matlin found out that I was about to submit an application for a bug. I knew where they were meeting, so I prepared to listen in."

"Howie found out? You mean you hadn't cleared it with him?"

Sara looked into Henry's eyes. "No, Henry. I've told you many times before. I know what I'm doing. I don't need someone holding my hand. Like you do."

Henry ignored the insult and continued. "What happened?"

"It turns out that our judge, Winerude, was out sick that day and Howie said that my application for the bug would have been passed on to another judge. Maybe one who wouldn't keep it quiet. So, Howie pulled my application, and I didn't get my bug."

Henry waited a moment to respond. "Sara," he said, shaking his head. "It sounds to me like Howie didn't undermine you. I'd say Howie might have saved your investigation."

At this word, Sara's face reddened with anger. "Don't you talk to me about being saved, Henry Perkins. I don't need saving and I don't want to be saved."

Henry shook his head silently. Same old Sara, he said to himself. Then she began to rise.

"Wait a minute, Sara. You haven't told me about the second thing that happened."

Sara hesitated. Then she sat down again.

"Well, we intercepted a fix on a murder case. Or an attempted murder case."

"What? Murder? What do you mean?"

Sara relaxed as she went on. "Remmelt arranged a bribe with a judge named Ryan in Brooklyn. Fifty thousand dollars. Some coke dealer named Johnson is being tried for attempted murder and Remmelt is his lawyer. But the fix is in now and Johnson is going to be acquitted after trial. He'll waive a jury, of course."

"Wow." Henry's face lighted up. "That's a great case."

Sara shook her head. "Good and bad."

"Why bad?"

"Howie has laid down the law. We can't let the guy be acquitted. Double jeopardy would apply, and the guy could walk."

Henry thought a moment. "I guess he's right. But why is that a problem?"

"Because it puts a time limit on the Remmelt investigation. I can't do anything about the bribe in the Johnson matter without revealing the source of our evidence. When I do, it will reveal the Remmelt wire and eliminate my chance to get into the DA's office. So, I only have until the Johnson trial to have the wire."

"When's the trial?"

"As of now, it's scheduled for some time next May. But it's likely to be moved up sooner."

Henry considered the situation. "Hmmm. That gives you about five months at best, I guess."

"Hi, Ed," said Henry, as he saw the Chief of Appeals walking down the hall with Justin Cole. "How did the argument go? I really wish I could have been there."

Scanlon had just that morning finally argued the appeal on the conviction of Justice Morris Bentzel, the judge whom Cole and Henry had caught in a sting operation shortly after Cole had joined the Office. Although Henry had helped Matlin at trial convict Justice Bentzel almost a year ago—and even worked on the appeal—he could not attend the oral arguments before the Appellate Division since Judge Winerude had directed that he be in court that morning with the required notice about the Hurd wiretap.

Just as Scanlon was about to answer Henry, Scoop Dixon walked by.

"Well, Scoop," said Cole, as the press secretary stopped. "You would have loved the expression on Mossman's face this morning when he stuck his foot in his mouth."

Dixon looked at Cole with a puzzled expression. "Who's Mossman?" he asked.

"He was one of the judges on the Appellate Division panel that heard the Bentzel appeal this morning."

"Oh, did you argue it?"

"No. Ed did. But I was there."

"What happened?"

"Well, they were giving Ed a hard time. You know, the usual stuff. About putting a false case in their court system."

"Yeah," said Dixon scowling.

Cole waved a hand dismissively. "I mean, how else are we going to catch a judge red-handed?"

"So, what happened?"

"Ed argued that this case was no different from an undercover case going after drugs."

"Yeah?"

"Well, Mossman—he was the one giving Ed the worst time. Then Ed says, 'This court has sanctioned undercover operations in many areas,' but Mossman cuts him off and blurts out, 'But it has to stop somewhere. And I say it stops at the courthouse steps.'"

Cole smiled broadly. "Then he realized what he'd just said, and he turned red. And that was the last we heard from Justice Mossman."

"This morning," said Dixon.

"What do you mean?"

"This morning."

"Here." Nelligan handed Henry a beer. It was quiet that afternoon in the Lion's Roar. Only a handful of people stood at either end of the multi-bay bar, well away from Henry and Nelligan. The jukebox was playing softly for the time being. In a half hour, the place would explode, and the volume of the music turned up. But for now, it was possible to talk.

"Thanks." Henry took a sip. Then he put down the mug. "So, what'd you want to say to me?"

"I've been looking over the line sheets, Perk. I see Black's gotten more calls from Cavaliere."

"Yeah. But I still don't see anything there."

"I don't know. My nose twitches. I don't think it's nothing. I think there's something there we ought to know about."

"I'll tell you what," Henry said smiling. "If we ever find out who Cavaliere is and he's somebody we should have been after, I'll buy you a martini. And if he's not..."

"You've got a deal," Nelligan offered. "A double."

"Deal," said Henry, clinking his mug against Nelligan's.

CHAPTER 28

Henry sat down at his desk and shook his head. In his hand was the extension he had been able to get of the wiretap on Justice Hurd for five more days.

"That gives you through Saturday," Judge Weinrude had cautioned Henry. "And barring something extraordinary, that's all."

Well, at least he had a few more days. His thoughts were interrupted by his door suddenly being opened. Barry Conlon.

"Aha, Perkins, old man. Stay seated. I've got a question for you."

"Wha…?"

"I see you have a worried look on your face." Conlon lowered his eyebrows in mock scrutiny. "A worried look I've seen many times before."

Conlon clearly had something on his mind. He dropped into a chair. He was holding a blue and tan paper container of coffee.

"Well let me give you a hint. Do the letters F-I-A-U bring a cloud to your eyes? Field Internal Affairs Unit?"

Henry smiled at the mention of the now-dissolved internal affairs unit charged with ferreting out corruption in the police precincts. It had often seemed more of a hindrance than a help. "Yup," he responded.

"And were there times," Conlon continued in his sardonic tone, "when, having locked in on the nefarious activities of some errant officers, you enlisted the assistance of the troops from the F.I.A.U., only to find that somehow your targets kept just out of reach and, no matter what you did, the evidence eluded you?"

"More than once. Why?"

Again, the hand went up. "And, in your many frustrated efforts, did the name of one Sergeant Edward Pelton of the F.I.A.U. become associated in your mind with said failures to make cases?"

Henry laughed. "Pelton. Wasn't he the jerk who went canvassing bars asking the bartenders if they paid off the cops?"

"Among his other activities, yes." Conlon raised a finger, "But maybe not because he was a jerk."

"What?"

"It appears that the good Sergeant Pelton had other motivations."

"Why? What happened?"

Conlon crossed his hands on his lap, smiling as he did. "Yesterday, we turned another key sergeant in my sergeants' club case. One of the coordinators, who helped run the thing. The one responsible for seeing that the group could continue taking their bribes in peace." Conlon wiggled his eyebrows. "The one who had the responsibility for arranging to protect the other sergeants while they were selling protection to the crooks."

Henry was starting to imagine where he was leading.

"And his answer was none other than our good Sergeant Pelton."

"You mean the sergeants' club was paying Pelton for protection?"

"Exactly. Pelton would report to Feeney—he's the coordinator I just turned—when the F.I.A.U. got any complaints on that precinct. And, for his part, Feeney would hand Pelton a wad of cash each month. Nice arrangement, huh?"

"Jesus. So, the anti-corruption guys were in on the corruption, too."

Conlon smiled broadly. "Now are you beginning to understand the reasons why you never seemed to make a case with the F.I.A.U.?"

Henry took a breath. "It gets worser and worser, don't it?" he sighed.

"Dan," said Henry, calling Nelligan two days later. "Come here; Mallon's got something you should hear."

A few minutes later, Dan Nelligan joined Pat Mallon in Henry's office. Henry turned on his tape machine.

"Hello."

"Hey, Bob. It's Al."

"Della Bove," said Henry.

"Hi, Al. It's in the works."

"Nah, I'm not callin' about that. I've got somethin' else. I need your help. Somethin' like those permits you got for that towin' outfit. I can't talk on the phone."

"Yeah?"

"And I've got another thing, too. To talk to you about. Can you come over today? Say at four?"

"Sure."

"Great. Gotta go."

He hung up.

"What do you think?" asked Henry.

"I'm not the lawyer; you are."

"You mean…?"

"Why not?"

Henry sat back in his chair and looked up at the ceiling. Eavesdropping on a political leader. But he wasn't sure, even if he did have probable cause, that he had time enough to get a bug in Della Bove's office before the meeting.

Henry put the cassette player on Matlin's desk. "With Della Bove's mention of the towing permits, I was able to make out probable cause and get a wire on Della Bove. But it wasn't in time for the meeting with Black. So, here's something to indicate what was discussed in the conversation we missed."

Matlin nodded.

Henry turned on the machine.

"Yeah."

It was Della Bove picking up his phone.

"With Della Bove's mention of the towing permits, I was able to make probable cause to get a wire on Della Bove. Listen here."

"Al?"

"Yeah, Erin."

"Al, I got a problem. And an idea."

"Shoot."

"I'm dumping Colonna."

"I understand."

"Too damned independent."

"I agree. So, who's the committee gonna back?"

"What about your boy Black?"

"Jesus, Erin. You only just talked to him about Civil Court. For next year. You think you oughtta send him right to Supreme? What about all the guys on Civil who've been puttin' in their time?"

"I know. But Black's doin' me a big favor with this Ben-Evans thing."

"Jesus Christ, Erin. You're talkin' on the phone."

"So what? You think that jerk Matlin's listening?"

"Erin..."

"Okay. Anyway. I'd like to talk to Black. Would you have him see me? Let's see...at two today?"

"Okay."

Pause.

"But you're sure you want to give it to Black?"

"Al. How long have I been county chairman?"

"All right, Erin," Della Bove sighed audibly. *"I'll have him there."*

When the parties hung up, Matlin stopped the machine. "That's all, I assume."

"Yes."

Matlin looked sternly at Henry. He looked at his watch. "The meeting's in less than two hours."

"Unfortunately, I don't think we have probable cause for a bug on Galligan. I'd hoped that Black and Della Bove would say something that might give it to me."

"I take it they didn't."

"No. Della Bove just left a message for Black to see Galligan at two."

Matlin sighed and wiped his eyes. "Well, let's hope that whatever Galligan says to Black turns up on the other wires."

Henry removed the tape from the machine and prepared to return to his office. He felt chagrin. As he reached the door, he heard the Special Prosecutor speak.

"It's not easy, is it, Henry?"

He looked back and saw Matlin with a small smile on his face.

"No," he responded thankfully. But he remembered his grandmother saying that even God's patience ran out at some point.

The next few weeks with the new Della Bove wire were like a country carnival for Henry. With the elections upcoming, there were numerous conversations about who were being made judges and even what they would have to pay for it. Somebody named Wanders was going to pay $50,000 for a judgeship. Another person named Higgins, who had done the Committee some favors, was being considered for less. There was a large government grant coming into Galligan's organization that was supposed to be for a senior citizen's center called Overland. Then there was a guy named Karl who needed "help" on a case he had in court. And one conversation was even closer to home. Someone named Mac asked if Della Bove could get him a piece of the air conditioning maintenance contract in the New State Office Building. Henry realized that they were talking about his building. The one in which the Special Prosecutor had his office. Politics was everywhere, even in their own air conditioning ducts.

But there was one conversation intercepted that Henry listened to several times. It was one between Robert Black and Senator Della Bove.

"Ya knows I really appreciate Erin's asking me."

Black was addressing Della Bove.

"And don't get me wrong, Al. I'm not bitchin'. But twenty-five grand is a pretty big hit."

"It's peanuts."

"No, it's not, Al. Look, I've been doin' things for the organization since I got outta law school. I handled all those election cases. I did that thing for Jerry. When he got busted that time. I got Kenny off…"

"You got a fee for that."

"Okay. But not for Jerry."

Pause.

"And I'm not gettin' a fee for this Ben-Evans thing, either."

"And you haven't won it yet. Don't forget that."

"Look at it this way," Della Bove continued. "You're goin' to Supreme Court. You know what fuckin' Vince Tonetti's gettin' over in Brooklyn? This year. And for Civil. Fuckin' Civil?"

"No."

"One hundred big ones. A hundred grand from one guy. For fuckin' Civil Court."

Pause.

"It's true."

Pause.

"But I gotta admit…"

A laugh.

"…the guy is, I hear, a hard case. Dumb as dirt. Couldn't barely pass the bar. But, anyway, you oughtta be grateful that you gotta pay no more than twenty-five. For Supreme."

Pause.

"And don't worry, you can make it back. Once you're on the bench."

"Oh, yeah? What about Matlin?"

"What about him?"

"Well, he's not exactly sleeping."

"Listen here, old buddy," Della Bove's voice was cutting. *"The right people are out there waitin', just waitin' for Matlin to slip up. One little stumble and he's gone. Take my word."*

"I wish..."

"You can bank on it. A few months, maybe even a year. And color him dead."

Pause.

"Hey, it's after hours," Della Bove spoke brightly. *"How 'bout a drink?"*

Henry listened to that conversation several times. And it brought a knot to his stomach. Not the part about Black's buying his judgeship. But the last part. About them lying in wait for Matlin.

He had also been rather surprised when he played the conversation for Matlin. The Special Prosecutor was happy that Black had said enough to spell out the judgeship deal. But Matlin had treated the rest of the conversation quite casually.

"Hey, Perk. Sun's over the yardarm." Barry Conlon put his head in Henry's office. Henry could see Larry Santarella and Marty Asner standing behind him. Asner lifted a hand as though hoisting a glass to his lips.

"Okay. I get the picture." Henry stood up and walked toward the door, on the back of which his coat was hanging.

The next afternoon, Henry leaned forward, turning on his tape machine. "Now what do you think about this conversation?"

"Hi, Al. It's Erin."

Nelligan nodded, pursing his lips as he did.

"Hi. How's it goin'?"

"Not so well, maybe."

Della Bove's voice dropped. *"Whaddya mean?"*

"Our little thing's taking too long."

"Listen, Erin. The only thing I'm worried about is Michigan and the Canucks. And the spics oughtta take care of that."

Nelligan hit the stop button.

"What're you doing?" demanded Henry.

"What did he say, 'spics?'"

"Yeah. Italians or Puerto Ricans, maybe he means."

"No, I don't think so. It doesn't make any sense." Nelligan hit the rewind button for a moment. Then he began playing the tape again.

"Listen, Erin."

Nelligan put his ear closer to the speaker.

"The only thing I'm worried about is Michigan and the Canucks. And the specks oughtta take care of that. Our guy will see to it."

Nelligan stopped the machine again.

"Sounds like 'spics' to me," said Henry. "That or 'specks.'"

"That's it. 'Specs.' Maybe specifications?"

Henry shrugged his shoulders. "None of it makes any sense to me yet," he commented, reaching for the play button.

"Maybe," Erin continued, *"But anyway, I want to meet our guy. So, I want you to get him to Ruggiero's. Next Tuesday at seven. Sharp."*

"Why not? It can't hurt."

Pause.

"Black, too?"

"Nah. We don't need him. He's done his part."

"Okay. I'll set it up. See you then."

When Henry turned off the machine, Nelligan spoke. "What do you think it is?"

"I don't know. Maybe the Ben-Evans deal?"

"No. Black would be needed for that."

"You probably think it has something to do with Cavaliere."

Nelligan laughed. "Maybe it does. Maybe Cavaliere's 'our guy.'"

"So, what do you think we should do?"

"I think we gotta cover it."

"The dinner?"

"Yeah."

"Will you handle it?"

Nelligan nodded. "I'll have to talk to Matt."

CHAPTER 29

"We didn't get it all," said Pat Mallon. He was giving a report on the dinner at Ruggiero's, which he had covered with a young female investigator, Nancy Gravett. "We got there on time, okay, but the place had screwed up our reservations and we had to wait. So, we didn't get seated until the subjects were halfway through dinner. And then we weren't anywhere near them."

"Couldn't you walk by their table?"

"We both did. But we didn't hear anything except someone telling a joke and something about the Giants' game."

"Damn." Henry shook his head in disappointment. But his mind was not on the dinner meeting. He was still rehashing the unpleasant confrontation that morning in Howard Matlin's office.

"There's no way we can get him to give us at least one more extension?" Henry had asked Matlin. "Or at least delay notice a bit?"

He had just admitted to the Special Prosecutor that the deadline for getting the court to extend the time to notify Justice Hurd that his telephone had been tapped had been missed and Justice Winerude had ruled as the law required. The law allowed such notice to be delayed in certain circumstances, but the time limits for obtaining and renewing the extension were strict. Meanwhile, Henry, while eagerly following up on several proposed judgeship deals revealed from the Della Bove wire, had overlooked the deadline.

Instead of answering, Matlin abruptly handed Henry the sheet of paper he was holding in his hand. "Read it again," he said.

Henry did. And it still concluded with the same words: "The order of this court extending the time to give notice of eavesdropping to Honorable John Hurd having now expired, the People are hereby ordered to give written notice to the subject of said eavesdropping, including the dates thereof. The notice is to be given within ten days of the date hereof."

Henry had looked up again at Matlin. What greeted him was not warmth. Nor was Nat Perlman happy. Perlman made no effort to hide his dismay.

Henry had wanted to argue but he couldn't. He *had* screwed up. Within ten days, he would have to tell Justice Hurd that the Special Prosecutor's Office had tapped his phone. That information would undoubtedly spread through the courthouse and even into Galligan's organization. It would likely cause Henry's other wires to dry up.

"…Horseman. Environmental Protection."

"Huh?" Henry's attention returned, but he realized that he hadn't heard anything investigator Gravett had just said. He looked at the young investigator who had accompanied Pat Mallon to Ruggiero's as his date. She couldn't be more than twenty-three, but she seemed so much wiser than most of the investigators in her age range. She'd only been working with him for a little over a week now. In fact, when she had been assigned, Henry wondered if it had been intended as a put-down or a joke of some kind by Matt Corey since he knew that Corey had made the assignment, and he believed that Corey did not approve of women investigators. Now, after just two meetings, he was convinced that Corey had inadvertently done him a favor. The joke was on Corey.

"I'm sorry, my mind drifted off." He looked at Gravett. "What did you say?"

Gravett for an instant looked puzzled. Then she resumed. "We identified the third person with Galligan and Della Bove. Or, at least, the car driven by the third person. We confirmed the person himself today."

"Who was it?"

"A city commissioner named Carl Horseman. He's a Deputy Commissioner-Engineer in the Department of Environmental Protection."

Henry recalled the investigation into summons-fixing in a branch of the DEP that the Office had conducted shortly after he had joined. But it couldn't have anything to do with that.

"You have no idea why...what's his name?"

"Carl Horseman."

"Why he was there?"

She shook her head. Mallon did likewise. Just then the door opened, and Dan Nelligan came in.

"What's up?" Henry asked. Nelligan held up a newspaper and glanced at the two investigators.

Henry looked at Gravett. "Give me a copy of your report, would you?"

"Of course," said Gravett, rising from her chair. Mallon followed her out.

"He did it," Nelligan said, handing Henry the afternoon *Post* opened to an inner page. Henry looked at the headline, "Environmentalists Lose One." The short article reported on a decision by Justice John Hurd denying an injunction sought by the Good Neighbors' Association against the Ben-Evans Company. Environmental advocates, the article noted, had hoped that the injunction would aid the growing attack on noise pollution. "A setback for the environmental effort," the article concluded.

Henry should have been pleased since the decision was necessary to show that Hurd was taking bribes. But he knew they still needed some more firm evidence to bring about an indictment and a conviction. And he knew that his chances of getting that evidence were diminished by what was coming. In less than two weeks Henry would have to give Justice Hurd notice that his telephone had been tapped and he knew that his best source of information—the wiretaps—would probably stop producing evidence. The fact that Hurd had performed his part of the transaction with Black now seemed hollow.

"Abso-goddamned-lutely nothing!" Henry wailed.

Nelligan shrugged his shoulders. "Doesn't surprise me."

Henry was complaining of the sudden silence two weeks later on all his wiretaps and bugs. Only four days had passed since notice had been given to Justice Hurd of his phone tap, and not a reportable conversation had occurred on any of his wires. "How the hell did they get the word around so fast?"

"That's why they call it an 'organization.'" Nelligan's smile was thin, but his logic undeniable.

"So, what do I do?"

Nelligan nodded. "I think you should talk to Howie. And I think I know what he'll say."

"Okay, Dan, it's in your hands. Get him in here."

Nelligan rose and headed for the door. Matt Corey remained seated, as did Matlin, who had asked Nelligan to approach Robert Black and convince him to meet with Matlin. Since the wiretaps and bugs had gone silent, it was the only hope for continuing the investigation.

Henry knew that the evidence generated so far would give Black serious reason for concern. His bribery of City officials in connection with the towing permits, along with two or three similar matters picked up by the wiretap and bug, were almost certainly enough to justify a conviction and disbarment. Black's agreement to pay for his judgeship and, perhaps, his approach to Justice Hurd, were good cause for his concern, as well. Still, Black was tough, and Henry was glad that it wasn't he who had to convince Black to come to the Office or to try to turn him.

"He's outside," said Nelligan.

"Bring him in," Matlin directed, shifting in his chair.

Henry took a deep breath. His heart was pounding. He recalled his previous failure when he confronted Detective Jack Keene. Fortunately, it wasn't he, but Matlin, who was going to look Black in the eye.

The door opened.

"Howard Matlin, this is Robert Black." Nelligan introduced Black and immediately took a seat.

The newcomer's eyes scanned the room, then came back to rest on the seated figure of the Special Prosecutor.

"Sit down." Matlin spoke gently but did not rise or offer to shake hands.

The lawyer looked about him, his fear apparent, but being fought back by an assumed air of confidence. "This is everyone?" he asked.

Matlin did not answer, but merely nodded toward the empty chair.

Henry took the opportunity to compare his vision of the man whose voice he had listened to for several weeks with the reality. He had been partly correct in his assumption. In coloring, skin, and hair, Black was about as expected. His skin was pale, while thinning black hair was left long on one side, to be brushed across the balding pate in a vain attempt to cover the evidence. His eyebrows were dark and full, hovering over sharp eyes inset deeply between high cheekbones. The nose was angular and extended out in an odd upward curve that, for a moment, reminded Henry of cartoonists' caricatures of Richard Nixon. Most startling was Black's size. Rather than slight and athletic, as envisioned, Black's small-framed body was pudgy, almost fat, as though, for the past several years, he had done little more for exercise than lift a glass or a fork.

When Black was seated, Matlin began. "You know why you're here," he said, putting it more as a statement than a question.

"No," said Black with challenge in his voice. He seemed prepared to joust with Matlin.

Henry looked at Matlin. His countenance had altered. The jaw was now firm, the mouth sternly straight. Into Matlin's eyes had come a fire, burning with anger and with condemnation. It was not a look Henry would like to receive. Apparently Black wasn't comfortable with it either.

"Well, uh, your man," he said, gesturing toward Nelligan, "said something about some permits. And, uh, some other matters." After mumbling his few words, Black sat back, trying to become comfortable.

"You are here," Matlin said in a flat, but ominous tone of voice, "because you are corrupt, and you've been caught at it."

The lawyer's head jerked back an inch, then became still.

"You've bribed several public servants, including police officers, with payments in cash. You've negotiated other bribes with other public officials. On the evidence we have, you can be certain of spending several years in jail." Matlin paused. Then he went on. "Your election as a judge is history. Dead history."

Henry sneaked a glance at Black. At Matlin's last words, the color drained from the lawyer's face. Matlin seemed to have hit his mark.

The room was silent. Matlin sat for what seemed a very long minute. His face was unmoving. Lips remained as lines chiseled between granite cheeks and chin. It was an upsetting sight. But most frightening, even to Henry, who was not their object, were the eyes. They burned their way like laser beams into skull and brain, piercing gooey webs of excuse and justification, and passing through into the soul, where they branded corruption as surely as Hawthorne's stiff-necked Puritans had branded a scarlet "A" on Hester Prynne.

"There are three alternatives," Matlin finally said. "One is jail." His hand lifted slowly. "One is there." Matlin was pointing to the window. His meaning was clear. His hand dropped again. "There is one other way open to you." The Special Prosecutor folded his hands on his desk in front of him. Then he completed his thought. "You can co-operate with our investigation."

Henry could see that Black was probably trying to calculate what Matlin knew and how much it could hurt him. But he could also see that the lawyer was succumbing to the firepower directed at him from Matlin's eyes. Matlin must have seen it, too.

"You will tell us your understanding with regard to the purchase of your judgeship from Erin Galligan." Henry was surprised. Not because Matlin had probably revealed the wiretap and bug, but because his tone of voice had suddenly become almost gentle, as though speaking to a child.

Black's head snapped back this time. But there was more.

"You will also tell us," Matlin went on in the same tone, "your understanding with respect to the transaction you negotiated with Justice Hurd concerning the Ben-Evans case."

Black gulped, perhaps because he had tried to swallow and failed. Immediately he coughed several times. But the diversion left Matlin unmoved. And Black could see it.

"The rest you'll learn as we go on."

Henry glanced at Black. The lawyer's mouth moved slightly but did not open or try to speak. Matlin still had the floor.

"Now, can we get started?"

"I, uh, what do you mean, 'started?'"

For an instant Henry forgot the tense drama in front of him, reflecting on how much Black's voice sounded like the voice he had been listening to for weeks.

"Now." Matlin looked at his watch, then back at Black.

"But, I…"

Henry was waiting for Black to ask at least about a lawyer, or about the deal he could strike. He was surprised by the next words.

"I know a lot less than you think I do."

"We'll be the judge of that."

"But I don't want to be put in an impossible position. Where you expect more than I can give."

"As I said, we can judge that. We know enough already to know whether or not you're telling the truth. So long as you do, you'll be fine."

Henry's mouth was open. He shut it. He couldn't believe what he was hearing. No protestations of innocence, no demands for counsel, no anguished bargaining or bluffs or pleas or other artifices. Matlin and Black were calmly preparing for Black's co-operation as though they were teacher and student, not prosecutor and putative defendant. The next words surprised Henry even more.

"You'll start now," said Matlin. When Black said nothing, he went on. "Mr. Perkins here will speak to you. In his office."

Me? In my office? Matlin's words stunned Henry. With no time to steel himself for the occasion, Henry, not Matlin, was to debrief Black.

He certainly was prepared in an academic sense. After all, he had spent much of the last two days going over the Hurd case and the judgeship matter, as well as other matters that implicated Black, and he had prepared a list of questions for Matlin to ask, should Black turn. But never for a moment had Henry imagined that he would be asking any of the questions, especially after all the mistakes he had made.

He stood. "Mr. Black, please come with me." His voice sounded small after Matlin's. But it seemed to work.

They entered Henry's office, and Henry stepped behind his desk, dropping his file in front of him. It was Black who spoke.

"I suppose we ought to introduce ourselves, since it looks like we'll be working together." He put out his hand. "I'm Bob Black."

Henry was standing by his window, looking at, but hardly noticing the display of lights that was Manhattan at night. Not only Manhattan. From Henry's office, one could see the Bronx, Queens, Westchester, New Jersey, and, on a clear night like this one, even Connecticut. He sighed and looked up as Dan Nelligan returned to his office with two cups of coffee.

"I can't believe that's all there is," he said, taking his seat as Nelligan also sat down. "I must have blown it." He picked up his notes on the debriefing of Robert Black.

"Come on," said Nelligan. "Don't be so hard on yourself."

Henry looked up as Nelligan continued.

"Of course, the guy's holding back."

Black's debriefing had been a disappointment. He was able to say that Hurd had paid $20,000 for an estimated $80,000 job. That helped. And he also admitted that he "believed" that his arranging of the bargain renovation for the judge was to be a bribe. But he insisted that no one had ever said so, in words, especially the judge himself. That meant that Henry still needed something more to make his case.

Asked about his judgeship, Black admitted giving Della Bove $25,000 in cash, which Galligan had demanded, but he couldn't swear the money wasn't for campaign expenses. So proof was still needed here. Maybe the party records Henry planned to subpoena would show the actual expenses as less than Black paid. As to the many other deals Henry had overheard on the Della Bove wire, Black had heard "rumors" about them, but he had no proof.

Henry had scored one slight hit. Pressed on "Overland," Black admitted that the party organization had obtained a large federal grant for a purported Overland Senior Citizens' Center, the funds for which went into the party coffers. But that involved diversion of federal funds and would have to be turned over to federal prosecutors. Asked by Nelligan about Mr. Cavaliere, Black said that he was an old friend.

"He's got to hold something back," Nelligan went on. "Otherwise, he's got nothing to sell later on."

"But that's not the deal."

"No, but it's the fact."

Henry scowled.

"Don't worry," Nelligan said, "we'll get everything he has eventually."

It was Friday night two weeks later and Henry had just emerged from the Metropolitan Opera, where he had seen a satisfactory, but not great performance of *Don Giovanni*. Since it was a pleasant fall night, Henry decided to walk up Columbus Avenue to 81st Street to take a bus across to the East Side.

The air was cool and nearly clear as it brushed against Henry's face. Although Columbus Avenue was just beginning to upgrade itself, it still reflected the mélange of cultures and lifestyles that had characterized it for years. There were Juilliard students and dancers walking briskly along, and old kerchiefed ladies waddling down the street bearing mysterious half-smiles that seemed to suggest memories of small towns in Poland or Rumania. There was still the occasional tiny family-run grocery store or food stand featuring something called "cucafritas," which someone had told Henry were parts of pigs, like the ears or cheeks. And the venerable 67 Liquors stood stolidly at the corner of 68th Street and Columbus, which one of Henry's college classmates said employed one of the most knowledgeable wine merchants in the city.

He crossed 72nd Street, heading north. Suddenly, from a restaurant just ahead, a familiar figure emerged. Then another familiar figure. He grimaced and slowed down as Sara and Justin Cole stepped onto the sidewalk and turned north ahead of him. Holding back until he was certain that neither one had seen him, he followed them up the avenue.

Sara was smiling as she talked to Cole, making Henry feel a cramp in his stomach.

Just then Cole stopped abruptly and faced Sara. Henry lowered his head and stepped into a nearby doorway and listened.

"Come on, forget that damned mob lawyer for a weekend," Cole was saying. "Screw him and screw the City. Let's get the hell out of town this weekend." Cole waved a hand in front of Sara's face. "Hey. Didn't you hear me? Let's get out of town. You know, leave this miserable city for the country. Where the air is invisible. And smells funny. Like clean."

Sara shook her head and turned north again. Henry could not hear her response, but it clearly did not please Cole. Henry crossed quickly to the west side of the avenue, keeping an eye on the couple, then following them at a discrete distance.

They walked north to Sara's street and turned east. Henry watched as they reached her stoop. Sara walked up the steps toward the front door and Henry could feel his jaw tighten as he waited for Cole to join her. But Cole did not follow. He saw Sara turn and look back at Cole, saying something. Cole shook his head and began to walk away. Sara turned back, took out her key, opened the door, and disappeared.

Henry continued his journey to 81st Street. *Maybe there was still hope for him,* he thought. As he approached the 81st Street bus stop, Henry didn't notice, as he sometimes did, the shame of all the lovely old buildings near the Museum of Natural History which had been turned into seedy welfare hotels.

"Hey, I understand we got two more judges!" exclaimed Henry as he entered the cloud chamber of Scoop Dixon's office Monday morning. He coughed.

Dixon smiled.

"I hear Lou Morotti got 'em." Then Henry's face clouded. "Justin Cole didn't have anything to do with this case, did he?"

"Not that I know of."

"Good."

"Actually," Dixon began, "Lou's got a few more of these guys under investigation. They're in cahoots with a couple of auto insurance companies. Just like these two. The companies use their influence to make sure these judges are assigned to the insurance cases, so they don't have to have real trials. The judges then dispose of the constant flow of insurance cases at the amounts the companies choose. Meanwhile, the insurance companies provide the judges with amenities such as cars and vacations."

"Great. I gotta go congratulate Lou. Two judges in one scoop." He laughed. "No pun intended."

Dixon's response was to blow a large mouthful of smoke in Henry's direction.

"Gee, thanks, Scoop."

Dixon laughed. He took a drag of his cigarette, exhaling the fumes into the already saturated air. Then he began to cough. It started with a sharp bark from Dixon's throat. Then it moved downward in his respiratory system through his bronchial tubes and into his lungs, where a gurgling sound took over. The eruptions now emerged in great thundering waves, roaring up from deep below, blasting by the larynx and into the oral cavity, from which they were expelled into the air. *Carrounph, carrouggough. Courroonnggllgh.*

Given the violence of the expulsion of air and fluid, Henry fully expected to see the inner lining of Dixon's lungs, charred, black, and cracking, suddenly ejected onto his desk into the piles of papers. It was several minutes before the storm let up and the wheezing subsided. Dixon was left speechless. It was Henry who spoke.

"Hey, buddy. You'd better think about giving those things up. Don't you think?"

Dixon looked up at him woefully. With the tears in his eyes generated by the coughing, he looked as if he were about to cry. Finally, he responded. "If I just had a reason. Something more than my lungs."

"Hello, Henry," said Sara, looking up from her desk. "What brings you here?"

Having seen Sara Friday night on Columbus Avenue, Henry simply wanted to put her back into his comfort zone.

"I need a break from politicians, and I wondered how you're doing with your wire on that mob attorney."

Sara smiled. "It's getting interesting, in fact." She leaned back in her chair, put her arms behind her head, and looked squarely at Henry with her sea green eyes.

His chest tightened.

"Our undercover guy is talking directly to Remmelt now. The lawyer. And Remmelt has told him he can get things done in the DA's office. We're waiting to see if anything happens."

Just then the phone rang. Sara answered, then frowned. "Alright, I'll be right down."

She set down the receiver. "Matt Corey," she said with a grimace. "He probably wants to tell me how to run my investigation." She stood up, as did Henry. "Which he isn't going to do, whether he likes it or not."

She hasn't changed, Henry thought as he rose to go. *Sometime that pig-headedness is going to get her into trouble.*

CHAPTER 30

"Ow!"

The pain of bumping his knee as he rose from his desk was almost a welcome distraction from what he had just read—the decision of the Appellate Division reversing the convictions of Justice Bentzel and his law secretary, which had just arrived.

"This is outrageous! These damned judges!" he wailed to Larry Santarella, who happened to be in Henry's office with him when the opinion had been delivered.

He read aloud: "'This errant prosecutor injected into our courts a fictional and false case, thus deceiving, and undermining the efforts of the loyal and well-meaning authorities entrusted with providing justice to our citizens. It is a misdeed which cannot stand. Both convictions are hereby reversed and dismissed. As the revered jurist Louis Brandeis memorably declared: "If the government becomes a law breaker, it breeds contempt for law," Olmstead v. United States...' bumpety bump U.S. blah, blah, blah—what horseshit! Our most significant accomplishment, just tossed in the trash. How else can we catch a corrupt judge? These judges are as corrupt as Bentzel himself."

Angrily, Henry stepped into the hall as Santarella left. Immediately he encountered Justin Cole striding down the hall.

"I'm sorry," was all he could think to say.

"What concern of yours is it?" barked Cole. "You didn't do squat on it."

"What I did or didn't do is irrelevant. It's the Office and what we stand for that's really been hurt. The Appellate Division looks horrible."

"You wouldn't know the difference," Cole snapped as he lurched off toward Matlin's office.

Rejecting the notion of going to Matlin's office himself, Henry turned back toward his own door. "They have enough problems; they don't need to hear my angry two cents," he told himself as he pushed open his door.

Still upset, Henry sat down at his desk, and started reviewing the useless transcripts of the brief grand jury testimony of the Bronx clerk and Justice Hurd's law secretary. They had both refused to waive immunity and had given him nothing. The door opened and Nancy Gravett entered.

"Hi, Nancy," said Henry. "What brings you here. Did you get more on that guy in the restaurant?

"No." Gravett shook her head. "It's something else." She looked at the chair in front of his desk. "May I sit down?'

"Of course. I'm still wrung out about Bentzel. But sit down anyway." Henry put down the transcripts and looked at the serious face of the young investigator across the desk. "What is it?"

"It may have something to do with Erin Galligan."

Henry sat up. "Galligan? I'm all ears."

"I assume you know about Galligan's summer home."

"You mean up in Maple Hill, New York."

"Right. And I also assume you've heard the rumor about how he got that summer home."

"I think so. I heard that an informant told us that some contractor gave it to Galligan or sold it to him for peanuts in return for Galligan steering no-bid road work to the guy's company."

"Yes," continued Gravett. "But it happened too long ago. And it's apparently outside the scope of our jurisdiction."

Henry nodded. "Probably."

"Well, this thing might not be in our jurisdiction either, but it's fresher and it looks interesting."

"Go on," Henry said, leaning back in his chair.

Gravett handed Henry a white booklet. "I assume you've seen these before."

"A registration statement, it looks like. To register securities with the SEC."

"Yes. It's for a company called Andersen Sonar Corporation."

Henry started to open the booklet, then closed it and placed it on his desk. "Why don't you tell me what you've heard, first?"

"Right. Well, Andersen Sonar is a small company in, guess where, Maple Hill, New York."

"The great metropolis." Henry chuckled.

"Yes. All of about five thousand people, if that. Anyway, the company has been around for years. Made its mark during the Second World War, when it made sonar devices for the Navy."

"Oh, wait a minute," Henry said. "Now you're ringing a bell."

He had read in the *Times* just a couple of days before about the award of a multi-million-dollar contract by the City of New York to a small company in Maple Hill, New York. Having heard Della Bove mention Galligan's home in Maple Hill many times, the mention of Maple Hill had led him to read through the rest of the story.

The contract was an unusual one. Sometime earlier, the City had passed an ordinance reducing the permissible noise level in public spaces, including streets, plazas, building lobbies, and enclosed malls. Of course, Henry had chuckled at the time; nothing had been said about the subways.

As part of the proposed enforcement, the City had decided to purchase devices which would measure levels of ambient noise. According to the article, bids had been received from three companies: a well-known Canadian company involved in the audio business; a Michigan company that made measuring devices for many uses; and Andersen Sonar. It was Andersen which had just won the contract.

"Anyway," Gravett continued, "Andersen is owned—or was owned—by a family named Andersen. Which is now old man Oscar Andersen and his daughter."

"What do they do, now that the war's been over for thirty years?" Henry smiled.

"Survive, I'm told. Just. They still get some small Navy contracts. And they make some device for deep sea diving."

"So, what's this?" Henry pointed to the registration statement, which indicated that it had been filed with the Securities and Exchange Commission.

"The new Andersen. Publicly listed."

"Why would you publicly list a company that's not doing anything?"

"But it wasn't going to be doing nothing much longer."

"Like making noise detectors for the City of New York, you mean."

"Yes," Gravett answered. "Whoever owned the stock before the contract was publicly awarded is going to make a lot of money on their shares."

"Hmmm."

Henry looked at Gravett. She was attractive, slender, with blond hair and a clear, but tanned complexion. And she had a lean, athletic body, like that of a good tennis player. He meant to ask her about tennis sometime.

But what interested him was her obvious intelligence. That, and the intensity of her interest. Henry felt confident listening to her.

"Where did you learn about registration statements and shares of stock and so forth?" he asked.

"Where else?" she laughed. "College. In California."

Henry smiled and nodded. "Anything else?"

"Well, for a registration statement, you need counsel."

"And?"

"Counsel for Andersen. He's interesting."

"Who is it?"

"Robert Black."

Henry sat up abruptly. "What?"

"Just what you heard. That's why I brought it to you."

Two days later, Henry shook his head and looked at Howard Matlin. "As I said, Black claims that he doesn't really know anything. But he says he strongly believes that Galligan and probably Della Bove are involved with the Andersen deal."

Henry was telling Howard Matlin and Nat Perlman about his new debriefing of Robert Black, after receiving the information from Nancy Gravett.

"But does he know anything about how Andersen won the contract?" Matlin asked.

"No. He swears he doesn't. He says that they talked him into letting his name appear as counsel for Andersen, but that he never did a thing. The underwriters did all the work, he says."

"The outfit called Layton & Porche?" Matlin said, looking at the memo Henry had prepared summarizing the substance of the registration statement.

"Correct."

"And he knows nothing of the restructuring of Andersen?"

"Only what Della Bove told him. That Andersen was 'refinancing' itself by going public, so that it could bid on the noise detector contract."

Matlin's face reflected his skepticism. "You couldn't get anything more out of him?"

"No," admitted Henry. "I tried. But that's all there is. Or at least, that's all he's admitting to now."

"The latter, obviously," growled Matt Corey, who was also in the meeting.

"Henry." It was Nat Perlman, sitting in his usual seat.

"Yes?"

"Why did you start this investigation?"

Henry was taken aback. "Because...because...it smells bad. And it has to do with Robert Black. And a company apparently connected to Galligan comes out of left field and successfully bids against two major corporations for a big City contract for which they had no expertise or even experience."

"You smelled something, is that it?" Perlman went on.

"Well, yes," Henry answered. He was beginning to wish that Perlman were not in the meeting. "And I recognize the cast of characters."

"But you haven't a hair of evidence that there's anything wrong."

"Not yet. But it smells bad."

"And if there *is* something wrong, have you considered where to find the jurisdiction to prosecute anyone?"

"Well..."

Perlman was probably right. The letting of a City contract was clearly not within the parameters of the original Executive Order establishing the Office. The Order designated "the law enforcement and justice systems" as the parameters of jurisdiction for the Special Prosecutor's Office.

"What about the superseder in the Bregner case?" Henry asked.

"That superseder," responded Perlman, "expanded our jurisdiction only to encompass any investigations involving the City that were already underway on the date the superseder was signed, which was almost a month ago. No one had even heard of Andersen then."

Henry looked at Howard Matlin.

"I wouldn't let jurisdiction stop us yet," said Matlin. "But Nat's right. I have a problem with your taking on this matter now."

Henry's face fell.

"Henry," Matlin continued, "I'm concerned that you aren't moving your other matters faster. The Hurd case has been on the front burner for some time now. And you were going to investigate subpoenaing records from Galligan's county committee about the making of judgeships. Presumably for money." He paused. "You seem to be spinning your wheels."

Henry swallowed hard, looking at Matlin.

"Have you explored the possibility of turning the Salerno brothers?"

Amazing how Matlin could remember names like that. "Uh, no. I figured they didn't know anything useful, so it would be a waste of time."

"And how about an evasive contempt case on the law secretary or the clerk? To pressure them into co-operating."

He had briefly considered it but didn't think it would work. "It's a very tough case to make strong enough to induce someone to cooperate," he said.

"True. But it isn't going to get any easier while you're waiting. And what about the subpoenas for the County Committee?" he continued.

Silence. It was Perlman who broke it.

"Henry, I think you'd better consider what Howie has said. And get back to your own matters and forget about Andersen."

For the next two days, Henry worked on preparing subpoenas for the records of the Bronx County Committee, for County Leader Galligan and for State Senator Della Bove, demanding all their records relating to the designation of individuals to become judges. At last, after reviewing them with Matlin, he had caused the subpoenas to be served.

The result was not what he had hoped.

All the recipients had challenged the subpoenas, claiming that they were overbroad, unjustified "fishing expeditions" outside the purpose and authority of the Special Prosecutor's Office. A flurry of publicity followed.

The investigation was vigorously attacked, as was the Office of the Special Prosecutor itself. Motions were made by all the affected parties, seeking to quash all of the subpoenas. Assaults came from several quarters, among them the Bar Association committee chaired by Max Olman. Even Potter Wilberton, III, president of the City's bar association, called Matlin to warn him about impugning the integrity of the judiciary.

When Matlin transferred the subpoena battle to the Appeals Chief, Ed Scanlon, along with Henry's colleague Hal Baker, Henry's anxiety eased. But the pressure on Henry did not.

The next day Henry was at his desk when there was a light knock on his door.

"Come in."

It was Nancy Gravett.

"Got a minute?"

"Sure."

She took a seat. "I thought you'd like to know what's happening in Andersen," she said matter-of-factly.

Henry took a breath. After his confrontation with the front office about the Andersen matter, he had heard that Matlin had decided to look into the matter briefly, even though it might be beyond the Office's jurisdiction. The investigation was assigned to none other than Justin Cole.

Henry hesitated.

"You're worried about the 'need-to-know' rule," she said, apparently reading his thoughts.

He nodded.

"I want to break the rule. For two reasons. First, I think you have a right to know, since you were the first person to take an interest. And second, I'd like your thoughts." She made a gesture of distaste. "Thoughts aren't something Justin Cole shares very well."

Henry sat back to listen.

"We talked to old man Andersen. And what we suspected was right. His company was just hanging on when, one day, a summer resident named Erin Galligan came to see him. Galligan asked him if he could make devices that monitor ambient sound. Andersen told him that, with a little retooling, they could make such a device. Then Galligan asked him if he'd like to bid on a big contract for the noise detectors. Andersen told him he couldn't do it because he didn't have the money to retool to make the devices. Galligan suggested that if the company were recapitalized, and some of the shares sold publicly, the money to retool could be raised. Anyway, Andersen eventually agreed and, as you saw, the company was taken public."

"With Galligan taking a big hunk of the shares, I'll bet."

She shook her head. "We don't know."

"You don't know?" Henry's eyebrows lifted. "You don't think Galligan did this as a good Samaritan, do you?"

"No. Of course not. But all the stock records show is the ownership of 150,000 shares by Andersen and his daughter, 200,000 by the public, originally issued through the underwriters, Layton & Porche, and the other 150,000, which are registered to a Goblox Associates at a post office box."

"What's it called?"

"Goblox Associates."

"Well, that has to be Galligan."

"Sure. But so far, we've got nothing to show it."

Henry sat back. "Well, thanks, Nancy."

"Hey," she exclaimed. "I forgot one more thing. Very important."

Henry sat forward again.

"Andersen told us that when he received the original proposal, he calculated how much it would cost him, and then he structured his bid accordingly. He gave Galligan the numbers. Then a few days later, Galligan asked him to give him a list of changes in the specifications that would make it cheaper for him to build the devices. So, Andersen gave him the list and, within a couple of weeks or so, Andersen got a revised proposal from the City that incorporated most of the changes he'd suggested. So, he was able to revise his bid downward. Substantially."

"You mean, somebody working for the City's in with them?"

"Looks that way," said Gravett. "And it looks like Galligan used whoever it is to get the specifications changed so that Andersen could win the contract. You can be certain he didn't do the revisions himself."

Walking down the hall later that day, Henry passed Sara's office and noticed the door slightly ajar. Sara was seated at her desk, reading something quite intently and apparently making notes. Henry started toward his own hallway but found his feet refusing to cooperate. He knocked on the open door and Sara looked up.

"Got a minute?" he asked.

"Not really, but come in. For just a minute."

"I was wondering how you're doing with the mob lawyer case."

Sara shrugged. "I had something else come up. Actually, I thought of you."

"Oh?" Henry brightened a bit and sat up.

"I heard that you were told not to investigate something you were on to."

Henry sank back again. Things got around.

"And the same thing happened to me."

"Huh?"

"I was on to something good, and they stopped me."

"What was it?"

"It was something Harry Rood remembered. From when he was with the police department." Sara put down her pencil. "Apparently there was an informant named Angie Squirelli who was murdered by a guy in the Colombo family and found in the trunk of a car at the airport with a bullet in his head. The cops got lucky. They recovered the gun with fingerprints of a guy affiliated with the Colombo family. A guy named Donofrio. Louis 'Puffy' Donofrio. I love these names."

Henry nodded. "Uh huh." He waited for Sara to continue.

"Anyway, the case was solid. Airtight. They even had an admission over a wire. And the jury took ten minutes to convict the guy of murder."

"So, what was suspicious? Why did Harry remember it?" asked Henry.

"The case got appealed. And, surprise, surprise, the Appellate Division threw it out."

"On what grounds?"

"That's just it They claimed that there was insufficient evidence to convict, or even to indict. So, as they put it, to 'preserve the sanctity of the law,' they reversed on the facts and dismissed the indictment. That way, it couldn't be tried again. So Donofrio walked and that was the end of it."

"Weird. When was this?"

"A little over four years ago."

"What have you done?"

"I brought in the lawyer who represented Donofrio in the appeal. Tried to scare the crap out of him."

Henry recalled the drug dealer she had turned. And the corrupt narcotics detective. She was good, he had to admit.

"He claimed that he was hired to write a brief and make an oral argument. And that's all he did. And then, surprise, surprise, he won."

Henry shrugged. "Tough story to break."

Sara shook her head. "It's pure bullshit." She sat back. "And I'm going to break it open."

"How?"

"Through Kondor himself. Paul Kondor. That's the appeal lawyer. A sleazebag. But not a sophisticated one. I had him scared. And I almost broke him." Sara's face grew angry. "Then I subpoenaed the DA's file, and the front office told me to back off. I assume they're scared of some adverse reaction from the DA's office. Or whatever." She sat up again. "I don't give a damn. I'm going after this one. Somebody did something very wrong and I'm going to find out what, who, and how."

"Sara, don't you think you ought to listen to the front office? Remember the stink you created when you subpoenaed that guy Donner in the Bermudez case without their permission?"

Sara gave Henry a piercing look. "You haven't changed, have you, Henry?" She looked away. "And I haven't. I don't need help and I don't need interference. I know what I'm doing, and I intend to do it."

She picked up her pencil. "Bye, Henry."

"Bad news." Barry Conlon opened Henry's door and looked in.

"What?" asked Henry, alarmed.

"Big reversal. Crocker."

"The judge we convicted?"

"Yup. Just reversed by the good old Appellate Division."

"Those bastards," Henry exclaimed, slapping his desk.

"On what grounds did they reverse? I understood we had the guy dead to rights."

"Something about insufficient corroboration of an accomplice. I haven't seen the opinion."

"What bullshit," said Henry.

"Geeze, Scoop, the papers are really letting us have it about the Crocker reversal—and after Bentzel, too."

Scoop Dixon's face was not happy. "It hurts, lad. It hurts."

Dixon drew a cigarette from his pack and put it in his mouth. Catching Henry's grimace, he took it away. "I can't quit. Not yet," he said, and began searching for a match.

"How's Justin taking it?" Henry asked.

"He seemed upset. But he never mentioned Howie or any of the shit Howie's taking for it. Just himself."

"How come I'm not surprised?"

Dixon took another drag of his cigarette. Henry slipped out before he was treated to another fit of coughing.

Every year they seemed to get bigger and more elaborate. Not that Henry minded. He loved parties, and Christmas parties were some of the best. Especially the Christmas parties of the Special Prosecutor's Office. Once again, the Office had taken advantage of the reception hall on the Executive floor of the New State Office Building. And once again, in a field of glitz, the now 150 employees of the Special Prosecutor's Office gathered, supplied with ample drinks and an assembly line of hors d'oeuvres. Once again, they'd invited a few reporters. At least, the friendly ones.

"Hey, Dan," he said as he saw Nelligan. Then he spotted the glass in Nelligan's right hand. "Ugh. What's that?"

"It's some special punch that Tim O'Leary made."

"O'Leary? Oh, oh. What's in it?" He looked more closely. "And how'd he get that color?" The liquid in Nelligan's glass was something between pea soup green and mud brown. "It looks horrible."

"It's good. Here, taste it." Nelligan held out a glass.

Henry hesitated. Then he spotted O'Leary watching him, a broad smile on his face. "Okay. Here goes," he said as he took a sip. He forced himself to smile. And then he didn't have to. It *was* good. And "punch" was a good name for it. It might be just what he needed right now.

One cup of the concoction led to another. Henry spotted Angie Palumbo with a glass of clear liquid in his hand, which he assumed to be vodka on the rocks.

"Not drinking Tim's stuff?" he asked.

Palumbo held his glass to his eye and peered at Henry through it. "Can you do this with that green shit?"

Two hours later, the party was really buzzing when a clinking of glasses interrupted the din. Howard Matlin climbed up on a chair, not far away. When the crowd quieted, he began.

"Three years ago, some of us here gathered in our new library for our first holiday party."

Henry remembered.

"At that time, we had already begun some investigations. And we even had a few indictments. But, most of all, we had hope. Hope that, during the months and years to come, we could carry out the mission assigned to us and begin an assault on the bastions of corruption that stood ahead of us. We all believed that we could make a difference.

"Three years later, we've done just that. We've battled our way into the police department, into the corrections system, into the prosecutors' offices, and into the courts themselves. And soon, we will certainly breach the final battlement, the clubhouse walls."

Applause interrupted him. Then he went on.

"It's been only a little more than three years that we've been in operation. But in that brief period, we've brought a lifetime of worry to the corrupt public servants who, before us, had no fears. Yes, there will be occasional setbacks."

Henry knew he was referring to the Crocker and Bentzel reversals.

"But we *are* making a difference."

Once again, applause.

Henry spotted Sabrina Wilcox of the *Times* and Mike Welling of the *News* standing nearby. He moved closer to hear their reaction.

"In a sense, we're still beginning." Matlin went on. "We've overrun the first tower, but the city is still in enemy hands. But don't lose faith; we're going keep going until we turn Sodom and Gomorrah into the new Jerusalem. I promise you that."

As the applause was dying down, Sabrina Wilcox turned to Mike Welling. "And what was waiting there in Jerusalem?" she said. "Golgotha."

CHAPTER 31

"I won't try to say that it helps. But it's part of being in government and, since we're in government, we can learn to live with it."

Matlin was addressing the staff of the Office on his first day back from his vacation, two weeks into the New Year, 1976. He was trying to put the best face he could on the 25 percent cut in the Office's budget which the legislature had just voted. When asked for a reason for the cut, the legislative leaders had pointed to the ongoing fiscal crisis in the State. The real reason, according to Scoop Dixon, was that, after the Bregner matter, lawmakers were becoming concerned that Matlin was a "loose cannon" who might next decide to aim at the legislature itself. No one was publicly admitting that thesis, of course.

On the day before the legislative action on the budget, an article appeared in the *Times* under Toby Copin's byline, quoting Chief Judge Sammons: "It must be asked," the Chief Judge had said, "whether Howard Matlin may be impugning the reputation of our judiciary without a proper foundation in fact." Having seen the real facts, Henry dismissed the article. It looked like the legislature had not.

"And so, we'll just keep doing what we were doing, and, despite the cutback, we'll make it."

A few staff members applauded. Most simply shrugged their shoulders, as Matlin had done, and went back to work.

Then came Toby Copin's article in the next day's *Times*.

"Where the hell did this come from?" Henry complained as he entered Scoop Dixon's office, causing the billowing of a cloud of smoke.

"I've been expecting you," said Dixon calmly. "Sit down."

"Dammit, Scoop, this is outrageous. Especially if it came from someone here."

Dixon did not get angry. He didn't even raise his voice. "Perk. Please sit down and we'll talk." He leaned over his desk and snuffed out his cigarette. "Here, I'm even putting out my weed for you."

With a sigh, Henry complied. "Okay. I'm sitting down," he said more calmly. "But I want to know who spilled the beans to that shit, Toby Copin."

It was only a half hour ago, on the Number 4 express, when he had seen Toby Copin's front page story in the *Times* spelling out his investigation into the handling of the Ben-Evans case by Justice John Hurd and revealing the fact of Robert Black's cooperation.

"You read the story?" Dixon asked calmly.

"Of course, I read the damned story."

"And in what paper did you read the story?"

"You know what paper."

"Yes. The *Times*." Dixon nodded. "And who wrote the story?"

"Copin. You know that, too."

"And what well-known and highly respected member of the bar represents the good Justice John Hurd?"

A light finally came into Henry's eye. He'd been so angry that he hadn't stopped to think. "You think it's Olman again?"

"Well, put it this way. What well-known and well-respected attorney was recently the recipient of an award by a journalistic society devoted to civil libertarian causes, which group is presently headed by a well-known and well-respected journalist whose byline is quite frequently seen on the front pages of the *New York Times?*"

"When was that?"

"Last Thursday night."

"You there?"

"Not happily. But yes. As a former staffer at the *Times*, I was invited. And I went." He smiled. "Damned good hors d'oeuvres, too."

Henry was angry. He ought to be. But it was hard to keep himself in high dudgeon while talking with Dixon.

"And Olman got an award?"

"Given by the society's current president, Mr. Barthold Copin to, as he put it, 'my good friend' Maxwell Olman."

"And then a leak. Same as Bregner."

"Same as Bregner."

"Same reason? Set up an attack on the Office?"

"No. Not according to Howie." Dixon paused. "Well, it didn't help. Howie's already gotten a call this morning. From Sammons. Chief Judge Sammons."

"And."

"Sammons was pissed off that Howie was after another judge and hadn't told him about it. Same as with Bentzel."

Henry shook his head. "But you say that wasn't the main reason for Olman's leak."

"Not me. Howie says it. He thinks that the article was meant as a warning."

"Huh?"

"Olman—I mean, Copin reveals in the article that Black is co-operating with the Office. Right?"

"Right. That's what made me so mad."

"Well, what better way to alert all the friends of the organization to the danger posed by any conversations with Black than to broadcast his role in the newspaper?"

"Jesus, you think Copin's that involved with the organization?"

"Of course not. Toby may be unpleasant and even less than scrupulous sometimes. But he's a journalist. And most of the time, he's a good one. He's just using a source to tell a story. One that everybody this morning is going to read."

Henry reflected on the situation for a moment. Then he started to get up from his chair.

"It's getting bad, isn't it?" he asked.

"Not as bad as it going to be," responded Dixon, reaching for his pack of cigarettes.

"Look at this shit," grumbled Henry. He had just walked into Ed Scanlon's office with the *New York Times*. Scanlon had asked him to join him and Hal Baker for a meeting.

"'If Howard Matlin,'" Henry read aloud from the *Times'* editorial, "is unable to keep silent about investigations which have resulted in no formal charges, perhaps the Governor should consider reminding his special prosecutor of his obligations to a justice system where one is supposed to be innocent until proven guilty.' Howie's gotta do something."

"What's he gonna say?" responded Scanlon. "He's already denied that anyone here leaked it, and nobody believes him."

Henry sighed and dropped the *Times*. He looked at Scanlon. "So, what's up?"

"The County Committee is appealing," said Scanlon.

Justice Winerude had, the day before, ruled on the motions by Erin Galligan and the County Committee to quash the subpoenas of the Committee's records which Henry had served on them. The judge had denied the motions and upheld the subpoenas. Now Galligan, Della Bove, and the County Committee were appealing to the Appellate Division Winerude's order to produce the documents.

"Now there'll be more delay in getting the records," Scanlon continued.

"So now, Ed and I have some late nights of work to do on the appeal," added Baker.

Henry and Nancy Gravett were having lunch out of the office at the Rathskeller. Henry had suggested it, as a better place to break the Office rules. And Gravett was filling him in on the Andersen investigation.

"What they did was simple," said Gravett. From a brief visit to the two competing bidders, a Canadian company, and a Michigan firm, Gravett had learned that a City engineer had visited their plants shortly after the bids were put out. Not long after the visits, revised specifications were received. In the case of each company, the revised specifications made it more costly for them to make the noise detectors, and their final bids had reflected the increase, making it easier for Andersen Sonar to make the low bid.

"And you think the revised specifications came from some City person who was helping Galligan to secure the deal for Andersen."

"Correct."

The waitress arrived with their lunch, setting it down next to the beers on which Henry had insisted. Henry took a sip of his Spaten. Then he leaned on his elbow and sighed.

"You wish you had this one, don't you?" Nancy said.

Henry smiled sadly. "What do you think?"

"Honestly, Henry, I think you've got enough to do at the moment."

Henry smiled, a bit ruefully. Nancy Gravett was, he feared, wiser than he.

"Hi, Nancy," said Henry, meeting her in the hall the next afternoon. "Anything new?" he whispered.

Gravett's face fell. "Cole's dropping the investigation. He says there isn't any jurisdiction."

Henry started to say something, but Gravett put up a hand. "Not now. Maybe later." She walked on.

"Can I see him, Harriet?"

"Sorry, Henry," answered Harriet Winsor. "He's out of the office. Won't be back until Monday."

Damn it. He didn't want to wait until Monday. All right. He'd been criticized by Nat Perlman. This time, he was in the right.

He knocked on the door of the Chief Assistant.

"Come in."

Perlman was at his desk, apparently reviewing some legal papers that weren't in order, since he was wearing his round wire-rimmed glasses and a sour frown.

"What is it?" Perlman asked.

"It's the Andersen case."

Perlman looked surprised. "What are you doing with the Andersen case?" He put the legal papers on his desk but did not offer Henry a seat.

"I'm not doing anything with the Andersen case."

Perlman's stern eyes were fixed on him.

"I've heard that someone else isn't going to be doing something."

"What are you talking about?" snapped Perlman.

He took a breath and began. "I'm talking about Justin Cole and the fact that he is dropping the Andersen investigation."

Perlman eyed Henry harshly. Then he responded in his usual restrained voice. "In the first place, as you should know by now, someone else's investigation is not any of your business." His quiet voice bristled with anger.

Henry opened his mouth to respond, but Perlman was still speaking.

"In the second place, where are the judgeship documents? Justice Winerude ordered the lawyers to turn them over this week."

"It's on appeal, as I assume you know."

"Have you given Scanlon and Baker your draft of the supplemental memo on the subpoena matter?"

"No; it's probably moot now..."

"Have you confronted the Salernos yet?"

"No. It wouldn't get us anything."

"Where are the financial studies on the other judges Galligan made?"

"I'm working on them with the accounting people..."

Perlman's fist struck his desk. Not hard. He didn't demonstrate his anger like Matt Corey. But the gesture spoke clearly.

"A while back," Perlman said, "I recommended to Howie that he remove you from these cases and put someone else in charge. To date, he hasn't acted on my recommendation, and I've been quiet about it. I think the time to speak up again may have arrived."

He picked up the papers on his desk. "Now I've got another problem. Someone has made a mess of a seizure order." He looked Henry in the eye. "Though, at least, he did it on his own. And he finished it."

In the hall outside, Henry realized that his knees were shaking, and the walls were spinning. All he wanted to do was to get back to his office without running into anybody.

Which he did. Though it didn't improve his state of mind. He was in trouble. Deep trouble. He wasn't about to make any cases that would secure the reputation of Howard Matlin or the Special Prosecutor's Office. He was about to be demoted. Or maybe even fired.

For what...? Why?

His head was swimming. He tried looking out his window, into the gloom of approaching evening, but it made him dizzy. He took his head in his hands, trying to rub out the pain and the confusion. But he felt fogged in.

Then he remembered. It was Friday night and he had tickets to the opera. *La Forza del Destino*. He didn't have a date but, so what? He'd go by himself. And then, tomorrow, he'd try to sort out the chaos and put himself together. Tomorrow.

Henry's neck lifted as he watched the chandeliers, like large crystal snowflakes, rise slowly toward the ceiling. His coat lay on the seat beside him, a testament to his subscription to both seats, one of which was now serving as an expensive coat rack. The lights dimmed and the audience applauded as the conductor stepped in front of the orchestra in the pit, took a bow, and turned. He raised his arms.

As he heard the three chiming notes that began the overture to *La Forza del Destino*, Henry sank back in his seat, wiping from his mind the thoughts of noise detectors and line sheets and subpoenas. The music softened and began to flow, first with menace, then with beauty, then with vigorous accelerando toward the rousing conclusion of the overture. Into the encompassing circle of sound Henry slipped, allowing the long arms of Verdi to reach sinuously around his shoulders and head, pulling him into the waters of Lethe, baptizing him into narcosis. The overture over, the opera began.

The great doors of the church were now open, the glow from within casting light sparingly on the ground in front. From out of the sanctuary slowly filed two lines of hooded friars, heads bent forward as they walked, each dark figure holding a candle in front of him. As they came together in front of the church, the glow from the many candles half-illuminated the obscured faces of the friars, while surrounding the gathering with a luminescent nebula. The priest who had led the columns placed a hand on the head of a slender hooded figure standing next to him. "*Il santo nome di Dio,*" he chanted.

Henry stirred in his seat, still enfolded in the music. But the waters of Lethe were leaking away, and he was becoming aware of himself again, sitting alone, surrounded by an unconnected crowd, on a balcony in a large, darkened hall. A place where he had come to rest momentarily, after wandering, drifting, sampling, dabbling. And failing.

"*Maledizione, maledizion!*" Curse him, curse him! The chorus was nearly shouting.

What a thought! To be cursed. But was it just a thought? Was it just some words sung loudly at him from a stage? Maybe he, himself, was cursed.

Had he ever succeeded at anything? Really succeeded? Certainly, he'd always thought he would. But the facts weren't bearing him out.

Instead, he was drifting. Tossed about by waves, propelled in and out by the tide, bumping against whatever floated along momentarily beside him. Not setting a course or even dropping an anchor.

"Maledizione, maledizione…!" Cursed! *"…maledizione, maledizione!"* Maybe it wasn't going to happen for him. A place to land. A way to make his mark. To build a home, a life. Perhaps he'd make no mark. Maybe there was to be no home for him.

The sound of the pizzicato triplets caught his attention. And then, ever so softly, the chorus of friars began to sing.

"La Virgine de gli Angeli, vi copra del suo manto…" The Virgin, among the angels, may she shield you from danger… *"e voi protegga vigile, di Dio l'Angelo santo…"* and protect you through the watchful eyes of God's holy angel.

His throat tightened as the lovely music—unearthly in its beauty—floated out toward him. And then, echoing the chorus, the soprano began to sing.

"La Virgine de gli Angeli, mi copra del suo manto, e me protegga vigile di Dio l'Angelo santo."

A tear slowly formed and crept over the rim of his eye. Then another took its place, as the first began making a path down the valley between his nose and his cheek.

"E me protegga, me protegga…" Protect me, protect me, the soprano sang. But it wasn't just the soprano singing these words, it was Henry Perkins. Inside himself, he was crying out; old, suppressed feelings erupting in a drawn and pain-filled wail that reverberated off unadorned walls of the empty space inside him, echoing their way into a vast beyond. "Help me, protect me."

The soprano and the chorus joined him now, throwing off the gentle mantle, rising to conclusion, their voices in *forte. "Voi protegga,"* sang the chorus. *"Me protegga,"* sang the soprano, *"e me pro-teg-ga."*

"And me," said Henry, as the curtain fell on the act.

He reached over to the other seat, picked up his coat and left.

Outside, the cold wind of the end of January whipped across the plaza, blowing water from the fountain onto the pavement nearby. He buttoned his coat and wiped his eyes, where the vestige of tears stung in the wind. Crossing the plaza, he turned left and walked, not quickly, not slowly. Not even consciously.

"Protegga me. Protegga me." For how many years had he been saying that? To how many people, while he drifted from one place to the next. Stretching out an arm, pleading for help, for guidance, for some hint of the direction he should take so that he wouldn't fail at whatever he was doing.

He picked up his pace as he passed the side door to Philharmonic Hall.

How many times had he asked for help? He didn't want to fail.

He reached the corner. The light was green.

How often had he looked for help?

The light across Broadway was green, too. He could make it if he ran. He did.

He made the island. Now he could walk.

What was he looking for? A mother? A father? Was he just trying to fill the void that two always-absent parents had never filled?

He crossed 66th Street and started up the avenue.

And then it hit.

Looking for help was part of the problem, not the solution. Looking for appreciation. Holding back until someone reached out a hand to show him the way so that he didn't have to risk losing.

But that wasn't what he needed. It wasn't a helping hand that would save him; it was…it was committing to and doing something that he knew was right, even if there was a good chance he would lose.

Push ahead. Like he was doing already. Fighting corruption that infested the City. He was doing now what he ought to be doing. But he was hedging his bets by holding back. To let someone show him the way. To avoid failing.

That was it. He was afraid to fail. Afraid even that the Special Prosecutor's Office itself might fail. So, hold back and maybe it wouldn't happen.

He had reached a corner. An empty corner with a brick wall. For some reason, he stopped. This was the place. Slowly, he felt his shoulders straighten as he stood up and turned. His lungs filled with the cold winter air. And forced it out again, warmed.

That was no way to live. Holding back. It was like keeping one foot on the boat and one foot on the dock. And when the boat moved, that position could only lead to one place: down into the water. That wouldn't work. He had to make a commitment. A commitment to what he believed in. So what if he lost? It was time to fight the fight and to do what he knew was right. Succeed or fail.

To do what he knew was right. That was the only choice. No more *protegga me.* He looked up at the street sign. "Columbus Avenue," it said. He smiled. He was on a voyage to the unknown. Like Columbus was. Maybe to sail on to a New World; maybe to go over the edge of the Old one. Only now it was Howard Matlin on the bridge, and he, Henry Jackson Perkins, was at the winches. Sailing on.

CHAPTER 32

The look of surprise on Howard Matlin's face turned to one of pleasure. His eyebrows settled back into place and the corners of his stern mouth turned up. And he smiled.

"See, Howie, there is justice somewhere," said Henry.

"He'll testify to all of that, you're sure?" asked Matlin.

"He's going in tomorrow morning. Before he has a chance to rethink it," responded Henry.

Matlin nodded.

Henry had finally gotten the break he needed. Sam Lorraine, Justice Hurd's law secretary, had read Toby Copin's story—the one based on Max Olman's leak. And he'd become frightened. He knew that he had talked with Robert Black several times, and he apparently had concluded that Black was acting in an undercover capacity and had recorded all their conversations. Fearing that he would be indicted with the judge, he had come into the Office unannounced and asked to see the person in charge of the Hurd case. Once seated in Henry's office, in front of Henry and Dan Nelligan, he had spilled his guts. And made Henry's case.

And there was more. The law secretary told about Hurd's meetings with criminal defendants while their cases were pending before him, about his taking an expensive Caribbean vacation, paid for by an insurance company which often had cases before him, and about other activities which, when further examined, promised to reveal illegal or, at least, unethical conduct on the part of Justice John Hurd.

And then the law secretary had gone on to tie Senator Della Bove into some of the corrupt transactions. Not only was Hurd going into the toilet bowl, but Della Bove was also likely to join him.

Henry stood up. "I've got to get ready for the grand jury tomorrow. If everything goes as it looks like it should, I'll draft the indictments tomorrow night and then you can review them the day after tomorrow." He smiled to himself but spoke to Matlin. "So, you can sign off on them."

Applause greeted Henry Perkins as he opened the door to Pete Flannery's office. He jumped back, surprised, since he thought that he had been called to his group chief's office to go over some time sheets.

"Oh, lord," he said as he saw the group.

"Way to go, Perk."

"Huh? Oh, thanks, Larry."

"Really great one!" exclaimed Hal Baker.

"I hope so."

"Are you kidding?" Barry Conlon put in. "From the paper this morning, it looks like you've got 'em by the short ones."

Henry looked around the office. Pete Flannery was sitting behind his desk wearing a mischievous smile. It was still early in the morning after the announcement of the indictment of Justice Hurd and State Senator Della Bove, but the room was almost full. In addition to Larry Santarella, Hal Baker, and Barry Conlon, Henry saw that Dan Nelligan, Tim O'Leary, Angie

Palumbo, Steve Wonderman, and Marty Asner had packed into the office. Near the wall, stood Nancy Gravett.

Flannery reached down and picked up a bottle of champagne. "Sorry it couldn't be beer, Perk. But you can lower yourself to sip some champagne just this once."

"A bit early in the morning," he laughed. "But I might be able to swallow it. Maybe with some investigator's coffee," he added, looking at O'Leary.

"Hey, don't look at me," protested O'Leary. "I only make punch."

A groan from several of those present recalled the effects of that effort.

"Great press," said Steve Wonderman. "It was the lead story in the *Times*. Front page, column eight."

Henry smiled. He had, of course, purchased on the way to work the *Times* and the *Daily News*. And, when he went to lunch, he'd buy the afternoon *Post*. It wasn't every day that your name was on the front page of every paper in New York City.

Wonderman was correct. The news reports had been good. As Sabrina Wilcox of the *Times* had put it, "the Special Prosecutor has unearthed that elusive but extant coupling between politics and justice." Mike Welling of the *Daily News*, always more colorful, had said that, "Howard Matlin has yanked up one of those roots of which he spoke when he first took office and he has turned up the dark, wriggling worms that appear only at election time."

"Just fuckin' Donegan," said Santarella. "Oh, sorry," he added, looking at Nancy Gravett.

"It's fuckin' okay, Larry," she smiled, provoking an approving nod from Santarella.

Johnny Donegan hadn't missed the opportunity to take a swipe at Matlin. "Another false step in Czar Matlin's forced march to Albany," he had called the indictment. Otherwise, Henry thought, his column merely rambled.

"Sabrina?" It was the first question at a press conference two days later.

"Mr. Matlin, you've just indicted the County Chairman and Senator Della Bove for selling judgeships. But you've only named one judge, or potential judge, who bought one. This Robert Black. Are there others?"

"First, Sabrina, the *grand jury* has indicted Mr. Galligan and Senator Della Bove, not me personally. But, to answer your question, yes, we believe so.

"Who are the others?" she asked.

"I'm not at liberty to say, at this point. But subpoenas have been served on the County Committee which, I am certain, will help give us some answers." Matlin pointed to the next questioner.

"Hi, Sara," Henry said. He was leaving the coffee shop where he had taken out a sandwich when he saw Sara Leventhal eating by herself. He sat down.

"I was curious. What's happening with your wire on the lawyer?"

"Still there" she responded. "We're monitoring his involvement with the Tutino people. Also, the trial for the drug dealer Johnson is still scheduled. The one Remmelt has fixed with Judge Ryan."

"Good. And what about the mobster's appeal?" Henry smiled. "Puffy Donofrio."

Sara's face showed anger. "The front office is still telling me to hold off. I want to talk to the lawyer who did the appeal, Paul Kondor. He knows what happened. But they still say no." She looked up at Henry with that now-familiar steely expression. "But I'm not waiting much longer."

"Sara…"

But she was already getting up to go.

"Jesus, what bullshit," said Ed Scanlon, tossing the opinion on his desk. Lou Morotti, standing in front of Scanlon's desk, looked at the Chief of Appeals. His face was befuddled and flushed with anger.

"What the hell are they doing?" Morotti demanded.

Scanlon shook his head. "They're saying 'No, no, you can't indict our friends.' That's what they're saying."

"Can I see the opinion?" asked Pete Flannery. He and Henry had been talking in Scanlon's office when Morotti had stormed in with the just-delivered opinion of the Appellate Division that dismissed Morotti's indictment of the two Brooklyn judges for conspiring with some auto insurance companies to resolve cases as they dictated.

"Why did they dismiss the indictments?" asked Henry as Flannery picked it up.

Scanlon snorted. "It's so ridiculous, it's barely explainable. In a nutshell, they said that we don't have jurisdiction because we didn't eliminate the possibility that the arrangements the insurance companies made affected interstate commerce more than they affected the justice system here, in which case it would be a federal case, not a state case."

"What?" exclaimed Flannery, putting down the opinion. "That's the most ridiculous thing I've ever read. He handed the opinion to Morotti and shook his head in disbelief.

"It sure is. But you know what it is—the boys on the bench are protecting their own."

The fallout was bad.

"MATLIN INDICTMENT DUMPED!" shouted the *Daily News.* "Matlin Improperly Indicted Judges," read the column header in the *Times.* The dismissal of the indictments was the lead story on all local news broadcasts and even made the nightly national news on one network. Many of the accounts quoted from the opinion, especially where the appellate panel had accused Howard Matlin of "riding recklessly over ground where he clearly was not intended to trespass." Johnny Donegan, of course, had a field day with the court's language, comparing Howard Matlin's "incursion onto forbidden ground" to Hitler's invasion of Poland.

And then the president of the Bar Association again criticized Matlin.

"How's Howie taking it?" Henry asked Scoop Dixon, sticking his head into the smoky room.

"Like a fool."

"What do you mean?"

"He laughed. Said he didn't expect anything better from a bar association."

"What about the dismissals?"

"About the same. What do you expect he said?" Dixon took a drag on his cigarette. "It's another nail for Howie's coffin."

Henry paused a moment. Then he pointed to Dixon's cigarette. "Speaking of coffin nails," he said, and turned to go.

"I need to talk to you." Dan Nelligan had opened Henry's door. "About the Andersen thing."

"Andersen? I thought Cole dropped it."

"He did. No jurisdiction, he said. But Nancy Gravett said you were interested in it."

"True. By the way, where is Nancy?"

"Checking out something for Matt Corey. In a super-secret investigation he and Howie are doing directly."

"So, what's up?

"In a nutshell, someone jiggered the specifications so Andersen would get the contract. Galligan apparently got from Andersen the kind of specifications they could meet. Then a City engineer went to the other bidders in Ann Arbor, Michigan, and Toronto, in Canada, and reported to the City on the state of those plants and the specifications they would have to meet. Then the City put out new specifications which made it easier for Andersen and harder for the other two bidders to do the job cost effective."

"I think I'd heard that. So, it means that the engineer's in on it, too?"

"No. Apparently not. Nancy talked to him and decided that he was unaware of how his reports were being used. He was just doing his job and reporting the results. But it's clear that *someone* used the reports to make it easier for Andersen to become the low bidder."

"Interesting," said Henry. "And I know that the new stock was issued, which shot up in value when Andersen got the contract. And some entity called Goblox got 150,000 shares. Probably Galligan, but we don't know for sure who Goblox is."

Nelligan nodded. "But here's the reason I'm here."

"Yeah?" said Henry.

"Black's name came up again."

"How?"

"Andersen apparently wrote a letter to Black that he had a problem that needed legal attention. There was a restriction on his company arising out of some earlier problem Andersen had had with the State, which prohibited his company from bidding on any public contracts within the State for two more years. Andersen had asked his company's attorneys to see if they could get a waiver of the restriction, but he had just been informed that they were turned down flat by the State. So, he told Black that he couldn't bid on the noise detector contract unless the restriction was waived. Black never answered, but three days later Andersen received a call from some commissioner in Albany informing him that the State had reconsidered and was waiving the restriction. Unfortunately, he had no recollection of the commissioner's name."

"Smells bad," said Henry. "And you were right, Black was holding out on us."

"I agree," said Nelligan. "But before we bust into this thing, we must consider the problem Justin Cole had. Where's the jurisdiction? How's the justice system involved in this thing?"

"That's true. It's a problem," Henry conceded.

"And what really stopped Cole is a letter he received from Andersen's attorneys saying that, in their opinion, the Special Prosecutor was acting outside his jurisdiction since the bidding process for City contracts does not relate to the justice system or to law enforcement. So they were instructing their client to have no further contact with our office."

"Oh, boy."

"And then," Nelligan continued, "the attorneys for the underwriters of the new stock, Layton & Porche, told Cole that they would not comply with a subpoena for their records of the deal because there was no jurisdiction. That's when Cole threw in the towel."

"What about the Bregner superseder?" asked Henry.

"No. That only expanded our jurisdiction enough to permit us to investigate and prosecute stuff already under investigation when Bregner broke. We began the Andersen thing after that date."

"Let me think about it," said Henry. "We can't just let Black and Galligan off the hook that easily."

"Well, you think about it. I gotta go," said Nelligan, "to Chicago on another matter." He got up from his chair. "I'll see you in a couple days."

It was mid-morning the next day and Henry was walking up the western corridor of the office toward the north end of the building, where his office was located. As he passed a certain office, by habit he glanced at the usually closed door and noticed that it was slightly ajar. Inside, he saw Sara Leventhal frowning as she leaned over some papers on her desk.

"Hi, Sara," said Henry as he pushed her door open enough to enter.

Sara lifted her head. "What is it?" she snapped.

"Rowrf, rowrf."

Sara's green eyes lifted and brushed across Henry's face. "Sorry," she mumbled. Then she looked away. "But I'm tired," she said. "And I'm waiting for an important call."

Henry started to get up, but Sara spoke again.

"Actually, don't go yet. There may be some good stuff coming."

Henry sat back down.

"There's an informant working with the cops in the Castegglio investigation. One of the mobsters has asked Remmelt to see if he can use his contacts in the District Attorney's Office to find out whether there is an informant and, if so, who it is."

"Wow! That could lead to something serious," Henry said. "By the way, what happened with that other matter—the appeal of that murder case that looks bad? Is the front office letting you go ahead?"

Sara's face hardened. "No. But I..."

Just then, the door banged open.

It banged shut again. But Matt Corey was inside now.

He stomped over to her desk, ignoring the presence of Henry. His face was red, his jaw clenched. Once in front of Sara's desk, he opened his mouth.

"Did you call Paul Kondor?" he bellowed.

"None of your business," she said.

To Henry it felt like Sara had just fired an empty gun at a charging bear.

"And were you just sitting here waiting for his call?"

She opened her mouth, apparently to argue. Then she sat back. "Yes," she admitted.

"Well, he isn't going to call you," growled Corey. "Because he's left the country, thank you."

"What?" Sara sat up sharply.

Corey's large head hovered over Sara's desk, a fierce and frightening visage. "You just blew apart maybe the best investigation this office has had. You just scared away the one witness who could give us the chance to nail a whole pack of scumbag politicians and judges in one sweep. You just screwed Howie Matlin worse than any of those rotten judges out there could ever do." He stepped back. "Howie wants to see you. In his office." He straightened up. "Now!"

With a stunned look on her face, Sara rose and walked toward her door.

"And you," Corey added, turning his angry face to Henry, "get lost. And keep your fucking mouth shut."

Later the same day Henry was entering his office, returning from the men's room when Nancy Gravett appeared. Henry was still troubled by the scene he had witnessed in Sara's office that morning. But he owed Gravett a word of thanks for her work in the Andersen case.

"Got just a minute?" Henry asked her, motioning to his office with his head.

"Not really," she responded. She looked tired and drawn. "But, why not?" She entered and dropped into a seat as Henry went around his desk to his own chair.

"What's wrong. You look really beat."

"I am wiped out," Gravett responded. "It's been a very bad day. Very, very bad."

"Why? What's wrong."

"Just about everything," she responded. Then she sat back and looked squarely at Henry. "Thanks to your ex-girlfriend."

"What?"

"Your former friend, Sara don't-tell-me-what-to-do Leventhal."

"Why? What did she do?"

"Will you keep this to yourself? Promise?"

Henry was taken aback. He didn't think that Nancy Gravett even knew Sara, except for passing in the hall and the like.

"I promise. What is it?"

Gravett thought a moment, then went on. "Oh well, you'll find out soon enough, anyway." She shifted in her chair. "I've been working with Howie, with Matt Corey and with Paul Meade, wonderful Sara's group chief, on a very secret and high-powered investigation. You've heard of Rockbay Village?"

"Sure," Henry responded. "It was supposed to be this huge high-rise development. Like Co-op City only ritzier. Hugh Vernon, the big developer, was putting it together."

"Correct. Then you know, I assume, that the license for Rockbay was turned down by the City because it would put too much strain on transportation, sewage, garbage removal, schools, and so forth."

Henry nodded. "Yes. And I remember that Rockbay sued and that the court ruled for the City. A big surprise, at least with a politically connected guy like Vernon."

"True," responded Gravett. "But Vernon got unlucky and drew an honest judge. And so, he appealed to the Appellate Division."

"And...?"

"The fix was in the works in the Appellate Division."

"How did you know?" Henry asked.

"An informant. I don't even know who it was. But the fix was being arranged by a City councilman and lawyer named Herb Scammet. And the guy to carry out the fix was an appeals lawyer named Paul Kondor."

Henry sat up with a start. "Paul Kondor?"

Gravett looked at Henry anew. "Why, you know him?"

Henry closed his eyes for a moment. Now he was in trouble. He had just given away the fact that he knew someone he had no reason to know except for what Sara Leventhal had told him. "I've heard of him," he continued weakly.

But Nancy Gravett was not that easily fooled. "How do you know about Paul Kondor?"

Henry looked at Nancy. Her bright face and eyes glowed with her intelligence and her unwavering honesty and rectitude. He couldn't lie to her.

"I know that Sara was trying to turn Kondor in a case that looks like a fix, also in the Appellate Division, of a murder case."

"And what else do you know?

"I know that Matt Corey was ready to skin her alive this morning because she'd called Kondor against the wishes of the front office. And I know that Corey said Kondor left the country and that Sara had screwed up a big investigation Howie had going."

Gravett sat back in her chair, still looking at Henry. "Well, then, now you know the investigation she screwed up."

Henry closed his eyes and sat back in his chair. Then he sat up again. "Why would Sara's calling Kondor blow the investigation?"

Gravett thought a moment. "Well," she said at last, "since you know as much as you do, I'll tell you."

"Kondor's phone was up," she continued. "By us. And his office was bugged. And we knew that he and Scammet were supposed to meet today to finalize the bribe. So, we were listening and waiting. Kondor was super-nervous. In fact, I think he probably could have been a weak link, if it had come to that."

Henry recalled Sara surmising the same thing about Kondor. Now he wanted to tell Nancy about Sara's insight. To defend Sara. But he realized that now, it wouldn't help anything.

"But why did Kondor leave the country, just because Sara called?" he asked.

"That's not the point," said Gravett. "Sara called him just as he and Scammet were about to do the deal. Scammet was there. When someone from the Special Prosecutor's Office called, Scammet apparently figured that he was being set up by Kondor and took off. The deal was finished, at least with Kondor. So, I guess out-of-the-country seemed a good place to go."

"And you knew that Sara called because she called on the wiretap," said Henry.

"Of course," answered Gravett.

"Oh, shit," said Henry. "Now what happens?"

"What else? It hits the fan."

CHAPTER 33

"You did as well as you could," said Henry as he, Chief of Appeals Ed Scanlon, and Hal Baker waited for the elevator in the lobby of the New State Office Building. "I'm cautiously optimistic."

"Me too," agreed Baker.

The men were returning from the Appellate Division, where Scanlon had just argued the appeal that the County Committee, Galligan, and Della Bove had taken from Justice Winerude's order that they turn over to the Special Prosecutor all records relating to the designation of candidates for judicial office in the last two local elections.

"Some of the questions were tough," said Baker. "But they were fair."

"Dereimer didn't ask anything," said Henry. "He never said a word even though he was Presiding Justice for this one."

Scanlon shrugged. "Who knows?"

"Ed," said Brian Hollander from the front desk as soon as the three men had stepped off the elevators. "Mr. Matlin wants to see you all. Right away."

The three men looked at each other quizzically and shrugged.

"How did the argument go?" asked Matlin as soon as the men had entered his office. Matt Corey was sitting in his usual chair, looking grim.

Scanlon shrugged. "Okay."

"Who was Presiding Justice?" asked Matlin.

"Dereimer," Scanlon answered.

Matlin looked at Corey and nodded.

"Has either of you ever heard of the Alpine Club?"

Henry shook his head.

"No," said Scanlon.

"Why?" asked Henry.

Matlin went on. "It's a club uptown to which a lot of politicians and judges belong." Matlin went on. "We received a call early this morning. Anonymous. But he sounded sane and seemed to know what he was talking about."

Matlin looked at Corey who nodded.

Henry stepped closer to Matlin's desk. No one had taken a seat.

"Whoever called told us that, last night, he saw Erin Galligan and Senator Della Bove having dinner with Justice Dereimer, who the caller seemed to know was presiding at today's argument."

The three men were silent.

Matlin continued. "He said that he walked by the table once or twice and heard my name mentioned."

"Holy shit," said Scanlon.

"Anything else?" asked Henry.

"No. That was all."

There was silence in the room for a moment. Then Henry spoke.

"Can we do anything?"

"Before the decision? Not much." Matlin lifted a hand. "All we would do is stir up a hornet's nest. And guarantee an unfavorable decision from the Appellate Division." Matlin smiled. "We have a strong case, so we'll just have to wait to see the decision."

It was Friday afternoon and Henry was on his way to the Lion's Roar for the weekly gathering. He was already looking forward to that first beer. As he was leaving, he passed a newsstand. Spotting the headline in the afternoon *Post*, he stopped abruptly. "MATLIN CHASING GHOSTS," it blared. He looked closer. The words "Says Councilman" followed in small print.

Henry bought the paper. Apparently, City Councilman Herbert Scammet, one of the more voluble politicians in the City, had held a press conference. He denounced Howard Matlin for what he said was Matlin's investigation into Scammet's ties with developer Hugh Vernon, a man Scammet dubbed "New York's most progressive businessman."

Scammet accused Matlin of trying to interfere with the Rockbay deal for political reasons. Or, Scammet suggested, perhaps Matlin had a financial interest he was protecting.

The story continued in that vein and referred the reader to an editorial. In the editorial, there was a summary of the setbacks the Office had suffered in the appellate courts, and it suggested that "if this apparently groundless fishing expedition into a highly respected city leader and a model entrepreneur was a play for some cheap publicity, the Governor should consider putting some brakes on his Special Prosecutor."

Reached for comment, Matlin had cited grand jury secrecy as a reason for "no comment."

Henry felt sick. He folded the paper and headed home.

The next day, which was Saturday, Henry finished his weekend chores. He had been to the dry cleaners, picked up a few items at the grocery store, and retrieved his clock radio from the repair shop, which had overcharged him for a simple part replacement. He was considering wandering into Mulroy's to watch the Knicks game and have a beer or two. But his mind kept returning to the thing that had bothered him all last night and morning.

How was Sara dealing with the attack which had hit the news the night before? Since her run-in with the front office, he knew that Sara had been troubled enough to have isolated herself from everyone in the Office. But that was her immediate reaction when the repercussions of her actions were internal. Now the consequences of the overturned investigation were out in the open, in the form of a wholesale, irrevocable attack from Councilman Scammet and a challenge from the usually supportive *New York Post*.

Henry knew that Sara was tough and generally immune to criticism. But something told him that, this time, her armor might be insufficient to protect her and that she was in jeopardy. It wasn't really his business, he told himself. She had chosen Justin Cole and, thus, it was he who would have to be there for her. But Henry had not been able to convince himself that Cole was either willing or able to play that role.

Before he had finished his thoughts, Henry found himself dialing Sara's home number, which he had for some reason kept in his little black book.

"Hello," said a familiar female voice.

Thank goodness it wasn't Justin Cole.

"Sara, it's Henry Perkins."

Silence.

"Sara?"

"Yes."

"Sara, I don't mean to intrude but I'm very worried about you. I'm sorry, but I am." Now what? He didn't know what to say next.

Still silence.

He readied himself for the attack. Into his head tumbled all the times Sara had criticized him for his attempts to help her. How many times had she angrily fended off his suggestions that she might need someone other than herself to help her out? Why did he think that this time would be any different or that she would not, once again, send him off with a blast of anger at being intruded upon?

"Where are you?"

Henry shook his head. He wasn't sure he had heard her right. "Where am I?"

"Yes."

"I'm in my apartment."

"Can I come meet you somewhere?

Henry's head spun. This was not what he expected.

"Sure. Coffee? Or a sandwich? Someplace near you?"

"No, let me come over to the East Side."

"Okay, meet me at the little place at 73rd and Madison in twenty minutes."

"I'll be there."

As he hung up the phone, Henry pulled himself up from the chair and focused on the fact that he had twenty minutes to walk to 73rd Street and Madison Avenue.

After they each had ordered tea, Sara settled herself in her chair and looked Henry in the eye. "I owe you an apology," she began.

Henry was startled. He tried not to show it.

"I criticized you for looking for help and set myself as the standard. No help, given or taken." Her head tilted sidewise. "Can you see how selfish that is?"

Henry didn't think he was expected to answer. He was right.

"I knew the best way to do things. I saw the correct vision. I knew what should and shouldn't be the goals. I...I...I..." She shook her head. "That's not the way the world works."

"I knew what was best. But, truth told, I didn't. Never did. Oh, sure, sometimes I succeeded. But that was as much despite me as not. But I couldn't let someone else's ideas get in the way. Just mine. Just one permissible view of the world. Mine. No one could help me because, if they did, they might get in the way of my one permissible view of the world."

She took a sip of tea.

"And where did that get me? Into myself. No real friends, no real relationships, no one to trust or to talk with or to share with. Just me. And if I step on your ideas or your wishes, tough. Mine are more important. And if I bull my way ahead, so what if I wreck your plans or your project or your carefully managed investigation? So what if I wreck your whole office, where I just happen to work? So what if everything I believe in gets trashed so that I can have my way?"

She stopped. Probably for breath. But Henry knew that he should keep silent.

Suddenly Sara's eyes began to water, and she seemed about to cry.

"What I really was, and still am, is afraid. I'm afraid that if I let someone else set the agenda, they won't do things the way I know they should be done. Instead, they might go off on a tangent and try to help someone. Like my father did. And they'll end up like my father, trying to help someone and dying in the process. Sacrificing himself, and me in the process." Now the tears did begin to run down her cheeks. "I lost him once. I don't want to lose him again."

"You mean...?"

"I mean we might lose. Howard Matlin might lose. You might lose. I might lose. We all might lose. And be sacrificed. Unless, as I kept telling myself, I keep things under my own control." She lowered her head. "And look where that got us."

"Well, Sara," Henry finally said, "for whatever it's worth, I still believe in you. I believe in us—in the whole Office, in the whole mission. And I believe in Howie Matlin. Whatever happens."

Sara sat back and took a deep breath. She picked up her cup of tea and drained it. Then she sat it down again and looked Henry in the eyes. "For whatever it's worth, Henry, so do I. And I'm going to do my part. Whatever happens."

CHAPTER 34

"I know there's something here," Henry said to himself as he looked at the slim file that constituted the discontinued Andersen Sonar investigation. "I know that Galligan's at the root of it and I know that Della Bove's involved, too. But there are no judges, no cops, no district attorneys involved. No justice system. And there was no investigation underway when the Bregner superseder was signed."

Galligan and Della Bove. Galligan and Della Bove. Something was gurgling in his mind.

Ruggiero's. The dinner they covered. Or at least observed, Henry recalled.

He rose from his chair and stepped over to his file cabinet. He pulled open the second drawer, the one containing the files on his wiretaps. There it was in the Della Bove section. "Restaurant meeting," it said.

He pulled the file and set it on his desk, opening and reading it while standing up. At once, he recognized Nancy Gravett's handwriting on a scrap of paper which she had apparently clipped to his copy of a report she had sent to the file, with copies to Matt Corey and to him. "Lic. No. NY E62253. NYC plt. assgd. Carl Horseman. Comm'r EPA. Thurs. din. w/ G and D-B. Accmp. Mallon. Saw but cdn't hear enuf to detm. purp. of mtg. Mtg set up in D-B/G call 9/30." The report to which the note was affixed merely spelled out the same information in sentences.

Closing the file, Henry stepped back to his file cabinet and opened another drawer. This one contained the line sheets from all his wiretaps, filed in manila folders by month and by wiretap or bug. He thumbed through the Della Bove wiretap, looking for September. *Ah, there it was.* Removing the file, he skimmed through the material until he came to the entry he was looking for.

"9/30," it said. "D-B arranges w/ Galligan to have dinner at Ruggerio's with 'our man.'"

That wouldn't do, he said to himself. He wanted to hear the conversation again. He looked at his watch. Almost eight. Maybe someone was still here who could give him access to the tapes. He got up from his chair and headed out his door.

It was almost an hour later before Henry was back at his desk. Fortunately, Sammy Parisi was working late, too. He was preparing to install a bug that night in another case.

In his own case, Henry fared well as Parisi had quickly located the reel of tape containing the conversation. "I'd make you a cassette, but I don't have time," said Parisi, handing Henry the reel. "You'll have to find the conversation yourself."

"Wait a minute," said Henry, putting the reel on a table. "I shouldn't have this. Isn't this the evidence?"

Parisi, flashing his familiar ear-to-ear grin, pointed to a room secured by a combination-type lock, like a safe. "There's the evidence. That's only a copy." He looked at Henry and laughed. "You don't think I'd trust some attorney with the evidence, do you?"

"Guess not," said Henry, scooping up the tape. "Good luck with the bug."

"Oh, it's not me who needs the luck. It's the bugee."

Parisi was still chuckling as Henry turned to leave the tech room. "Hey," Parisi called after him. "Don't you need this?" He pointed to a reel-to-reel player which would be needed to play the tape.

Once back in his office with the player and the tape, Henry put the reel on the machine and began searching for the conversation, using the line sheets as a guide. At last, he found it and sat back to listen.

"Hi, Al. It's Erin."

"Hi. How's it goin'?"

"Not so well, maybe."

Della Bove's voice dropped. *"Whaddya mean?"*

"Our thing's taking too long."

"Listen, Erin. The only thing I'm worried about is Michigan and the Canucks. And the specs oughtta take care of that. Our guy will see to it."

Once again, Henry pressed the "pause" button. This was what he was looking for. He smiled, briefly recalling the debate he and Nelligan had had about whether Della Bove was using some ethnic slur or saying something else. What Della Bove was talking about was now clear. He was referring to the specifications for the noise detector bid and to the fact that the change in specifications would make it more difficult for the Michigan and the Canadian companies to submit a successful bid for the noise detector contract. Henry restarted the machine.

"Maybe," Galligan continued. *"But anyway, I want to meet our guy. So, I want you to get him to Ruggiero's. Next Tuesday at seven. Sharp."*

"Why not? It can't hurt."

Pause.

"Black, too?"

"Nah. We don't need him. He's done his part."

"Okay. I'll set it up. See you then."

Henry turned off the machine and sat still for a moment, reflecting on what he had heard. Then he looked at Gravett's report. "Carl Horseman. Comm'r EPA."

EPA. Environmental Protection Agency. The City agency that was buying the noise devices. Could this Horseman person be part of the scheme? And did Horseman have anything to do with Robert Black?

Henry's eyes fell on the pile of line sheets in front of him. He spotted the word "Cavaliere" on one of them. Cavaliere. Horseman. His little bit of Italian from one college course put the two words together. Coincidence?

Quickly, he rifled through the line sheets until he found one of the "Cavaliere" conversations. There was a mention of a "waiver." Then he looked further and found mentions of "specs" and "modifications" and "financing."

If Cavaliere was not Horseman, Henry would be very surprised. And if he was, then the Andersen Sonar matter was part of an investigation before the Bregner superseder and therefore the case fell within the expanded jurisdiction of the Special Prosecutor's Office.

"Bingo," said Dan Nelligan as he took a seat in Henry's office the next morning. "I found a tape of a talk Horseman gave recently. It's the same voice. Mr. Cavaliere."

"No doubt?" asked Henry.

"None. I told you so." Nelligan grinned. "My nose is never wrong."

"Well, I owe you a martini for this one."

"A double," corrected Nelligan.

"You realize what this means. We were on to Mr. Cavaliere, aka Mr. Horseman, and his shenanigans well before Whelan signed the superseder. If there was any doubt about jurisdiction for the Andersen matter, good old Mr. Cavaliere has removed it."

Henry let the scowl linger on his lips as Robert Black took a seat in front of him. He hadn't shaken hands with Black, nor had he returned Black's friendly greeting. Briefly, he recalled Matlin's similar treatment of Black and its effect. He resolved to be as successful himself.

He looked across his desk at the pudgy figure facing him. Now he realized why Matlin's intense focus must have unnerved Black, for the lawyer's eyes were darting everywhere. Everywhere but meeting his own gaze. Quickly, Henry glanced at Nelligan, to make certain he was ready. Then he fixed his eyes on Black's.

"Right now," he began sternly, "our deal is off."

Black's head jerked. "What do you mean?" he asked.

"You lied to us."

Finally Black looked at Henry. "How?" He looked away.

"By telling us that you knew nothing about the alteration of the Andersen specifications and Carl Horseman's role in it."

He heard Black suck in a lungful of air. He almost had him, he thought.

"Our deal was no lies. You lie, and every bet is off, and we go for the maximum." He saw the thick eyebrows wiggle. "Matlin told you that when you first came in. Now I'm telling you. For the last time."

Henry folded his hands in front of him and stared at the lawyer. The room was not hot, but the man across the desk was beginning to sweat. Henry watched as stubby fingers reached up and pulled a dampening shirt away from the neck. Then the fingers dropped to the front of the shirt where they began to fiddle with a button behind the tie. Still Henry riveted his eyes on Black's, even though the latter's eyes were assiduously avoiding his scrutiny.

The room was silent. Nelligan didn't move, nor did Henry. Out in the hall, someone laughed loudly. Black took the opportunity to divert himself, looking at the door from behind which the noise had come. But neither Nelligan nor Henry acknowledged the distraction. Neither moved a muscle.

Black returned to adjusting his shirt collar. But that seemed to fail him, as well. Suddenly he took a deep breath, apparently making up his mind.

"I knew about the Andersen deal. Some things I didn't tell you. But not all the things you want to know."

"Try us," responded Henry.

It was over an hour later when Black left. In that time, he had made the Andersen deal clear to Henry and Nelligan.

The specifications for the bids were redrafted by Commissioner Horseman at the instance of Erin Galligan. At least, that's what Black had been told. Goblox Associates was, to Black's understanding, a creation of Galligan and Della Bove. It existed to hold a large block of the new Andersen shares of stock. Black believed that Horseman must be sharing in the Goblox holdings, unless Galligan was paying him in cash for his part.

The incentive for Galligan and Della Bove was obvious. In view of Andersen's low volume of business, the newly issued shares had been sold for a few dollars each, raising just enough money from the public to establish a market in the stock and to finance the retooling of Andersen's facilities. But as soon as it was announced that Andersen had won a large contract with the City, the price of the shares shot up, making the holders of blocks of shares a good deal of money.

What Black told Henry and Nelligan, they already knew or had guessed. He merely confirmed their suspicions. The problem was that most of Black's information was hearsay, largely from Senator Della Bove. The investigators still had no proof that Galligan and Della Bove owned Goblox Associates. Nor had they proof that Commissioner Horseman had received a bribe from Galligan or Della Bove to induce him to alter the specifications. Without proof of ownership of Goblox and of such an undertaking, no case could be made.

"You believe him that he doesn't know the stuff personally?" asked Henry after Black had departed.

"Yeah, I do." Nelligan responded.

"So do I," admitted Henry ruefully. "And what that means is that we still don't have a hold on Horseman."

Nelligan nodded.

"At least not yet," said Henry.

Nelligan smiled.

"I want to know why I've been dragged in here. And why I was told to come without an attorney."

"Commissioner Horseman, you were not dragged here. And you were requested, not told, to speak to us informally. You're free, at any time, to refuse to talk to us and to consult an attorney." Henry was keeping his voice as informal sounding as possible.

"Perhaps now is the time to consult counsel, then." Horseman rose from the chair in which he had just seated himself.

Henry weighed the alternatives. And tried one.

"May I ask who your attorney is?"

Horseman hesitated. Henry thought it might be that he hadn't consulted one.

"You needn't tell me," said Henry, hoping to evoke the opposite response.

"I don't see why I can't tell you," Horseman responded. "I've consulted Mr. Maxwell Olman."

Just what he suspected. And that told him how to proceed next.

"Well, Commissioner. As I said…" he paused casually and waved a hand. "Sit down. No sense in being uncomfortable while we chat."

Horseman took his seat again.

Henry looked at him. Horseman had a narrow face, with ears that clung to his skull as though sewn in place. His eyes were close set, but they seemed to be forcibly separated by the prominent nose that jutted out below a forehead that, itself, was bifurcated by a vertical peak. The mouth was small and, at the moment, pursed. Looking at Horseman's head, Henry wondered if perhaps some large babysitter had accidentally sat on it as her infant charge lay on his side.

Going to the animal phyla, Henry thought first of a rat. But then, Henry corrected himself, Horseman looked more like a weasel than a rat. A frightened weasel.

"So, as I said," Henry continued in a casual tone of voice, "you can talk to a lawyer." He lifted a hand conversationally. "Even Olman." He let his hand fall. "Galligan's lawyer."

Horseman sat up abruptly. But Henry continued talking in the same easy manner, almost lolling in his chair.

"And you can see what he wants to advise you. About the shares of Andersen Sonar that you were supposed to get for your troubles, but that Galligan hasn't given you."

There was a jolt across the desk. It reminded Henry of a film he had once seen of an execution in an electric chair. Somewhere in Florida, he thought it was.

Nelligan started toward the Commissioner, apparently thinking he was going to fall off his chair.

Henry went on. "Maybe Olman'll tell Galligan to give you the shares now, huh?" Henry sat up straight and fixed his eyes on the wilting figure of Deputy Commissioner Carl Horseman. He almost felt bad. This one wasn't even a challenge.

"What the hell is this?" asked Henry as he dropped the morning's *Daily News* on Scoop Dixon's desk.

Dixon looked like someone had just reactivated his hemorrhoids and then treated them with a hammer. He merely shook his head.

Dixon fumbled in his desk drawer and pulled out a fresh pack of Camels. With what Henry thought were shaking fingers, he ripped open the cellophane wrapper and the foil fold, tapping out a cigarette.

Henry opened his mouth to address the cigarette's introduction. Then, looking at the pained expression on Dixon's face, he decided to hold his comment.

"This is really bad," said Dixon at last, blowing out a cloud of smoke as he did. "The State's highest judicial official, the mighty Chief Judge Arthur Sammons openly, publicly denounces, as he pompously puts it, 'the outrageous and illegal methods' of the Special Prosecutor for putting a false case in his holy system—a case you friggin' worked on."

"I know. But I was asking about this crap." He dropped a column by Johnny Donegan on Dixon's desk.

"Holy shit, I didn't even see that." Dixon smiled bleakly and snuffed out his cigarette. Then he picked up the paper Henry had set on his desk and began reading the Donegan article. It accused Howard Matlin personally of locking an unidentified witness in a closet, depriving him of food, drink, and his required medicines for twenty-four hours, in a vain attempt to force the witness to falsely accuse an unnamed judge of corruption.

When he had finished reading, Dixon looked up at Henry, a puzzled expression on his face. "I have no idea," he said. "But I'm gonna find out." He rose from his chair.

Thirty minutes later there was a knock on Henry's door.

"Come in."

It was Scoop Dixon. "I've talked to Howie, to Matt, to Nat, to all the group chiefs, to Harry Rood and to Sammy Parisi. And no one has the slightest idea of what Donegan's talking about."

"Guess you'll have to deny it," said Dan Nelligan, who was sitting in front of Henry's desk.

"Sure. But who believes a prosecutor when he denies something like this?"

Nelligan smiled.

"What's funny?" asked Dixon.

"I thought Donegan was on the wagon. Looks like he fell off. And got the D.T.s again."

CHAPTER 35

Howard Matlin looked terrible. There were circles under his eyes, as though he hadn't slept well for some time. And, in the whites of his eyes, little red lines seemed to confirm the impression. Nevertheless, he smiled when Henry Perkins sat down.

"What's doing, Henry?" he asked.

Immediately Henry felt reassured. He could see that, even though he was the subject of attack from many sides, Howard Matlin was still in control. Comfortably so. Henry relaxed.

"Want to put out a contract on Donegan?" he laughed.

Matlin smiled. "I'd rather Sammons disappeared."

"Hear, hear," said Henry.

"Have you learned anything about the Andersen deal?"

Henry smiled broadly as he related the role of Commissioner Horseman in the transaction and the way in which Horseman's presence gave the Office jurisdiction.

"Good work," said Matlin. "You're making progress."

The knocking on Henry's door was loud.

"Come on in. Before you break the door."

Immediately Larry Santarella entered with a smile. Behind him stood an unsmiling Hal Baker.

"Hey, baby," blurted Santarella. "You made the tabs." He held up a copy of the afternoon *Post*.

"What is it?"

"Read for yourself."

Henry looked at the article. It was a short piece, on page 8, squeezed in between an advertisement for a mattress sale and a picture of some woman in Central Park with her skirt blowing up above her waist. It was entitled "Matlin Aide Accused."

"Read it," urged Santarella.

He did. Some group calling itself "Friends of the Judiciary" had issued a press release attacking the Special Prosecutor's indictment of Justice John Hurd as "an unwarranted attack on the unquestionable integrity" of New York's judiciary. It had referred to the assistant handling the investigation as *Harry Porkins*, and it called him a "Matlin-like zealot."

"Shit, man," protested Henry. "They spelled my name wrong."

"Hey, Larry. I wanted to ask you something," Henry spoke quietly to Santarella, as they returned from lunch in the State cafeteria later that day. "What's wrong with Hal? He doesn't seem himself."

Santarella's cheerful expression faded. "Marital problems."

"Hal? But his wife's great."

"I know. But with all the shit gettin' flung at us lately, and with Hal burnin' the midnight oil in that subpoena battle, I guess she's not too happy."

Henry looked at him. "You think there's anything I can do?"

Santarella stopped and turned toward Henry. "Yeah. Keep your fingers crossed for him. And go catch whoever the fucksticks are that you're after."

"Mister Porkins, I believe?"

Henry jumped. He had been staring out his window, watching the tiny planes take off and land at distant LaGuardia airport. It rested his eyes.

"Sara." He *was* surprised. This was, he believed, the *first* time Sara Leventhal had entered his office. "What brings you here?"

"Well, first off, I wanted to ask what it felt like to be a Matlin-like zealot."

"At least they could have spelled my name right."

"But I also wanted to fill you in. A lot has happened since we last spoke."

Henry recalled vividly the scene in the coffee shop nearly two weeks earlier. He had left Sara alone since then, allowing her to deal with her problem in her own way on her own timetable. "Sit down." Henry pointed to the chairs in front of his desk.

Sara sat. "First off, the mob appeal. Matt Corey went after Paul Kondor and convinced him to come back."

"Wow. That's great."

Sara nodded and smiled weakly. "Reluctantly, I have to agree."

"And then...?"

"And then I got my shot at him. And just as I suspected, once he saw the hot spot he was in, he folded and told us everything."

"Everything?"

"Well, everything he says he knows. And the unfortunate part is that I believe him that it's all he knows. And so does Harry Rood, who sat in on my interrogation."

"So, what did he tell you?"

Sara shifted in her chair. "First, as soon as Donofrio had been found guilty of murder, Kondor was contacted by Sonny DiPiano, a mob buddy of Donofrio. They wanted Kondor to handle the appeal. Nothing more."

"Nothing about a fix?" asked Henry.

"Not at first. Not until Kondor told DiPiano that Donofrio was a dead man—that the case was a loser, that the evidence against Donofrio was overwhelming and that he'd never seen a stronger case."

"So, what happened then?"

"DiPiano said he'd get back to him the next day. And he did. And he set up a meeting with a guy who could 'help out'   a guy named Jack Peacock."

"Who's he?"

"He *was* Vince Tonetti's bagman."

"Tonetti? The Brooklyn boss?"

"That's the one."

"I thought this thing was in Queens."

"The murder was at JFK, so it was prosecuted there. But Donofrio was a Brooklyn mob guy."

"Oh. So then what happened?"

"Peacock said the matter could be handled for a hundred grand. And DiPiano agreed without hesitation."

"And who got the hundred grand?" asked Henry.

"That's what Kondor says he doesn't know. And that's what I believe he's telling the truth about."

"So, what have you got?"

"Fortunately, a little more than that."

"What?"

"Well, the good news is that DiPiano, for whatever reason, worked through our boy Paulie. Kondor. He gave Kondor an envelope to give to Peacock. And Kondor admitted opening it before he gave it to Peacock."

"And what was in it?" Henry asked.

"Just what DiPiano had said. A hundred grand in cash."

"And I assume he gave it to Peacock and then Peacock gave it to Mr. X. So, when do we get Peacock in here?"

"Never," said Sara.

"What?"

"Peacock died about a year ago."

"Oh, crap. So, we're screwed."

"Not yet."

Henry looked at Sara questioningly.

"As I said, Kondor gave us a little more. Peacock told him to meet him with the envelope on a certain corner in Brooklyn near the courthouse at a certain time. When Kondor showed up, Peacock was sitting in a cab. He called out and Kondor went to the cab and gave him the envelope."

"And?"

"And then Peacock turned to the driver and said, 'Kennedy Airport, Swissair,' and the cab took off. That was it. The next thing Kondor knew, he won the appeal, and the conviction was reversed and the whole case thrown out."

"Jesus," said Henry. "That's amazing. So, what can we do now?"

"I've already started it. I'm issuing subpoenas to Swissair from JFK to Switzerland for passenger lists on that date, which Kondor was able to pinpoint for us."

"Well, it's a start."

"I'm sure it will take a while to get responses. But it's a start. What about your Andersen case?"

Henry smiled. "Well, we found that it is in our jurisdiction."

Sara lowered her eyebrows. "How?"

"Before Bregner, Dan Nelligan and I were already looking into the City guy who turned out to be the guy who fixed the bid specifications so that Andersen would win the contract."

"And who was that?"

"An EPA commissioner who has admitted his part in the deal."

Henry's head snapped up as he opened the *New York Times'* Sunday magazine. There was a horrible picture of Howard Matlin, his face half in shadows, and an article entitled "Howard Matlin: A Modern Torquemada" by Toby Copin. Most shocking of all was the article's claim that it was based upon an interview of Howard Matlin by Copin. Unsurprisingly, the article was a vicious attack on the Special Prosecutor.

First thing Monday morning, Henry was in Scoop Dixon's office. "There isn't a word of truth in this whole thing," Henry complained. "Where did Copin get this stuff? Not from Matlin, as he claims."

Dixon shook his head sadly.

"I mean, he says that Howie admits that he didn't have any evidence against Bregner. He has Howie admitting that the Vernon thing was a fishing expedition. And, of all things, he 'quotes' Howie to the effect that friggin' Hurd is probably innocent. There is no way Howie said any of those things."

"I know. And we've already lodged a formal protest and demanded a retraction," Dixon sighed. "But a lot of good that will do."

"But, Scoop," Henry moaned, "I don't get it. First off, did Howie talk to that asshole Copin?"

Dixon nodded affirmatively.

"But why? Why in the world would Howie even give the time of day to that slime bucket?"

Dixon looked back across his desk at Henry through reddened eyes. He took a drag on his cigarette. Then his face puckered. The smoke must have tasted sour by now, after twenty-four hours of hell. That's what he told Henry his life had been since the Sunday *Times* had reached most New Yorkers early the day before.

"I tried to talk him out of it."

Henry eyes widened. "You mean the Copin interview wasn't your idea?"

"Perk, I may look like shit today. But do I look like an idiot?"

"It can't have been Howie's idea. Can it?"

Dixon shook his head.

"Then who?"

"You don't wanna know."

"Bullshit, I don't want to know. If you ask me, it must have been Erin Galligan's idea. Or Max Olman."

"No. It was right here. Home grown."

"Who the hell was that stupid?"

"It was Cole."

"Justin Cole?" Henry's response was almost shouted. "Justin Cole?"

Dixon merely nodded his head.

"What the fuck was he thinking of?"

"He had this idea that, if Copin heard our point of view directly from the horse's mouth, he might soften his attitude toward the Office."

"Horse's mouth? Cole must have been looking up the other end of the horse."

CHAPTER 36

Henry's office door burst open.

"Did'jya hear the news?"

Henry jumped as Barry Conlon swept in the door.

"What news?" He was alarmed. It must be bad.

"Winerude just dismissed the Bregner case."

"Dismissed the whole case?"

"That's what Hal Baker just told me. And he'd done somethin' on the papers."

"Shit!" Henry put a paperweight on the documents he was reviewing and stepped toward his door. "Where's Baker?" he asked as he stepped past Conlon.

"I don't know. He was pretty shook up. Maybe he's with Matlin and shit-for-brains Cole."

Henry turned and faced his old drinking buddy. "Hey, Barry. He may act like a shit sometimes, but he's one of us. And, anyway, that indictment had Howie's name on it, not Cole's. And it's Howie who'll take all the shit." He left Conlon shaking his head.

Cole wasn't in his office, so Henry swept around the front of the building and past Matlin's office. Dixon was gone, too. Probably with Matlin. He had another idea.

Her door was closed, as usual. He knocked.

"Yes!"

The response was barked through the door. Good old Sara. At least she hadn't completely changed. He opened her door.

She was not at her desk. Instead, he saw her pacing in front of her windows, a grim look on her face.

"You've heard, I see," he said.

Her eyebrows contracted and her mouth opened. "Heard what?"

"What are you pacing around about?"

"Our informant in the mob case was murdered."

"Omygod!"

"And Remmelt told somebody that he got the name from the DA's office, and he gave it to Ralph Castegglio. Who presumably had the informant rubbed out."

"Oh, my lord, Sara."

"Just like happened to my father. Exactly the same."

"My God." Henry shook his head. "Who was the source in the District Attorney's Office?"

"We don't know yet. But we're working on it. If we can."

"What do you mean?

"The Johnson trial—that's the attempted murder trial that's been fixed by Remmelt and Judge Ryan. For fifty grand?"

Henry nodded. "I remember."

"It's been moved up to the last week of April and could be moved up sooner. And we can't let it go to verdict because of double jeopardy. So, once we move on that bribe, it'll reveal the source of our information, which is the wire on Remmelt. And that's the end of anything on the wire."

Henry took a deep breath. "Woooh."

"And that," Sara continued, "would be the end of our chance to confirm who leaked the informant's name."

Henry looked at her for a moment. "Then I guess you don't need any more bad news."

Sara returned his look, her eyes tired and red. She sighed loudly. "No. Give—let me have it. What is it?"

"Bregner. Justin's case. Winerude just dismissed it."

"Oh my God!" Sara exclaimed. She was clearly stunned.

"I haven't seen an opinion," Henry went on. "I thought maybe you had one."

She walked to her phone and picked it up, punching three numbers as she did.

"He's not there," offered Henry. The unanswered ringing confirmed his statement. "I think he's with Matlin. And Dixon and the rest."

She put the phone down and looked at Henry for a long, silent moment. Her face was still, but inside Henry sensed that something cataclysmic going on.

"This will kill him, Henry."

Suddenly he wanted to ask her why. Why she cared so much about Justin Cole, who, as far as he could see, cared about no one but himself. Why would she feel sorry for someone who, just a short time ago, with his Copin interview, had proved his capacity to hurt Howard Matlin—the very man who had provided Cole with the stage on which he had become a star? Someone who, with equal likelihood, would also hurt Sara?

But Henry didn't say a word. He realized that Sara did care. She actually seemed concerned about Justin enough to share his disappointment.

"I'm sorry," he said.

"Come on," Sara said at last. "Let's see if we can find a copy of the opinion.

"I can't believe it," Sara groaned.

They were standing in front of Justin Cole's desk, on which they had just found a copy of Justice Winerude's opinion dismissing the Bregner indictment. Looking on together, they read it. Henry was aware of Sara's impatience with his slower pace. He recalled that long ago, Sara had mastered speed reading. But she said nothing until Henry was finished.

Picking up the opinion, Sara read aloud. "'The Special Prosecutor failed in the grand jury to disprove the possibility that the money given to Bregner by Colbert was in repayment of some prior obligation yet undisclosed. Thus, the prosecution has not eliminated all possibilities but those that incriminate, and the indictment must fail.' And this idiot was on Law Review? At Yale?" She threw the opinion on the desk.

"Since when is a prosecutor supposed to try his case beyond a reasonable doubt in the grand jury?" She looked at Henry but was talking to herself. "Eliminate every possible defense; that's what trials are for." Sara glanced down at the opinion again, then looked up. "What absolute crap!" She was too angry to continue.

Henry shook his head and tried to lighten the atmosphere. "At least, with judges like that, we could save a lot of time and money. No need for juries or trials."

A noise behind them caused both to turn around. Justin Cole had arrived. He stomped into his office and walked around his desk, glaring, first at Sara, then at Henry.

Henry stepped back.

"I don't want to talk about it," Justin snapped.

Sara shrugged her shoulders. "Fine."

Blam!

They both jumped. Cole had just slammed his fist into his desk, causing his pen and paperweight to fall to the floor.

"I'm going home," he announced.

"Fine. I'll get my coat," said Sara.

"Alone," Cole glared at Sara.

Sara stood stock still facing him. Not moving a muscle. Henry held his breath and tried to fade further into the corner. It was Cole who moved first. He strode around his desk and removed his coat from the back of his door. Then, without a word, he walked out.

Sara didn't move until Cole was gone. Until Henry couldn't even hear Cole's footsteps anymore. Then she turned in the direction of the elevators, where he was by now, and lifted her left hand. She closed her fingers, all but the middle one. Then she lifted her right arm and brought her hand firmly down on her left forearm.

"Let's get back to work," she said.

A brawny forearm, thick with black hair that covered the skin until both disappeared under rolled up white sleeves, plopped a mug of coffee on the counter in front of Henry. "Here," said the counterman as he turned back to the grill to scramble Henry's eggs.

Henry unfolded the *Times* and looked over the front page. His eyes stopped quickly.

"Bar Committee Accuses Special Prosecutor of Wiretapping Abuse." Right on the front page.

Henry's coffee cooled while he read. By the time he finished, his eggs had arrived and were cooling, as well.

Henry, however, was not cool. He was very angry. The article discussed a report of the Criminal Courts Committee of the Bar Association on what it called "egregiously excessive" wiretapping by the Office of the Special Prosecutor. In its report, the Committee had cited only rumor and hearsay as its evidence since, as it had claimed, facts were "withheld" from it. The Committee's report, of course, failed to mention the fact that the wiretaps in question were still under court seal and thus could not, by law, be revealed.

Equally salient to Henry was the name of the chairman of the committee and the man who announced and elaborated on the findings. Max Olman had embellished the report with his own attack on the Special Prosecutor for his "addiction to listening in on the innocent conversations of private citizens." Olman had neglected to note that his client, Justice John Hurd, had been indicted for bribe-receiving because of some of those "innocent conversations."

Swallowing his eggs without sufficient chewing, and his coffee without tasting it, Henry paid and left for the grand jury.

It was still raining hard as Henry emerged from the coffee shop and opened his umbrella. In the street outside, the curb had become the bank of a river that roared toward the corner. At the corner, water had already begun to spread over the cracked sidewalk, forcing pedestrians who wished to avoid wading through the black, ankle-deep runoff to detour between two cars, one parked legally, and one behind it, extending several feet into the crosswalk. As people converged on the nearby subway entrance, umbrellas squeezed together, sometimes sliding, one under the other, threatening eyeballs with probing metal prongs where supports had been denuded of their black nylon coverings.

Traffic was snarled, seemingly hopelessly. Horns sounded, long and painfully, as lights turned from red to green and back to red again, all without any apparent effect on the matted agglomeration of vehicles inching toward the next corner, where the same scene would be repeated.

In the overflowing gutters, sodden newspapers collected, some floating on top of the mess, some sinking to the bottom to join broken umbrellas and other items of flotsam clogging the sewers that might otherwise have removed at least a portion of the accumulating water.

In some parts on the country, the mayhem in the streets might be considered sufficient provocation for an appearance by the National Guard. In New York City, however, it was just another early April morning.

The subway platform was nearly unapproachable, with crowds backed up, almost to the token gates. As usual when it rained, the subway came to near collapse. For some mysterious reason, trains were slowed to a crawl by the traffic jams overhead, as though their rights of way were somehow impeded by rains that fell elsewhere, and signals were plagued by failures, apparently in some sympathetic response to the saturated streetlights above.

Maybe it was a good thing it was raining, for it gave Henry time to forget the article he had just read and to begin to focus on the grand jury session ahead.

The rain was still falling in fits and starts, splattering against Howard Matlin's window as Henry settled into his seat in front of the Special Prosecutor's desk. Also present were Dan Nelligan and Matt Corey. Henry was speaking.

"Porche confirmed everything we knew from the documents." Henry lifted the document he was holding on his lap. "And he gave us this."

Matlin read the document quickly.

Henry continued. "That's a memo that Galligan told Horseman he would show him. The one that Horseman said proved that he owned the five thousand shares of the Goblox holdings which he was giving Horseman for his role in the Andersen deal. And it also confirms that Galligan and Della Bove owned the shares nominally held by Goblox Associates. Obviously Galligan did what he said he'd do. And he also gave a copy of the memo to Porche."

"Honor among thieves," laughed Nelligan.

Matlin nodded. That's Galligan's and Della Bove's signatures on the memo?"

"Yes," responded Nelligan. "Both have checked out."

Matlin handed the memo back to Henry. "Well, that's our proof that Galligan and Della Bove own the other hundred and forty-five thousand shares."

"Except," said Henry, "They don't."

Matlin's eyebrows dropped. "What do you mean?"

"Remember the waiver problem?"

"Yes," responded Matlin. "There was some restriction on the Andersen company that had to be waived. Black was asked to do it but someone else did it three days later."

Henry marveled at Matlin's memory. Especially during these difficult times. "That's right," he said.

"So, someone got some shares to handle the waiver?"

Henry handed Matlin a piece of paper. "Here is a report from the registrar and transfer agent for the Andersen stock."

Matlin took a few minutes to examine the document. Then he looked up and turned to Matt Corey. He held out the document, which Corey took.

"Matt, that's a record from the company that's paid to keep track of the ownership of stock. What it shows is that there were a hundred fifty thousand shares registered to Goblox Associates at the post office box we know of."

Corey nodded.

"But it goes on to indicate that there was a second registration of the stock Goblox owned. Now, according to this document, instead of the whole hundred and fifty thousand shares being registered to Goblox, there are two listed owners. Goblox has one hundred twenty thousand shares." Matlin looked at Henry. "And five thousand of those were to be Horseman's?"

"Correct," said Henry.

Then Matlin looked again at Corey. "So, thirty thousand shares are now registered to something called 'Seaward Holdings.'"

Matlin turned back to Henry. "Do we have any idea who owns Seaward Holdings?"

"None."

"But everybody here would agree that the owner of the Seaward Holdings shares is likely to be the person responsible for obtaining the waiver of the State prohibition against Anderson Sonar to bid on this deal and now is, in effect, a full partner in this deal. Am I right?"

Everyone nodded.

"Clearly," said Matt Corey, verbalizing the obvious.

"Does Seaward Holdings have an address?" asked Matlin.

"Yes," said Henry. "It's a bank. In the Bahamas."

Nelligan sat up and smiled. "The Bahamas? That's my turf."

CHAPTER 37

"It sounds to me," said Howard Matlin, "like you're almost there." His tired eyes tried to smile.

"Almost," responded Henry. "Except for one thing. No one will talk to us about how Andersen got the waiver so we can see who the other partner in this deal is."

Henry and Dan Nelligan had met the day before with the State bureaucrat who had formally issued the waiver of the bidding restriction on Andersen Sonar. But he had done so, he said, only because he was ordered to do so by his boss, the Commissioner of the agency. And both Henry and Nelligan said he was credible. The Commissioner himself, however, was refusing to speak with Henry or anyone else at the Special Prosecutor's Office.

"Did you give him a subpoena?"

"Not worth it, Howie." Henry waved a hand. "The guy had his lawyer tell me that he had nothing to say without immunity. And even then, he'd have nothing to say."

"Perhaps you could take a contempt on him."

"I'd have to give him immunity to do it. Since it seems likely that he's the guy who got the stock, we would lose our target."

Matlin nodded his head. "You're right. You shouldn't immunize him."

Henry was silent.

"There's another possibility," said Matlin at last.

Henry looked at his boss. His eyes still glowed with the fire that had burned its way through the law enforcement and judicial systems of New York City. But the eyes glowed barely. There was a sag in the jaw that seemed to pull down the formerly firm cheeks and jowls. The mouth seemed to have lost its ability to smile, content to rest expressionless beneath the nose. Even his eyes were affected, with creases spreading outward from each one, and sagging circles underlining them.

"I could call the Governor and have him order the Commissioner to cooperate."

Of course. Henry hadn't thought of that. But something stopped him and told him not to accept Matlin's offer.

"Let me see what I can come up with first. I've got a couple of ideas." He didn't have any ideas. But it was all he could think of saying.

"Fine," said Matlin. He uttered no protest and made no other comment. Henry thought he saw a flicker of relief in Matlin's eyes.

"I'll let you know as soon as anything happens," Henry offered reassuringly, and he rose to go.

Dan Nelligan rose with him and accompanied him through the door. Once in the hall, Nelligan turned and took Henry gently by the shoulder. "Thanks for not taking Howie up on his offer," he whispered.

"Why?" asked Henry.

Nelligan pawed the ground with one foot, lowering his head as he did. Then he looked at Henry. "This is between us," he said, still whispering. "The Governor's not returning Howie's calls."

An hour later, Henry was walking by Matlin's door when he ran into Sara emerging from the Special Prosecutor's office.

"Sara."

She stopped and looked at Henry. Her face was drawn, and her mouth was turned downward in a frown.

"What's wrong?"

"I just had to give Howie some bad news."

"More bad news? Is there something else that can go wrong?"

"It looks that way," responded Sara. "The Johnson trial—the drug dealer who tried to kill a cop and for whom Remmelt arranged a bribe with Judge Ryan..."

Henry nodded. "I remember."

"The date's been moved up again. Ryan had a case plead out. The trial's starting next Monday."

"Woooh," Henry sighed. "That doesn't give you much time for your other stuff, does it?"

"No." Sara turned and headed toward her office.

Henry started down the hall himself but glanced in Scoop Dixon's open door. There, engulfed in smoke, he saw several assistants gathered around the press secretary's desk. No one was smiling.

"Sara," he called.

She stopped.

"Come with me to Scoop's office. I have a bad feeling."

For a moment Sara hesitated. Then she joined Henry and walked to Dixon's office.

"What's happened?" Henry said, poking his head in as far as the smoke would permit.

"You haven't heard?" It was Barry Conlon, who looked like he had just been told his mother had died.

Henry's heart thumped and he felt his stomach tighten. Something was very wrong.

"No. What happened?"

"The Governor's just appointed a commission," said Paul Meade, Sara's group chief.

"A commission to investigate our office," added Lou Morotti. "At the request of the Chief Judge."

"What? That's ridiculous."

"You're right," agreed Dixon. "And it's so ridiculous that they're starting hearings Monday."

"Monday! How can the Governor appoint a commission one week and start hearings the next?" protested Henry.

"Simple," answered Hal Baker. "By planning this thing in advance. And announcing it when everything was set up."

Then Sara spoke. "Maybe you're overreacting," she said at last. "Maybe this will be a chance to let the public see what we're really doing."

The group looked through the smoke at Sara as though she had two heads.

"You must be kidding," said Morotti.

Then Dixon spoke. "If anyone thinks for even a minute that our side is going to be heard from, they are in for a big disappointment. Even Howie didn't think of that when we discussed it." Suddenly Dixon was seized by a fit of coughing. It began with a dark, gurgling choking sound that grew in volume. In a matter of seconds, it had driven both Sara and Henry away.

Once they had escaped the smoke and the cough, Sara took a deep breath. Then she gagged.

"Sara, what's wrong?" exclaimed Henry.

She looked at Henry with wide eyes. "He knew. Howie knew about this when he was talking to me. And he never said a word."

"Oh, God. Save me from this asshole." Henry couldn't keep his thoughts to himself. He leaped up from his desk and started toward Scoop Dixon's office.

But he didn't get there. In the hall, almost immediately, he bumped into Sara. And he unloaded on her first.

"Sara. Did you see Donegan's column?"

She made a face. "I never read the *Daily News*. Too many gory pictures."

"Well, there should be another one today. Of Johnny Donegan's decapitated head."

She smiled for an instant. "Okay, what does he say?"

Henry lifted the newspaper. "Of course, it's about the Governor's appointing that stupid commission." He began to read aloud. "'Like a tiny crocus after a long, dreary winter, the Constitution has once again poked its irrepressible head through the ice bound soil to endow the land with the spring of freedom.' What shit."

Sara smiled weakly. "You have to admit, the guy can write."

"Yeah," responded Henry. "Too bad he can't think."

The next day, Henry was even angrier when he learned that Mike Welling, the reporter who had covered the Special Prosecutor's Office for the

Daily News since the Office's inception, with consistently favorable comment, had suddenly and inexplicably been transferred to the obituary page.

"Why in the world would they take probably their best local crime reporter and put him doing obituaries?" Henry wailed.

He had to wait until Dixon stopped coughing for an answer. "Did you read the editorial today?"

"In the *News*?"

Dixon nodded and handed him his copy.

Henry read it and looked up. He felt like he had swallowed something rotten. "'Trampling on rights.' 'Disemboweling the Constitution.' What the fuck are they talking about. Where are the specifics? Where're the rights we've trampled on? How can they say these things without citing any specific examples? And they call us the McCarthyites. They'd better take a look in a mirror."

"You done?"

Henry hesitated. Then the corners of his mouth lifted. He'd like to have continued grumbling for another hour, but Dixon had undermined his anger. "Yeah."

"Well, let me brighten your day some more then. The word is that the lead witness at Monday's first hearing of the Commission is your favorite attorney."

Henry looked at Dixon dubiously. "Not..."

"Max Olman."

Henry shook his head. "An objective review? That's what's they're supposed to be doing?"

Now it was Dixon who shook his head. "Nobody ever said politics is objective," he said as he fumbled for a cigarette. A fit of coughing interrupted him and drove Henry from the room.

Henry shifted uncomfortably in his seat. He had just finished telling Matlin about his failure to get anywhere with the reluctant Commissioner.

Matlin took it all in. At least he seemed to. The problem was that Matlin's head must have felt like a punching bag, with all the bad news it had absorbed recently.

Henry felt terrible. Yet there was nothing he could do. Nothing to ease the pressure, to deaden the pain, to lessen the threats hanging over the wounded head. Nothing except to try to finish his case, so that he could prove to the world that the people Howard Matlin wanted to make into defendants ought to be defendants. Ought, in fact, to be in jail.

Matlin was speaking. "Henry, we've been under a lot of pressure lately."

Henry felt his mouth open slightly. This was the first time he'd heard Matlin acknowledge the strain. He was speaking again.

"And I just wanted to make sure that you were holding up all right."

It took a second or two for the words to penetrate. And when they did, they hit Henry hard. Howard Matlin was under more pressure, was having to endure more pain than any man he had ever imagined. And yet, just after Henry had added another pound per square inch of pressure, Matlin had stopped feeling whatever he was feeling and had asked Henry if he was all right. Henry wasn't certain he could pull himself together enough to respond.

He got up, nodding. It was the best he could do. Then he stepped toward the door.

"Oh, by the way," Matlin said.

Henry turned around. Just as he did, the afternoon sun reached a point in the western sky that projected a beam of light onto the desk in front of Matlin. The light struck some object on the desk and reflected into the face of the Special Prosecutor, lighting as well the air around it. For just an instant, his head seemed to shine, surrounded by a nimbus, like a head in one of those flat, pre-Renaissance panel paintings he had seen in museums in Europe. Suddenly Henry felt as though he was in the half light of a gallery of the Louvre, staring at a twelfth-century painting, shot through with the tiny cracks of age and deterioration, dimmed by the turning of the once-bright colors to pigments of sorrow and night, except for the central figure—the face of a man hanging on a cross, his head looking out at the world with a message of profound suffering and eternal hope.

"I'm calling a staff meeting at five thirty. Can you be there?"

Matlin's voice, speaking in a routine manner of an ordinary sounding meeting dispelled the illusion. Of course, Henry recalled at once, they often had staff meetings on short notice. To discuss something as mundane as the Christmas party. Which is why Henry was disquieted by his own reaction. The hairs on his neck rose.

Half an hour later, Henry strode into his office to find Dan Nelligan waiting for him. "News already?" he said hopefully. Perhaps he'd heard something from the Bahamas.

"It's news," Nelligan responded. "But not news you're gonna like."

Henry stopped dead and looked at Nelligan. "What?" he demanded.

"Sit down. I'll give it to you. It's very short."

He did as Nelligan suggested, not daring to speculate on the newest tragedy. From Nelligan's expression, it could only be a tragedy.

"Here, read this."

A glance told Henry that it was the Appellate Division's opinion in the appeal which Galligan, Della Bove, and the County Committee had taken from Justice Winerude's order enforcing the Office's subpoenas for the County Committee's records on the filling of judgeships. It was material the Office needed to continue its investigation into the purchasing of judgeships.

He read.

"The Special Prosecutor has made no showing to contradict Appellants' position that this is a fishing expedition, without basis in fact, without any objective cognizable by law. The orders appealed from are reversed and the Special Prosecutor's subpoenas are quashed in their entirety. Dereimer, P.J. All concur."

Henry looked up at Nelligan in disbelief. His mouth hung open loosely until he spoke.

"Quashed in their entirety. Nothing. We get nothing." His fist hit his desk firmly. "Holy fucking shit! I don't believe it."

"You don't?" responded Nelligan. "Did you see who wrote that masterpiece?"

Henry looked at the opinion again. "Dereimer." He looked up, his face reflecting his sudden comprehension. "The dinner."

"Cozy, isn't it? He dines with Mr. Galligan and the Senator one night and gets rid of their subpoenas the next day."

A knock on the door interrupted what threatened to become an intemperate outburst.

"Yeah!" he shouted.

The door opened. It was Barry Conlon. "Five thirty. Matlin's meeting."

"Oh, yeah," he said softly. "Thanks."

They all filed in quickly. Some laughing. Some sullen. Most ill at ease. And expectant. There was a sense of foreboding in the air, of something no one wanted to hear. Perhaps, Henry thought, trying to dismiss the feeling, he was becoming punchy. Perhaps he needed a fresh view.

He looked around the room. The staff members were sitting on risers, permanent risers used for the grand juries sitting in Manhattan that sloped down to the floor below. At the side of the floor were some chairs which could be brought out for witnesses to sit in or for the stenographer. But they were out of the way. Down below, in the center of the floor, sat a single table with a single chair. Alone. Waiting.

Just then, the door opened, and Howard Matlin walked in. At once, a deadly silence descended on the group.

Henry took another quick survey of the room. Everyone seemed to be there. Down in front were the group chiefs, together with Appeals Chief Ed Scanlon, Nat Perlman, and Matt Corey. Hal Baker, looking glummer than usual, was sitting with Larry Santarella and two other assistants in his group. Henry spotted Sara, down and to his left, sitting next to Justin Cole.

Matlin cleared his throat. "When we started some three and a half years ago," he began, "I said that we would not settle for picking a few rotten apples from a few trees. I said that we would dig up the roots instead. The roots where the corruption started that led to trees producing rotten apples. I said it. And I meant it."

Henry could almost hear his own heart beating.

"I meant it. And you meant it. And, in the few years since that time, we've all proved that *we* meant it. We've dug deeper and pulled up more rotten roots than anyone in any city in this country. At any time."

There was no applause. No comment. Just one 120 solemn faces, riveted on one lone figure.

"Now, it seems, some people think that we've dug too far. Pulled up too many decaying plants. Uprooted too many comfortably rotting lives." Matlin paused. "Well, those people are about to have their say."

Several people sat up abruptly.

"I predict that I will be fired soon. Removed from office. And a lot of you might be hurt when that happens. So, what I am asking is that, if there are any of you who have families, careers, reputations you want to keep safe, you consider withdrawing from the Office today, or any time in the next few days. If you do, you'll do so with my most sincere and my most urgently offered blessing. You've all given too much of your efforts, pledged too much of your loyalty, sacrificed too many opportunities to add to it the punishment of a tarnished reputation, a damaged career, or an unsettled family.

"You can go. And go loved, appreciated, and safe. I urge you all to consider my offer."

The moment he had finished, he walked quickly from the room.

Henry was stunned. Even though he fully expected something terrible, he had not expected Howard Matlin to announce his own execution. Suddenly, he remembered something from Catechism class when he was a youngster. He remembered the teacher telling how, one night, Jesus gathered his disciples together and told them that they were going up to Jerusalem and then he foretold his treatment after they arrived—his suffering and his death. He recalled that, at the time, the idea of someone predicting their own death had horrified him, and that he had stopped listening to the teacher for that evening. Now the idea seemed to horrify him again, only this time, there was no one to stop listening to.

"Never."

It was the first word spoken since Matlin had left.

"Never," said someone else.

Suddenly, someone applauded.

"Never!" shouted Pat Mallon.

"Never!" echoed Jock Zabiskie.

The chant was picked up, first by a group of investigators sitting in the front rows. Then it spread upwards, like the football cheers that pass around a stadium.

Hands clapped, louder and harder.

"Never, never, never!" went the chant, shouted from 120 voices. "Never, never!"

At last, Nat Perlman rose and turned to face the crowd. He raised his arms for silence. And at once the shouting and the clapping ceased.

"I think we've given Howie his answer."

A burst of applause greeted Perlman's remark. After a moment, he raised his arms again for silence. When the applause died out, he spoke again.

"We've given Howie his answer. Now let's go back to our desks and translate that answer for the public. Into indictments and into convictions. So that no one will dare touch our Special Prosecutor except to shake his hand."

When the applause died, so did Henry's spirits. He looked at Dan Nelligan, sitting next to him, and saw the same loss of spirit. In his mind, he pictured an opinion, ending the judicial investigation, lying on his desk. He saw a commission gathering the following Monday morning, carrying in their hands, loaded dice to roll in front of cameras. And he pictured the Special Prosecutor, sunk in his chair, light fading from his face as his image dissolved into a darkened painting, waiting to be shipped off to a museum.

"Dan," he turned to his friend, who looked back at him. "Let's go get drunk."

CHAPTER 38

It was Monday morning and Henry was sitting in his office. "A nice objective view for the start of the Commission hearings," he said aloud. The *Daily News* editorial, anticipating the Commission's proceedings, dubbed Howard Matlin "a vehicle gone out of control," and called for his removal by the Governor.

He reached for his phone to buzz Dan Nelligan and share his unhappiness, but then he remembered that Nelligan was on his way to the Bahamas to look for clues about the mysterious new partner in the Andersen scheme—the new owner of 30,000 shares of Andersen Sonar Corporation. "Maybe I can talk to Scoop," he said, and got up and left his office.

He turned right and began the walk around the floor to Dixon's office. In the western hall, as he passed by Sara's door, she emerged.

"Oh, hi, Sara."

She looked at him distantly.

"You look preoccupied," he offered.

"I am. I'm on my way to Howie's office with the latest bad news."

"What do you mean?"

"The Johnson trial is starting tomorrow. It was delayed for a day. But it won't take very long. We have to arrest Judge Ryan and Remmelt before Ryan actually acquits Johnson. And then our investigation becomes public knowledge and our spotlight into the DA's Office goes out. Along with our chance to nail down Ross and maybe even Donner."

"Yeah. Unfortunately, you're right."

"See you," Sara said over her shoulder as she headed for Matlin's office.

"Hey, Larry." It was Tuesday morning and Henry spotted Larry Santarella walking from the subway to the office. To most, it was a beautiful April morning, and spring was clearly blossoming. But the sun hadn't fully penetrated the street between the subway exit and the New State Office Building. And to the two attorneys from the Office of the Special Prosecutor, there was no spring apparent.

"Jesus, Perk," Santarella said without a greeting, "did you see who that bunghole Commission heard from yesterday?"

"Yeah. Lead witness was our friend Max Olman."

"Him, sure. But how about putting on that crook Bentzel and then his law secretary who negotiated the bribe? As legitimate witnesses."

"I know. And of course, no one bothered to ask either of them if they took any of the money." Henry laughed weakly. "At least, they could have given us a perjury case to work with."

"Who's the Commission hearing today?" asked Santarella.

"I don't know. Maybe Scoop'll know."

A half hour later Henry was taking a seat in front of Howard Matlin's desk.

"How are things going?" Matlin asked, almost casually. In fact, the Special Prosecutor was drinking a cup of coffee and looking over some papers. Business as usual.

"I just talked to Dan Nelligan in the Bahamas," Henry said.

Matlin looked up. "And..."

"Nothing definite yet, but he thinks he's very close to getting what we want. The owner of the thirty thousand shares, belonging to whoever made the Andersen deal possible. I'll talk to Dan again tomorrow."

"That's good. And, if we get what we're looking for, are you ready to indict the others? Galligan, and all."

Henry nodded. "I am. All the evidence has been presented to the grand jury. All that's needed is whatever Nelligan can find and a charge on the law and a request for indictment by me."

"Very good."

Henry rose to leave. As he did, the office door opened sharply, and Scoop Dixon entered.

"Jesus, Howie..."

"I already saw it, Scoop."

Henry was surprised. From his demeanor, he wouldn't have guessed that Matlin had already read the editorial in that day's *New York Times* that urged the Commission to act quickly in the "Special Prosecutor scandal."

Henry looked at Matlin again. The Prosecutor's head was erect. But he could see the muscles along the side of his neck straining as they held his head up.

"You mean the editorial, or the report on the Commission?" asked Dixon.

"Both."

"Well, I've got something else."

There was a sinking feeling in Henry's stomach. More bad news.

"Yes?" It was all Matlin said.

"Sabrina Wilcox's been transferred."

"Transferred?" It was Henry.

Dixon looked at Henry, then back to Matlin. "The *Times* pulled her off our beat and they're sending her to the West Coast. Immediately."

Again, it was Henry who spoke. "First the *Daily News* banishes Mike Welling to the obituary page. Now the *Times* sends Sabrina Wilcox to California. I'll bet Toby Copin doesn't move."

"Of course not," said Dixon. "In fact, he's been designated to cover our office exclusively from now on."

"Are you serious?" exclaimed Henry.

Dixon's face was redder than usual. "Of course, I'm serious. Would I joke about something like that to Howie?"

For a moment, they both seem to have forgotten the figure at the desk—the object of the mounting forces of The Establishment's resistance.

Henry now looked back at Matlin. His head was bent at an angle, as though looking at something on his desk. It was a peculiar angle and one that stirred something in Henry's memory. Then he saw. It was that same odd angle at which so many artists had placed the head of Jesus as he hung from the cross.

The shadows from the morning sun darkened Matlin's lowered face and, for an instant, Henry thought he saw blood running down Matlin's cheeks. Turning away quickly, he left the room. Before he was tempted to look at Matlin's hands.

"Another triumph for objectivity, I see, Scoop." Henry was carrying the afternoon paper, with its list of the day's witnesses at the Commission.

Dixon stuffed the cigarette he was holding into his mouth and took a deep drag. By way of response, he blew out forcefully a stream of bluish smoke. "I especially like their calling Toby Copin. To 'represent' the press."

"Well, asking the head of the ACLU what he thought of our office's wiretapping wasn't exactly rolling it down the middle, either."

"Have you heard what they've got on tap tomorrow?"

"No," answered Henry. "What are they doing, resurrecting Al Capone to give his opinion?"

Dixon laughed. "Not that I know. But one guy is the head of the police union…"

"Oh, he'll be objective," Henry said sarcastically.

"…and then they've got some 'special' witness. They won't say who."

"Can't wait to see who it is," said Henry, withdrawing from the office. "I'll see you later."

Even the last car was crowded, but at least Henry could read his paper. In the center cars of the express, after he changed at Grand Central, people were so jammed in that one could not read a paper, even one folded over in the vertical manner made necessary by the New York subways. So, at rush hour, Henry always walked to the rear of the platform and rode in the last car.

Not that he was enjoying the Wednesday morning paper. Another terrorist bombing by the Red Brigade in Rome. Another town's water too polluted to drink. A third week of Congressional hearings on the oil embargo. And the second day's testimony in the Commission.

Having read the partial report in yesterday's afternoon paper and knowing who had testified, Henry hadn't expected anything good. And there wasn't anything good. At least the *Times* did not have Toby Copin reporting on his own testimony.

As the train started south out of 14th Street, Henry turned to the editorials. And jumped.

"Matlin Must Go," was the heading of the lead editorial. He read on.

New York can no longer endure the specter of unrestrained and unprincipled abuse of power as it has in the person of Howard Matlin. For over three years, Mr. Matlin has been controversial. He has lost sight of the need of all branches of government to function, not in a pervasively antagonistic manner, but in an orderly and co-operative way. By acting otherwise, he has undermined the public's faith in our justice system. For over three years, he has been overzealous. He has carried on his fanatical mission without regard to the rights of citizens, whether public servants or not.

The goal of honest government is a desirable one and we reiterate our firm commitment to that end. But such a goal cannot be reached by promoting divisiveness or by trampling on due process, as Howard Matlin has done.

We call on Governor Whelan, once again, to exercise his authority and his esteemed good judgment, and to remove this thorn from society's side. The sooner Howard Matlin is gone, the sooner this City and State can be restored to decency, and our legal system can begin again to honor its sacred trust.

As he sat there in the crowded subway car, his stomach in his mouth, Henry pictured himself, sitting in his office in his old law firm some three and a half years ago, enthusiastically reading the editorial in the *New York Times* on the appointment of Howard Matlin. At the time, it had made such an impression on him, that Henry now actually remembered it. A few words of it came back to him: "It is not enough that Mr. Matlin be well-intentioned… He must be zealous…He must violate the sanctuaries of the privileged as often as necessary, so that he can clean up the puss of corruption."

So much for consistency, Henry grumbled to himself. For the remainder of the ride, he stared at a sign advertising canned pinto beans in Spanish.

As he stepped off the elevator in the New State Office Building and entered the waiting room of the Special Prosecutor's Office, Henry recalled the time that he and Howard Matlin had encountered the lady with the reticule who had leaped from her chair and rushed at them like a bird. A flicker of a smile crossed his otherwise glum face.

There were other glum faces, as well, including that of the new investigator who sat at the front desk. Yet, once inside, Henry could sense the activity in the offices around him and, by the time he reached his own office, he had almost put the editorial out of his mind.

There was a message on his desk. He picked it up. "Dan Nelligan called. Will call again at ten." Henry looked at his watch. A half hour to wait.

"Dan!" he nearly shouted when the call came.

"Yeah, Perk. I've got some good news."

Henry decided to say nothing about the *Times* editorial, or the other events of the past two days. "What is it?"

"I think I've located some information. On who owns those shares."

"Who?"

"Can't say yet. But I'll be back in New York with some documents and, if I'm lucky, a witness."

"When?"

"Tomorrow afternoon. Have the grand jury sitting, cause it's the only way this guy'll talk."

"Tomorrow afternoon?"

"Yeah, I'll come right up there."

When Nelligan had hung up, Henry started calling. He would have to call himself to arrange for his grand jury to meet, since he was the one who had told everyone they could skip the Thursday session this week.

A little later, Henry took a break from calling the grand jurors to answer a call of nature. As he emerged from the men's room, he saw Sara walking briskly toward her office. "Sara," he called.

She turned.

"What's happening?"

Sara let out a big breath. "Castegglio's meeting with Remmelt today. In Remmelt's office." Sara repressed a smile. "To discuss the DA's Office and what happened." She resumed her serious expression. "If things go right, we might confirm who gave up the informant."

"What about the Johnson trial? What's happening there?"

"It's going very quickly," Sara answered, turning back toward Henry. "The prosecution should be finished sometime tomorrow. Then summations, which shouldn't take too long since there isn't any jury."

"When will it be finished?"

"Well, the judge is a Catholic, I guess. Because he told the lawyers that, since Friday is Good Friday, he wants everything done by noon that day. So, I guess we'll have to arrest everyone Friday. And that gives us about a day and a half to wrap up the rest."

"Well, good luck," Henry said. But Sara was already on her way.

It had taken almost two hours. And some arm twisting. But Henry finally had his quorum for an afternoon grand jury session Thursday. Now he would descend on Scoop Dixon to share a grumble about the *Times* editorial.

As soon as he stepped into the office, he realized that something was different. Dixon was sitting behind his piles of papers. His eyes, like his face, were red. The office looked like the back room of a junk shop. But he could see the window. And, beyond the window, he could see the river and New Jersey.

The smoke...there was no smoke. He looked at the desk and saw Dixon's ashtray. Empty.

"Scoop. Where're your weeds?"

The bloodshot eyes lifted. Underneath the eyes his mouth spread into a smile, almost like that of a little boy who had been caught studying when he had told his friends that he was going to play baseball. "I quit," he announced. "I quit 'em."

Later, Henry wasn't sure what he should do, though he wanted to do something. There were documents and testimony he could review in his cases, especially Andersen. But he had already done that, thoroughly. And he was fully ready for the grand jury the next day. With the office literally under siege, he felt almost foolish attending to business as usual while the battle for existence roared overhead. But since he could think of nothing he could contribute to the battle at this point, he had come to something of a standstill. He felt as though he were caught in that becalmed space between two converging currents, where small floating objects quietly collect while, on either side, waters go rushing off in one direction or the other. Thus, it was, at around eight o'clock that evening, he found himself wandering the circumference of the floor, vaguely intending to get himself a cup of coffee and, perhaps, some inspiration.

He didn't see her right away. But when he did, he was taken aback.

He had never seen her looking that way. Not sad or tired. Stunned was a more appropriate term. She looked as though she had just learned of the sudden death of a family member. But since she had no immediate family that he knew of, he surmised that it might have something to do with her investigation. So, he spoke to her.

"Hello, Sara."

She looked at him, gradually focusing on his face and taking in his greeting. They were standing by her office door, a fact she also seemed to realize gradually.

"Come in, please," she said.

Henry was a bit surprised by her invitation, but he entered with her. She closed the door behind them.

"I just came from Howie's office," Sara said as she dropped into her chair.

Henry took a seat himself.

"He'd been waiting to see what happened with the Costegglio conversation. But I brought him a bombshell."

Henry didn't speak. He sat down and waited for Sara to go on.

"Henry, we've confirmed who gave the informant's name to Remmelt and the mob."

"Who?" Henry asked.

"It was definitely Martin Ross. The DA himself."

"Ohmygod. What did Howie say?"

"Nothing. He picked up the phone, called Matt Corey and asked him to come in early tomorrow. So, we could prepare to arrest Ross tomorrow afternoon."

Henry shook his head. But he didn't get to say anything more. For just then the door burst open, and Justin Cole stumbled in.

It took Henry no more than a second to realize that Cole was drunk. Badly drunk. His raincoat was on, but it had caught on something and one of the side panels was ripped. His tie was loosened and there was a brown stain on his shirt front that was repeated on his tie, as though he had spilled a cup of black coffee all over himself. But the eyes alone, wet, and red, would have been enough to signal inebriation.

Cole started for Sara's desk but suddenly he spotted Henry. Half turning, he glared down at Henry. "What the fuck're you doing here, shithead?"

Henry's fists clenched and he began to rise. But Sara motioned him back into his chair.

"I did it. I fucking did it," Cole blurted out, dropping into a chair. "It's all outta the fucking bag now." Each time he said "fuck," several large drops of saliva emerged from his mouth and began a course down his chin.

"What are you talking about, Justin?" Sara snapped her question like a schoolteacher, reprimanding a student.

He was silent for a moment, weaving around in his chair. Then, apparently, her question sunk in. "I'm talking about this stupid place. And fucking Matlin."

Once again Henry made a move toward Cole and, once again, Sara stopped him.

"I still have no idea what you're talking about," she said.

Again, he paused. Then he leaned forward and addressed her with a combination of words and hurled spit. "I told that stupid Commission who's who and what's what. That's what I'm talking about. I'm not taking the blame."

Suddenly Henry saw. The "special witness." It must have been Justin Cole.

"You talked to that Commission?" Sara said, saving Henry the trouble.

"You bet I did. And I told 'em everything. I told 'em about all the fuck-ups by idiots like Morotti and that asshole Meade. And how fuckin' Matlin fucked up all the cases. Not me! Fact is, I made every fuckin' case in this office that's worth more'n flyturds and Matlin is the one who screwed 'em up. I warned him not to cross the line, but he insisted on violating peoples' rights. Against my advice!"

"You rotten shit!" Henry couldn't believe what he was hearing. Except that he could. "You just destroyed Howie Matlin!" He started from his chair, but a noise stopped him this time. It came from the other chair in front of Sara's desk. At first, it sounded like gagging or coughing. But Henry took only a second more to recognize it. It was a sob.

"It-umph-t's finished. It's all exposed for the crap it is.", Before Henry could react, Cole was out of his chair. Without another sound, he ran from the room.

Sara jumped from her own chair and started around the desk. She strode past Cole's vacated chair and toward the door. Then she stopped. For several seconds, she stood, as though frozen. At last, her arms dropped to her sides. Then her body straightened, and she turned slowly and walked back to her chair and sat down.

CHAPTER 39

The door to Henry's office opened and, for only the second time he could recall, he admitted Sara Leventhal. Not that he hadn't seen her that long before. It was after eleven the night before when he finally walked her to a cab and saw her off home. She had recovered from the long crying session in her office, and she wanted to ride home alone.

He had listened while she poured out all the hurt that had been bottled up for so long. So many years of fighting battles, too many of which were mostly in her mind. So many years of driving away the flesh and blood of love and friendship. So many helping hands slapped away, and so much opportunity for caring left behind.

And then all the unpleasantness of her relationship with Justin Cole. Her attraction to him *because* he wasn't a caring person; that he wouldn't try to enter her space. But how his self-centeredness had gradually made her feel as though she were being frozen out of his life altogether.

By the end of the session, Henry felt more drained than Sara probably did. In fact, as she unburdened herself, Sara seemed to lighten up, to gain back the buoyant spirit that, through all the bad times, Henry had always believed she had. Before Sara left, Henry saw something in her eyes that made all his waiting and all his foolish caring worthwhile. He saw joy. As she began to see hope for herself, her eyes began to glow. Until she suddenly jumped up and asked him to see her to a cab. Then he had felt joy, as well.

"Can I see you for just a minute?" Sara asked, holding the door to Henry's office ajar.

"You can see me for more than a minute, if you wish." After all, he didn't have his grand jury until two o'clock.

"A minute's all I've got. And I need your help."

"Sure."

"But first, I want to thank you for last night. For listening to all that shit."

He started to say something ordinary, some cliche. Then he changed his mind and said what just came out. "It *was* shit. Awful, smelly shit. And— sorry for being crude—but it's out now and its flushed. And hopefully it's made you feel better."

She smiled. "That's the nicest, horrible thing anyone's ever said to me." Immediately she laid a packet of paper on his desk. "And now for the favor. If you have the time." She almost smiled. "I'm going to be with Howie as we wait for the arrest of Martin Ross."

"Well, I've got a grand jury at two. I have to leave around noon. Until then, I'm free, if you need me."

"It shouldn't take that long. I could get an investigator to do it, but I'd feel better if you did it."

"Okay."

He wasn't permitting himself to reflect on the fact that she had come to him for help. At this stage, he would simply take things as they came.

"You remember the Donofrio murder case where Paul Kondor was the fixer? The murder case that was fixed in the Appellate Division?"

"Yes, of course."

"Can I sit down?"

430

"Sure." He pointed to a chair.

"Then you'll remember that Kondor paid a hundred thousand dollars in cash to Jack Peacock, who took it to the airport, presumably to whomever took the bribe."

"Yes."

"Well, I subpoenaed the passenger lists to Switzerland for that day." She picked up the packet of paper she had brought in. "And here they are."

"And what you want is for me to search either for Jack Peacock to see where he went or someone else I might recognize who might have done the fixing and taken the bribe."

Sara nodded. "That's it."

"Might take longer than you think," Henry said eyeing the stack of paper.

"I hope not. They're pretty uncomplicated. And what else can we do?"

Henry shrugged his shoulders. "Not much, I guess." He reached for the pile of papers. "And maybe we'll get lucky."

"Thanks, Henry," Sara said, backing toward the door. "I've got to meet with Howie now. And plan the arrest of District Attorney Martin Ross for being an accessory to murder."

At eleven forty-five he found it. At eleven fifty, he was in Sara's office with his coat on. He would continue right out to the grand jury.

"I didn't find Peacock," he said.

Sara's face fell. "Well, I'll have to try something else."

"But I did find someone we know," Henry continued.

"Oh?" Sara's head lifted quickly.

"This person took a plane on the afternoon of May fourteen from JFK to Zurich, Switzerland. And came back the next morning."

"Holy smokes! Who?"

"The Honorable Chief Judge of the State of New York, Arthur Sammons."

Sara's eyes opened wide. "Wait a minute, Henry." She rummaged through a file on the floor beside her desk. In a moment she straightened up and placed a document on her desk. It took only a second for her to find what she was looking for. "Ha!" she said and looked up at him.

"This is the opinion reversing Donofrio's conviction and dismissing the indictment. It concludes 'Sammons, P.J. All concur.'"

Suddenly Henry was very angry. It sounded just like another opinion he had recently read at his own desk. From another presiding justice who had sold out.

"Sammons was the presiding justice for that?"

"Yes, it was before he went up to the Court of Appeals. He was still on the Appellate Division."

Henry backed toward the door. "I've got to get to my grand jury. But I think we've found who took the hundred grand in cash. I wonder what happened to the 'sanctity of the law' on that one?"

Nelligan was taking the car to the garage. It was a good thing, since Henry needed to be alone. Even if it was only for the walk from the street to the elevator. He wasn't certain that he would be able to walk much farther than that.

This last twenty-four hours had turned the world upside down. If he were watching it on television, he would turn off the set. Couldn't happen, he would say. But it had just happened. To him.

First, he had learned that the most celebrated District Attorney in New York City had, in fact, helped organized crime murder an informant. Then he discovered that the Chief Judge of the New York Court of the Appeals was a cash bribe-taker. And now, he was trying to absorb what had happened at the grand jury, not two hours ago.

Nelligan had arrived, not only with documents, but with a witness. The witness had testified, and the documents had verified, that the owner of Seaward Associates—the person who had facilitated the corrupt Andersen Sonar deal—was Governor James A. Whelan.

As he stepped off the elevator, he saw that something was wrong. There was no one at the desk and no one in the waiting room. He used his key to let himself in and turned down the center hall toward Morotti's office. But there was no one there, either.

It was eerie. An office, with typewriters still turned on, with half-drunk cups of coffee sitting on the desks, with papers and books open to places people had been reading or writing. But no one was there. It was as if some extraterrestrial spaceship had descended and emptied the office.

He turned to walk back across the building to the western side when, to his left, he heard a noise. It seemed to come from the investigators' area. Quickly he walked to the southern end of the building. Now he could hear voices.

As he entered the investigators' area, he was surprised to see so many people crowded into the room. It was a large space, but it seemed that the whole office staff had gathered, and they were packed around the desks.

"What's going on?" he asked Tim O'Leary, who was standing near the door.

"The Boss's been fired."

"When?"

"Half an hour ago, or so."

Henry looked around.

Matlin wasn't there. Nor was Corey or Perlman or Harry Rood. "Where is he?" he asked O'Leary.

"In his office. With Perlman and Dixon. They'll be in in a minute."

"Where's Corey?"

"I can tell you that," said another voice.

Sara looked as bad as Henry felt.

"He's out with Harry Rood. Supposed to be arresting Ross."

"Ssssh," said someone. Others took up the plea for silence, while John Cappelli turned up the television set that had been running silently on top of a file cabinet. At that moment, Henry saw Dan Nelligan enter the room. Nelligan spoke with George Reed. He looked at Henry, then at Sara. He nodded and stepped toward a group of investigators near him.

"Good evening. This is Fred Mellen with the six o'clock news. Governor Whelan today fired Special Prosecutor Howard Matlin. We go live now to Albany, where the Governor will speak."

Henry felt someone's shoulder press against him. It was Sara.

On the screen the familiar face of Governor Whelan, standing in front of a microphone, appeared. "Good evening," the Governor said, drawing out his vowels dramatically.

"Three and a half years ago, I acted in the face of a crisis in confidence in the enforcement of law in New York City. I did then what I thought was best. I was mistaken. Instead, New York City has been subjected to three and a half years of abuse and intimidation, which have left it injured and crying out for justice.

"I have now acted. The long night of terror is over. Howard Matlin is gone. I have removed him summarily from office, and he can do harm no more."

He turned to his left and stepped a few inches to his right. "I have with me here, the Chief Judge of the State of New York who will say a few words. Chief Judge Sammons."

Sammons stepped into the center where Whelan had stood and faced the cameras. "I only want to reiterate what the Governor has said. It has been a long, dark night for New York. But now, the day is breaking, and the sanctity of the law will be preserved."

Sara and Henry looked at each other and almost smiled. But the bitter taste in Henry's mouth and the tears in Sara's eyes prevented it. Then they turned back to the television, where Whelan had again taken center stage.

"Howard Matlin is gone. And the People are free again. In his place I have appointed a man whose effectiveness, whose regard for constitutional rights and whose integrity are known throughout the city and state."

He turned to his right and motioned to someone. Then he edged to his left to make room for a familiar face. "District Attorney Martin Ross," he concluded.

Sara screamed. It was not a loud piercing scream, but it was enough to rip a hole in Henry's heart. She ran from the room.

Instantly, he followed until he caught up with her in the hall outside. He reached out a hand and touched her shoulder. She turned and dropped against him, laying her head on his shoulder as she did. He closed his arms to support her while she cried.

"Hey, the Boss is coming." It was Paul Ahern, calling them back into the room.

Henry grabbed some tissues from a box on a desk nearby and handed them to Sara, who blew her nose loudly. The noise caused her to smile, and she deposited the tissues in a wastebasket, signaling that she was ready to return.

They had just entered the room when Howard Matlin stepped in behind them. With him were Nat Perlman and Scoop Dixon. The two assistants edged into the crowd, which now formed something of a semicircle around their leader. Silence was immediate.

"You've all heard the news by now, so I won't comment on that. I only want to say a few words about you. The most significant part of this whole undertaking. You."

Henry felt his hand touched. Then Sara's hand was in his. It tightened its grip as Matlin went on.

"You come from many different places, with many different backgrounds, different talents, different lives. But there was one thing you all have in common. And it's the reason I hired each one of you. In every case, when I first saw you, I saw stars in your eyes, and I knew that you belonged here with us.

"Now, I see some tears in those eyes. There might even be one or two in my own eyes. But remember this: Stars last a lot longer than tears. And they give off a lot more light. Tears dry up and go away, but stars, no matter where they are, burn on and on. That's what I want most to see. Wherever each of you goes, if you just let the stars burn on, then the light will never go out.

"Thank you for your faith, for your help, and for your friendship. No one has ever been better served."

He turned and left the room.

CHAPTER 40

Henry had to stop again and straighten his skis. Damned difficult balancing one bag with skis, another with boots, and then a great big duffel bag containing all the rest of his stuff. For two weeks of the worst skiing he'd ever had. And he still had to go through customs.

It was almost two hours later when he stumbled into his apartment. He turned on a light and dumped his things on the floor in the living room. The place smelled musty and stale. Like he felt.

He went right to the phone.

For two weeks he had suffered intensely. Guilt. The worst he'd ever felt. If he hadn't been so far away, with a no-change return ticket in two weeks, he would have rushed back to New York to ask someone's forgiveness. Howie Matlin's, if it were available.

He hadn't waited even a day. The very night that Matlin had been fired, Henry had called a travel agent and booked himself into a group leaving the next day for Austria. Some cancellation or something. All Henry knew was that he had to get away.

Until he'd arrived. He climbed from the train the next evening and stepped into the Alpine preciousness of a ski village. Brightly clad figures sauntered down snow-covered roads, laughing and chattering in a half-dozen languages. Steep roofs, still covered with thick blankets of snow that clung like the frosting on the gingerbread houses he had eaten as a child. The narrow streets lined with small hotels, restaurants, ski shops, and a few mundane stores that sold groceries or hardware. The streetlamps casting soft light on the snow and on the buildings, making everything look so cozy and inviting.

It must have been a cheerful greeting to the disembarking passengers. But to Henry Perkins, it was the beginning of two weeks of hell.

The fact that the spring skiing was terrible probably made things even worse, though it was fitting, he felt, that an unusual alternation between cold and warmth left the snow either ice or slush. The only fact that mattered to Henry Perkins was that he had run off, that he had abandoned the man who had changed his life, just as soon as the man was down. And no fluffy powder or delft blue skies could erase that fact from Henry's conscience.

Dan Nelligan answered after two rings.

"Dan, it's Perk."

Silence greeted him. For an instant, he thought that he had called the wrong person. Then he heard the familiar voice. "Have a good time?"

"Dan. I've done nothing but kick myself for two weeks. Please don't make it worse."

Again, there was silence. Then it was broken. "Weelll..."

"How's Howie? How's he taking it?"

"He made it. That's the main thing."

"Made it? What do you mean?"

"He's alive."

"Well, I'd assumed that. I wanted to know how he's taking the firing."

"Jesus, you *have* been away. You don't know what happened?"

Henry felt a thud in his stomach. "No. What?"

"Perk, Howie almost died. No. He did die. For a couple minutes, or something.'"

"What the hell are you talking about?"

"The next day. After he was fired. Howie had a massive heart attack. So bad, his heart stopped beating for a while. They had to revive him."

"Oh my God," moaned Henry. And he was off drinking Austrian beer while Howie Matlin was dead and resurrected. "Oh my God."

"Hey, Perk."

Henry felt even worse now. In fact, he couldn't feel any worse and live, he thought.

"Perk," Nelligan said again.

"What?" His voice was drained of emotion.

"There's nothing you could have done. Except worry like the rest of us. You aren't a doctor. So don't go banging yourself on the head."

"Jesus, Dan. I couldn't feel worse if it were me in the hospital."

"Well, speakin' of hospitals, here's the good news."

"Good news?"

"Yeah. Howie's comin' home tomorrow. Up to his house in Fuller. And Matt'n we're drivin' up. You wanna come?"

"You'd let me? After what I did?"

"Hey, man. I don't know what happened two weeks ago. It's too long ago to remember. So, I don't wanna talk about two weeks ago. I'm talkin' about tomorrow. You wanna come?"

"Just tell me where and when to meet you."

They headed north on the West Side Drive. In the bright spring sunshine, the Hudson River glittered, a band of sparkles spread beneath the sunsplashed Palisades. Ahead of them, Henry could see the George Washington Bridge reflecting the morning sun and looking like a pair of diamond necklaces stretched out in parallel, lying across two hangers, with their opposite ends resting in the unlikely repositories of Fort Washington and Fort Lee.

Already Matt Corey was slipping into character. For a few minutes, Henry had been unnerved, not by Corey's hostility, but by its opposite. Corey acted as though he was glad to see Henry, as though it was important to him that Henry had joined Nelligan and him for the trip upstate to Matlin's home. Then, as Nelligan maneuvered the car onto the Drive and headed north, Corey seemed to relax and become himself again.

"And you know who they made Chief Assistant?" Corey's head twisted halfway around in the front seat, looking back in Henry's direction. "Donner. Bert Donner." He laughed harshly. "That's who's gonna be lookin' for crooked prosecutors. Well, he's the guy ta find 'em."

"Sara must be upset," Henry ventured.

From the face Corey made, Henry was visibly reminded of the former Chief Investigator's opinion of Sara Leventhal. The truth was, he couldn't exactly blame Corey. Sara had been difficult for a long time.

"And for chief investigator...oh." Corey's voice dropped. "You wouldn't know him, probably. But anyone who'd worked with him at the DA's Office would laugh."

"A crook, too?"

"Crook? Nah. He's a library boy. Always readin' books on law enforcement. New methods of crime detection. That kinda shit. He wouldn't know a real bad guy if he fell over him while the guy was pullin' a bank job. But he's just right for those birds. He's a guarantee that they don't catch anybody except, maybe, some patrolman who's screwin' somebody else's wife."

"What's happened to the case against Hurd? Anything?"

"I don't know," Corey grumbled. "But they dismissed a whole shitload of our cases. Somethin' about the 'interests of justice,' or some crap like that."

"It's gone," volunteered Nelligan. "That's one of the cases that Ross dismissed on his own motion."

Henry shook his head. "Three and a half years. Down the drain."

"Maybe not completely," said Nelligan. "The feds're takin' a look at Galligan. Maybe they'll get him on somethin'."

Henry sat back, contemplating the wreckage of his and the others' three and a half years of labor. At least there were a few bad cops in jail, he reflected.

"It's interesting, isn't it?" Henry said at last. "What good guys we were while we were prosecuting cops. And then how bad we got as soon as we went after the politicians and judges."

"Yeah," grunted Corey. "It's like Howie said one time, not too long ago. He was talkin' to some lawyers' group and somebody asked him about one of those dismissals—a judge, I think it was. Howie says it was a terrible thing that happened to him. While he was puttin' cops inside, he was a whiz with his evidence. Then he went after the judges, and somethin' happened to his brain, and he suddenly forgot all the rules."

Henry laughed. After that, he stared out the window in silence.

As they traveled northward, the heavy lines of southbound traffic, crawling toward Manhattan and work, thinned out. Out the window, Henry noticed the predominance of green over other colors. The tiny, new leaves were out now, and they were wresting the landscape from the dreary blue gray of winter.

Yet spring was a fact of nature, not of his soul. There, there was no season, as in a nether world. It was as though he had been cut off from the life source that had nourished him for these past years but had been offered no substitute. He had accepted the fact that his quest was over. He had tried and failed. Or, rather, he had fought and lost. But, having lost, he was unresolved about the future. Indeed, he had no idea where to go next, or what to fight for.

It seemed to him that there was something more he needed before he could begin again before he could accept what had happened to him and go on with the next phase of his life. What he couldn't help feeling was that the path out of this limbo somehow involved Howard Matlin. Not that he needed Matlin, as he used to need him. But that it was from Matlin that a signal would come.

After the news of the changes in the Special Prosecutor's Office had been related and chewed on, they all lapsed into silence. Once or twice, Nelligan had a discussion with Corey about directions, but otherwise both investigators seemed as meditative as Henry. Each one knew, Henry surmised, that his destiny had somehow been altered by his association with the man they were going to see. And now it had been changed again, in a manner none of them could yet know. There was a lot to reflect on while they rode.

"Oh, shit. Look ahead, Matt." The car slowed to a stop.

Henry snapped out of his thoughts to see what had provoked Nelligan's protest. Up ahead, blue and red lights flashed. Between their car and the flashing lights was a long line of cars, similarly brought to a halt by the accident. They were in for a long wait.

Caught in the middle of the line of traffic, there was no alternative but to wait until the police and tow trucks had cleared the automobiles involved in the crash. It was almost an hour before they were permitted to pass by.

"Doesn't look like anyone was hurt," Henry commented as they finally drove by several dented cars, now lined up at the side of the road. He spotted a group of men, apparently including the local ambulance team, standing near the road, chatting unhurriedly.

"Shit," grumbled Corey, looking at his watch. "We're gonna be late." He looked at Nelligan. "Step on it," he said.

Henry settled back, hoping that Nelligan could get them there without their becoming themselves the occasion for a gathering of the kind of local public services they had just passed. In a few minutes, he slipped back into his brown study.

"What the fuck's that?" exclaimed Corey.

Henry, who had been deep in thought for over half an hour, sat up, startled, and looked out the window. They were already weaving their way through a residential neighborhood, a development of homes, all about twenty-five years old, all with their neat, green spaces in front, with hedges or small trees dotting otherwise unmarred lawns. The streets were quiet, winding paths that separated the homes on either side. A police car with a flashing blue light, blocking access to one street thus appeared quite out of place.

"Looks like a roadblock of some kind," responded Nelligan.

"But that's Howie's street they got blocked."

Nelligan pulled the car up to the stopped patrol car and started to roll down his window. But Corey beat him.

"What the hell's goin' on?" he boomed.

A young officer, who had already approached the driver's side of the car, looked surprised. "I'm sorry, we can't let any cars through now."

Nelligan had taken out his badge and was showing it to the officer. "Police business," he said.

"Yeah, everybody's got somethin', buddy." The remark came from an older cop, who had apparently smelled trouble and sauntered over to back up his junior officer. "Nobody's gettin' through."

"What the fuck?" The bellowing was followed by a violent opening of the door on the passenger side. Then all Henry could hear were some words softly spoken. A laugh from the older officer was succeeded by the younger man's stepping back and waving them through.

Corey climbed back into the car. "Get a move on," he growled.

Nelligan said nothing, but Henry wanted to know how Corey had accomplished the feat. Suddenly, however, he recalled something that made it irrelevant. "Wait a minute!" he cried.

Nelligan stopped the car. "What is it?"

Henry ignored him. Quickly rolling down the window, he called the younger officer over. "Did you see a red Toyota with a sunroof go through here?"

443

The officer thought a moment. Then he turned toward the older offi-cer. "Hey, Sarge. You see a red Toyota go up there yet?"

"Nah," said the sergeant. "I'd'a noticed. Wife's got one." He shook his head. "No red Toyota."

In his disappointment, Henry forgot his question for Matt Corey. Even when it was answered for him, he didn't care anymore.

"Know that sergeant?" Nelligan asked Corey.

"Yeah. From when I was up here with Howie. Dumb shit, but a good drinker."

Sara had told him she would come when he had called her. She had said that she would drive up in her car and meet him at Matlin's house. But now she couldn't get through.

"Hey, Dan, can I have him let someone else through?"

"Who?" growled Corey.

"Uh, Sara."

"Keep drivin', Dan. We're already late." Then he turned around and looked at Henry. "If she can't talk her way through that feeble excuse for a roadblock, she isn't worth dog meat." He turned around and mumbled some-thing to himself. It sounded to Henry like "not that she is, anyway." But he wasn't in the mood to argue.

Henry felt that he should do something to ensure that Sara could get through when she arrived. Then he thought again. He looked at his watch. They were almost an hour late. If Sara was coming, she would be here by now. Indeed, she had told him that she was leaving early to do some errand and would get there well before him. Apparently, she had changed her mind and wasn't coming.

He recalled the night of her unburdening to him after Justin Cole had announced his treachery. He pictured her head, leaning against his shoulder, crying at the news of Matlin's dismissal. And he felt her hand slipping into his as Matlin had said his farewell. Now it all meant nothing.

The car rounded a turn and came upon the reason for the roadblock. There were several cars parked in front of what he assumed was Matlin's home and several people gathered on the front lawn. The first license plate Henry spotted broadcast the letters, NYP. "New York Press." Corey saw it, too.

"Goddamn fuckin' vultures. Stinkin' reporters. Dirty shits can't leave the guy alone, even when he's down." Corey was shouting by now. "Stop the car, Dan!" It wasn't a request.

Nelligan pulled the car up in front of a parked car just past Matlin's house and Corey leaped out. He strode off toward the crowd of reporters milling about in front of the house. Apparently, Matlin still hadn't arrived, as they were hanging out close to the street.

"Come on, Perk," yelled Nelligan over his shoulder. "We've gotta stop him before there's bloodshed." Nelligan had jumped from the car, and he was already following Corey. Henry started to run around the car to join him. Then he stopped.

Corey could handle himself, he thought. Better than Henry could. And so what if a reporter or two ended up with a broken nose? It would only be justice.

Henry's head was lowered now. He wasn't thinking about Corey flattening some photographer from the *Daily News*. He was thinking about Sara and the fact that she had let him down. He should have known better than to have gotten his hopes up just because she had turned to him as the only available shoulder when her world had fallen apart. After all, she had just learned that her lover had betrayed her trust, that her mission to vindicate old wrongs at the District Attorney's Office had crashed on the rocks and that what had happened to her father was, in a manner of speaking, happening to her boss and to her. Henry had simply been a convenient crying towel, he feared.

He shook his head and forced a smile. It was time to go see how many noses Matt Corey had bloodied. He lifted his head and took a step around the car.

"Henry." It came from the other side of the car. Quickly, he stepped around the car and saw her, striding toward him.

"I was afraid you weren't coming," she said.

He didn't repeat the thought. He didn't even think to ask her how she had gotten here. He was too happy to worry now.

She came quickly and took his arm, pulling him toward Matlin's lawn. "Hurry up. There he is now."

Henry looked back down the road and saw a van pulling up. "Saint Mary's Hospital," it said on the side of the van. He began to trot beside Sara.

The first thing he saw when he reached Matlin's lawn was Matt Corey standing motionless. No blood on his hands, no fallen reporters at his feet. In fact, there were no reporters anywhere.

He looked around. There was Sammy Parisi, Paul Ahern, Sid Wise, Jock Zabiskie, and Arnie Gordon, the office manager. He saw Freida and Rose and Kristine, the three group chiefs' secretaries, and nearby, Morotti, Meade, and Flannery. Down front was Harriet Winsor, Matlin's own secretary, standing with Nat Perlman, and next to them was Scoop Dixon, which immediately explained the press plate for Henry. Across the front walk were Tim O'Leary and Angie Palumbo, and near them, Larry Santarella, Hal Baker, and Barry Conlon. And Rood and Gunther and Scanlon and Wonderman and Capelli and Zabiskie and Asner and Mallon and Olean and Hollander and Kaplan. Nearly every person who had worked for the Office of the Special Prosecutor was standing there on Howard Matlin's front lawn, clapping, now cheering as the former Special Prosecutor, helped by two strong-limbed nurses, inched his way up the walk toward the house.

The skin on his once-swarthy face sagged, and his jaw, like the underside of his eyes was edged in shadow. A weak smile hung on his lips as his face turned slowly to one side, then the other. For a moment a tear appeared at the edge of his nose, and then as quickly was gone, burned away by the fire that rekindled in his dark brown eyes. As Henry watched, shadow gave way to more finely etched lines, which emanated from the outer point of each eye and crept upward from the corners of his mouth. His body seemed to straighten as it shuffled up the sidewalk toward the front door.

Reaching the three steps, Matlin began the difficult ascent. Gingerly he placed his leg on the first step. Then, with an assist from the two ladies at his elbows, he mounted it. The next step was similarly conquered, and finally the last. At the summit, he straightened himself and turned slowly around

Henry felt Sara's arm next to his and he reached for it. With his fingers, he felt his way down her wrist to her hand and he took it in his own. A squeeze ratified his action.

He watched while Matlin turned himself toward the crowd. The nurses stepped forward to support him, but Matlin waved them away.

Henry watched the brown eyes sweep the assemblage, stopping and moving, stopping, and moving. Then, for an instant, they stopped and fixed on Henry's eyes. Something passed through the air and then Henry knew. He knew that he could, he would continue to fight. Somehow. Somewhere. He was going to carry on. He felt Sara's hand squeeze his arm.

Matlin's eyes moved on until they had covered everyone gathered there. Then they lifted above the crowd, above the street lined with automobiles, above the houses and trees and all the landscape. And the arms began to move. Henry saw them rise slowly, as though lifted with great effort. But up they rose, unfolding, and finally stretching out full length. Out over each one of them. Out, a thousand miles into infinity.

THE END

ACKNOWLEDGMENTS

Thanks are extended to Eva Talmadge, writer, book editor, and former NYC literary agent, who brought out the best of Sara. Also, the author is grateful for the loving help and support of his wife, Peggy.